BAD WATERS RUN DEEP
THIS TIME THE GHOSTS DON'T WANT PEACE, THEY WANT WAR!
A LORNE TURNER MYSTERY

First Published in Great Britain 2022 by Mirador Publishing

BAD WATERS RUN DEEP

THIS TIME THE GHOSTS DON'T WANT PEACE, THEY WANT WAR!

A LORNE TURNER MYSTERY

JOE TALON

PROLOGUE

HE BEGAN HIS EXISTENCE IN a moment. An act of creation born from the miracle of life. In a time before they caged words and set them down on parchment or vellum.

A simple life of existence lay before him. The life of a god at the birth of a river.

People came from miles around to offer trinkets and edibles in exchange for a little of his will, his blessings, falling into their lives with benign intentions. Harvests grew strong, the fruits on the trees grew fat, and the hunt knew success. Illnesses swept through the encampment, but with due reverence and care given, he gave his aid. He mollified the demons that brought plague or pestilence, and the people once more knew peace.

They grew strong and fat on the land, protected by him.

Season rolled into season and word spread of the joy found in his small valley. More people came with gifts, and he returned their worship. Some of these people remained among the original tribe and it grew, driving commerce with others. All the while, he enjoyed the fresh spring water of his home and the gifts of his community.

Other tribes came wanting trade with this bountiful valley, speaking foreign tongues and with strange ways, but they soon learned why the community on this windswept hill kept faith with their god and his river. Old lives and new merged and the world around the valley grew strong.

With that strength came change.

It brought covetousness. Those who had little, who didn't appease their gods nearly so well, came to the valley with war in their dark hearts.

Blood soaked the land and filled the river. When the new tribe settled, they built walls, denying easy access to the god's quiet place.

A man came who said, 'I will speak for you to the people and the people will speak to you through me.'

He took the trinkets and demanded gold. He took the libations and demanded slaves. He took the people from the god and gave back hollow words of praise. The god did what he could with the crops, but they failed. He did what he could with the fruits, but they turned bitter. He did what he could with the livestock, but they grew thin.

Then one day, the old people grew tired of this, and they rose up to defend their land and their god. They defeated these incomers with their swords and shields. They took the blood and bone of their enemies and gave great thanks to their river god. He grew in strength once more and peace returned to the valley.

This cycle continued through gifts of stone, of bronze, of iron, and into the world of steel.

Until one day a man came with a new word from a new god. One with a son who had lived among men in a land far from the river god's valley and yet his words spoke to the hearts of many. Many joined the new God-Son in his mission.

Still peace held sway, but the river god felt the loss as a mother does the death of a child.

Until the day when a new man in steel came to the valley. He became a king of this place and stamped his power on the god's valley in buildings of stone. He slaughtered those that stood against him. Worse was yet to come, because his faith in the God-Son was absolute and he built churches. He prevented the libations and trinkets. He did not care about the gifts the old river god could give. His only interest lay in the power of the God-Son and the backs of the slaves farming his land.

Darkness and loneliness surrounded the old river god. He brooded, knowing this time would not pass, as it had before.

His river still ran, but his gifts did not run with it. The new power in the valley burned the old river god, and he grew sullen. He resented the new God-Son and his priests in robes of black. Then worse still, a great and cruel evil kept the old river god pinned in place, imprisoned for all of time. The old river god wept his rage and frustration, but could not act.

He just needed the pain to go away.

He just needed the pain to go away.

That is when it began. When he started to rebel against their control. He had given it all to his people, but they did not listen, and they did not heed his warnings.

He rose, as he had not done for eons. He rose and walked across the land. He took their children. He murdered their menfolk. He destroyed their farms.

Condemn the old river god perhaps, but now he has no pain. Birds bring new trinkets; the magpies and crows are the best. The squirrels and otters bring him libations. He does not make them strong, because they would be hunted, but he gives them sanctuary. At this time, it is all he can offer.

He is bountiful in his love. He is vengeful in his pain. Heed his warning for he will rise up and take back what was once given freely.

1

THE LIGHT GLINTED OFF THE church windows, looking like shards of diamond bright feathers. I wiped the sweat off my brow. My back cracked the moment I straightened, and I glared at my nemesis.

"This is your fault," I said, pointing a gloved and sweaty finger at him.

Ghost grinned at me with his pink tongue long and wet, the heat affecting him as it did the rest of the moor. I shook my head. Again, I picked up the large mallet to bang the post into the drought burdened soil near the wall which separated the farm's garden from the graveyard. We'd never needed a fence between Stoke Pero farm and the church, but the latest addition to the family liked the deer and ponies too much. Keeping Ghost safe proved even more difficult than keeping Heather safe.

With her first year at college almost over, we'd be celebrating somewhere nice, or that was my plan. I heard the rumble of her bike coming from the top road and banged the post into the ground with renewed vigour. We wanted to leave Ghost in the garden without having to tie up the enormous lump. He'd ripped out the first post I'd tied him to the moment Heather left the farm. That was before the beast grew to the size of a pony. Now, we needed a fence strong enough to do battle with his enthusiastic love.

I knew how he felt.

The post shuddered under the weight of my blows and the cracked soil. My muscles ached, the pain making my mind drift into the zone I'd created when I had to overcome physical discomfort for a mission. I smacked down once more, and the soil turned from brittle lumps to a soupy mush of mud.

"What the…" No water main crossed this part of the garden. I'd checked. Had I found some hidden spring?

The hole filled quickly and with it came the scent of rotten bodies. Gagging, I backed off.

"Hey, gorgeous," Heather called out. I didn't know if she spoke to me or the dog—we often found ourselves interchangeable.

I turned to yell at her to keep the dog away, shocked by the discovery of the foul water. The drought was hitting Exmoor with brutal efficiency, killing off the weak and old at an alarming rate. We'd found too many wild animals suffering this year. Is that why this water smelt so bad? Were bodies trapped somewhere diverting a water source?

Heather climbed off her beloved Dixie. We'd traded in the original bike for a Suzuki 400 Bandit. Bright red and with just enough guts for me to know she could keep up with traffic and not be pushed off the road.

"Don't bring the dog—" I glanced back at the hole smothering a gasp. The stake stood in dry soil. Summer air, hot and heavy, clean and smelling of the moor, rushed back. Making sure to hide my shock, I smiled as Heather came over. She greeted the dog, and offered me a kiss.

"I'm all sweaty," I said, pulling away. Confusion filled my head, but I didn't want to disturb her, so forced the odd vision away. It made no sense and must be a product of my PTSD, but not one I'd experienced before. Good to know my brain could still create new ways to freak me out.

She huffed and grinned. "Me too. Safety gear in this heat is doing my head in. I'll be glad when I don't have to do those miles every day. Talking of which, did the National Park letter come through?" Her eyes, slices of captured summer sky, looked both hopeful and worried.

"It's on the table," I said.

The squeal of pleasure made me flinch, but I grinned as she raced into the house. Ghost pounded after her, his windmilling tail and scrambling paws making a mess of the flowerbeds. I sighed. An Irish Wolfhound-

German Shepherd mix was never going to be easy. I just hadn't reckoned on this level of chaos. The young dog had been used as a tool by Thomas Moore the previous November in an attempt to scare me. Possessed by something that made him a slavering monster. Removing Moore's influence had given us a devoted hound, which I liked. Just as well I hadn't killed him on sight.

Walking into the kitchen, I saw Heather sat with the envelope in her hand, expression grim.

"What if they don't want me?" she asked.

I pulled the gloves off my hands and headed for the sink. Over my shoulder I said, "Of course they'll want you. Even if they don't, you keep on with it. We don't give up on our dreams in this house—remember?"

A soft smile spread over her face. "We keep going until the job's done."

I nodded. Two of the mantras we lived by, they kept us sane and focused.

Taking a deep breath, she ripped open the envelope. My anxiety matched hers. A job with the Exmoor National Park Authority would help keep her here in Stoke Pero. I worried she'd wake up one day and wonder why she'd shackled herself to a broken old soldier.

She pulled the letter out and scanned it. Her face said it all. Tears filled those beautiful eyes and my heart dropped to the floor in sympathy.

"I'm sorry, love."

Without a word, she left the table and walked off into the house.

I'd go in a minute. Sometimes my presence didn't help, because I wanted to fix the unfixable. Picking up the letter, I read the refusal of her dream job. In a personal paragraph at the bottom, the park ranger she volunteered with most often recommended a list of additional experiences he could provide that would ensure she made it next time. Telling her now wouldn't help. Now, by the sound of slamming doors upstairs, she just needed to vent some of the disappointment. The wardrobe seemed to be having the worst of it.

Ghost and I made tea, and I found some of Lilian's carrot cake, to help soften the blow. Tucking the letter into the back pocket of my combat shorts, I padded on bare feet up the stairs to our bedroom. Heather had a nasty habit of only seeing the bad things in her life, her 'failures', and it made the future too murky. I tried to pull back the veils.

I'd lost count of my many failures as a soldier in the elite regiment of the Special Air Service. It came with the territory, but it also meant I never gave up. I needed to give Heather that gift, if nothing else.

"Sorry," she growled.

"It's okay. Did you read the letter properly?"

"No. What's the point? It's just bollocks to fill up space."

I fought the urge to sigh in frustration. "Keith has a list of recommendations that'll help for the next position. He really wants you to be a ranger, Heather. You just need to finish your course, do some more specialist volunteering, and they'll give you the job."

"That'll take another year and we need the money now," she exploded. Her dark hair, brushing her shoulders, curling in waves, made her look soft and vulnerable. Two things she definitely wasn't, unless something hurt her, and this hurt her.

We did need the money. We always needed the money. The old Nissan Warrior I'd inherited, along with the farm, had to be replaced at some point. Upgrading the oil-fired boiler before the winter also loomed on the horizon. We'd never afford to fill the old tank when the weather closed in on the moor. My life revolved around the words *need* and *money*.

Broaching a subject Heather hated, I tried to say, "Security work—"

"No. No, Lorne. I will not have you put in that position. You are not working the circuit."

She meant the security circuit so many ex-Special Forces guys relied on when they left the army. Different people I'd served with had approached me a few times, but the PTSD meant I might not be reliable. Still, I could train people, at a push, if I had no choice.

"Okay, well, maybe we'll look at it again in a few months. See how the summer goes when the schools break up? We've done good so far this season."

She sat beside me on the bed and took the cake. "Thanks," she mumbled.

"You'll get there, kid. I know it." I put an arm around her shoulder and kissed her hair. She smelt of town air and tension. "Get showered, get dressed, we're going to Minehead, and we'll have fish and chips on our spot. We'll take Ghost."

"Can we afford the petrol?" she asked with misery falling off her fork, along with the cake crumbs.

I chuckled. "I think we can manage that. We might be rural poor, love, but at least we're rural."

She smiled and placed her head on my shoulder. "I've been poor so long I don't know of another way to live."

"Just as well, considering you're shacked up with me." I stood up. "Get a wiggle on. Maybe we'll go for a swim in the sea."

She laughed and normality returned to our home.

EATING CHIPS COVERED IN VINEGAR and salt was one of our treats. Even during the hectic tourist season, the old town of Minehead remained relatively sane. We sat on the sea wall and watched the Welsh coastline, the gulls and the windsurfers. This was my idea of heaven. A simple life.

The tide tickled the rocks and sand and looked comforting after all the dry streambeds and watering holes I'd found on the moor over the last few weeks.

I pushed back my worries and concentrated on the moment. The PTSD made life difficult enough, without me brooding on our current troubles. I glanced up at the beach and the figure of a boy caught me by surprise. He stood still, just above the tideline, in what looked like winter clothing. He was clearly soaking wet. No adults seemed concerned, and Ghost didn't react to his presence. The boy stared at us, but we sat too far away for me to see any definition in his face.

The sound of my mobile phone going off disrupted my concentration, and I glanced away for a moment. When I looked back, the boy was gone. A shiver passed through me and the chips lost some of their appeal.

Watching Ghost's attempts to chase off the gulls from every corner of the beach made Heather laugh. The dog never strayed far from her. I didn't have anywhere near the loyalty from him. She said it was because I could look after myself and didn't need guarding. I realised she hadn't seen the boy.

Pulling out my phone, trying to keep the chip fat off it, I frowned. "Number unknown." The boy must have been a trick of the light, a random shadow making him look fully clothed for winter.

"Could be more work," Heather said around a mouthful of fish and with some hope.

I accepted the call. "Turner."

Heather rolled her eyes.

"Is that Exmoor's Psychic Agency?" asked a man, more plum jam than local cider to his voice.

I blinked. The previous year Heather decided we needed a new business, using my hitherto denied psychic sensitivities. We'd had a few calls over the months and even a little work, but nothing to take to the bank for a mortgage payment and I'd almost forgotten about it.

"Um, yes. That's right. How can I help?"

"My name is Medway, Michael Medway. I'm the head teacher at Syndercombe Academy near Clatworthy. Do you know it?" he asked.

"I don't have kids, so no, I'm afraid I don't. Clatworthy's familiar though, or the reservoir."

"Well, that's a start, I suppose. I'm calling because I think we need a little help from… A psychic. Really, I can't believe I just said that." He muttered the last sentence and the word 'psychic', came out like it tasted bad in his mouth.

He annoyed me. Never a good start.

I took a breath. "Why do you think you need us?"

"The school is for teenage boys who board, and they have it in their heads the place is haunted. The parents want something done, as if we have a rat problem, or we'll be losing students. Someone gave me your card. I would like to meet with you and perhaps you can write a report stating the place is not haunted. It's more for peace of mind than anything else."

The patronising tone did not sit well with me. People did not patronise me. Since last November, I'd avoided everything that resembled an *official* weapon, but I'd be glad to make an exception for this bloke.

"Mr Medway, if you wish for a report, why not write one yourself? I'm sure your art department could help," I snapped out in my best sergeant-major bollocking voice.

He sucked in his breath to retort.

Heather plucked the phone from my hand. "Mr Medway? I'm Heather Wicklow, Mr Turner's business partner. Perhaps we can come and make a preliminary evaluation of the premises? Then, we can discuss anything Mr Turner feels might endanger or scare the boys. These things are often difficult for us mundane people to understand. I've worked with Mr Turner for some time now, and I've been party to some startling experiences." She talked to the phone with her best voice, Devon accent hidden to the point of being non-existent.

She held silent for a moment. Then said, "Yes, I'll be with Mr Turner. I'll be happy to discuss the terms of our contract with you when we arrive. What date is convenient?"

More murmurs from the phone I couldn't hear. My eyes started to search the beach, looking for the boy. He'd been blond, a pre-teen, but…

Heather's voice broke through my search. "Tuesday will be fine, Mr Medway. We'll see you at ten. Yes, I look forward to meeting you as well." Heather hung up and glared at me. "Really? You're going to turn down good money from a private school at this point?"

"He annoyed me."

She sighed. "So?"

I shrugged and stared out at the sea.

A small hand occupied some space on my thigh. "I know you don't want to do this business, but it could be a very good income stream. Most restless spirits aren't like the ones in Scob, or tormented soldiers from World War Two. Neither are they controlled by megalomaniacs like Shaw and Moore." Our previous year had not been full of spirits who wanted to walk into the light. They wanted to avenge their untimely deaths and as for what the *Gnostic Dawn* and *Fraternity of the Nous* had done...

"I feel like a fraud. It's embarrassing," I muttered, a petulant child. Watching the distant shoreline of Wales was preferable to looking at the woman I loved.

She nudged me with her shoulder, making me look at her and the smile. "We can make money, boss. We can take it from the rich and keep it because we're poor." Her blue eyes shone with a devil of a glint in them.

"I can take advantage of the rich," I admitted.

"Then that's how we think about it. We are going to go to the school, have a nose at how the other half live, and leave with a fat cheque after wafting about some sage and holy water."

I laughed. "You plan on conning Ella out of the water?"

"Totally." She grinned with the savage delight of a naughty elf. "She'll never notice if I raid the font after the christening on Sunday."

"You're a wicked girl."

"Yes, I am, which is why you love me."

This time, her phone went off. She plucked it out of her daysack with a smile on her face, the warm breeze colouring her tanned, freckled face a soft pink. Glancing at the screen, the colour drained away, like someone turned a tap under her chin.

I looked at her screen. It simply said, 'Aliens Live Here'. She declined the call and stuffed the phone back, saying nothing.

"Heather?" I prompted, every one of my instincts on alert. Something nasty lurked in her phone.

"Wrong number." Voice tight, shoulders tighter, food forgotten in her lap. "Ghost, come back, we're leaving," she called out to the dog. Then, looking at me, she said, "I've homework to do. Let's get back to the farm. I need beer."

She jumped down from our perch and went to catch the dog. I watched her swipe at her face, and I knew our world had hit a brick wall we'd have to climb over. If it proved too high to climb, I'd smash a hole in the bugger.

2

THE FOLLOWING DAY, WE WENT for a run, all three of us. Heather had been pensive and restless all night, and needed the freedom of the moor. I didn't push her to tell me what the problem might be, but it didn't make it easy living with her secrets. We'd both woken early—mostly due to me doing battle with something horrible in my dreams—and opted for exercise over conversation. The long dry winter, spring and summer left the moor ragged and desperate. The park authority had taken to leaving water troughs in dry streambeds to help the deer and ponies. I'd seen every type of animal using them. None of the locals had ever known it this bad. Even the River Barle struggled to make Tarr Steps look picturesque at the moment.

Heather and I did what we could around the farmhouse, keeping buckets in the shower, so we used the grey water for the plants. Without being prompted, Heather doused for underground springs, and we found one. More of a leak at this point, but a few of us got together to build a system of shallow pools in the dry soil and diverted the spring. It meant the moorland animals could share in the bounty the domestic farm animals enjoyed.

The trees, usually redolent in their finery this time of year, endured. As if they drew into themselves, shutting down their soft energy, silencing their presence, while the sun battered them instead of loving them. It felt alien and scary. I remembered this terrible sucking dryness all too well, and I didn't want it for my moor. My homeland. This land should smell of rich loam and cool winds. Everything I tasted in the air as I ran over the moor brought back memories of hard, bitter rock-lands and wadis made of the memory of water.

When we reached the long drop back to Stoke Pero, Heather stopped. We carried water for the dog and for us, so I sat while she fussed over Ghost.

I judged now was the time to broach the call. "So, who is 'Aliens Live Here'?"

Dropping a small nuke would have done less damage.

Her eyes darkened and her skin flushed. "Irrelevant." Standing, she turned her back and took in the view.

Tumbling moorland, turning to farmland, turning to woodland, all of it parched. A blanket of browns and greens torn from a fairy tale and placed in this world to give us back our lost magic. The sky above, though, was a hard blue, almost as hard as Heather's eyes when she looked back at me. Bird song dripped notes through the heavy air.

"I'm guessing you won't let this go?" she asked, voice guitar string tight.

I lifted my cap and wiped sweat off my brow. "No."

Coiled, like the adder sniffing for danger, she crouched to cuddle the lump of dog at our feet.

A mad fluttering of wings made us all startle. Partridge, taking umbrage at our presence, called out a warning. Ghost barely blinked.

Heather's shoulders slumped, and she sat on the struggling grass. With slim fingers she plucked at the brittle blades, still not meeting my eyes. I'd rarely, if ever, seen her like this and I didn't know if it was the phone call she'd declined or the career disappointment.

I sat beside her in silence for a while, forearms resting on my bent knees, and stared out over the sun-bitter landscape. Eventually, I said, "You know you can tell me anything, right? I mean, you have to put up with my nonsense." I tapped my head with my knuckles. "Let me carry some of yours for a change."

She sighed and relented on her silence in a rush of words. "When I moved in with Ella, then with you, it was like a brand-new penny in my soul. All bright and shiny, untainted by the fingers using it, hoarding it, marring its bright surface with their avarice."

I waited in silence. When Heather used big words and enormous images, it usually meant a deep trouble lay behind it. Minor troubles came with vast amounts of profanity and stomping.

"But the past always mars the present and taints the future. I should know that, living with you."

I winced. The truth hurt but remained unarguable in its honest understanding.

"Sorry," she said. "That was cruel." Her eyes softened and reminded me of the summer skies of my childhood. Islands of peace in the maze of memories that haunted me.

"It was honest, not cruel. Who hurt you, Heather?" My heart ached to see her tormented like this. She didn't deserve it.

"The number belongs to my parents' house."

I didn't react. Instinct kept me still. We'd lived together for over a year and been romantically entangled since the previous summer. This woman would be my wife, and at some point, we wanted children. After all the things we'd shared in that time, she rarely mentioned her family. I didn't even know if they knew where she lived. I knew she'd left home at seventeen, and I knew a lot about her life after that point, but her childhood remained a mystery.

"Talking to them never ends well," she added in a small voice. "I don't want to know what the problem is, and I don't care."

Both were lies, but it would be tactless to point it out—I lied about my mental health issues all the time and waded daily in the murky waters of denial.

I wanted to fix this, because that's what I always tried to do with Heather's problems. "Maybe you could phone them? It'll give you control over the conversation."

She snorted. "You don't know my father."

True. I knew he was a consultant for rural businesses in and around Exeter, but that was it. Respecting Heather's privacy, I'd never tried to find out more. Perhaps it was time I did, and I considered ringing Paul to help.

My old mucker had resigned from GCHQ just before last Christmas to care for Willow. I popped in to visit most weeks, but it was hard seeing her struggle with her new life. The bullet Shaw delivered to the back of her head missed her brain but shattered her skull. Her motor skills and speech needed to be relearned, and she'd had a few mini strokes. Paul cared for her in a way I'd never imagined him capable of, and Willow fought to get her life back every day. She'd find it, or most of it, I had no doubt. She just needed time.

Willow's past had haunted her for years before leaving her with the brain injury.

Heather's past now wanted a chunk of her new life, and I needed to limit the fallout.

My past zoomed in and out of focus with alarming regularity, often leaving me confused and disorientated, sometimes in a supermarket, sometimes in the house. Running proved to be safe and reliable. I did a lot of running.

"Let's go home. We've some planning to do for Friday evening when we take out that group for woodland photography." During the long dusk of summer, we'd be taking a small group of tourists into Horner Wood so they could photograph badgers and foxes, maybe some owls.

I stood and hauled Heather upright, Ghost rising with us, looking eager for the next stage of his adventure. Everything was an adventure to Ghost.

These days, photography was the only shooting I wanted to do. I'd promised Ella I'd decommission my stash of guns, and I'd done just that, giving her the firing pins. The weapons ought to be handed over to the police, but I figured burying them in the small field I still owned at the back of the barns would do for the moment. Besides, old soldiers from the SAS struggled to release their trust in their toys—even if those toys caused a mental breakdown.

Running hard, we raced each other back to the house and Heather, with Ghost at her heels, hit the yard a good twenty metres ahead of me.

"My knees can't go downhill," I complained, panting and grinning just as much as the dog. I never begrudged her a win. I'd spent years at the top of my game. She deserved the same confidence.

She raised her hands and did her victory dance. Then she stopped. I tracked her gaze and saw a black Porsche Cayenne in the layby below our place.

A tall, slim man leaned against the bonnet. Despite the weather, he wore a suit and tie. The pale linen blended with his colourless skin, the blue tie the only flash of existence in this world. He walked towards the farm gate. As he drew closer, I noted the colour of his eyes matched the tie.

Ghost shifted to stand in front of Heather. His head lowered and a long, low rumble vibrated from his chest. He wasn't much of a barker and didn't lunge at people, but he'd never growled at anyone either.

I didn't need more of a signal to act. Stepping in front of Ghost to cut the man off, I made him look at me rather than Heather.

"Can I help? Are you lost?" I asked.

He barely glanced at me, all his attention on my fiancée.

"I am not lost. Apparently, my daughter now resides at this address. You are?" his voice reminded me of ruperts I'd suffered under in The Regiment. Harrow, Eton, Oxford, Sandhurst, and daddy pulling strings to have their little darling control Regiment men.

I loathed him already. Asking me who I was on my land did not endear me to the man.

"I own this farm. That's who I am." I felt the stare. One that we all develop over the years. One that says, *'I've killed men like you. Don't press me. I'm likely to do it again.'* My inner beast, quiet for a long time, happy to sleep in his dark corner at last, rose and padded forwards. The savage hyena energy whipping out, making Ghost take a step back from me.

Heather reached my side and placed a hand on my arm. The beast calmed.

"Lorne, this is my father, Clive Mordent. Father, this is Lorne Turner, my business partner and fiancé."

Not the way we usually introduced ourselves to people. Marriage was heading our way; we just didn't have the money and hadn't found the time. She wore a ring though, my mother's, which we both liked.

I also wondered about Heather's name being Wicklow and her father

Mordent. More questions for when we didn't have an enemy on the borders.

Clive Mordent looked me over. The bald head, the scars, the short but lean frame. He obviously thought little of what he saw. I, on the other hand, saw money, real money, along with confidence, education and power.

Heather's eyes were shades darker than her father's, but they shared the same firm jaw and high cheekbones. Her height must come from her mother, along with the dark hair.

"Perhaps we can speak in private?" Clive asked his daughter.

Heather's tension curled my stomach and made me want to stomp on this bloke.

"No," she forced out. The effort it took for her to keep her shoulders firm shocked me. Heather rarely, if ever, backed down, but I could see her desire to cave in and do as ordered.

Her father's jaw clenched. "At least invite me in. It's hot."

"Is Mother in the car?" Heather said.

"Yes."

I noticed the engine was off, which meant the air-conditioning wouldn't be running. He kept his wife in a hot car, and she let him. Another black mark.

Heather didn't move. Locking her gaze somewhere near the man's throat, she said, "What are you doing here?"

"I called. You didn't pick up."

"That's because I was busy. I have a business to run."

A sneer covered Clive's face. "Yes, that's how we discovered where you currently live. Why are you using your grandmother's maiden name?"

Heather's eyes narrowed. "Because she loved me. And when I marry Lorne, I'll take his name, because he loves me."

I watched tears spring into her eyes. "Heather," I spoke only to her. "Go inside, give Ghost something to eat. We've things to do today and I need you on your game. I can deal with this."

Without a word, she turned and left, taking the dog with her, going around the back of the house.

"I need to speak with my child," Clive said.

"And I'll relay your questions. Leave me your business card and I'll email you Heather's reply." Movement from the Cayenne caught my attention.

A woman, small, dark and impeccably made up, approached. Her floral summer dress clung to her tiny frame, and I had the impression of a fairy trapped between the pages of a book she didn't want to be a part of anymore.

With a tentative smile, she approached. "You're Lorne?"

"I am. You must be Heather's mother?"

She nodded, but her eyes remained fixed on the house, as if she could peel away the bricks and see her daughter's life.

"Iris. I'm Iris." It sounded like she wanted me to confirm this for her.

"It's a pleasure." No handshakes, just nods. I didn't want to touch either of them, so it worked for me.

I realised her dark hair now came from a bottle, but the texture and length reminded me of Heather's before the fire at Scob had melted a chunk.

Iris touched Clive's arm. "Maybe we could go in and talk to Heather? She's obviously just been for a run. I've never seen her looking so well." This part she aimed at me.

"Heather works hard." I guessed Heather didn't want these people knowing too much about her life, but I felt the need to show them how far she'd come in the eighteen months since I'd taken her from the grotty bedsit of her old existence.

Clive prevented me from saying any more. "Look, we are here for one reason. It's quite simple, I need to know if she's had contact with her brother. He's missing, and we need to find him."

Heather had a brother?

"I can tell you for a fact she's had no contact with her brother. I would suggest you email us any further questions. The email is on the website."

Iris touched her husband's arm again. "Perhaps we could just talk to her for a minute?" The small fluttering voice made me nervous.

With Heather never sharing her childhood, I'd always wondered what made her leave home. Her desire for an alternative lifestyle, the rebellious nature tattooed all over her body, or something darker. Far darker. Whatever happened in the family home, she'd stuffed it in a box and thrown away the key.

I focused on Iris and smiled. Not one of my scary ones, though she looked a little alarmed at the scars covering the right side of my face. "Maybe we could meet up in Exeter for coffee sometime? Just email me and I'll discuss it with Heather. She's really very busy right now. Work, college, the business, her volunteering for the National Park."

Iris's eyes, a pale, washed out version of her namesake, widened. "She does all that?"

"I couldn't run my business without her." I saw no reason to be hard or cruel to the small woman. Heather might be small in stature but never in personality. Iris, though, she looked to be made up of broken promises and shattered dreams.

"Is she happy?" Iris asked, her voice too small and delicate to come from a grown woman.

"Iris." Clive's snapped word made her take a step back. He locked eyes with me. "If her brother gets in contact, I want to know immediately. The police are looking for him. It's serious and I have no wish to be dealing with his mistakes."

"I see. Well, I'll let her know," I said. Softening, I looked at Iris. "I'll tell her you asked after her."

Clive's face tightened further. His lips thinning and fighting a well-practiced sneer. "Goodbye, Mr Turner."

3

I FOUND HEATHER IN THE living room, her fingers buried in Ghost's fur as she watched her father trying to turn the Cayenne around in the lane without shattering our gate. I usually left it open, but my need to keep him out of Heather's space made me shut it after they left. That and I felt like being petty. It left little room for the oversized sports SUV.

"You okay?" I asked from the doorway.

"I need to shower and change. Our clients are due in an hour, and we haven't eaten. It's going to be a long day." She moved to push past me, but I blocked her.

Tension thrummed in the air, whipping around her head and shoulders, ready to knock the unwary off their feet.

"Look at me, love."

When she managed the briefest eye contact, the rage fairly burned the summer sky colour to diamond blue. "What?"

I was going to say, 'Calm down and talk to me', but I figured I needed my balls, so I opted for a safe, "I love you and we're safe here. This is our home."

A war surfaced. I didn't know if she wanted to punch me or burst into tears. Both might happen as the day went on, so I moved out of her way.

In return I received a muttered, "Love you too," before she raced up the stairs.

Ghost and I shared a long look, and I had the oddest feeling he wanted to say, 'Women are a mystery to me too, mate', adding a shrug.

WHEN I'D RELAYED THE MESSAGE to Heather about her brother, she'd just muttered, "Good luck to him. I hope he stays hidden."

When I'd broached the subject of us talking about the issues she clearly had with her parents, I'd received a, "No. We aren't talking about it."

I'd rung Ella.

"You need to leave it, Lorne. She'll talk when she's good and ready. If you push, she'll push back harder, and you won't like it. Heather's created a new life for herself and if she doesn't want her old one taking over, who are we to judge?"

"I don't like there being secrets between us."

"It's not a secret and don't you keep heaps of your past hidden from all of us?" she asked.

"That's different."

"No. It's not."

"Operational details—"

"Don't have to be shared, Lorne, for you to tell us who you were before you came home. But you don't want to be that man, so you don't tell us about him. What Heather's doing is the same. Try to keep that in mind."

I sighed but knew she probably understood more than I did, which meant I just watched Heather slowly come back to me, rather than force her to open her box and shed its contents all over the kitchen floor. There was every likelihood that if I made her open the box, we'd never get it all stuffed back inside. It's why I still refused to go to therapy, despite promising myself several times a week to do just that.

COME TUESDAY MORNING, WE TOOK the bikes over to Clatworthy for our meeting with the head teacher of Syndercombe Academy. The sun was as hard and bright as every other day. A hard coin set in a sky blue enough to hurt. I didn't want to take the old Nissan. It might not make it home. We'd left

Ghost behind in his new fenced garden and he seemed happy enough with his shed.

All weekend I'd had moments of odd panic, my throat and lungs feeling full of water, or sensing it swirl around me like I had in Scob during the flood. Then Monday morning almost caused a total meltdown. Heather left for work, leaving me with Ghost, and I filled his water bowl, then a glass for me. I stared out at the parched lawn while I lifted the water to my lips. The smell snuck up my nose a moment before I swallowed the first foul mouthful.

I'd seen and experienced poisoned wells in remote villages. Places in which enemy combatants would dump the body of a dead animal in the only water source. The contaminated fluid stank. I'd never tasted it, not until now.

The glass shattered as it hit the quarry tiles and I yelped in shock. The dog dove for the back door. Perplexed, I checked the tap. Clean water pattered out to fill the sink. I checked the dog bowl. Clean. The shivering started, as if I was cold. I'd sat on the floor for a bit, working hard on my breathing and staying in the present, until I'd been able to clean up the mess. I hadn't told Heather when she'd come home that evening.

The rest of the day and the following morning, I sniffed everything before I drank. Nothing weird happened, and I relaxed. A good burn on the bike would shake the cobwebs loose.

The quickest way from Stoke Pero was over the top of the Brendon Hills. I loved the B3224. The road between Weddon Cross and Raleghs Cross was far too much fun on two motorbikes. Completely failing to be sensible, we arrived early in Clatworthy village for the meeting.

Pulling up outside the church, I lifted my visor. "You good?" I asked.

Heather grinned. The bike helmet squashing her face in the most adorable hamster-like way. "That was fun and you're naughty."

I winked and looked at the church. A small grey building with a tower. It looked at us with a ferocity I rarely saw in churches. The graveyard was neat and the gravestones few compared to most churches in the area. Trees gathered around the site, and it felt as if the two did battle in some centuries long conflict over the space. When I mentioned to Ella our planned location and why we'd found it necessary to be there, she'd said the church dated back to the twelfth century, making it Norman and properly old.

"It's a pleasant village," Heather said, looking around. "It's very…"

"Expensive."

Heather chuckled. "Yeah. Barn conversion central with a healthy dose of retired London types."

I wished I could say the village contained locals, but the expensive cars, mock Georgian porches and silence, spoke of money. Only the wind and the chorus of bird song surrounded the village. Few of us, born in places like this, had the luxury of staying. The farms hereabouts would be different, but the labourers' cottages and the barns would no longer be for those with generations in that graveyard. Change came hard for some, but if it weren't for incomers, these villages might die as the youngsters moved away to find new jobs and more exciting lives.

After checking the satnav on my phone, I realised we needed to take Glass's Rock Lane, before a small fork in the road took us up Mill Lane. The roads at this point ran narrow, with dark green hedges and towering old trees cutting off the sun. For centuries, these narrow lanes felt like the capillaries of rural Somerset, taking people into the quiet and lonely places of the bucolic landscape. Riding slowly on the bikes, we kept close together. If I opened my arms out, I'd be able to touch both sides of the lane. Grass and moss covered the centre, making me aware of how treacherous it would be in the winter.

Mill Lane opened up and Heather wobbled on her bike as her head went up. The vast wall of the reservoir towered over us. A concrete megalith, totally at odds with the rolling hills and small valleys inundating the slopes of the Brendon Hills.

"Bloody hell," she muttered, over the rumble of low revs.

"Here," I called out. The signpost for Syndercombe Academy came into view.

The large, beautifully painted, wooden sign had a crest on it and the name of the school in some fancy font. Deep blue and gold dominated. The crest had three lions rearing up in black on a golden shield. What that had to do with Clatworthy, I had no idea. Heraldry never meant much to me.

We turned up a driveway, its surface ridged concrete, and rode a short distance to a large parking area. Shorn dry grass fields hugged the drive and the car park. The school stood before us.

Red brick, black slate roof, white mullioned windows. It reminded me all too vividly of The Rectory in Scob. I didn't enjoy thinking about that place. However, this building didn't have gothic gargoyles staring down at us. It had beautiful shiny paintwork. The ivy racing up the side had the good courtesy to appear manicured. The windows, facing south, captured a little of the natural sunlight permitted in the tight valley. In the winter, this place must be gloomy, with the sun low over the hills and the vast wall of the reservoir to the west casting an enormous shadow.

Heather put her bike on the stand and removed her helmet, ruffling her hair. "Yuck, too hot," she said, undoing her jacket. "You see anything?"

"No. Don't feel anything either."

"So, no Friday the Thirteenth vibe?" she asked.

"Not even a Harry Potter vibe," I said.

She laughed, a carefree sound I'd missed since her father's visit.

Checking over the building more carefully, I realised it just looked... bland. A large Victorian house with nothing more sinister than five million cubic metres of water sat to its left. The trees behind it were deciduous and mostly beech, their summer-darkened leaves tickled by the wind's many fingers. I sensed no coiled horror lurking behind the windows, no monsters in the woodland, no whispering dead in the soil. My djinn, Al-Ahmar, didn't fill my mouth with dust and sand. The beast remained quiet. No sensation of black feathers being dragged over my scalp.

I'd never seen a more boring building.

The only advantage it had over every other Victorian manor house came from its location. I had to admit to being a little awed by the reservoir. At one point in Afghanistan, our unit helped ensure the safe arrival of a huge turbine for the Kajaki Dam. We killed a lot of Taliban on that trip. This dam was older and happier. With less dead on its conscience.

I shook the memory away and concentrated on the colour green, rather than the parched grass of the lawns. My heart remembered the brutal journey up that Afghan valley, and it beat too fast, making me dizzy. The rush of faces in those sand blasted, bullet blasted, villages of...

"Lorne?" Heather appeared in front of me. "Breathe out. Everything is fine. You are fine. We are here." She pinched the spot between my thumb and forefinger, causing an ache in my trigger hand.

I focused on her face. Just her face and the memories washed back. The harmless and benign English countryside took over and my heart slowed.

"All good?" she asked.

"Yeah. Sorry. The dam... I erm..." I shook my head. "I'll tell you about it later."

She nodded. "Just don't look at it if it's disturbing." She eyed it with suspicion.

Senses spiked by the sudden influx of memories; I zeroed on a man walking out of the large double doors at the front of the school building. My body primed for a fight as he strode towards us.

"Ms Wicklow?" he called out. A frown marred his face as he looked at me.

"Mr Medway, yes, I'm Heather Wicklow and this is Lorne Turner."

Michael Medway wore cotton trousers with a seam ironed into the legs sharp enough to cut bread. A shirt the colour of tinned salmon, open at the neck, gave the impression of country casual. A round belly hung limp, just like his hair, over a belt and it strained the buttons of his clothes. Grey eyes, hard as the slate tiles of his school, took in our bikes and gear. The disapproval wafted over me, and I wanted to snarl.

Two men judging me in the same week left me wanting to behave like a child and prove my skills. I squared my shoulders and stepped forwards.

"Mr Medway, it's a pleasure."

"Mr Turner." The face mirrored the plum jam voice and belly. A man about my age, but one who hadn't run up and down Welsh mountains in the pouring rain, before being deployed to deserts so dry the snakes thought twice about moving too fast, stood before us. A red wine nose, jowls a boxer dog would be proud of, and stranded hair high on his scalp the colour of fine-grained sandpaper with just enough energy to flutter in the breeze.

Mr Medway turned back to Heather. I didn't blame him. Most people found her easier to talk to, including me.

"Perhaps we can go inside? This heat doesn't agree with me. We're so close to such a large body of water we suffer from constant humidity when the temperature exceeds twenty degrees."

Heather smiled. "That would be lovely. Thank you."

I trailed along behind, still not sure what the hell we were doing here, what he expected us to do, or why he needed us. The few occasions I'd used my 'new' skills over the months since facing down Thomas Moore, I'd felt the whispering call of the dead in various locations and even managed to find them some peace. This place just felt like a big house full of rich children.

We walked through arched double doors, mock-medieval, into the dim and cool interior. I looked around at trophy cabinets, pictures of past head teachers, all men, of course, and a grand staircase, wide and high right in the centre of the large entrance. It opened to a gallery with more faux medieval gothic decoration. The wooden grain on the stairs shone deep and dark in the flood of sunlight brought into the school through two large arched windows on either side of the doorway.

4

MEDWAY HELD HIS ARM OUT, indicating we should follow him. "Come through to my office and I'll explain what we want you to do and how we ended up needing you at all." He shook his head. "I still can't believe any of this is necessary."

A figure moved on the landing, and I sucked in a breath, expecting something to happen. Expecting the taste of rotten water in my mouth.

"Wellie?" asked the shadow.

I squinted as the figure jogged effortlessly down the stairs, the familiar name ringing in my ears.

"Crusty?" I called out in shock, the moment the man became more than a shadow.

Our bodies collided in a hug that spoke of brotherhood and shared memories that bound us tighter than blood. Though there'd been a lot of that as well, it just belonged to other people most of the time, until it didn't.

"Damn me, you look... As ugly as ever," Crusty said with a laugh.

"Yeah, well, I don't look old. What happened?" I ruffled his once ginger hair. It now resembled a stray snowdrift but showed off his blue eyes.

He chuckled. "Teaching makes you go white. Tally are a doddle in comparison." He winked.

"Oh," Heather said. "That makes sense."

I had my arm slung over Crusty's shoulder. He stood only a few inches taller than me. "Heather, meet Crusty, Damien Heaney. Crusty, this is my fiancée, Heather Wicklow."

His eyes widened as he shook her hand. "Well, you lost the prize, but he won it."

She laughed. These days strange men were less of a threat and she maintained her relaxed stance. "He has his moments. It's lovely to meet someone from Lorne's past, but can I ask a question?"

"Sure."

"Why Wellie?"

More of Crusty's laughter. It rolled around the entrance, making Mr Medway scowl, but warmed my heart. I had no idea a Regiment friend lived so close.

"I shouldn't reveal Regiment secrets really, but on this one occasion... He's a farmer's son," he said, as if that explained everything.

Never slow, Heather chuckled. "Farmers wear wellington boots."

Crusty's wide open smile lit up the big room. "You'll do."

"Damien, perhaps you could reminisce on your own time? The boys are expecting you in the gym."

I watched Crusty fight the desire to give Medway a disrespectful salute. "Of course, Michael. Maybe Lorne can come and watch us playing lacrosse before he leaves?" He turned to me. "Come and find me. You can't go without a catch up."

"Roger that."

He clapped me on the shoulder and ran out of the building.

"How long did he serve?" Heather asked.

"We were the same intake, the only two that made it through first selection that time. He served eight years before doing his back. Several months later, he could move, but he decided he'd done his time. We held the bond of brotherhood." Memories washed over me, most of them good. I worked harder these days to keep the positive memories front and centre.

I trailed after Heather into the head teacher's office, but my brain had followed Crusty out to the playing fields. To see someone so familiar in this place baffled me. We'd shared more intimacies than lovers do in some respects. Caged in scrapes for days and nights, using small plastic bags and bottles for our bodily functions, huddled together for warmth, treating wounds, sharing meals. We form strange bonds while serving, but when a man leaves, everything changes. Not just for him, but for those of us still deployed. Crusty left because he cracked several vertebrae falling down the side of a mountain in the Hindu Kush. I'd tumbled down after him and pulled him out of the line of enemy fire by his webbing.

I never knew if my actions ended his career. If I'd waited for the medical evacuation, rather than moved him with a spinal injury, perhaps they'd have saved him from the rods holding his spine in place. I'd gone to the hospital when I returned from deployment, but he made it clear his time was done, that included his friendships. Sadly, it often happened that way. It meant we never shared our memories because only our fellow sufferers could possibly understand.

With so much tumbling around in my head, I crashed into Heather's slim back, not expecting her to be still.

"Sorry," I muttered.

"Concentrate," she hissed.

I tried, but to be honest, this bored me and the thought of chewing some fat with Crusty did not, so I wanted out of the stuffy office. It was hot too, despite the fans and open window. The odour of books permeated the sticky air, rubbing shoulders reluctantly with lemon scented polish strong enough to make my nose tingle, and slightly sour man stink. The office had a wall of photos with Mr Medway shaking hands with notable people, his long list of certificates and images of him on yachts looking nautical. Clearly, he'd rather be at sea than teaching.

The other walls held books. Mostly military history, which didn't interest me, and biographies of soldiers from previous wars and centuries.

"Would you like tea?" Mr Medway asked.

"Water would be nice," Heather said with a smile.

Medway moved behind his large wooden desk to a small refrigerator. He took out three glasses and a jug of water. "We don't believe in plastic where it can be avoided," he said by way of explaining.

"Very wise," Heather agreed. She really wanted to make a good impression.

The room held two small leather armchairs, accompanied by the necessary occasional tables and a large rug, the same shade of blue as the school's emblem. The desk held an expensive computer and little else. Medway must have some minion to do the paperwork.

I took the offered glass of water and sniffed it, expecting the scent of wet dead to drift up. Instead I found it smelt of mint and lemons, matching the furniture polish. Heather and Medway both gave me strange looks. I managed a weak smile in return. Nothing haunted this school. The watery visions I kept experiencing must be to do with the drought. A latent desire for fresh water to give the land back the mud and green I loved, rather than the dry, parched version of England that reminded me of hot deserts the world over.

"Please, do sit down," the head teacher indicated two straight-backed chairs. Probably meant for miscreants when justifying bad behaviour. Or parents he didn't like.

We sat. I held my glass, nervous of the desk's polished surface and water marks. He didn't offer a coaster, and I didn't want to make Heather tut.

"What seems to be the problem?" Heather asked. "I understand we're not the kind of company a man like yourself would usually employ, so what's happened?"

Medway pursed his thin lips, making them bright red for a moment. "I want you to know that I have no patience with supernatural nonsense. We teach religious education here, but I am an atheist. Just as I don't believe in an almighty deity, I do not believe in goblins and demons."

I fervently wished I had the luxury of the same denial.

He sighed. "However, this is a school of boys, and they have imaginations I cannot control. It started after Christmas, and grew worse as we neared the Easter break, which was very early this year. Before we broke for the holiday, the term ended with a death." Medway clasped his hands together and looked down at them. "I still don't understand how we missed it. The summer term has been very stressful, not just because of the exams and sporting events but also this... ghostly madness." His gaze met mine for the first time. "I suppose it was fortunate your friend Damien found one of our twelve-year-olds in the reservoir. At least he's used to seeing dead bodies. The police investigated, and the inquest found for death by misadventure. On the quiet, they said probable suicide, but without a note it was kinder on the family to call it an accident. Ofsted also came and cleared us of any wrongdoing."

I must have looked blank because he added, "The Office for Standards in Education, Children's Services and Skills. They keep us on our toes and make sure we meet the care and educational needs of our pupils."

"I'm sorry for your loss," I said. "It's always a tragedy when a child loses their life." I also felt for Crusty. Regardless of how many dead we counted, the death of a child always tore a hole in your heart and remained vivid in your memories.

"Yes," Medway agreed. "It broke our hearts. He was a popular boy, part of the chess club and a member of the lacrosse team, which is unusual. Some of his friends, several weeks after we lost Ryan, decided to hold a séance with a Ouija board, of all things. They'd made it during Technical Design classes. It was a Saturday night, so we only had the full-time boarders here, twelve boys in total ranging from eleven to sixteen. Five of them took part, the others deemed too young and impressionable." Medway's eyebrows moved around on his large and shiny forehead, looking like dark caterpillars attempting to escape a gardener's fingers. "It seems they are all impressionable."

Heather crossed her legs. Like me, she found the heat suffocating. We'd stripped out of the motorcycle gear, but smart trousers and a t-shirt still proved too much. "What happened next?" she asked.

A long-suffering sigh later, Medway explained. "Damien was the first to catch on during the following week. He's very good at seeing patterns of behaviour and changes that could demonstrate a potential problem." Medway once more graced me with a look. "I suppose it's in your training manual."

My jaw clenched. "Something like that," I growled. Heather glanced at me with concern.

"He's still berating himself for young Ryan, of course. Says he should have read the signs, but we all missed them."

This man didn't understand Crusty at all. If we had a duty to perform and we failed, then someone died, it lived with us forever. We trained so we didn't make mistakes. We didn't have the luxury of second chances. I understood why Crusty couldn't let Ryan's death slip off his shoulders. He'd been told to care for these lads, and he'd carry that burden until someone told him to put it down.

Heather tried to move things on. "So Damien found the Ouija board?"

"It began with some of the younger boys claiming to have seen Ryan in the dormitories. Dripping and covered in weeds, accompanied by a terrible smell." That caught my attention but before I could chase it down, Medway continued, "Then the screaming nightmares started. The older boys, of the full-time boarders, started losing focus in classes, claiming they couldn't sleep because of the banging. A member of the kitchen staff claimed a spirit stabbed her hand with a knife." Medway shook his head. "All foolishness, of course, but what can you do? A sort of hysteria set in. Damien discovered the boys responsible, and we brought in a trauma specialist to help them deal with the grief we thought they suffered. Then the older boys started to 'see' spirits walking the wood during their morning runs and invading the school at night. It's madness. I finally agreed to seek some help from the Church, but they decided they needed more time than I can afford and had a number of hoops to jump through. Which brought me to you, because of a business card and web search."

I shifted position, the sweat on my back sticking me to the chair. "You want us to find out if your school is haunted?"

Medway snorted. "It's not haunted. Your job is to *prove* it isn't haunted by waving your magic gadgets about and showing the boys this is nonsense. I need the placebo effect of your presence."

I felt my eyebrow twitch up. "Is that what you told the Church when you rang them?"

Medway's nostrils flared and his mouth pursed again. He looked like a part of Ghost's anatomy I worked hard to avoid, even if I couldn't escape his constant flatulence. Working hard, I managed to smother the desire to chuckle.

"I made my position clear," he stated. "Their medieval procedures for this kind of thing could have offered some comfort to the boys, but they wanted a full psychological assessment of each child and the parents to be informed. I have no wish to upset the children or the parents with such idiocy."

I thought about Ella and how her faith had saved my sanity, if not my life, on more than one occasion during recent events. "The Church knows far more about this than I do, Mr Medway."

"I don't doubt it, but I need this resolved now and you're all I have in the area."

My body tensed. Heather, forever attuned to me, placed a hand on my arm before I reached over the desk and started rearranging Medway's wandering caterpillar eyebrows.

Heather headed me off at the pass. "Why don't you let us look around the school? Maybe spend the night? That way, we can make a full assessment of the situation and by meeting some of the boys, we can start calming things down. If there is anything supernatural amiss here, then we'll soon root out the problem. I understand your disbelief, Mr Medway, but..." Heather allowed the sentence to hang. "There could be some problem you're not seeing because you're too close to the boys. It could be as simple as hormones going a bit nuts because of the weather, or a leaking pipe in the walls. We'll figure it out."

Medway, obviously preferring Heather's soft voice to mine, nodded. "Very well. I have a conference in London to attend for a week, so I don't have to watch this foolishness. Most of the boys left yesterday for the summer break, but some will be with us for the next few weeks. Damien will also be here along with Polly, our school nurse and cook, to act as guardians to those left."

Heather nodded. "Then we can stay tonight?"

I looked at her. "What about Ghost?"

"I'll phone Ella. She can take him."

Seeing Ghost with Ella never failed to worry me. Despite being a gentle giant, Ghost was young… and a giant.

Medway put in, "I would like this resolved quickly. We'll sanction a bonus if you could have this finished by the end of the week."

I blinked. Today was Tuesday, and I didn't have any clients for the survival courses until Saturday. "Done," I said.

5

STANDING IN THE SUN, OUTSIDE the school's main building, I said, "Well, this is going to be easy money for a change."

Heather glanced at me, shielding her eyes. "You sure?"

I nodded. "Nothing here but the squirrels. Give Ella a ring about Ghost and then we'll go find Crusty."

"I'll make a wild suggestion that you don't call him that in front of the kids," Heather said, pulling out her phone and walking away a little to call Ella.

I leaned on the bike and looked over the building and grounds. Taking it all in. From the front, the building looked isolated, but behind it stood the dorms for the boys and a large gym and refectory. To my right, sheltered by a ribbon of conifers, I saw the playing fields. A long strip of well-tended grass now looking a little brown and patchy in places.

If it weren't for the money, which we needed, I wouldn't be here. Trying to use an ability I only admitted to with reluctance didn't make me a happy little soldier. Heather kept up her argument that it helped people, that I'd been given this gift for a reason, that wasting it or denying it just made my life more difficult, but I really didn't like it. Knowing what lay on the other side of a door we needed kicking in before some arsehole blew us up or shot at us, that was one thing. Actively going to someone's home—or school in this case—and finding spooks who didn't work for the notorious GRU, or ISI seemed fraudulent to me.

Still, if this place wanted to give me money, then I'd take it. Finding security work that didn't require me to use a firearm would be very difficult, unless I wanted to patrol a car park for Lidl in Bridgwater, so I needed to knuckle down and accept my new role in life.

I watched Heather laugh at something Ella said, and it made me smile. If toeing the line meant keeping Heather happy, then I'd do everything I could to make this work. Whatever talent I had for the supernatural, I'd use it and keep a roof over our heads. Heather needed time to reach her goals, and I wanted to give her that safety.

She walked towards me. "All sorted. Ella's going to stay at the farm overnight. It's easier than trying to move Ghost down to her place. He just knocks everything over."

I chuckled. "Yeah, it's a small bungalow."

"It really is. She says she's dropping in to see Willow today. They're planning a gentle walk to Eddie's place and Lilian is doing them lunch."

Too many of Willow's friends couldn't handle her dramatic change. To be honest, I struggled. I'd lost a lot of friends over the years to bullets and brain injury of various kinds, and it was always hard to reassess the changes in the person you knew. To learn to love the new version of that person. Willow had lost a lot of weight. Grey grew back with her brown stubble of hair. Her eyes had a haunted look which mirrored the sadness in her heart. She struggled with walking, short-term memory, and performing any delicate task. Paul loved her, cared for her, and had become her power of attorney for the moment. She'd be due some hefty compensation because of Shaw escaping custody. A *For Sale* sign now hung outside the shop, where I'd first met her, and that made me sad as well.

The tiny village of Luccombe rallied around thanks to Ella, and Willow found welcome in the community.

"Good. I'm due to go help out later in the week. She wants to start doing yoga and meditation again, but is worried about doing it alone. I said I'd join her, and we'd make it a class when she had her confidence back. Something she could teach, get her back out into the world."

Heather raised an eyebrow. "I thought yoga and meditation were, and I quote, 'a lot of old bollocks, what's wrong with a twenty mile yomp?'"

I had the good grace to blush. "Yeah, alright. I can't imagine trying to twist myself into a pretzel either, but she needs the help."

We watched as a sleek Mazda MX5 in bright red pulled up. Medway's window came down and his head appeared. "I'm leaving now. Damien will see to your needs. Remember, you have until the end of the week to clear this up. I'll want a full report and invoice on my desk for the governors."

Heather stepped in front of me, doubtless picking up on my desire to rip the man out through the window of his motorised skateboard. "Of course. We'll have it all squared away by Friday."

The man sniffed, looked at me as if he'd scraped me off his shoe and drove off, the fat wheels scattering gravel. Something sorely tempted me to give him a two-fingered salute.

"How the hell does someone like him afford a car like that?" I asked. "It's brand new."

"Lorne!" bellowed Crusty in a voice designed to carry between mountain tops. "Has the miserable bastard gone yet?" Still in gym shorts and trainers, my old mucker ran towards us.

"He's fled the scene alright."

"Good, then maybe you can tell me what the hell you're doing in my neck of the woods?" He nodded after Medway. "He's been really on edge since we found Ryan. Spending less and less time at the school. Is that why you're here?" Damien's blue eyes searched mine, and I knew I'd have to tell him the truth. Then I'd have to wait for him to stop laughing.

"I need scran, mucker. Any chance we can find some fodder and I'll explain?"

"Sure, let me round the lads up and we'll take you to the canteen. Polly's here somewhere." Damien flashed one of his smiles and we followed him.

It turned out Damien didn't want to take the piss out of me. We sat in the kitchen with five boys, three of the poor buggers at twelve, one at fifteen and the last at sixteen.

Polly, the nurse and 'kitchen skivvy', her words, sent the lads outside with sandwiches.

Heather offered to help with the scran and asked, "What brought you to Somerset?"

Polly laughed; a warm sound designed to wrap you in a blanket of joy.

"You're right. I'm not a native of these parts." As if her North London accent didn't give it away. "After my mother was caught up in the Windrush scandal and I finally convinced the bloody government we had a right to remain in the UK, I'd had enough of city life. I wanted a fresh start. The bastards wanted to send her back to Jamaica after sixty years of being here legally. They lost the paperwork, but we had to prove she had a legal right to stay." Clearly Polly still had issues. I didn't blame her.

I wondered briefly when my actions during the War on Terror would be deemed a war crime and I'd be hunted by the country I served after I'd followed orders.

Polly continued, "When I managed to get it all sorted, I needed a real break and hiding away down here offered me that opportunity. Besides, some of these boys need to see some ethnic diversity." She winked at Damien, and I realised something more than friendship must hover between these two lucky ducks.

Damien asked, "So, come on, Wellie, what are you doing here?"

It took a while to explain how things had changed for me after I left The Regiment. Carving out a new life in this strange world of hauntings and occult mysteries, alongside my more prosaic business.

When I finished talking, lunch had been over for a while and Damien found us some beers. "You're basically a ghostbuster?"

"I wouldn't go that far. I'm more of a…" Glancing at Heather, I hoped she'd bale me out.

"Enabler," she provided. "He senses them. His instincts provide him with an answer and off they go into the light—or wherever. Those of us who are sensitive can also pick up on what's happening, sometimes see it. It's like he gives them the strength they need to make their intentions known."

I grunted. "That bit sucks. Sometimes it's difficult, with the PTSD, to know the difference. It's still a juggling act and I still drop the balls." The recent manifestation of poisoned water being a case in point.

"Is it bad?" Damien asked in a quiet voice. He wasn't asking about the spirit visions.

Our eyes met. I knew what he meant. "Yeah, fella, it's bad."

Polly's hand closed over Damien's, and I knew he had his share of nightmares.

I didn't tell him about Al-Ahmar, my hitchhiking djinn. If he made himself known, after months of silence, I'd find a way to square it, but I didn't want to confuse the issue.

"You always had a sixth sense. I lost count of the times you saved our lives by pushing one of us out of the way just seconds before something happened."

"Didn't always manage it," I muttered, studying the metal top of the industrial kitchen table. "I let you down."

Damien snorted. "Fuck off, did you. If you'd left me on that mountainside, rather than dragging me into the gulch, I'd be dead. They'd have used me for target practice. I'd rather have a dodgy spine and discharge than be dead. Besides, I did the circuit for a while once I found my feet."

I hadn't known he'd been in security. At least I hoped he meant that circuit and not the one for mercenaries. I raised a smile. "Cheers, mucker."

"Right, let's get you around this place. See if you can pick up on anything and I can fill you in on anything Medway left out. Which is probably quite a bit. Boys!" The bellow made us all start.

Polly shook herself. "I wish you wouldn't do that."

Five boys trooped in from the garden. "Sir?" asked the eldest. He stood just shy of six feet and his shoulders filled the t-shirt he wore. Hair the colour of old gold flopped over his cornflower eyes. By the time he reached university, he'd be shattering hearts. Even I could see it. One of the younger lads knew it too and stood just behind him with a forlorn gaze. Bless him.

"I'm about to give our guests a tour of the school, Adam. Maybe you could join us as one of those responsible for Medway having to hire a local psychic to debug our sanctuary?"

A scruffy lad, one of the young ones, piped up. "Can we come, sir?"

Damien narrowed his eyes. "I don't know, Olly, can you?"

Olly conferred with his cohort for a moment. "Yes, sir, we can come."

I hid my smile. I didn't have any experience with children this age—or any age, to be honest—but Damien handled them well. He'd been a teacher longer than he'd been in the army, so I guessed it was practice.

The boy, who had gazed so adoringly at Adam, rolled his eyes. "They'll just talk rubbish, sir. You know what they're like."

"I hope not, Robert. Mr Turner here used to work with me, so he won't put up with your bollocks."

The swear word made the younger ones grin.

Polly shuddered. "I'll stay here and start on dinner. I don't need any more ghost stories, thank you very much."

"Just a quick question, Polly," I said. "Medway mentioned a member of staff who thinks a ghost stabbed her hand?"

Polly rolled her expressive eyes. "Tessa, bloody woman. No, it wasn't a ghost. She's trying to find a way to sue the school."

"So she didn't find a knife stuck in her hand?" Heather asked.

"Oh, she did, but I'll testify to the fact it wasn't a ghost," Polly said, before vanishing in the larder. "She did it to herself so she could skive off work."

I glanced at Damien.

He grinned, looking like a feral old wolf for a moment. "I think Polly did it because the woman pissed her off—closet, or not so closet—racist. Tessa's too scared to come after Polly, so she's going for the school. The ghost thing is bollocks for certain." He chuckled and walked off.

Heather shrugged and said, "Seems fair," then followed Damien. I kept in line with her. The boys trailed out behind us like ducklings and quacked almost as much.

Adam asked from behind me, "You were in the army, Mr Turner?"

"I was."

"As an officer?"

Damien snorted from the front.

"No, son. Well, a non-commissioned officer. Sergeant-major before I left."

Adam squared his shoulders. "I want to go to Sandhurst. I want to be a Paratrooper."

Damien and I shared a look. He said, "Maybe you should talk to Lorne about it, Adam. He'll be able to give you some real insight into the consequences."

It surprised me. Damien had loved the army. Loved being in-country and fully operational. He'd never really been into the hearts and minds stuff. He looked like an action hero and behaved like one.

We'd both changed.

The afternoon sun made us lazy, and we drifted from empty classroom to empty classroom like prospective parents. Then we followed the long, covered hallway between the main school building and the low modern dorms nestling among the trees. Nothing in me reacted to the place. Each large room full of various amounts of school equipment was just that, a room designed for education. The dorms had been retro fitted for two to four lads sharing a space large enough for beds and desks in a private room. No locks on doors. The school specialised in teaching a modern curriculum but supplemented it with a great deal of outdoor activity and practical skills. They had only one hundred and fifty pupils, most of whom boarded during the week, a few of which hardly ever went home.

Along the way, the lads told us about sightings and things happening.

When we reached the end of the tour, Damien turned to me. "Anything?"

I shook my head. "Either my senses are off kilter or there's nothing here to feel." I looked at Heather. "You?"

"Giving it a bit more time might be a good idea," she said. During the tour, she'd grown quiet and distant from me, as if uncertain of her place with Damien being such a big part of my life. He'd known me longer, been around me during a time in my life when I'd still loved the army. He had privileged information about me that excluded the man she knew. The man she loved. I'd been so different then, but I didn't know how to explain.

We did a brief walk into the woods, the atmosphere damp and hot. The summer-dark trees held the air hostage under their mighty boughs. This woodland kept its age deep in its roots, deeper still in the wide trunks of the trees, and the vast array of forest flora. I liked the dimness, the bitter scent of summer dry soil. I sensed nothing in the woods. None of my usual triggers went off and boredom settled in.

By the time we returned to the school, Damien had duties, and the boys had homework. He gave us a room to share with separate narrow, uncomfortable beds. I'd bunked alone for years, so it didn't matter too much.

"We need to set up equipment, Lorne," Heather said, perching on her bed.

"Really? There's nothing here, love." I lay back, hands behind my head, and closed my eyes. The room, shaded by large pine trees, remained fairly cool and I had a need for a nap.

She sighed. "Fine, I'll set up where the boys think they saw most of the activity."

I opened an eye. "Set up what?"

Over the last few months, we'd been picking up various packages from Ella's—not even Amazon wanted to come to the farm if they could avoid it— containing paranormal equipment. I now had a vague idea what an EMF meter did in relation to ghosts, a sophisticated thermometer, and a thermal camera. I'd used thermal cameras in the past to trace enemy combatants through all kinds of terrain. I kept letting it wash over me, in the same way many men let the accumulation of women's shoes wash over them. When I'd mentioned this to Ella, her eyes turned from hazel to agate, and I'd received a brief but pointed bollocking.

Heather grabbed her motorcycle panniers and left the room. I dozed off. When I woke, she hadn't returned, so I went hunting and headed to the kitchen. I found Damien.

He grinned at my appearance. "You looking for your lovely lady?"

"Yeah."

"She's with Polly and some of the younger lads picking veg for dinner from the garden. I have to say, mucker, you're punching well above your weight with that one. She's a spitfire."

I flicked the kettle on. "Yeah. I'm a lucky man, so hands off."

Damien held his paws in the air. "Not my type, mate. I like 'em like Polly, with a lot more meat on their bones. Heather looks like a strong breeze will have her over."

"She's a great deal tougher than she looks," I said. "You and Polly are…?"

"We are," he said with a grin. "She's a cracking woman."

"I'm pleased for you. Us old soldiers need hearth and home to keep us settled."

Damien blew out. "To be honest, it all feels like it happened to someone else. I've been out so long it's only the dreams that remind me of that life. Even the few years I spent on the circuit. Seeing you was a shock."

"You did rather drop out of our lives."

He shrugged. "Not much point staying in touch when all your mates are off saving the world and you're stuck in a hospital. Your deployments were long. Besides, I knew at some point you'd be facing promotion and your dedication to the job went beyond that of most of us."

"Much good it did me," I said, making us a cuppa.

The evening meal, like lunch, happened in a languid haze of chatter and memories. Heather wanted to sleep before doing a stint watching the sites she'd chosen for her equipment. I sat in the kitchen with Damien and a bottle of scotch. Things became a bit hazy after that.

6

THE MORNING ARRIVED ALL TOO soon.

We stood on either side of the small room and Heather's eyes blazed like a blacksmith's forge full of blue fire.

"What do you mean, you're leaving?" she snarled, voice low and as hot as her eyes.

"I mean, nothing happened. I didn't so much as have a bad dream. This place isn't haunted by anything other than the testosterone and the imaginations of teenage boys." My head pounded, my eyes ached, and my mouth felt like a badger had taken a piss in it. I'd forgotten what drinking with Damien could be like.

Heather's lip curled. "I'm not bloody surprised you slept. All I could hear was you snoring, and it stinks like a nightclub after a stag party in here. I'm not leaving, Lorne. This isn't done. Those lads, if you'd bothered talking to them, rather than Crusty," she said his name like it came from the toilet bowl, "might have taught you something."

My eyes narrowed, mostly because she'd opened the curtains and the sun now poured into our room at a low angle. "I wouldn't expect you to understand what I went through with him—"

Her hands reacted violently to this, and my brain hurt as I tried to track them. "Oh, of course I wouldn't understand. I've only been living with you for a year. Listening to your every murmur and trying to help you find a way to settle your memories so you can have a normal life. A happy life. No… I know nothing about your time in the fucking army."

We rarely, if ever, swore at each other and we'd never had a knock down row like this. I was bewildered and lost, and I didn't like how it made me feel. It meant I overreacted to Heather's anger.

"For fuck's sake, Heather. This is a ridiculous business. How the hell did you talk me into it? If you want to know the truth, I'm sick of being pulled in this direction. I don't want to be psychic. I don't want to be a ghost hunter."

"Ah," sarcasm dripped from those sweet lips. "You poor thing. You don't want to see the dead. Well, I don't want to listen to your screams when they march through your bloody thick head. Fine. You want to go, go. I'm staying and helping these boys because someone has to give a shit. Maybe you and Damien can run your fucking survival business together. He'll doubtless be so much better at it than little old me." She yanked opened the door to the room and the sound when it smashed home almost knocked me off my feet.

Anger rippled through me. Layers of it lacing together like a Gordian knot and just as unfathomable. I didn't want to be angry. I didn't want to be here. I didn't want to see Heather so upset. I didn't want to be angry with her. Everything felt off-kilter in this place, like someone had rubbed me raw with sandpaper. I needed out.

I picked up my bike gear. Packed my dirty t-shirt, socks and toothbrush, then left the dorm room. When I arrived in the kitchen I found Damien drinking coffee.

"I'm off, mucker. I'll give you a ring and we can have another catch up."

He blinked. "Erm. Okay. Heather is…" He looked around as if she'd turn up like my shadow.

"Don't know, she's staying."

"Right. See you soon then." He frowned, brain function far below premium.

I climbed on my bike, probably still over the limit, and roared off. I didn't head home. I headed for roads I knew had no police speed traps on them and opened the bike up. Two hours later and I was heading for Cornwall. I'd also calmed down. I pulled into a Little Chef on the A30 somewhere in Devon and ordered a full English with two cups of tea.

Sitting in the small café, I watched the traffic and realised what a twat I'd been to my girl. Something was wrong, and I'd made it so much worse. It had to be the meeting with her father and her missing brother. Heather felt unsettled, and I'd humiliated her by being the cynic around Damien and trying to remember the man I'd once been, not the one she loved. I also realised way too late that we just didn't behave like this, even on a bad day, and despite my belief the school wasn't haunted, there could be something in there able to destroy rational behaviour.

I ate the food without tasting it, knowing I just needed fuel, and wondered how to fix our first argument.

Nothing came to mind except a grovelling apology. Gulping my tea, I stared through enormous picture windows at the traffic whizzing past and the fields beyond.

Shock swept through me with the same speed the swallows danced overhead.

"What the…" I put my mug down.

A boy stood in the centre of the road. A boy in winter clothing, soaking wet, and just staring at me through the glass. I banged my knees trying to scramble out from the bench seat, which made me glance down at the table to check my tea. Dirty, stinking water flooded the empty plate and filled the mug to overflowing. In confusion, I glanced back at the boy. A lorry descended on the tiny figure. I felt the scream gathering in my throat and I wanted to smash the glass of the window, so I had a more direct route to the child.

The lorry arrived. He didn't stop. He didn't blow his horn. The boy just ceased being in the road.

My body shook. The release of unused adrenaline turned my stomach and made the fry-up a terrible choice for a hangover cure.

The water on the table also vanished. I stared at the clean plate and half-empty mug.

Placing my palms on the smooth surface before me, I focused on slow breaths, wishing with all my heart Heather sat next to me, talking me through the rising surge of panic.

"Fuck, I'm being haunted," I muttered. I knew I needed to get to the school, but I needed some time at home. I also needed to see Ghost. When I felt stable again, I rose, paid and left the small café.

I filled up my tank at the petrol station, flinching at the price, and headed for the farm at a more sedate pace. By the time I reached it, the heat of the day bore down, and I needed nothing more than a gallon of cold water, a shower and another sleep. I'd forgotten Ella and Ghost waited for me.

Muscles aching from fatigue, unused to alcohol abuse that bad, I schlepped up to the backdoor.

"Hi, honey, I'm home," I called out.

Ghost launched himself at me and I braced. At least he was pleased to see me. Ella, not so much.

"Heather's been on the phone."

I had the feeling that might happen, though I wished she'd keep our problems to private. Or maybe that was a guilty conscience speaking. I liked it when she told people how proud of our achievements she was, or how much she loved her life at the farm.

"I screwed up."

"Yes, you did. I suggest you apologise and grovel."

"It wasn't that bad," I said.

"Lorne, you basically told her the business she's set up on her own and worked hard to make professional was a waste of time and you hated it. On top of that, she's dealing with her family issues."

"You'd know more about that than me. She doesn't tell me anything."

"That's because she doesn't know how to, Lorne. Also, you got pissed and behaved like the man who used her as a punching bag when he drank."

I threw my bike lid at the chair by the old range that Heather liked to use when huddling for warmth on a wintry morning. It bounced on a cushion and smacked onto the floor. "I did not hit her!"

Ella reached me in three strides. "No. What you did was almost worse.

You cut her out. Closed her down. Got good and drunk with a crony and ignored her." Ella poked me in the chest, not the least cowed by the flare of temper. "You are the centre of her world, you fool. She's still learning how to function out there and you scared her by being like the people she ran from." Ella's face was almost as white as her dog collar, except for two spots of high colour on her cheeks. I'd never seen her like this.

"Shouldn't she be telling me this?" I muttered.

"Yes, but she can't. She doesn't have the words, and this needs fixing fast. Heather's vulnerable in a way you can't possibly understand. You've never been a victim, Lorne. Being a white knight isn't enough. You want to protect her? Then you need to open her up and make her really trust you. Right now, she doesn't."

That hurt. That hurt a lot.

I sighed. "Fine. I'll fix it." I knew I ought to tell Ella about the ghost boy, but I didn't have the willpower.

Ella's hand covered my wrist, and she gave it a good squeeze. "You stink like a brewery. Get a shower and get your head down. Go back to the school tomorrow. I've a service in Luccombe tonight so I'm off home. Take Ghost with you. He'll help."

An idea occurred to me. "Could you come to the school and do one of your blessing things?" I asked.

"Only if there really is a problem in the place. Prove there's a problem, then I'll help," she said. "But I'll also need the permission of the local vicar, so we'll have to think about that as well. Oh, and while we're at it, Paul rang. Willow's had a terrible couple of nights. Yoga is off. She doesn't want to see anyone. I think Paul could do with a chat."

"Christ, when did I become the emotional hand holder?" I muttered.

"Since people began to care about you and look after you. It goes both ways. I'll see you later." She left.

I stared at the dog. "Guess I'm walking you now."

Ghost turned in a tight circle and wiped out one of the kitchen chairs in the process.

While walking the dog over the parched moor, I had a good idea. Heather needed help with her family, and I thought finding her brother might be the key to that little conundrum. I knew just the man to help me find a missing brother.

When I reached the farm and fed Ghost, I called Paul. He spent twenty minutes explaining the latest problems with Willow, mostly mobility problems again, before promising to find this mysterious brother of Heather's. I crashed out soon after that.

THE FOLLOWING DAY, I ROSE before dawn. I packed a little of Heather's summer clothes in a daysack, the dog bowl and some food in a bag for life, and risked taking the old Nissan Warrior back to Clatworthy. On the way, I stopped off in Minehead and went to the jeweller's in the main street. I found a cuff bracelet of racing wolves in silver made locally and knew she'd love it. Armed and ready for operation, *Forgive Me*, I headed to the wild country.

It took an hour because of traffic, so I knew the occupants of the school would be awake. When I pulled up, the place looked the same as the day before but…

I frowned, my instincts waking up and taking notice for the first time. The shiver of a black feather being dragged over my scalp forced me to suck in a sharp breath. A snide giggle made me turn so fast I smacked my elbow on the wing mirror.

"Shit." It bloody hurt. I rubbed and flexed my fingers, trying to bring back the sensation. A shadow shot off into the trees, human shaped. "What the hell is going on?" I murmured.

The sky over the woodland nearest the school erupted in a flurry of black wings and harsh alarm calls. The crows rose and wheeled off away from the reservoir. I watched them twist and curl in the sullen air and wished I could go with them. How could somewhere change so fast in just a day?

Did it hide from me? Was that possible? Something held sway here, and it wasn't the sunlight and innocence of the day before.

That's when another dose of panic took over. Where was Heather?

Ghost jumped down out of the truck the moment I opened the door, and a low rumble filled the space between us. It alarmed me.

I clicked his lead on the collar. "Yeah, you and me both, mucker. We need to find your mum."

He looked up at me.

I checked my phone. No signal. Odd, but not really a surprise. All mobile reception in rural communities could be hit and miss.

"Come on." I jogged towards the school, veering off and heading to the back. I figured the kitchen and dorms would be the best place to find the others. Ghost kept an easy pace with me, for once not distracted by every smell in the area.

When I came around the back of the main building, a small, dark-haired figure stood outside with a mug cradled in her hands. Ghost rushed for her, and I had the good sense to release the lead before he wiped me out. Heather yelped, recovered, and I smiled as she cuddled the dog. Once he'd been sorted, she looked at me.

Her eyes, usually bright and full of life, had the same desperate haunted cast I'd seen the first time we'd met in a biker bar full of violence and hate.

A wobble started on her lower lip.

I needed to be first. "I'm so sorry, Heather. I was out of order. I made a mistake and I want to apologise," I said. Then I realised I stood there as if trying to explain a fouled operation to my CO.

Unlike my commanding officers, Heather folded instantly and threw her arms around my chest, burying her head in my shoulder. "I'm so glad you came back. I've been so worried. I shouldn't have lost my temper, either."

The world, previously tilted at an odd angle, shifted back and centred. I breathed out.

I wrapped her up in my arms despite the heat. "What's happened?" I asked.

Heather unpeeled herself from my shirt. "It's been a horrible night, Lorne. This place is wrong. It's not like Scob was, or even the hospital in Horner.

Whatever is here is hunting people down. It's active. I can feel it sticking to me."

I brushed hair from her face. "Okay, okay, we'll sort it. I'm sorry I didn't believe you. Me, of all people." Lifting my mouth I tried a half smile. She didn't punch me, so I explained about the boy and apologised again, this time for not telling her sooner.

"I think it wanted you gone," she muttered.

"Do you believe that's possible?" I asked.

She shrugged, a wet thing lacking any form of vigour. "I don't know. Not in any of the reading I've been doing over the last few months."

Other than her college work, most of Heather's reading had revolved around the occult and paranormal.

"Where's Crusty and Polly?" I asked.

"Far as I know, he got drunk again last night. No one else is up yet. It was a rough night with the boys. I ended up with the younger ones. We dragged several mattresses into the one room and kipped on the floor."

"It was that bad?"

She nodded. "Come on, I'll explain over breakfast."

7

WE SAT IN THE INDUSTRIAL kitchen, and I took over breakfast duties, guilt gnawing a hole in my masculinity. I should have listened to Heather. What use am I if I can't help those who need me? Pride and arrogance kept me away. I once had a sergeant who'd thought it wise to impart a pearl or two of wisdom in the ears of his new privates when they joined the SAS. He'd said in thick Glaswegian, 'Pride and arrogance are two of the many things that'll get you killed in this regiment'. He wasn't wrong.

Heather sat, with Ghost's head on her lap, at the table nibbling toast. The dog ate more than she did and the paleness under her summer tan worried me.

"What happened?" I prompted.

"It started after sunset, close to eleven. Lights flickered, not unusual apparently, but then I kept noticing this terrible smell. I asked Damien about it, but he said it was the drains. It didn't smell like drains to me. I've lived in bedsits. I know how drains smell."

I'd have to take her word for that, though I'd smelled enough open sewers in my time and latrines. It did coincide with the horrible, stinking water I kept experiencing. I really could be a total bloody fool. Whatever haunted this school had reached out to me days ago.

Heather drew circles on her plate with some toast. "It reminded me of manky pond water with a hefty dose of dead sheep in the mix. The first of the boys, Killian, knocked on my door and asked if he could change rooms as the smell in his was so bad."

"Why didn't he go to Polly?" I asked.

"Couldn't find her. I guess she was with Damien somewhere else. Besides, I don't think the boys like wandering around the school at night. The smell in his and Mason's room made me gag when I checked it. That's when the knocking started. It raced over the ceiling, like someone stamping on the roof, making us all jump. The other youngster, Olly, appeared in the hallway and all the lights went out. I had my phone on me, so they reached me, and we retreated to my room. The banging went on for a while, then nothing. The lights came back after that."

"What about the older lads?"

Heather shook her head. "Adam and Robert are in a different set of halls, and I didn't see them."

"What if it was a prank on their part?"

"If they were playing a prank, I don't really see how. Running over a roof wouldn't make that much noise, though we can try it if you want. The really horrible bit came when something started knocking on the door. I called out a few times, but when I went to open it, Olly stopped me. He said I'd be letting the smell in and when that happened, things could go wrong." Her voice petered out.

"What did he mean?"

"Apparently, Killian and Mason used to share a room with Ryan, the lad that died. They think it's him come back from the reservoir after the Ouija board game. Olly was there, despite being banned by Adam." She peeled off another piece of toast dripping with honey and gave it to Ghost.

"What do you think? Could it be Ryan?" I asked.

She focused on me for the first time. "I think it's far worse than some poor child."

"What makes you say that?" Intrigued despite myself.

Heather gazed at the dog, her fingers tight in his thick ruff. "I'm struggling to believe what they said, but…"

"Just tell me. It might be weird, but we know there's often a grain of truth in the weird." I watched her and felt surprised by the obvious distress.

"They said the spirit board told them to find the treasure. To find it and destroy it."

I stirred the milk and oats together slowly. "Treasure? Where?"

She shook her head. "That's the problem. It just said 'river' apparently. So the younger kids, they've spent their time off from school searching for this treasure. The older ones thought it was bollocks. Apparently, it started out as a bit of fun. Then it wasn't. Killian and Olly, even Mason, think Ryan might have gone looking for the treasure alone. That's how he ended up in the water. They all said he was obsessed. Driven mad towards the end, always trying to get out of classes so he could go looking."

"That's sad. Maybe he was unhappy here." I switched subjects. "What have your instruments told you?" I watched her feed more toast to the dog, so rummaged in the cupboards and found the makings of porridge.

A heavy sigh told me enough. "They didn't work, and I don't know why. There's nothing in the talcum powder, none of the tripwires have triggered, the cameras have caught nothing. The sound recordings picked up bugger all but hard static. The boys didn't want me leaving them long enough to take EMF readings or to use the Geiger counter."

We had a Geiger counter? It was the previous comment that made me frown. "What do you mean by hard static?" The pan heated quickly, I stirred in a pinch of salt and some honey.

Heather dragged her laptop towards her and began waking it up. Where mine needed the computer equivalent of caffeine, sugar and several cigarettes to start, her new computer chirped to life with all the joy of a blackbird in spring. I found its eagerness to please disturbing.

"Here, listen," she said, voice subdued, shoulders hunched.

A rough sound of white noise bounced around the kitchen. Ghost's ears pivoted, and he tried to climb into Heather's lap, licking her face in worry.

"Yeah, alright, big man, I don't like it either, but we'll have none of that," she said, pushing him down.

"Do you have your earphones with you?" I asked.

She fished them out of a side pocket. I put the porridge in a bowl and handed it over; she'd struggle to share that with the dog, and turned the laptop towards me. With a bit of fiddling, I found the sound level I could tolerate and listened to the strange hiss of noise.

By bringing the bass right up, I caught something in the background. I knew from previous experience white sound could hide all manner of data and as I fiddled with the frequencies, I thought I detected verbal noise.

While I worked, the kitchen filled. Polly arrived with Adam and Robert, all of them giving me a nod of welcome. I couldn't help but notice how quiet and pale the two lads looked. The three youngest also arrived and Ghost distracted them while Polly prepared breakfast for the lads.

"What are we going to do?" Olly asked.

I pulled back the headphone. "About what?" I asked, trying to find out more intel.

Olly glanced at Heather. "Didn't you tell him?"

"I did, but he'll want to hear your version," she said, her patience surprising me.

"Why? Doesn't he believe you?"

Heather smiled. "He believes me, but witnesses of the same event can have different perspectives, and good detectives collect all the information. Once they have everything, they can discard the differences between accounts, or use them if appropriate, and that's when they have more chance of finding verifiable facts. Those facts can then lead them in the right direction to solving the riddle. So he needs your accounts."

Killian spoke next. "I want to go home." He had soft green eyes and freckles a few shades darker than his hair.

Polly took his hand as she laid the table. "I know, sweetheart. You will when your parents return from the embassy in Thailand. It won't be long."

"It's three weeks! I could be dead by then!" Killian yelled. He stood up with such passion, he knocked over his chair. The next thing I knew, he'd raced off outside with Ghost in hot pursuit.

"Shit," I mumbled, yanking off the headphones and dashing off after the lad.

The last thing any of us wanted to deal with was another dead boy. I'd be keeping careful watch over this little tangle of hormones until we had the problem pinned down.

"Killian, wait. Ghost! Bloody well stop," I barked.

Fortunately, the dog would never be a hair missile, more of a hearth rug. He soon ran out of emergency energy and came back to me. Together we kept pace with the running boy but didn't push to overtake him. I figured giving him some space to run off his fear would help our conversation. He needed a clear head.

When we reached the end of the playing fields, the lad slowed to a walk. I did the same thing, though Ghost rejoined the child. He looked small and lost among the shadows of the big pine trees on the edge of this bit of the school property.

Killian threw himself to the dry ground. I sat next to him, the dog between us. Small hands buried themselves in Ghost's ruff.

The lad sniffed. "I haven't seen my parents in over a year. Not in real life."

"I'm sorry, lad. I know a lot of fathers who missed their kids while we served overseas."

"My dad won't believe me about the ghosts in the school. He thinks it's all rubbish. Doesn't believe in anything. He thinks I'm weak."

Talking to children wasn't really one of my skills, so I took it carefully. "I'm sure that's not true."

The boy looked at me with such disgust I knew I'd just fumbled the ball and scored an own goal.

"Fair enough," I muttered. "I don't know what I'm talking about. To be honest, it doesn't really matter what he thinks. It's what you do that matters. If you think there are ghosts here, tell me about them and we'll try to solve the problem together."

Killian thought about this for a while, his fingers in silent communion with Ghost's fur. "It started before Ryan died. He shared a room with me, you know that?"

I nodded. "Heather told me."

"He was my best friend."

"I'm sorry. I lost my best friend when I was twelve. It hurts." Let's hope it didn't haunt him the way Tommy haunted me all those years.

"What happened?"

I debated about whether telling the truth would help, but decided if I wanted Ryan's secrets, I needed to give something in return. "Some evil people stole him from us and never gave him back. He died a stranger in a strange world we didn't understand."

Killian thought about this. He seemed the type to think about a lot of things. "I'm sorry."

"Thanks."

"Ryan was amazing. Funny, kind, clever, he loved dogs. His mum was amazing. I used to stay with them, but she..." Killian bowed his head. "She doesn't want to see me anymore. His sister died as well. I guess that makes it worse."

My heart broke for the little man. I put a hand on his shoulder. "It'll change, son. I promise. She's in a lot of pain right now and although that pain will never go, she will learn to see the joy in those who love her. It just takes time. You need to be there when she's ready."

Killian nodded. "I'll try. Ryan, he used to..." Killian sniffed and wiped his nose on his arm. I fought my chuckle at the familiar behaviour. "Ryan used to love telling stories, especially ghost stories, but then they happened for real, and it all got really heavy."

"When was this?" I asked.

"January. It's freezing here in the winter. We spend a lot of time in the common room. He was given a tarot pack for Christmas, and he started doing readings for everyone. It was fun, but then the nightmares started."

"What happened in the nightmares?" I tried not to think about the ethics of giving a twelve-year-old a tarot deck. Willow wouldn't approve.

"He'd see dead people in an old church he didn't know. There'd be water swamping everything. He kept drowning in his dreams and joining the dead people. Then a monster would come and start eating the dead people. He always woke up when the monster tried to eat him. It was always the same dream. I told him that he needed to throw away the cards, but he wouldn't."

"Do you have them?" I asked.

Killian shook his head. "Monster Medway confiscated them when they cleaned out Ryan's stuff. I expect they're in his office."

I had to hide my chuckle at the nickname for the head teacher. I also knew the cards wouldn't be in his office for much longer. "Okay, Killian, what happened next?"

"Ryan stopped eating properly. He became real quiet. We all thought it was because his parents had split up. That can happen, right?" Killian looked at me as if I could give him answers to questions he didn't want to ask.

I nodded. "Yeah, it can happen. None of this is on you. Understood?"

A slow nod. "I keep trying to tell myself that." He sighed. "I'd hear him whispering in the bathroom. We have a small bathroom in our dorm because there are three or four of us in there most of the time. It makes it cheaper for the parents if we share. None of us are properly rich, most of us are army brats or our parents work for the government. Ryan would lock himself in there and whisper to someone. I couldn't hear what he said, but sometimes I heard him crying."

Jesus, this story gave me the heebie-jeebies.

"Then one day, I woke up, and he wasn't in his bed. I went looking for him but couldn't find him. That's when I saw Mr Heaney carrying him. He was blue." Big tears rolled down the lad's cheeks and the pain in my chest expanded. "He was all white and blue." Killian bent over Ghost's back and sobbed.

I rubbed circles on his heaving spine and stroked his red hair.

"I'm so scared. I don't want to die," Killian wailed.

"I won't let that happen," I whispered. "I promise I won't let that happen."

Dangerous promise, mucker. Dangerous promise…

My inner cynic could go—

Killian whispered, "I've been web chatting in our group and then I PM'd

~ 64 ~

Big Chris. He was in the dorm next to ours. He's still getting nightmares, and he's scared." Killian spoke between controlled sobs. "He's not the only one. All Ryan's mates are having bad dreams. What if it gets them as well? They're all over the place now."

It hadn't occurred to me that whatever scared the boys here might have followed them home. It followed me, so why not them? Bearing in mind how bloody scared I'd been the previous morning in the café, it must be even worse for the lads.

"Lorne?" Heather called, snapping the thought off too fast to grapple with properly.

I rose. "Over here." My voice could carry across an Afghan mountain pass. She'd find us.

Heather jogged over. "You left your phone in the kitchen. Damien's up. I think we need everyone in the same place for a while." She gave me significant eye contact, and I took a deep breath, the morning already making me sweat.

"Okay. Come on, Killian. Let's go back. We need a plan, and I'm going to need your help."

The boy sniffed but tears still tracked down dusty cheeks, making marks. I had a terrible moment of seeing him in some conflict somewhere in the world, ten years from now, in full combat gear. Those same freckles were stained once more by tears. The body of a friend in his arms.

I closed my eyes. Projecting into the future by mirroring my past was not a good way to remain in the present. I needed to remain in the present.

Heather took Killian's hand and Ghost walked to her other side. I trailed along behind them.

8

BY THE TIME WE REACHED the school, Killian had recovered most of his twelve-year-old's enthusiasm for life and coaxed Ghost into a game of chase.

"Good idea bringing him," Heather said.

"I figured he might remind you I'm not always such a prick," I said. I felt the heat rise in my cheeks.

She chuckled. "The doggie equivalent to the UN?"

"Something like that." My hand moved to the pocket containing her gift. I hadn't found the right moment to give it to her yet.

Her hand slipped into mine, preventing the retrieval of the gift. "I'm glad you brought him. I'm even happier you're here with me."

A voice equal to mine bellowed from the kitchen, "Wellie, get your arse in here."

I felt Heather stiffen next to me.

She mumbled a quiet, "I need to check on Ghost."

"Fuck," I breathed out as I watched her jog after the dog before he vanished into the trees. I needed to find the right moment for the present and Crusty being around wouldn't help.

My phone chose that moment to pick up a signal. The ring startled me. "Bloody hell." I slid to green.

"Turner?"

"Well, it's not the fucking Pope," I said.

"Wow, what crawled up your arse and died?" asked Paul.

"Sorry, it's been a long day."

"It's ten-thirty. How is that possible? Even for you?"

I chuckled. It felt good talking to Paul, a part of my army life who knew the current version of me and accepted most of it without a murmur of complaint. "I've annoyed Heather."

"What? More than usual?"

"Yeah."

"You're an idiot then."

"And to what do I owe the pleasure of this conversation?" I asked, derailing his criticism of me.

"I've found her brother. Or I've found a likely location. He's in a place called Wiveliscombe." Paul mangled the name of the town.

I rubbed my eyes. "Of course he is."

"Is that a problem?"

"No, not at all. We're about ten mikes away in Clatworthy. And it's Wiv-e-lis-combe to a local, or Wivvy. We used to go there with the Young Farmers' Association for a piss up and punch up with the rugby team."

"Sounds delightful."

"It was a good proving ground before the army, that's for certain. Can you narrow it down for me?"

"I've put together an information packet for you. Check your email."

"Thanks, Paul. How's Willow?" The familiar knot in my gut tightened. She had one all to herself since she'd been shot.

"She's okay. The heat is affecting her, so we're going to Northumberland for a few days. I wanted to let you know I'll be on cut-down services until I get back."

"So no hacking drones?"

"Just try to stay out of trouble, okay?"

"Roger that, fella. You drive carefully."

"I will. We're going to take it slow."

"See you on the flip-side."

We hung up. I didn't like the thought of my makeshift family moving around the country, which I had to admit was ridiculous, but true, nonetheless.

I headed into the kitchen to answer Damien's summons with decidedly mixed feelings about my old friend.

Damien was forking scran of sausages, eggs, beans and toast into his mouth as if we had to leave immediately for a week-long mission on hard rations. Polly slid a plate towards me. I debated whether it would fit with the porridge I'd had earlier, but what the hell? A fry-up is a fry-up and shouldn't be missed.

I mumbled my thanks and ate while studying Damien. I'd made a point of just enjoying his company rather than seeing the man as a stranger and assessing him as such. Memories can overlay the people we know in the present, so we don't see how time and life have carved lessons into their bodies and minds.

My old mucker looked his forty-five years this morning. His face sagged and had a puffiness indicative of long-term heavy drinking. The veins on his cheeks showed the same abuse and his eyes had a yellow cast to the whites that I recognised. It gave the disturbing illusion he hid something dark behind the bright façade. Was it memories or something more? I knew one thing: if Damien's physical health under the surface wasn't great, what was his mental health like?

"You going to give your gullet a rest, mate?" I asked, watching another sausage vanish in record time.

"So, what happened to you yesterday? Thought you'd be back last night," Damien asked.

I glanced at Polly. She smiled, her dark eyes kind but worried. I wondered if she'd spoken to Heather.

"Family business," I said. "Sounds like the night proved eventful."

Damien snorted. "Everyone is so gullible. I didn't hear anything."

"I'm not surprised," Polly said, eyeing the recycling on the kitchen unit by the back door. Several empty bottles of spirits lined up in regimental order.

Damien scowled, ignoring her. "Want to go for a run around the reservoir?" he asked me.

I eyed him with some scepticism. "Not in this heat, but I'd be happy to go for a walk. It would be good to get a feel for the area." Something here felt off, but I couldn't catch hold of the energy. It slipped through the room in ribbons of sickly yellow, dull grey and beige, a sludgy muck.

Damien grunted.

Heather and Killian came into the kitchen, chatting happily with the dog in tow. The boy seemed a lot more relaxed. I realised for the first time the kitchen didn't have any of the children in it. Not being used to them being around, I hadn't noticed. The dog, smelling potential, sat near me with his 'dad I love you' face.

"He's beautiful," Polly said.

"This is Ghost." Heather ruffled his head, then rested her hand on my shoulder. A sense of solidarity drifted off her and made me relax a little.

Adam, the oldest boy, arrived along with Robert. They both looked tired and frayed around the edges.

"Do either of you know the local vicar?" I asked.

Adam nodded. "Yeah, good bloke but he's in charge of several large parishes so we see little of him in the village."

"You go to the services in the village?" I asked.

Adam nodded. "Medway doesn't approve of religion on school grounds, so those of us who are of the Christian faith go to the local church. We have a few Muslims here, and I talked Medway into giving them a room for prayers, but it was a battle." He glanced at Damien and me, the colour rising in his cheeks. "I... erm... I didn't mean..."

I chuckled. "Don't sweat it, kid. I didn't fight Muslims. I fought terrorists."

Damien grunted, but I didn't know if it came from approval of my philosophy or dismissal. It added another layer of concern.

"Maybe you could give him a ring and let him know I'd like a chat if he's in the area? Also, do you know of any older residents in Clatworthy I might talk to? Locals, not incomers."

Adam's eyes grew distant, but it was Robert who answered. He had a sweet voice made for singing in choirs. "Mrs Langford. She comes in once a week to teach extra music to those of us who are interested." Robert checked with Adam for his approval of the suggestion. The boy had it bad.

Adam nodded. "If it happened in Clatworthy, that woman would know."

"Good." I also needed to get into Medway's office, but I'd leave that one for the moment. "Want to help investigate ghosts?" I asked Damien.

He snorted. "Seriously, mucker? You really are losing it." He pushed his plate away. "Well, if no one wants to run in this weather, you bunch of pussies, I'm going back to bed for a few hours."

We all watched in silence as Damien left the room.

Polly sighed as the tension eased. "I'm sorry. He had an awful night."

No one said anything. They'd all had a terrible night, but the children didn't get to sleep with a belly full of booze.

"Do you want me to give Mrs Langford a ring?" Robert asked, breaking the tension.

"That would be great. Heather, we'll need…"

"I know, notes taken. We'll have to leave Ghost somewhere safe."

"I'll keep him safe," Killian announced with a smile and bright eyes.

WE STOOD OUTSIDE A SMALL, neat bungalow on the edge of some beautiful farmland rolling off towards the Brendon Hills like summer waves of green and brown rather than blue lapping a distant shoreline.

In the extensive garden, rose bushes took up a lot of the space, with sprinklers flicking water at their greedy roots. They crowded the green lawn. Adam and Robert led us through the small gate. Heather remained quiet. I hadn't told her about her brother being so close. Right now I didn't know if my interference would be welcome, and I figured earning a few more gold stars before I mentioned the brother might be wise.

I focused on trying to look harmless as an elderly woman opened the front door.

"Hello, Mrs Langford, this is Heather and Lorne," Robert said, stepping to one side for the introductions. A woman in her sixties, made of iron girders and determination, focused sharp brown eyes on us.

Mrs Langford's gaze narrowed, assessing us. Dressed in casual summer wear made it hard for Heather to hide her subtle but long tattoo, and for me to hide the worst of the scars on my arms and legs. We didn't look too friendly.

"Hello, Mrs Langford, thank you for agreeing to speak with us," I said in my best 'trying to explain something important to Top Brass so I could save lives' voice.

"You're down at the school?" she asked.

"Yes, we're trying to help sort out a problem there and we thought you might give us some background as a long-term resident of the village," Heather said.

The woman's narrow lips pursed, and she cocked her head to one side as if listening for something inside herself. Eventually she said, "I've lived here all my life. Grew up in a labourer's cottage. If you want to know the history of Clatworthy, then yes, I can help." Her Somerset accent rolled like the farmland hereabouts. "We'll have tea in the back garden, and you can ask your questions."

I tried to hide my smile, but she caught it.

"What's so funny?" she asked, her challenge clear.

"I admire a woman who won't allow strangers into her home and has the good sense to give herself the space to run, if necessary," I said with total candour.

Heather smacked me on the arm, thinking I sounded rude.

Mrs Langford's expression switched to amused. It took at least five years off her age. "Well spotted. Most of the silly buggers who come to my door have no idea what I'm doing. Doesn't change the plan though, so go around the side and I'll meet you."

"Yes, ma'am," I said.

We went around the side of the house, the scent in the hot air full of the roses. I saw a small decking area surrounded by raised beds containing more roses and various ornamental grasses and bark. Clearly Mrs Langford didn't much like gardening except for nursing her roses. The boys sat on the steps while Heather and I took two of the metal garden chairs. The ones designed to be as uncomfortable as possible.

Mrs Langford came through the back door, a walking stick in one hand and a heavy limp marring her grace of movement. When she caught me looking at the stick, she grimaced. "I need a hip replacement, but I can't afford to pay for it privately. It'll be a few years away."

"I'm sorry. Bad joints are a unique torture," I said.

"They are." She looked at Robert. "Perhaps you can help carry things through from the kitchen?" The thick rural accent didn't hide the precise diction.

"Of course," Robert said. He hurried after the older woman, and I caught a softening in Adam's eyes. Perhaps things in the romance department had a little more balance to the scales than I'd thought.

When we settled down with homemade lemonade and biscuits, I started to ask questions.

"What can you tell me about Syndercombe Academy's background?"

Mrs Langford's eyes widened a little. "Well, you're very blunt. May I be just as blunt?" The challenge was obvious.

I felt my mouth twitch. "You may."

"What happened to your face?"

Adam and Robert stared at her, then at me.

Everyone I met always wanted to know, so I'd seen this coming. "In exchange for the truth, I want everything you know about the academy and the history of the village here."

"It's not Clatworthy village that's the problem," she said. "It's Syndercombe."

I frowned in confusion.

"The academy is the only house left of the village of Syndercombe. The village is in the reservoir. It's why I never left the area."

Heather sucked in a sharp breath and shivered. I swallowed as the terrible prickling over my scalp and back began. The sensation of hard black feathers.

I needed the information the older woman had, the gatekeeper to the secrets in these old hills. "I was shot in the face. The burns are from Syria." I pointed to a neat hole-like scar on my upper arm. "9mm round from a handgun in Afghanistan." I turned the arm over and indicated a long, jagged scar on my underarm. "Knife wound from slavers in Thailand. We were supposed to be on a training exchange with their Special Forces when we stumbled over a camp. Couldn't exactly leave the women and children there, so..." I shrugged. It had been a short, bloody, and brutal fight, but we saved the victims of slavery. It took some explaining to the Head Shed though; engaging 'civilians' went against protocol. I'd not been in charge, so the shit didn't fall on me.

Mrs Langford nodded. "You're a soldier."

"I was. Sergeant-major 22nd Regiment of the Special Air Service."

She released a surprisingly deep chuckle. "My great uncle served with Stirling when he was in the Scots Guards."

"A hard man to please by all accounts." David Stirling formed the SAS during the Second World War.

Mrs Langford nodded once. I'd obviously passed her test. "I feel as if I've been fighting a battle here, unseen and alone for all these years. I've grown tired and perhaps a little lazy. I have to hope that my negligence didn't lead to young Ryan losing his life."

9

ADAM AND ROBERT EXCHANGED FROWNS and Heather leaned forwards. She said, "You can't be held responsible for that."

"Let me tell you the story and we'll see if you think the same when it's over," Mrs Langford said, her sadness darkening her voice. She gazed at the boys for a long moment. "I love teaching at the school, but I'm there for more than just one reason." Her eyes focused on me and Heather. "You see, the dead live with me, just as I believe they live with you." She stared directly at me.

I shifted on the metal chair. "They make interesting company," I admitted. There didn't seem to be any point in hiding or denying, not anymore.

"This story starts with the Norman invasion of England in 1066."

I blinked. "I don't think we have time to cover a thousand years."

Mrs Langford chuckled. "It's only a little of that time we need to worry about. Syndercombe and its surrounding countryside found themselves gifted to Turstin fitz Rolf as a reward for his bravery during the Battle of Hastings. He is one of the few provable companions of William the Conqueror, making him an important man. Being a Norman, ruling a Saxon enclave like Syndercombe, and soldiers being what they can be, meant things in this rural idyll of England became savage. Turstin fitz Rolf was very much a man of his time."

It took little imagination to understand how the Norman victors would have treated the locals. They didn't even share the same language. A thousand years since then and the weapons might have changed, but little else.

The narrative continued. "We don't have records of what happened to the local people during this period, but there are myths and legends that some wrote as folk tales during the eighteenth century. Stories passed down to each generation. Turstin was a Christian man, as was William of Normandy, and they believed they fought with the Pope's blessing and therefore God's. But," at this point she held up a finger to draw attention to her words, "he found little evidence of the Christian faith in this valley."

Robert's eyes widened and he sounded breathless when he asked, "Were they worshiping the devil?"

Mrs Langford drew in a deep breath and shrugged her shoulders. "Who knows, really? What was written by the Norman monks was kept at Glastonbury Abbey and subsequently destroyed during the Reformation. Who knows the actual truth now? It was all taken from oral tradition. They said the people in the valley worshipped a demon who lived at the river's head. They gave him the blood of innocents, and, in exchange, their land grew the best crops in the area, fed the best cattle. The people here grew rich on the excess."

She paused and nibbled a biscuit. Adam, just as caught up in the story as Robert, prompted, "What happened next?"

"Turstin would not have the worship of demons in this place. He wanted to drive the devil out—or so say the monks—he ordered churches to be built in stone. Then he placed two fortresses in the valley, one at the top, one at the bottom, so all the locals had to pass the gates to do business and he could check their intentions remained godly. When he discovered some of the locals went against his orders, he used a priest who spoke the local dialect to remonstrate with the people. When they still disobeyed, he had several hung, their bodies left to rot at the site of the river's head."

Heather frowned and pointed out the obvious flaw in the plan. "Wouldn't that pollute the water?"

Mrs Langford laughed. "It's a story. We have no proof, other than the words of a monk. Anyway, as Turstin grew old, he feared the people would turn against God and the power of the demon would hold sway once more. In an effort to confront the demon and hold the land on the Christian way, he martyred himself, falling on his trusty sword and ordering his burial at the head of the river."

Even I had to admit, this was a cracking good story. However, I wasn't here to waste time. "But what's any of that got to do with now?"

Sharp brown eyes studied me. "Everything." She sipped some lemonade before continuing, "I won't bore you with all the stories I've collected over the years, except for the period before they completed the dam. This is my account of that time, as an eyewitness, despite being a child of twelve when the valley was flooded.

"The entire area was in upheaval at the time, as you can imagine. The village and church were to be buried forever, the families moved out and much-loved land lost. All because the towns and villages in the area grew so fast after the war and needed water. My parents argued about it a great deal. My mother, the local, wanting things to remain the same. My father, a farm manager, seeing it as progress. I just wanted to witness everything that was happening, so I would often sneak off and explore as the dam rose to tower over the remains of the village.

"When a dam is built, it's important it's tested and controlled for the first five years of its life. Cofferdams and diversion channels are used to control the water, but the weather during those last years of the nineteen-fifties in this area was wet and cold. We had a lot of snow and when the dam filled, it filled fast. The village, of course, was fenced off, but I wanted to be the last person to see the light come through Syndercombe's church windows." Her eyes grew distant. "Sometimes, I think the souls of the place called me back, needing help, but a twelve-year-old girl can't offer much in the way of help. When I returned to the church, the water was already at the edge of the village. I walked into the church, but it wasn't the one I remembered. I stood in a far earlier version, small and plain. A low vaulted ceiling rose over my head and simple frescos in bright colours decorated the white walls. I stared about in amazement."

"What happened?" asked Heather.

Mrs Langford's eyes locked on Heather's and the brown became darker. "I saw a man in mail armour, head bowed, sword bloody in his leather-gloved hand. Bodies littered the ground around the small nave and chancel. Slaughter covered the stones. Each tunic of the men and women was ripped open, and an inverted cross burned, not cut, burned into their chests and belly. I remember gasping, and that man, that Norman warrior, he…" Her eyes grew distant and filled with tears. "He stared at me with such horror on his face. He said something, he said 'Adiuva me', which is 'Help me'. I recognised it because I was in the top class at the grammar school for English, so I studied Latin."

Mrs Langford drew in a deep breath and her hand trembled as she sipped again at her glass.

"I think I saw an echo of something terrible. I think Turstin sacrificed himself because of what happened in the church."

"Did he do it?" I asked.

Mrs Langford shrugged. "I don't know. I have thought about it so often, dreamed of it even. Possibly, one of two things happened. In a fit of rage, he committed this act on his people who still disobeyed him, consigning their souls to Hell, or he found the bodies and someone else did it. Or *something* else."

"What happened after this vision in the church?" I asked.

"When I came out of the trance, everything had changed around me. The church of Syndercombe, like most parish churches, had been rebuilt during the fourteenth and fifteenth centuries, then added to by the Victorians. Before the flooding of the valley, they'd stripped the building of anything precious, like the pews, some of the stained glass, the heavy church doors and so forth. In the shell of that building, I now saw the bodies of men, young men I recognised from among the immigrant workers. They'd brought in Irish labourers to help with construction. Six men lay dead on the floor of the church, their shirts ripped open and inverted crosses on their chests. I saw no blood, and I did not see how they were killed. I thought I saw ropes holding them to the stones of the church.

"When I came to my senses, I felt the water lapping at my feet. Hours must have passed while I stood, trance-like, in that church. That's when I ran. The dam and the flood waters meant I couldn't return home the way I'd come. I'd have to go around and cross the River Tone further up the valley. I ran and ran, it rained and rained. It grew dark…" Her voice petered out once again, hands knotting in her lap. "My father found me huddled under a tree, half drowned and half dead, almost frozen. I tried to tell him about the workers, I tried to tell people, but they took it as the ravings of a fevered mind, and perhaps it was. I was a child and a girl. Rural Somerset, in those days, barely noticed the sixties racing towards them. We still had very Victorian values and behaviour. No one went to check the church until I did."

"You went back to the church?" I asked in surprise.

Mrs Langford straightened, and her eyes brightened. "I did. During the drought in the seventies, the village became visible, so I gained my diving certificate."

I chuckled. "You learned to scuba?" I had to admire the woman for that.

She nodded. "I did, went on to dive all over the world on various holidays, but my first solo dive was the church. It's against all the rules and many laws." She stared hard at the boys, who grinned. "Nevertheless, I dived to the church to look for bodies or bones. I found neither, which is no great surprise. The river feeding the reservoir can cause strong currents, but I found the remains of rope. Someone had tied rope around the stone pillars. It crumbled as I touched it. Perhaps I'd imagined the men I'd found dead that day, but the rope made it more likely. It was then that my husband and I researched the area more thoroughly. During times of crisis, over many centuries, we tracked reports of missing people or strange happenings around the villages of Clatworthy and Syndercombe. For instance, just a few weeks ago, a woman was here looking for her husband and his friend. Apparently, they came down here to do some business and she hasn't heard from them since. They are detectorists. She said the police weren't interested. I fear poor Ryan isn't the first to drown in the last six months."

Heather nodded as I glanced at her.

I said, feeling very uncomfortable with the explanation, "There's a possibility that certain things, energies, have hit a critical mass in vulnerable places because of actions taken on Exmoor by a man called Anthony Shaw."

"The occult police officer on the news?" Mrs Langford asked.

I nodded.

"You're the ones who stopped him?"

Again, I nodded.

I watched her organise her mental library to take this into account. "That makes sense. I think that timing works very well."

"So what connection does Syndercombe Academy have?" Adam asked.

Mrs Langford smiled at the lad. "It's the only surviving property for a start. It was also built on a much older site. The original Norman fort is believed to be under the school."

"Wouldn't they have wanted to build somewhere to dominate the land?" asked Robert. Then his cheeks coloured as we all focused on him. "That's what we're taught in school."

"Like the Iron Age fort up there?" Adam added to back him up. Robert now blushed for a different reason.

"The Iron Age fort is said to be haunted," Mrs Langford explained. "Remember, this period was rife with superstition. The Normans would have built a fort to control access to the valley, and the academy is the perfect location. They may well have built again on the higher ground."

I needed to round off this meeting. "I have to say, Mrs Langford, your help is greatly appreciated and more comprehensive than anything we'd have found on the internet."

She shrugged. "I can't tell you what is down there under the water, or how to stop it. When I heard the boys had used that terrible board thing to try to contact Ryan, I was horrified. Something in that building is fighting to get loose. I think it escapes periodically, creating death and chaos, then returns to wherever it comes from. People don't understand how old places like Syndercombe really are, and what that can mean."

I understood all too well after my experiences in Afghanistan, Syria, and now here, at home. "You've certainly given us a lot to think about."

"I'm just glad most of the boys have left for the summer and those who are left..." She looked at Robert with a parental loving eye. "Will soon be leaving. The building needs to be empty again for a while. We have to hope that will settle down the energy."

Heather asked, "Is that why you never left the area?"

Mrs Langford nodded. "I have never felt able to leave and once they turned the big house into a school... Well, that was that. Whatever small gifts I have that might involve the supernatural, I had to believe God gave them to me to protect those I could from whatever was under that school. This time, I believe, we have you two to help us."

"One last question," I said to her. She arched an eyebrow at my sharp tone. I modified. "If you don't mind?"

A soft, amused smile graced her face.

I felt like I'd just been gently reprimanded by my mum. "Um... Do you know any stories about treasure in these parts?"

Mrs Langford's eyes widened. "Treasure?" She stared at the boys, both flushed red. "There's a silly story I picked up about a hoard because of the hill-fort overlooking the valley, but I don't think it's credible. There's been no coins or jewellery found in the area, so I'm not sure it was wealthy enough for something like Sutton Hoo to be buried in the hills. We don't have cairns or henges. No Roads of the Dead, like the one at Avebury. If that's what they were."

I nodded. "Okay, well, thank you, Mrs Langford. Your time and expertise are appreciated."

Suddenly, she reached out for my arm and a vice-like grip held me still. "The treasure may or may not be real, but I know something here is wrong. There's an imbalance in this valley and over the last few months, it's become so much worse. I'm grateful you're here because I'm not strong enough to face it... Whatever it is..."

Her theory might well be correct, but I needed time to think. Then I had to tell Heather about her brother being nearby.

1 0

ON OUR RETURN TO THE school and Ghost's over-the-top relief that his parents hadn't abandoned him forever, I drew Heather to one side.

"At the risk of further antagonising you, I have a confession to make." I fingered the bracelet I'd bought as a peace offering, the solid metal making an odd shape in my thigh pocket.

Heather sucked in a breath. "Lorne, it's hot. I'm exhausted. Could we save any confessions for another day?"

"I know. I'm sorry, but I don't want to hide this from you, and I'm worried you'll think I'm doing it on purpose. I found your brother." The last sentence came out in a rush. I waited for the explosion now I'd set fire to the det cord.

Heather looked at me in surprise. "You found Barnaby?"

"Yes. Sorry. I just wanted to help."

"You or Paul?" she asked, her eyes narrowing.

"Erm…"

Her mouth twitched in an effort to hide a smile, and I relaxed. "Paul then. You asked your GCHQ special consultant, resident clever clogs and all-round smart arse to find my brother?"

"I thought it might be important. It might give you some control back after your father found you. I also want to know what the hell is going on. I've never tried to invade your privacy around your family, but you're hurting, and I can't help if I don't understand." I took her hands, deeming it a safe move.

"Heather, we're supposed to be getting married one day soon, and I know nothing about your childhood. It worries me and I think it's time."

Her gaze dropped. "Where is he?"

"In Wiveliscombe, just down the road." Heather wasn't a local to the area, so wouldn't know all the small towns and villages just yet.

"I know Wivvy. Smoke sells drugs down there and had a grow site for a while."

Of course he did. Smoke was the president of the motorcycle gang Heather was involved with before she ran into me. Although not intrinsically evil, the man wasn't a good guy.

"Paul gave me a pin for Barnaby's mobile phone. Do you want to go and find him?"

Heather wrapped her arms around my waist and placed her head on my shoulder. "We should stay here and deal with this. You need to talk to Damien."

"You come first, Heather." I breathed in the soft lavender musk of her hair. It felt good having her back. "I think we visit him. Take a break away from this place together. Grab some lunch and have a think about what to do before tonight. I'll be guided by you."

Her arms tightened around me, and the small body pressed tighter. "I love you."

"Good. We'll take Ghost with us."

She relaxed in my arms, and I smiled.

We left the boys helping Polly in the school's garden and Heather clutched a shopping list for the local Co-Op. Ghost padded with obvious relief between us and jumped into the back of the truck without any form of coaxing.

"I don't think he likes it here," Heather said, watching the dog settle on the backseat before she clipped his safety harness on. I didn't tell her I'd forgotten to strap the dog in on the way over.

"What do you think about Mrs Langford's story?" I asked.

Heather shrugged and twisted in the front seat so she could look at me. "I believed her. She makes a credible witness no matter how dark her story is.

What we do with the information is the next stage, but I don't know how we investigate further. It's that which'll give us the answers we need to stop this thing from scaring the boys and possibly hurting them."

We headed from Clatworthy village to Huish Champflower, then Maundown and Langley Marsh, into Wivvy. A picturesque trip through villages kissed by wealthy outsiders and burdened by the rural poor in equal measure. A bitter-sweet combination of commuters, retired folk and old families.

Heather tracked us on the sat-nav. "He's in Plain Pond, but it looks like a field or something. It's near the sewage works."

"Nice," I muttered.

A sudden idea invaded our current quest. "Maybe we need to see if we can find some architects' plans for the academy? That might show where the old Norman building was. It sounds like this fitz Rolf was a man in some trouble. He might be the area's first recorded victim or perpetrator."

Heather blinked to re-establish the connection with my pogoing thoughts. "I also think we need more information about what happened to Ryan. I tried talking to Damien about it yesterday evening, but he clammed up and hit the vodka so hard I thought the boys swapped it out for water."

"He's always been a drinker," I mumbled, feeling the need to defend him, but we'd been separated by time and experience. We weren't Wellie and Crusty any more. We were Lorne and Damien, with jobs in the real world.

I saw the sign for Plain Pond and drove into an estate of nice ex-council houses and bungalows from the sixties with sizeable gardens and lots of space. The cars, though, looked older and small. Cheap to run and cheap to repair. "Do you think he lives in one of these?" I asked.

"Not according to the pin," Heather said as I pulled up.

We slipped out of the truck, locked up, and looked around. The air smelt hot and damp, the lack of a breeze making it almost stale. I put Ghost on the lead and Heather followed the trail from the phone's app. Taking a track behind the houses, we saw allotments, full of summer's bounty and a large truck covered in flowers and rainbows.

Heather and I shared a long look. "That's the location of the phone," she said.

"He's living in a van?"

She shrugged. "I guess so. How the mighty have fallen."

"What's that mean?"

"Barnaby is, or was, the golden boy. I might have a pile of GCSEs behind me with A and B on them, but he has A stars across the board and attained a first at Oxford in Philosophy, Politics and Economics. He went to work in The City earning silly money, while I lived in a bedsit in Exeter drinking and doing drugs." She stared at the multi-coloured van while she spoke, her hand tight on Ghost's lead. "I am very much the failure."

"He lives in a truck, Heather. You are building a future designed by you. I don't think you're a failure. You're a survivor of whatever put you in that bedsit."

"My father, the great Clive Mordent, is a clever man and a controlling one." She finally looked up at me and in those chips of sky-blue, I saw the haunted sadness I'd witnessed the night we first met.

"Coercive control?"

"The very worst kind. I think that's why I ended up with the bikers. His control was absolute, so anything they dished out was easy to handle in comparison." She placed a hand on her belly. "I don't think I can do this. Let him have his peace."

Ghost shifted, telling me someone was behind us. I turned, protecting Heather with my body. Not a conscious decision, an automatic one.

A man approached. Tall, slim, with a thick black beard and long black hair in tangles over his shoulders. He wore sandals, baggy cotton trousers so faded the rainbow colours looked like hews of mud. A loose-fitting shirt of cream cotton covered a thin chest. Numerous leather bracelets and necklaces with pendants finished the ensemble. He had a shopping bag in both hands, and I saw cans of Stella beer poking out of the top.

Blue eyes widened in suspicious surprise. "You're not from the allotment. Are you lost dog walkers?" The accent held no trace of Heather's Devon, but

I knew this was her brother. I realised he must be her older brother. The tanned face had more crow's feet marching over it than his sister's.

Heather turned slowly. "Hello, Barny."

His mouth dropped open. "Heather?"

"Hey. How are you?"

Barny glanced around us. "Where's Dad?"

Heather relaxed a little. "Don't panic. He doesn't know I'm here." She nodded at me. "Lorne found you. He's good at finding people."

"To be honest, Paul found him, but okay," I muttered, stepping forwards with my hand out. "Hi, I'm Lorne Turner, a friend of Heather's."

Barny looked me up and down, put the Stella cans on the ground and took my hand. "Hi, I'm the big brother. How did you find me?"

I glanced at Heather. Did I confess to having a friend who could hack this bloke's mobile phone? He looked like a lot of drugs and beer formed part of his five-a-day fruit and veg requirements, so paranoia would be a problem.

"He tracked your phone," Heather said, cutting through my thought process. "I have interesting friends and Lorne's my fiancé, so play nice." Why was she provoking him? What kind of reaction was she expecting? I didn't understand this family dynamic being an only child.

"You hacked my phone?"

"Tracked it. I have a friend who works in the…" I realised the damage I could do if I said, 'security services' so I held the words back and finished with, "…data analysis world."

"What are you doing here?" he asked Heather. If he were a hedgehog, he'd be rolling into a defensive ball of spikes about now.

"Father came to Lorne's farm. He found me online. Or Mum did. He's looking for you. Says you have problems with the police. Lorne thought it wise I found you first."

Barny took a long look at me, but his eyes fixed on his sister once again. "Does he know?"

Heather gave a one-shouldered shrug. "Broad strokes."

"So he's not going to drop me in the shit? Living here is good. I have a nice life. I help guard the allotment, work on it, water it, and get paid in vegetables. Then there's the website building for the local businesses. I'm left alone."

"Why are the police after you?" Heather asked.

The tension between the siblings churned my battle senses, and I found it hard to breathe at a normal rate. "Look, we came to warn you, that's it. We can leave," I said, sounding harsher than I meant to.

They both ignored me.

"I got busted for possession and failed to attend court." Barny made no excuses.

"What kind of drugs?" Heather asked.

Barny's eyes grew distant. "Crack. I had enough on me to be charged with dealing."

Heather sucked in a breath. "Were you?"

He shrugged.

"In London?"

"Bristol. I left London five years ago. Father didn't tell you?"

I could almost hear Heather's teeth crack she held so much tension in her jaw.

She ground out, "I haven't spoken to them for years. If I hadn't been on the website for the business, he'd never have found me."

Barny's eyes grew sad. "You should move again. Now he knows where you are."

"It's my farm and we're not going anywhere. Your father doesn't worry me," I said.

I became the centre of attention.

Barny said, "He should."

Heather reached into her daysack and removed a business card. "This is us. If you ever need to talk, you can ring me or email. I won't tell Father where you are. So long as you're happy in your life, that's all that matters."

Barny snorted. "I miss the penthouse suite and the posh cars, but this life has its charms. Where is this farm?"

"Exmoor, near Dunkery Beacon."

"You came all the way down here for me?"

Heather shook her head. "We have a job up at Clatworthy."

"Huh." Barny nodded. "Yeah. I keep hearing about some weird shit up that way. Took a walk there a few weeks back. I don't like moving the van too often. She gets grumpy. I spent the night on the old hill-fort, smoked some weed, took some stuff. Weird night, man, full of dark dreams."

Having been forced to take a pharmaceutical version of LSD thanks to the Winter Sun, I understood exactly how a haunted place could make you feel if you hovered, untethered, under the influence. Bad. Very bad. If it hadn't been for Al-Ahmar, my hitchhiking and, for the moment, silent, djinn, I'd be dead.

Heather cocked her head, almost relaxed for the first time. "What kind of dreams?"

Her brother appeared to be mildly astonished by her question. "If you want to know, you can come to the van, and I'll tell you. It's beer o'clock and they don't like me very much in the White Hart."

Heather snorted. "The locals don't like anyone else in the White Hart. You should try The Bear."

By silent consent, we walked to the van.

"Yeah, but Lucy isn't too happy with me in there, either. I'm a bit behind on her latest website update."

"So what happened in this dream of yours?" Heather asked.

"Want a beer?" Barny returned, rather than answering her question.

"No, it's too early." Her impatience made Ghost wiggle about, bored by the lack of activity in the sultry morning.

I felt like I needed to hurry things along or we'd be here until sunset, and plans needed to be made back at the academy. The whisperings of some ideas formed in the back of my head.

I breached the silence. "Listen, we need a proper catch-up. I don't doubt that, but we're on a timetable. Maybe we could cut to the point?"

Brother and sister focused on me, and it felt like being dunked in the ice-cold water of the Arctic—a sensation I knew all too well.

Heather relaxed her grip first. "He has a point. We're kinda in a hurry."

Barny shrugged. "Okay, we'll do it here." He sat on the step outside his van.

I spotted a box with a tatty cushion on it, so hauled it over for Heather, settling myself next to Ghost on the ground. I watched in horror as Barny cracked a can open and took a long drink. After an expressive belch, he grinned.

Heather rolled her eyes. "What the hell happened to you?"

"I broke," he said with sad simplicity. "I snapped clean in two and ran. Ain't no mystery to that one, little sis."

Heather's eyes filled with empathy. "I'm sorry. The burdens placed on you were impossible. I know that now. I'm sorry if I made life harder for you." She placed a hand on his thin knee.

He reached out and touched her fluffy hair. "It wasn't your fault, little pickle. You had your burdens to carry as well. We have better lives now."

I worked hard to hide my incredulity. This was better? Living in a bus and working as an impromptu guard for an allotment? We should introduce him to Spud. They could swap stories of the hidden worlds they explored. Or maybe not.

Barny shook himself. "Okay, where we at? The dreamtime I had at the lake. Yeah, that was bad. To start with, things seemed really mellow, the trees and water in harmony despite the dam blocking the natural flow of water. The area seems to have become used to it, you know?" He focused on me with a sharpness I found disturbing.

"Not really," I lied.

A knowing smirk crossed his full lips. "Yeah, whatever. Anyway, the evening turned to night, and I was riding high."

"When was this, Barny?" Heather asked.

"That's the thing. I didn't know until several days later, but it was the night the boy died up there. Around Easter." Barny's face collapsed, and big fat tears rolled down his cheeks. "I think I saw it happen." He gazed into his sister's face, begging for something I didn't recognise. But Heather's instincts, as always, ran true.

"Whatever you saw, it wasn't your fault and there was nothing you could have done, Barny. You need to tell us everything and we need to find out what's going on because the boys in the school up there are having a really rough time of it."

The man's face cleared, and he sniffed. "Yeah, totally, okay. Well, I heard this rending sound, like a rusty gate to hell being opened and this thick black oil surged up from the centre of the lake to spread out over the surface. I realised then that it was polluting all the drinking water. It shone like a sick rainbow in the moonlight for about an hour. I kept thinking something was coming up out of the oil, but when I focused on the movement, it just vanished. Like some great sea serpent rising up and down, trapped by the sides of the combe. I've had bad trips, but nothing like this. It felt real, you know?"

Heather nodded. "I know. What did you take?"

"Mescaline and MDMA." He sounded almost apologetic.

I just blinked. Having been dosed by the Winter Sun, and almost losing my mind in the process, I couldn't imagine voluntarily sending yourself crazy just to reach a higher plane of existence.

"I'd make a wild suggestion here, bro," Heather said. "Don't do it again."

Barny shook his head, the black locks flicking around. "No way, man. That was bad."

"How did this oil stuff make you feel?" I asked. Willow always said that I needed to heal from the PTSD by understanding the feelings behind the events I relived. There was a reason our friendship had strained to breaking point on several occasions.

"Like I never want to shower, or drink the water from that place again."

He seemed to have succeeded on the first objective all too well.

I touched Heather's shoulder. "I think we have all we need for now. I'll give you two a few minutes. Meet me back at the truck." I took hold of Ghost's lead. "Come on, buddy, your mum needs some alone time."

Walking back towards the truck I thought about Barny's words. The coincidence of him being up there the night of Ryan's death struck me as odd, but then my life these days was odd. I just had to roll with it and hope it would all make sense in the end. Heather arrived back at the truck and climbed in without a word. I drove us out of Wivvy.

"You alright?" I asked after two full minutes of silence.

"Not now, Lorne. I need to think. Can we talk about what we need to do?"

When I glanced at her those blue mirrors of the sky looked puzzled but not over burdened by emotion. Satisfied she didn't need a bailout from some mental quagmire, I nodded. "Okay. Here's the plan. We need to get under the water. I can use Damien as a dive-buddy. We'll either be free diving, or he might have some equipment for us to use at the school. Either way, we're trained well enough for something this simple. The reservoir is low so it shouldn't be difficult. I need to see this church. The other thing I want to do, and I need you for this, is to break into Medway's office. I think there's more to this lad, Ryan, than we're being told."

"Even by Damien?"

I navigated slowly around two horse riders. "Yeah, something isn't right in that quarter."

"Glad you noticed," she muttered.

"What's that mean?"

She sighed but studied her hands. "I know he's important to you. I know you shared a lot, but he's been out of the army for a long time. You haven't seen him since he left. I'm not sure he's the man you remember, and you aren't the man he remembers. I just don't understand how he and Polly slept through all that madness last night. I also don't understand why the boys came to me for help and not them."

"You were closer?"

A one-shouldered shrug. "Maybe. Just be careful and watch your back."

11

WE REACHED THE SCHOOL AS the boys came in to eat lunch. It had been a busy morning already. Polly's wide smile made my nerves jangle.

She sounded almost manic when she said, "Great, you're back for lunch. We have home-grown salad, ham and fresh bread with cheese if you want it?"

"Where's Damien?" I asked, eyeing the jugs of tap water on the table. I briefly wondered how I'd convince everyone Ghost needed bottled water in his bowl. Not like I could find him a puddle in this weather. Maybe I could get Ella to bless it over the phone?

How is this my life?

"Damien's in the shower. He's been out for a run. What did you need?" Polly asked.

I wanted to assume Polly and Damien stood on my side of this, at least for now, and Heather's instincts might be tripping her up because of the argument.

"Well, I'm planning a few new ways to spend the afternoon and need his help."

"Help with what, Wellie?" Damien said, looking fresh as a wilted daisy as he wandered into the kitchen, stealing food from a plate and earning a rap on his knuckles from Polly. He patted her backside, and she giggled. These two were happy and normal in some ways.

I said, "I want to dive to the church in the reservoir. I also want into Medway's office. Can you make that happen? I'm assuming it's locked."

Damien's eyes widened. "I thought we were ghost hunting? That all sounds a bit serious."

"Things are serious, Damien. A boy died."

His eyes narrowed and darkened. "I know," he growled. "I found his body."

"Then help me. I need more information."

His shoulders relaxed just a little. "Yeah, okay. I can help with both. We have dive gear, but you can't go down there alone. You'll need a dive-buddy. And yes, before you ask, I can get you into Medway's office leaving no evidence behind."

I grinned. "That's what I like to hear. Lunch, Medway's office, dive."

"Yes, sir." He rolled his eyes. "He's a bloody dog with a bone when he gets an idea in his head." Damien said this to Heather.

She just smiled politely and turned her attention back to Ghost.

After lunch, where I had to prevent Damien from drinking beer, he accompanied me and Heather to Medway's office.

"I happen to have a key," he said, jangling a set in front of my nose.

"Does Medway know?"

Damien gave me a 'look,' and I chuckled.

As he unlocked the door, he said, "It pays to have a nose at the performance reviews before being hauled into the office for a roasting. Listen, if we want to dive, I need to test the equipment, so I'll leave you to it."

"Thanks," I said, watching him go and surprised that he didn't want to help with our raid.

"You're going to test your equipment for this dive, right?" Heather asked, her face a mask of worry.

"It's a bit like checking your own parachute. It's just something you do for yourself."

Heather nodded. "Good."

Her paranoia annoyed and concerned me by turns. I trusted Heather, but

Damien had been a brother for a long time. We'd shared a part of our lives very few people could ever understand. I knew Heather had a tendency towards jealously, but I thought that was about her lack of confidence and my previous relationship with Willow. I didn't think it would extend to something like this.

Pushing these thoughts back, I focused on the task at hand. Sometimes I found navigating my romantic relationship harder than any engagement I'd endured on the battlefield. Right now, I needed to focus. We might be in the office, but I wanted access to the filing cabinets and Medway's computer if possible.

"Can you start on the PC, and if you need it, give Paul a ring?" I asked her.

She chuckled. "He'll be pleased."

"He can hack as easily from Northumberland as he can from Exmoor."

"And maybe Medway has the code on his screen," Heather said, pointing at the yellow piece of paper.

"You're joking?"

"Well, I'm assuming that's why he has a note that says, 'Battle of Medway', written in faded blue ink, stuck here."

"When was the—" I stopped, Heather was already on her phone.

"43AD." She typed it in, then frowned at the rejection notice. She tried another word, "Vespasian." Her face broke out in a grin. "Who needs GCHQ to hack a computer?"

I chuckled and left her to it. She'd be far faster than me at corralling the ones and zeros. Not seeing a filing cabinet in the office, I headed to the door at the back of the room. It wasn't locked and turned out to be the admin cupboard. Inside, I found the filing cabinets and enough stationery to satisfy even Paul's OCD collection.

The drawers, of course, were locked, but the simple single mechanism controlling access didn't hold up to my use of a paperclip, a thump and a yank. The first drawer slid open, happy to comply with my brute force.

"Try not to break anything," Heather called. "We need the money. Medway won't pay us if he thinks we've broken something."

"Roger that," I replied, already scanning through the files. As I assumed, these had to be the paper copies of student files, nicely labelled and filed first by year, then by last name. Not being familiar with the schooling system and it having changed so much in thirty-five years, I found this confusing to start with but realised year seven meant a child around twelve. Ryan's age. After that, it was easy.

Jobs like this, when I was serving, would always be complicated. Either the files would be in a foreign language, or we'd be facing high-end security, or men with big guns, or all three. I almost felt cheated.

I found Ryan's file, under the name Hudson, and pulled it out. The heat in the small admin area had built quickly, so I returned to the main office.

Heather glanced up. "You found it?"

I nodded. "You?"

"I found things that a head teacher shouldn't be watching on a school computer, but nothing illegal yet." She pulled a face and wiped her hand on her t-shirt.

I grinned as she poked the mouse with some reluctance. Refocusing my attention on the file, I scanned. The first page was the child's original application to the school aged eleven and parents' details. Then a basic health check and insurance documents. After that came the academic stuff. He was a bright and well-liked kid, then the disciplinary record.

Ryan had been a straight down the line kid until Christmas. When he returned from the Christmas break, he'd been on detention every week at least once, covering almost all his classes. All his teachers sent reports to the head about his behaviour. I frowned. Never once had Damien been forced to discipline the boy.

A small note on the page, next to the English teacher's signature, stated, 'Confiscated a pack of playing cards, like the role-play games'. I sighed. They weren't role-play cards.

The kid had died three days after this final detention.

I looked around the room. "Where would Medway keep confiscated items, do you think?"

"In that room you've just been in. I bet there's a box full of stuff," Heather said, half lost inside the computer.

I put the file down and returned to the stuffy cupboard. Sure enough, a large wicker basket sat at the back of the small room, its lid half open. I briefly wondered how many of Heather's belongings sat in a forlorn box like this at her school or at home. My heart ached for the child, lost in time. It was becoming obvious she'd ended up with the bikers for some pretty dark reasons.

Flipping the lid of the contraband box open, I found all sorts of things, none of which surprised me. Catapults looked like the most obvious contraband, some homemade, some bought. I found a very good one, tested the elastic and put it to one side. I hadn't used a catapult for years. Slingshots also appeared to be popular, so I snaffled one of those as well. I could teach Heather to use both—it would make up for not using firearms. A series of very violent computer games and some porn lay together in the box. I left them alone.

Finally, and with a sense of reluctance rising from my overactive instincts, I picked up a wooden box. It was probably twenty centimetres by fifteen.

"Heather," I called out, "I think I found something."

"Me too, you need to get in here," she said.

I held the box as if it contained an unstable ordnance. Something inside me, it reached out to the contents in the box, as if they held a conversation whispering at the very edge of my perception.

"Love, you remember the psychometry episode I had with Ki's scarf?" I asked, putting the box down on Medway's desk and wiping my fingers on my shorts and t-shirt.

"Of course, you nearly fainted."

I tore my eyes off the box. "I did not."

She just raised an eyebrow.

"Okay, I nearly fainted. Well, I think whatever is in there is likely to do the same thing. Can you open it?"

She reached for the box. "What's in it?"

"I think it's the tarot deck Ryan was using."

Heather snatched her hand back. "No, I'm not opening that unless we have some serious mojo between me and it. Like Ella and a shed load of salt or something." She eyed the box. "Come and have a look at this."

I watched the box as well. It wasn't anything remarkable to look at, just a plain wooden box in a style churned out by their million in a Chinese factory to look ethnic and Nepalese or Indian.

Circling the desk, I leaned over Heather's shoulder and peered at the screen. "What am I looking at?" Other than the obvious, it was a spreadsheet.

"The accounts for the school. They are deep in the red. The school is drowning in debt."

"Assets?" I asked.

Heather shrugged. "Difficult to see, but the building is heavily mortgaged. The school fees aren't enough to cover the debt once they pay the bills and wages."

"Can we tell how long this has been going on?"

"I'm not an accountant, Lorne."

I kissed her head. "No, but you are brilliant."

She sighed. "Mr Manipulation strikes again. Years, and before you ask, as far as I can tell, a shell company is bailing them out at the end of each financial year. It settles their debts, and they start all over again in the new financial year. The school is a charity, of course, so it's all transparent until you try to track the shell company."

"Okay, make a note and we'll get Paul onto it. He'll need something to do other than eating ice-cream. Anything else?"

"Detailed files on each of the students. I've taken a copy of Ryan's and those of the boys currently in residence. I've also found files on Polly and Damien."

"That's—"

"Efficient and expedient." Her steady gaze dared me to argue with her. "If Damien wasn't an old friend, you'd want all the intel on him you could gather. Apparently, his drinking problem isn't going unnoticed. Medway keeps private notes on everyone. The accounts are being sent somewhere else, but I can't track the email address. It's a random series of numbers and a Gmail account so it could go anywhere. Yes, I'll make a note for Paul."

I squeezed her shoulder. "You're amazing."

"I'm learning," she mumbled, moving files around. "If Medway checks his usage history, we're going to be busted because he'll see someone opened the files. I can't hide it and wiping cookies from the internet browser will just make him suspicious."

"Don't worry. He'd have to be super vigilant to see you've been in there. Close it all down. I want to get in the water long before evening begins."

"I don't think we should be here tonight," Heather said, while concentrating on the computer. "I also think the boys should be gone."

"We can't take the boys out of the school. We'll be done for kidnapping. Besides, Killian told me something that might make it a moot point."

Heather's focus sharpened. "What did he say?"

"The lads who knew Ryan best are still having nightmares about something chasing them, drowning them, stuff like that, even though they've gone home. Killian's had several web chats about it."

"Something here wants them, Lorne."

"And we'll stop it."

"What if we can't?" she asked, finally looking at me.

"Then we'll have made a mistake."

12

ARMED WITH WHAT I KNEW to be Ryan's box of tarot cards and a USB drive containing several files we'd stolen from Medway's computer, we went in search of our dog.

Killian and the others had him in the common room, sitting on the sofa sharing biscuits while the lads played on a PS4.

"I hope they aren't chocolate biscuits?" Heather asked.

All four sets of eyes turned in guilty alarm and several, 'No, ma'am' arrived, mumbled around the crumbs. I chuckled as they received Heather's best stare. Ghost slid off the sofa, padded over and gazed up at her. Within seconds, she'd folded. I wish I had the dog's skills.

Killian caught sight of the box in my hand, held carefully with the edge of my t-shirt, keeping my fingers off its surface.

"What are you doing with that?" he asked.

"Nothing you need to worry about. We just wanted to check up on you," Heather said. "Now, who is going to try to beat me at Call of Duty?" She rubbed her hands together with glee.

I wished them luck. She thrashed me every time.

"Who knows where Mr Heaney is?" I asked them.

Olly piped up, "Gym, that way." He pointed to a door on the other side of the room. "He's with Adam and Robert."

Heather settled down with the lads and I did a time check. It had been a long day, and we'd had a late lunch. At 16:53 hours we had almost five hours until full dark. I wanted us all to be in the school and barracked by then.

I strode down the hallway, through some double doors, past some changing rooms and into the central gym. Robert leaned against the doorway. He heard me coming.

"Lorne's here," he told whoever banged about in the storeroom.

"Send the silly old sod in," Damien called out.

"Thanks, I love you as well," I said, joining Robert on the other side of the doorway. "What are you doing?"

"Trying to find all the scuba gear. We stopped doing it because of the insurance costs."

"Your licence still valid?" I asked him.

He glanced at me. "Is yours?"

"No."

"Well then."

We shared a maniacal grin. Old soldiers reliving some mad memories. Not every deployment sent us to the deserts of the world. Sometimes they used us to back up UK or US Marines or our SBS brothers.

Together we checked the regulator set, tanks, seals, weight belt and the all-important gauge consoles. I went through everything several times. We had wetsuits, fins, gloves, masks and snorkels in separate bags. I found some glow sticks and Damien had a light. Other than the unknown currents, I didn't think we could go too far wrong on this mission. The water levels around Syndercombe village wouldn't be as high as usual, so in theory, I could make it to the surface without the gear if necessary.

When we left the small room carrying the diving rigmarole, I found Heather watching us from the doorway.

Damien leaned in close and whispered, "I don't think your woman likes me very much."

I patted his shoulder. "Then talk to her. I'm not her keeper." Though the level of distrust in Heather's eyes as she looked at Damien made me think it might be wise to brave a private word. Instincts or jealousy, it didn't matter which, she couldn't condemn the man without more proof than that provided by a bottle of vodka.

LUGGING THE BAG OF GEAR and the air tank, I trooped with Heather, Damien, Adam, and Robert to the minibus. We could have swum around the reservoir to the village's location, but to be honest, I didn't want to spend that long in the water. The school's boat, which the boys assured us was watertight, had to be the most sensible option. They kept it at the fishing lodge, which suited us perfectly. The old road, now underwater, that brought Syndercombe and Clatworthy together had the fishing lodge on one side and a gate on the other to prevent people from driving into the reservoir.

I'd also been told by Olly, who seemed to enjoy regurgitating facts, that the reservoir plunged to a depth of thirty metres in some places. Deeper than I wanted to go, without a better air mix and more practice. I didn't plan on being underwater longer than necessary or much deeper than ten metres. It should be possible to find the village, with the drought in place lowering the water levels, without a problem.

Damien drove us through the narrow lanes, the trees bowing their crowns together over the pitted tarmac as if trying to absorb the mark of man and return the land to nature. I felt anxious about the dive and wished I hadn't suggested it. Whether from the near drowning in Scob, or Damien's vivid energy lashing around the minibus, making him drive too fast, I didn't know what made me so uneasy. I still hadn't experienced anything other than scary vibes in the academy personally, which meant I was doing this because of Heather's report. I kept having to remind myself that I trusted her judgement, but for some reason it didn't come easily.

Just like with our argument, I wondered if this had more to do with the school and the things happening in it, than with our dynamic. Whatever buttons we had to trigger negative behaviour, they were being pushed. Could that be why Damien drank? Not just his memories?

He talked fast and hard, as if on patrol. It rubbed against me, like sandpaper grinding against velvet. All of us stayed quiet in the minibus, picking up on the manic aggression leaking from him.

Glass's Rock Lane, open to the sky with summer rich hedges rather than crowding trees, led us to the junction for the lodge. The minibus bounced as Damien took the corner too fast.

"Mate, come on. We've got kids in here," I said, my seatbelt biting my shoulder.

Damien ignored me and shot down the narrow road towards the water. We soon pulled up outside the fishing lodge and I breathed out as the handbrake went up. Over my shoulder, I saw Heather check on Robert, who looked shocked. Adam watched Damien with a strained expression I didn't understand.

The tension among us separated Damien from our group and it felt strange, tugging on my sense of loyalty in a confusing muddle of emotions. He stomped off to the lodge to sign for the keys, and Adam led the way to the large rowing boat painted in the school's livery. The boat looked a little forlorn, and I guessed, since Ryan's death, it hadn't been used. The water spread out in front of us, a dark sheen under the sun's glare. Not a ripple disturbed its surface, and the murky depths kept their secrets from those on land.

I looked around, taking in my surroundings, trying to find a sense of place. Hillsides rolled off to form the Brendon Hills and then Exmoor in the distance, admittedly out of view from my current location but there in my mind as my hearth and home. This relatively small mass of water filled an ancient combe at the head of the largest river in the area, the River Tone. One that had held the life of many small communities for centuries along its winding meander through the valley. It's not until you spend time in countries as dry and harsh as Iraq, Afghanistan, and Mali that you begin to really understand the value of water. Our benign environment had protected and provided for countless generations along its many waterways, and this drowned village was just one of them. Gone now perhaps, but still held in the memories of the land.

The thick trees bordering most of the water's edge held still in the sultry afternoon air. Not a broad leaf or fur tree's needle, stirred. No crows scolded, no sparrows chattered, no squirrels flitted. Everything lay heavy and still. Waiting.

I dumped the bag and tank on the ground, rolling my shoulders, relieved to be free of the weight for the moment.

Heather approached, her eyes dark with worry. "You don't have to do this."

"It's just recon, Heather. I'm going down to get eyes-on so I can see what's happening. It might give us clues to events in the school. Come on, give me a hand. This isn't my wetsuit, so it's difficult to use."

I stripped down to my briefs and started to talc up, making the suit slide more easily over my skin.

"Jesus, Turner, that's a lot of scarring," Damien said, having reappeared from the lodge. He took in the mess over my right flank.

"It was a big mortar," I muttered.

Adam looked pale. "Does it still hurt?"

"Sometimes, but it's mostly phantom pain, or because I've over exerted myself," I said, wiggling into the suit, the heat not helping. "Bits of it are numb, bits oversensitive."

"Welcome to the army," Heather said. "Whatever the recruitment posters tell you, this can be the result."

I chuckled. "Alright, Heather, you don't have to terrify the lad. He wants to sign up and most soldiers come out with barely a scratch."

She looked at me. "Is that why you wanted me to stop being in the Army Reservists?"

I didn't have much of a rejoinder for that, so kept my mouth shut.

The wetsuit didn't fit well, so I was in for a cold trip down to the old village.

Heather zipped me up and chuckled. "You look funny. Not very 007, sweetheart."

"We can't all look like Greek Gods as we emerge from the water," I said, faking umbrage.

"Looking like Sponge Bob would be a start," she murmured, then danced out of the way as I tried to swat her arse.

After a brief discussion, we decided Heather and Adam should row us out, Robert remaining on land in case of a problem. Rowing in a wetsuit with high humidity and afternoon heat radiating off the water and land didn't fill me with joy. Besides, if something went wrong with the dive, I needed someone I trusted in the boat.

"Don't pull on your oar too hard, Adam. You'll be unbalanced with Heather on the other side," Damien instructed.

Heather's eyes narrowed and I could almost see the ticker tape coming out of her ear that read, 'Challenge accepted'.

We shot across that water with the attack speed of a shark. The bend to the left was because of Heather, who had previously done a lot of kayaking on the River Exe at school. To be honest, I was glad she had control of the oars. I'd never been much good at rowing.

She smiled at Damien as she brought us to the neat halt, facing the way we'd come. "I can see the outlines of some walls," she said with total innocence.

I chuckled and peered over the edge. The black mass of tar-looking water had changed as we'd crossed its depths. The fresh water now appeared clearer, more benign, with a green tinge reminiscent of a romantic painting. As my eyes adjusted to see underwater in the boat's shadow, rather than into the sunlight's reflected glare off the surface, I saw the walls of a lost home. My heart pinged, and I realised this village would look like all the abandoned places I'd been through. A gun's sights trained on their broken walls, hoping the only lives in the place belonged to lizards.

A brief touch of my hand brought me back.

"You okay?" Heather asked.

I nodded. "Yeah, just a memory, not an episode."

"You feel anything like an episode down there, get back. Drop those weights and get back to me," she said with a gentle tug on the weight belt around my waist.

"Still love me then?" I asked, doing the last checks with the regulator and lowering the face mask.

"Always, even if you look like a demented fish-rabbit in that get up." She puffed out her cheeks to demonstrate what a fish-rabbit looked like.

"You ready?" I asked Damien, who went through his checks with Adam.

He nodded.

We mounted opposite sides of the boat to keep it balanced and, as he always had, Damien marked us off. On three, we rolled back into the water's icy embrace. Muscle memory kicked in, as it did with anything I'd learned to do in the army, and I cleared the mask before submerging.

13

THE WATER FILLED THE WETSUIT, making my breathing tight for a moment as I adjusted to the sudden cold. The visibility looked good. A few metres on either side of me remained clear and in the distance the green tinge turned dark. I spotted Damien and gave him the 'okay' signal. He nodded. Under my flippers I saw the walls of the cottage, about three metres down. I pointed to the walls and Damien nodded again.

We both bent at the waist and shot off into the hidden interior of the reservoir.

Damien took the lead, and I watched his bubbles to check they remained regular and even. Within moments we made it to the bottom. The long weeds attached to the stones of the nearest cottage and the broken beams of the old roof waved at us. I felt a current, obviously from the nearby streams, but this far from the dam wall, nothing tugged hard. Being only sixty years old, more or less, the reservoir's hidden cottages sat on the edge of a tarmacked lane.

With a brief gesture to show his intention, Damien followed the lane into the heart of the village. The path drifted under our bodies, sometimes clear, sometimes hidden by thick watery undergrowth and murky waters. Rainbow and brown trout flickered in and out of view, their beautiful lean strength mesmerising. Watching fish in their natural environment always filled me with joy, their effortless grace in a world so alien to us, humbling.

As we sank further down, I checked the gauge on my wrist and discovered that I neared my ten-metre limit. I pushed hard to catch up with Damien. Touching his arm to grab his attention, I held my fist to ear height—military speak for 'stop' whether on land or underwater. He gave me the thumbs up to show he was listening. I then pushed my hand out, palm down, and swished it from side to side, telling him we needed to level off.

Damien gave me the thumbs down and even behind the mask, I could see he was annoyed. If I didn't have a mouth full of regulator, I'd be sighing. He always wanted to push the limits. Damien then used his open palm to indicate we should go north of our current location. I hoped Heather would track the bubbles from the boat.

Once more I gave the levelling off signal. We needed to find the church, but not at any cost. If I panicked over something, even at this depth, I'd suffer for it by hitting the surface too fast. Damien gave the okay signal, but I sensed his irritation, and he still sank lower than I wanted to go as he raced into the dark. Did he feel like he had to prove something to me?

I shook my head and swam off after him, but maintained my depth. When you lose someone in your regiment, someone you're close to, they can become lionised in your memory and Damien fitted that category perfectly for me. If he'd made his twenty-year service, he'd have been my commanding officer, I had no doubt. I was a good all-rounder for my unit, but Damien was better and a natural risk taker where I'd been more steady, especially after the first year or two of regular deployments. Probably how I'd survived so long.

In a small community like Syndercombe, that didn't have too many houses, we'd find the church easily. Though, I began to feel more uncomfortable with the mission, because the further we went from the boat, the darker the water became, which meant it was deeper. Damien had found a couple of waterproof torches, so I stopped swimming, tugged at the one clipped to my belt and switched it on. I saw fish buck away from the light and Damien's feet vanishing into the blackness of the water.

My breathing shifted, the rise of bubbles beside my face changing their pattern.

Good timing, idiot. Let's try not to drown.

I closed my eyes and trod water, then pinched the skin between thumb and forefinger. Sharp aching pain oozed from the spot, and I counted my breaths. Yeah, this hadn't been one of my best ideas. The water closed around me, suffocating and claustrophobic.

Maybe you need to think about why this is happening?

Good point. Why the panic attack now? I'd had no flashback. If my skin wasn't so numb from the cold, would I have that creeping sensation of black feathers being dragged over my flesh? Was something trying to prevent our exploration?

These thoughts pushed the panic back and logic took over. I twisted and kicked hard, shooting off after Damien.

Within moments, my torchlight found him, floating just a few metres ahead, the broken spire of a small church parallel to our position. He turned in the water and gestured to the hole in the spire. I shook my head. I pointed to my chest, then pointed towards the ground. He needed to follow me for a change. Habits are bad, and I was in the habit of allowing Damien to take charge. However, I had far more experience. A little faith in myself might serve me well right now.

Aware we'd be going deeper than I intended, but not by much, I swam down to the wall of the tiny church. Though larger than the one at Stoke Pero and Culbone, it still wouldn't comfortably fit more than thirty souls at a time. When I thought about what Mrs Langford had told us, I knew the door to the place had been removed and it would be safer to use than drifting through the roof. Snagging our equipment on a broken beam or tile tempted Lady Death a little too enthusiastically for my tastes. I had a woman to marry and a dog. Life wasn't to be thrown around quite so carelessly these days.

We found the hole fast enough, on the other side of the church to the one I'd chosen. The inevitability of that helped keep me present, but I felt the whispering dread pushing back through the water. No fish surrounded us, and no weeds attached to the exterior of the church. The water felt colder in this spot with the tug of a current making it hard to remain still. I paused, using the torch to trace the keystones in the arch of the old doorway. This church had no porch, so we'd be going straight into the nave.

For the first time in months, I wished for Al-Ahmar's company. My desert companion, the djinn I'd learned to co-habit with, remained quiet inside me. He'd been gone since the events at Hinkley Point. Something of a relief and a worry. My nightmares had changed, the terrible events in Syria taking a backseat over some fresh horrors my subconscious needed clearing out, but the PTSD absences remained the same.

Now, I wanted the company because Ahmar had a habit of being able to drag my body out of the shit, even if he couldn't always protect my mind.

A strong finger poked me in the back, and I realised I'd been frozen in my thoughts for too long. We had to go inside. I ducked my head under the thick stonework and entered the lost building.

Darkness. No ambient light from above made it through the broken roof. I paused on the other side of the doorway and flicked my torch around, feeling Damien against my tank, nudging me forwards. Out of habit, I shone the torch towards the altar end of the church and almost screamed.

Bubbles blew out of my mouth and the regulator hissed as I fought the instinct to holler in shock.

I heard Damien behind me, his tank hitting something metal in the church's wall, setting off a chime in the water. More bubbles filled the surrounding space. I fought for control, but it wasn't easy.

A face turned white dead eyes towards us. Bloated pale skin split and oozed fleshy substances into the disturbed water. Thick fingers, a rope clasping them together in mock prayer, reached out for the living among the dead's watery home. I flashed the torch around and realised at least one more body floated inside the ancient church. This one lacked the flesh around the naked teeth, eye balls missing, making it appear something trapped the corpse in an endless howl of blind terror.

The currents of water inside the building, now disturbed by our presence, shifted the dead closer to our position. I tried to push back, away from those blindly seeking fingers, the tips torn and ragged. Had these victims tried to save themselves by clinging on to something? I should stay. I needed to find out. That's when the shadows, those formed by our torches, shifted contrary to the natural order. My tank butted up against something solid.

Damien grabbed my arm and tugged us back the way we'd come. I followed with no argument, trying to hold on to my fraying control. We needed to reach the surface, but we also needed to spend a few minutes at a depth that would help rid us of the nitrogen and other gasses that caused the brain and body to feel bad. A full case of the bends would only happen over thirty metres, but even at this depth, the body didn't like the toxic mix of chemicals as we rose.

I had just enough awareness to check our depth, twelve metres, before Damien kicked for the surface. I reached for his leg to slow him down. A cascade of bubbles escaped his mouth as he screamed and lashed out at me. I jerked back to avoid his fin and foot catching me in the face.

He was going to hit the surface too fast. Kicking down hard, I arrowed upwards, twisted, and reached out for his shoulders as we came face to face. I grabbed him again and pushed down. His eyes roved wildly, and his bubbles flew away in a frantic burst. With one hand, I tapped his mask, then mine, asking him to look at me. Placing the same hand on his chest, I made a slowing down gesture. Damien's hand closed over my forearm, and he hung on. For his life, he hung on. I nodded.

Thinking it wise to move us away from the church, I kicked gently. Damien was now obedient and still in my grip. We drifted from the village and back the way we'd come, into the light.

WHEN I SURFACED, THE SIDE of the rowing boat was within arm's reach. My numb fingers closed over the gunwale, and I released Damien for the first time in what felt like hours. We spat out the regulators and I lifted my mask as Damien struggled with the harness holding his air tank. It wouldn't be easy to climb up with the tank attached.

"Heather, help him," I ordered.

"Are you okay?" she asked.

"No. No, we aren't, but we need to get out of this water. Get him out first. Adam, help her."

I remained in the water, relearning how to breathe genuine air and calming my racing heart. They hauled Damien over the edge, the boat rocking, and I tackled my harness. Heather leaned over and helped.

"What happened?"

I stared at her. "We found bodies in the church. Recent dead."

Her eyes widened and her mouth fell open. Adam swore and Damien just sat slumped over in the stern, shivering.

I kicked hard and hauled myself over the edge, making lighter work of it than my companion.

"You okay, fella?" I asked him, putting a hand on his shoulder once more.

He looked up at me. "I try not to remember what the dead look like, Wellie."

Nodding, I said, "I know, Crusty. I know."

Damien rubbed his hands over his face. "What the hell is going on here?"

"That's not our job. We need to call the police, get professional divers down here." I turned my focus to Heather. "How fast can you get us to shore?"

She took both oars and rowed hard. It didn't take long to reach the small pontoon. Wordlessly, she tided us off, then handed me her phone. Robert shared quiet words with Adam, helping him lift out the gear.

I'd considered calling the emergency services, but there seemed little point, so I looked up Detective Inspector Kate Mackenzie's number.

As senior investigating officer on several high-profile murders in the area, she'd be the best person to call. The phone rang.

"Good afternoon, Heather, what can I—"

"It's Turner, Mackenzie."

"Don't tell me, you've found a body." She laughed, and I heard Ella in the background. Good, she was in the area.

"I need you down at Clatworthy Reservoir. I've found at least two bodies. There might be more, I don't know. You'll need a dive team and body bags."

My eyes flickered to the treeline behind the fishing lodge. Shapes drifted among the shadows. I nudged Heather and pointed. She frowned but followed my direction, squinting.

"Adam, on me," she barked and jumped out of the boat. "Robert, stay put."

"Be careful," I snapped out as she hared off down the shallow beach.

"Lorne? What's going on?" Kate asked, her voice terse.

"Hopefully, nothing. Look, there's no rush, the dead aren't going anywhere, and they'll be no evidence that can degrade any further. Here's what I know…" I went on to describe what we'd found.

"Why are you down there?" she asked.

"Would you believe we're here because of ghost stories?"

She sighed. "Knowing you is never dull, Turner. Alright, I'll muster some troops and see if we can get a dive team down there before dark."

"I think leaving it for the morning is better, Kate. The dead really aren't going anywhere but—" How was I going to say this without sounding like a bloody idiot?

"Spit it out, Lorne. Nothing you say will surprise me anymore."

"This is a lot more dangerous than just a few corpses in the reservoir. Leave it until daylight. Call who you have to, but trust me, you want the sun on this job."

Silence for a long time, then a quiet, "Okay, I'll call my DCI and let him know. Do you need Ella down there? I know she's your Robin when you're in Batman mode."

She'd been part of more than one crazy adventure we'd had over the last eighteen months. Though her sarcasm annoyed me.

"We're at Syndercombe Academy. If you need a base, it's the best place. Almost empty at the moment."

"Okay, I'll bring Ella down now, that sound good?"

Oh, yes, that sounded good. Having a priest around might be the best piece of advice I could have right now. "Yes, I think that's wise. Sorry. I know you guys don't get too much time together."

"Hey, when duty calls, it calls. I'll see you in an hour or so."

"Roger that," I said, hanging up. While I'd been talking to Kate, I'd kept Heather in my line of sight. She'd now vanished into the treeline, and it made me nervous. "Damien, I need to change. I can't run in this suit."

When no response came, I glanced at him. Damien hadn't moved. I nudged him with my foot. "Hey, I need some help here. Adam and Heather have gone into the woods and there's clearly a problem in the area we don't understand. Get it together."

Damien's white hair, still stuck down to his scalp, looked thin and his skin sagged, making him suddenly older. "What's going on, Lorne?"

"Right now? You're getting up and I'm getting dressed. Move." I hauled him up and pushed him onto the pontoon. We covered the short distance to shore and my pile of clothes. I changed. "Stay here, gather the dive gear together and stow it in the van. I'll be back soonest." The moment I had my boots on my feet, I dashed off into the woods.

It took a handful of seconds to find Heather's trail, and I followed it without a problem. She wasn't trying to hide. Dodging through the trunks of hornbeam and ash trees, I tumbled into a field and stopped when I spotted Heather and Adam. A fence separated us, so I put a hand on the nearest post and vaulted the barbed wire.

"Heather?"

She didn't move, and she stood stiffly. Adam remained at her side, taller by a head at least, and equally still. I scanned the surrounding area, my senses on high alert. Nothing moved in the heat of the late afternoon. Not a leaf, not a bee, not even the ever-present summer flies.

I stepped around the pair. "Heather?" I asked again. Her eyes stared into the distance, but I knew they registered nothing, because they were white. Like the dead.

1 4

"HEATHER…" I DIDN'T KNOW WHAT to do. She wasn't there, in her body. I didn't know if I should shake her, hold her, or murmur some kind of prayer over her. "Heather, listen to the sound of my voice. I need you to come back. Wherever you are." I glanced at Adam. He was in the same state.

Fear rose like bile in my throat. What the hell had I seen in the treeline to cause this? Even a year ago, I would have denied the possibility of this being something other than a weird effect of heat, water, chemicals in the air—anything other than the supernatural.

These days, sadly, it was my go-to, which disturbed me.

"What do we know, Turner?" I muttered aloud. "What can I do?" I looked at her hand, the engagement ring bright in the sun. My mother wore that ring until her farmer's fingers grew too thick.

"Bugger it," I said. "Sorry if I make a mistake." Focusing on Heather's face, I reached for her left hand with my right.

Shadows filled my vision. Dozens of them in the field around us. Some almost black, others pale as wisps of dreams. The clearest wore tunics, with heavy cloaks, long hair and boots made of wool and leather. They resembled images I'd seen in the history books, an archaeologist's version of the Celts, or something similar. They appeared to be moving at a slow rate on a well-worn track that didn't exist in my time. A track leading to the summit of the nearby hill.

I sucked in a hard breath, tightening my grip on Heather's hand while reaching out for Adam's as well. The shadows didn't seem to be on any nefarious business, they just... existed in this place. How though? How were they being tied to this land? How were they affecting Heather and Adam? How was I supposed to get my people back?

Without the djinn's help, I understood little about my 'gift'. Now I knew it existed, and it wasn't down to my training in The Regiment, the sixth of my senses had grown considerably in strength. Whether it was because of the djinn's presence locked in my soul, or the terrible snap in my reality causing catastrophic psychosis and long-term PTSD, I didn't know, but things were changing for me.

Willow always said to use simple visualisation to help me manipulate the vibrational energy I sensed. So, what to visualise to help Heather and Adam? They'd stumbled into something occupying the same space. I couldn't force them to move, and it probably wouldn't be wise. I needed to rid them of the shadow form occupying this space. Sucking it into me and pushing it into the ground, because 'grounding' was important.

Huh, so you do listen.

I ignored my inner sarcasm monster and focused on seeing Heather and Adam at the kitchen table in the academy when we'd enjoyed lunch. Both of them were laughing and full of animated life.

Outside of that bright memory, I saw the shade of another being occupying their space in the here and now. A separate energy. An extra layer of reality with enough strength it could take some control of a living being.

Trying to keep calm, I thought of a vacuum cleaner and sucked.

Not a pretty image perhaps, but it worked. I drew in a sharp breath to help with the images I conjured in my mind, held that breath, and watched the darkened shadow inside Heather merge with me as if I had the gravitational pull of a black hole.

Once it had succumbed, I pushed the shadow down. Down through the centre of me, using the clear visuals of my chakras, that Heather and Willow kept banging on about. The colours made it easy to see clearly, I had to give them that, and it worked. The dirty shadows clinging to Heather and Adam plunged through me, turning the world ice-cold for a long moment, before they separated into my legs and down through into the earth. It felt like moving treacle, their reluctance to leave the warmth of my body very clear, but with an ever-widening bubble of blue and white, I pushed them out. Gradually, the others in the field faded, and I wondered if I'd just dreamed the last few minutes.

Heather stumbled into me, and Adam dropped to his knees in the summer scored grass.

"Oh, God, Lorne, what's going on?" Heather whispered, clinging to my arms.

Adam burst into tears. I put a hand on his head. "It's okay, son. It's okay. You're safe now." I brought Heather down to Adam's side, and the lad sought comfort by burying his head in my shoulder. I'd comforted more broken soldiers than I cared to remember, so I quietly hushed him and patted his back.

Heather drew away first. "What happened?" She swiped at the fall of tears on her cheeks. They came more from shock than grief, I thought.

"I'm not sure, but I'd like to put some distance between this place and us," I said, pulling them both to their feet. The sun burned my naked scalp and neck. Thirst made me a little dizzy as I stood. We returned to the cool interior of the small woodland strip separating the field from the water and the shade instantly revived our flagging spirits.

"Lorne, I really need to know what happened," Heather said.

I noticed she hadn't released Adam's hand. He looked terribly young. "I'll start from the beginning, in the water…" The explanation of what I'd seen and experienced took us back to the minibus. I finished with, "That grassland is like a minefield, I think. Those trapped spirits are stuck, and you stumbled into two of them, absorbing them. Whatever is here must be growing stronger."

"Where's Damien?" Adam asked.

Robert appeared from the shade of the small fishing lodge. "He just ran off." The lad pointed north at the long side of the reservoir. He looked relieved to be united with his friend. Adam stood close and their hands brushed.

I found the minibus door unlocked and the keys on the front seat. The dive gear sat in the back, stowed with military precision. Half of me expected to see Damien sat under a tree with a hip flask of vodka, but no sign of him lurked in the darkening shadows. I walked around the gravel car park but too many tracks littered the ground for me to pick out any in particular, and the earth was too hard for him to leave a trace.

This worried me. I spent a full five minutes scanning my surroundings. He could be anywhere.

Heather approached. "Lorne, I think we need to go. He'll know this place better than you. Maybe he just needs some alone time. The boys have to get back and the police will be down soon, right?"

"Only Kate and Ella tonight."

The colour in Heather's face shifted. "Why did you let Kate bring Ella? This place is toxic. She doesn't need to be here."

I gripped Heather's arm. "Maybe we need her here."

It didn't take long to drive back to the school, longer than it took to arrive because I valued my life, but within fifteen minutes, I had them safely tucked up in the kitchen. A long, cool glass of water later and life felt a bit more normal. The boys stayed with us, and Ghost lay under the table with a fan on him, the thick fur making him vulnerable to heat exhaustion.

"The police are on their way to the school," I said as everyone took a seat around the table.

"Why?" asked Polly. "And where is Damien?"

"I don't know where Damien is right now. He left the water okay, that's the main thing. What we found in there might have triggered some stuff for him…" The more I'd thought about that on the journey back to the school, the more likely it was the reason for his disappearing trick.

We'd been on our second deployment in Afghanistan with The Regiment, still a bit wet behind the ears, and I'd been too close to an RPG explosion. It had blown my ear drum, confining me to barracks for a couple of days. You can't have good comms with just one ear functioning. The unit Damien and I patrolled with most often went out into a village called Abi Jan near Lashkar Gar on the Helmand River. What they'd found in the village proved too much, even for the most hardened of us. For Damien, it made the war personal. He was never the same. Seeing those drowned bodies might well have brought back too much pain with me around to add to the mess.

I spread my fingers over the surface of the wooden table, feeling the smooth grain under my fingertips. The lack of callouses on my trigger finger a relief.

"Let Damien sort things out before he returns. What we need to do is protect ourselves before night. I suggest we use this opportunity to pack up our stuff and leave the school. The police can deal with the bodies we found in the water, and I can put everyone up at the farm until we contact the boys' families. Does this seem like a plan?"

The younger boys shared solemn expressions, but it was Killian who spoke up with Olly's urging. "We think we should stay and find out what's going on, because this isn't going to stop. Moving us to your farm will just take the problem with us."

"I can protect you at my place," I told them.

"No," Robert said, crossing his arms. "I want to know what's happening here. So does Adam, right?" He looked at his friend.

Adam nodded, despite his obvious reluctance. "The others are right, sir. We should stay and see this through."

"You've all watched too many films," I said. "This won't work."

A series of loud pops, like small arms' fire, came from outside.

Ghost shifted under the table, his head coming up so fast it hit my knee. He growled, then began the most horrendous barking, surging out from under the table.

"Shit, Ghost, shut up!" Heather tried to yell over his noise.

I'd never heard him like this, but I knew what a service dog sounded like when facing a known enemy. Rather than try to stop him, I opened the back door, and he shot out in a race of fury and revenge. I ran after him and skidded on the gravel as we stopped. Ghost pulled up sharpish, circled and came around me to sit at my heel. He shivered.

All the tyres on all the vehicles were blown.

Heather, Robert, and Adam arrived next.

"What the hell?" she hissed. "My bike."

I held my breath, waited for three heartbeats, then winced as she screamed, "Bastards!"

The rant that followed our discovery would have made a Glaswegian sailor pale with its colourful ways to use various implements that aren't meant to be inserted into the human body.

Eventually, she turned to me and said in a low growl, "I'm going to find out what's going on here and I'm going to make that something scream."

I thought this might be the place for a 'Yes, dear' but opted for the safer, "Roger that."

"How the hell is this possible?" asked Adam, his face pale. Since finding the bodies under the water, the lad had been quiet.

I watched Heather with half an eye as she stalked around the truck, now sat forlornly on its wheel hubs. Thank goodness Heather had put Dixie on her full stand. The bike remained upright and undamaged.

"We'll need to call a garage," I muttered, unwilling to answer Adam's question. Heat could blow tyres. I'd seen it happen, but never all four, and it wasn't that hot on the gravel. Approaching my truck, I knelt and examined the hole. Neat, tight, the worst of the damage pointing inward. I traced the hole with my forefinger. Someone, or something, had done this to the vehicles. The minibus and Polly's small city run-around were in the same state.

How could someone do all the tyres so fast? Ghost had reacted to something instantly, something violent. I'd not heard anything moving around outside. Rising from my crouch, I searched my surroundings, allowing myself to relax. Gravel didn't hold footprints very well, and dry earth left even less evidence for me to follow, but my gaze drifted over to the woodland. The treeline started maybe twenty metres from my current location. I approached, using the most direct route, and felt the heat of the afternoon slide off my shoulders as the shadows slipped into place.

"You want us to stay, don't you?" I whispered, peering through the dense layer of trees and scrubby bushes.

A low groan filled the space between the trees. I didn't react. I just said in the quiet voice, "Who are you? What are you?" I wished Al-Ahmar would rise through me and give me a clue as to what we faced. The djinn, though, remained silent, absent, and it left me feeling vulnerable. I opted for the direct approach. "What are you?" I repeated with more volume and purpose.

The day flashed black, a lightning strike in reverse, the trees white, the surrounding space a void. I had time to suck in half a breath before an image screamed out from between those white trees. An image formed of pain and hate.

I backpedalled, hit a rut in the hard ground and smacked onto my arse. From several miles away, I heard Heather calling my name, but I just sat in the dirt, my body quivering.

"Lorne?" She touched my shoulder. "Lorne, what happened? Remember to breathe."

Good point well made. I sucked in a breath. "It's loose," I managed. "It's loose, and it's coming for us." With Heather's help, I scrambled up off the ground. "We have to move. Get everyone inside. Now!"

The boys were scattered about the damaged vehicles, their voices coming in and out of my head like a badly tuned radio. Heather didn't question or argue; she called Ghost in to her side and began shepherding the children back to the school's kitchen.

Adam approached me. "Do you need a hand?"

"I'd like to say no, but the world refuses to stay still," I muttered.

Offering me his arm, without comment, Adam acted as a crutch.

Once I made it into the kitchen, things eased considerably, and the world righted itself. Heather and Polly handed out squash to the kids, and I took a glass. The cool lemon sugar a welcome distraction for a moment.

"What happened?" Heather asked, her voice leashed but her body primed and tense.

"I think it gave me a glimpse of what's plaguing this place. How it fits in with the bodies we found in the reservoir, I don't know, but we're in trouble. They punctured the tyres from the outside, as if someone knifed or shot all of them simultaneously. Clearly an impossible task. When I went to the treeline, I heard a low moan, almost words. That's when it showed itself..."

I realised my hands trembled, and I closed my fists. Focusing on Heather, I said, "Remember what I said about Al-Ahmar? The first time I saw him?"

She nodded. "The face with the screaming mouth and black eyes."

The others remained silent, watching us, not understanding.

"It's like that," I said. "Only twisted, white against black, barely recognisable as a human type face. Teeth, lots of teeth like a misted creature on the surface of the mirror screaming in hate." A full body shiver took over. "It wasn't running away, like Ahmar, it isn't running from rage and hate and blood and bone." I covered my face with my hands. "It isn't running from the anguish caused by the black flags, it just wants to..." My hands dropped from my face, and I knew the horror of my understanding spread like a virus through the others in the room. "It just wants us."

15

POLLY CHUCKLED, HER VOICE BREAKING the brittle silence like a splinter burying itself deep into the skin. "You can't be serious?" her London accent made her voice sharp. "Look, I've been around Damien enough to know PTSD—"

"It's not PTSD. I know the difference, now, between my sensitivities and my mental health issues."

She scoffed and if I'd had the energy, I'd have challenged her, but in that moment, I simply couldn't be bothered. We heard a vehicle pull up, and I knew it would be DI Kate Mackenzie and Ella. I really didn't want Ella here, tangled up in this. Phoning them had been a mistake. Kate should take Heather and Ghost away. That, at least, I could manage.

"I'll go," Heather said.

"We can't leave, can we?" Robert asked in a small voice, eyes wide. "It's too late."

I focused on the boys. Their bravado had vanished. Adam sat at one end, Robert the other, Olly, Killian and the near silent Mason between them. Lost boys.

"To be honest, I don't know. Maybe we can leave by walking out of the place."

"But what if it comes with us? Like it has some of the others?" Killian asked.

The back door opened, and Ella walked in with Kate and Heather. Her dog collar shone like a beacon. Ghost went to greet his friend.

"Then maybe we use our own supernatural contacts to help break the connection," I said. "Let's not panic just yet. It's scared us, but that's its job. Maybe we need to remember it's just doing its job."

Adam nodded, clearly liking the analogy. "Which means we can accept it and that takes away the fear."

Killian didn't look impressed.

I made the introductions. Polly eyed Ella but gave a civilised smile.

"I think it's time you gave me more details, Turner," Kate said. "Perhaps we can do a formal interview in a nearby room? Also, what the hell happened to everyone's tyres?"

"Did you come down in Ella's Rav or your BMW?" I asked.

"Mine, why?"

"I hope your tyres are insured," I muttered. "Come on. We need to talk."

I led the way to a classroom.

Kate grabbed my arm the moment the heavy classroom door swung shut. "What's happening here, Lorne?"

Sitting on the teacher's desk, I said, "I'll take you through everything we know so far, because, to be honest, I don't know what's going on and I need help. I'm not a detective, and I don't know what to do next."

"You mean there's not an assault rifle you can pick up and threaten someone with?" Kate asked, the dripping venom understandable but not welcome or funny.

"Not fair, DI Mackenzie."

She just raised a dark, neat eyebrow.

I shifted in discomfort. We both knew I sailed far too close to a hurricane to be trying to win that battle.

As I lay everything out for Kate, perspectives shifted, and my oversight of the issues clarified. Basically, we had a sunken village where someone left bodies many years ago. Mrs Langford's memories made it clear those bodies might relate to some form of sacrifice. We had evidence of the academy becoming a focal point for supernatural activity. We had more bodies in the water and a dead boy.

"How many do you think are down there?" Kate asked when I finished.

I shook my head. "I don't know, and I didn't want to hang about to count. Two for certain, one more damaged than the other, both tied in a way that's reminiscent of a ritual. Or maybe that's just me overreacting to what I saw. There's a Mrs Langford in the village you'll want to talk to. She was a child when this place became the reservoir. She saw something back then, but no one believed her. I'm not sure she believes it now but by the time she was old enough to find out more for herself, the human remains had gone."

Kate sat in silence, gazing first out of the window of the classroom, then at her hand on the wooden table top. "I'll talk to my DCI again, get a budget okayed for an initial assessment. Once we know what we're dealing with, I'll be able to make more decisions about how to proceed. My priority has to be the safety of the children." Her sharp brown eyes focused on me. "Where's this friend of yours? Damien?"

The summer twilight had begun outside. It might last over an hour in this weather, but it wouldn't stop the night descending.

"I wish I knew," I confessed. The uneasy feeling about Damien spread more sticky tendrils of doubt through my head and heart.

"Are you armed?" Kate asked with all the suddenness of a wasp's sting.

I blinked. "Um, no. Well, not with a firearm, if that's what you're asking? I have nothing like that here or at home."

Her eyes narrowed, and I realised Ella had never confessed to my weapons' stash. Her continued loyalty to me always surprised me. I never felt like I'd earned it.

"Seriously, Kate. I have nothing, not any more. I've found some things confiscated from the lads, and I can use them if necessary."

Kate spread her fingers out over the table top, obviously a mental ritual because the hesitation behind her next words made it clear she'd considered them. "Lorne, I'm just going to say this—is your friend a threat, and can you take him out if necessary?"

I blinked several times. Considering Damien as a threat didn't sit well with me, but to have Kate echoing Heather also nudged my conscience. "Honestly? He could be if he's tangled up in this madness. Back in the day, he was a better soldier than I was, but he's been out of the game a lot longer than me. I'm fitter, faster, but he always had a ruthless edge I lacked. He's a lot bigger and knows the territory here in a way I don't. That's my honest opinion and a real threat assessment. I know he was a good man and would never hurt children, or women, but…"

"If he's not functioning by his own accord…?"

I shrugged.

"Okay, so we have one potential human threat out there and something bad in here. Maybe we should—"

Ella rushed into the room, banging the door on the way, making us both start in shock. "Kate, someone's been at your car."

"Fuck!" The detective inspector exploded out of the chair and dashed off, almost knocking Ella over.

I didn't bother chasing her.

Ella took her place at the table. "You okay?" she asked.

"I don't know. This was supposed to be a simple haunting, and it's turning into a nightmare. One of my oldest friends is out there, possibly losing his mind, and I'm babysitting a bunch of kids who should be with their families."

"Ahmar giving you any clues?" she asked, the tension in her voice saying more than the words.

"He's still quiet. Whatever happened to him during the confrontation with the angel has knocked him out of the game. I don't know if he'll ever be back."

"Maybe that's just as well."

I wasn't so sure. He'd saved my life and given me intel more than once. From thinking I was going mad under some kind of possession, I'd learned to co-exist with my desert spirit and I found I missed him. I certainly needed his help now.

"Ella, I don't know what's happening here. I'm finding this place is confounding my senses. I don't know if it's a trapped spirit who wants out, or something bigger."

"Like what?" she asked.

"After what we witnessed at Hinkley Point, who knows? If someone had told me six months ago angels really existed, I'd have laughed. But if angels exist, then so do their opposite number. All this hocus-pocus I'm trapped in has checks and balances. You can't have light without the dark and I seem to operate somewhere in the shadows caused by the two meeting."

A soft smile lightened her pixie face. "That's a very apt and eloquent way of explaining the situation. We've trusted your instincts before, so what are they telling you now?"

"Run."

She snorted. "I'm guessing that's not really an option, or we'd be doing it already."

"No, not really an option." I sighed and rubbed my face. It had been a long day. "The boys seem to think that whatever is here will follow them home, even if we get them out of the area. It won't be difficult to walk out of the valley, but I can't afford to let them leave with something clinging to them."

"I could bless them. That should help."

It wasn't a bad idea, and it made sense. "Whether or not we leave, I think that's a plan."

"Okay, then we'll start there and formulate other options. The others can help. I think leaving with the boys is the best we can do, even if it's just to get them to the church in Clatworthy for the night."

"Have you spoken to the vicar?" I asked.

She nodded. "He's away at a symposium, but he's happy I'm here. We've met a few times at diocese functions. He's a good man, but badly overstretched. He tried to help the head teacher here, but went through official channels and that gummed up the works."

"Medway, he's the head teacher. He told me about contacting the Church. Apparently, he thinks it's failing as the fourth emergency service. Besides, he doesn't believe in the supernatural."

Ella chuckled. "They never do until it comes knocking. Come on. You need to eat. We don't know how long the night is going to be."

Back in the kitchen, I looked around for Heather. No sign. No sign of the dog either, so I guessed she'd taken him out to do his business.

Polly stood at the kitchen counter, making a range of thick sandwiches. A cake sat to one side cooling, and the boys helped by making coleslaw. Busy work.

Her manner seemed strained, and she flinched as Kate came back into the room looking like a vengeful goddess, her dark skin flushed and her eyes sparking. "Some fucker's broken into my car and ripped out the damned wiring."

The boys smirked at the language.

"We'll be walking out then, if we leave," I stated, then almost stepped back out of the room as the full force of DI Mackenzie's glare hit me. It felt like being doused in artic water and lava at the same time.

"Stating the bleeding bloody obvious won't help my frame of mind, Turner," she snapped. "This is your doing."

I opened my mouth to argue, caught Ella's warning look, and snapped my gob shut. "I need to find Heather," popped out instead. Walking around the unhappy DI, I left the kitchen. I knew Kate didn't like me very much, and we probably had different priorities, but being blamed for destroying her car annoyed me.

"Heather? Ghost?" I called out.

Nothing. She wouldn't have gone far; the area was too dangerous. I pulled out my mobile phone. No signal. "Bloody typical."

"Heather!" I called out, concern rippling through me. I whispered, "Where are you?"

Movement behind me had me turning and primed for combat within a single breath.

"Lorne?" came a voice I half recognised. A tall, thin man made of dirty cotton rainbows and long black hair, hurried towards me.

"Barny?" I called as I strode towards him.

"I need your help, mate."

Approaching, I saw he held out his hands. Blood covered him and most of his tatty shirt. "It's the dog. I can't carry him. He's too big."

My stomach rolled, dropped, and threatened to leave the premises. "Where?" I asked.

Barny pointed back up the lane, the only vehicle access to the school. I started running while he was talking, but soon heard him coming after me. I found Ghost lying in the road. A thin whine filled my heart with terror.

"Okay, buddy, okay. We'll get you sorted. I need to look."

Barny pounded up behind me, sounding like an asthmatic elephant, but he must be fit because he recovered quickly. "I think there's something around his legs."

I was already kneeling beside the big dog. He gazed at me with total faith in my ability to save him. I'd seen that look in Heather's eyes once or twice. It always scared me. The narrow lane was dim, the sun only a hint of orange on the horizon. "I need light. Take my torch app and shine it on the dog." I handed over the mobile.

He took up position beside me and held the phone steady. He was right. Wire held the dog's legs trapped in a tangle. Barbed wire.

"Okay, Ghost, this is going to hurt, but we're going to get it done fast," I found myself explaining to the dog, who twitched and whined. I pulled off my t-shirt, ignoring Barny's sharp intake of breath, and tied it around the dog's muzzle and head. Did I really think he was going to bite me? Better safe than sorry with a dog. To be honest, he just lay there, as though having my scent that close to his nose helped keep him calm. Next, I pulled out my portable toolkit. A small pouch with a multi-tool inside. The pliers started cutting at the wire. When I'd made enough cuts, I pulled the evil wire out of Ghost's tangle of fur. It looked far worse than it turned out to be. Dogs don't bleed like humans when we're cut.

Barny stroked Ghost's head, helped where he could, but basically kept the drama under control, just like his sister would in any crisis.

When the last of the barbed wire came free, Ghost struggled up and shook himself. I removed the makeshift muzzle and wiped blood off the multi-tool and my hands. "Can you walk, big man?" I asked the dog.

With small, tentative steps, the dog moved. He wasn't happy, and I winced when I saw fresh blood on his legs, but he'd reach the school. "Ghost?" He turned towards me at his name. "Where's Mummy?" I asked him, feeling like a dork.

The poor animal whined but couldn't offer me any intel.

I turned to Barny. "Did you see her?"

"No."

"What are you doing here?" I asked instead.

"I thought… Well, I thought I might be able to help, so I walked up. Seeing Heather, it shook me up, but, you know, she's my little sister. I've been getting weird vibes since this morning. She needs help."

An unending series of swear words filled my head, but I pressed my lips together. None of this was Ghost's fault or Barny's. This lay at my door. I hadn't kept my unit together. "Get him to the school. You'll find a vicar in there. Tell her Heather's MIA and to help the dog. She needs to keep everyone together in the same room."

Barny nodded, a man of few words, and coaxed Ghost towards the school.

I took my phone back and scanned the area for clues as to where the dog had come from. A narrow track, more for foxes than deer, vanished into the wood. When I knelt and pulled at the dry grasses, I felt the sticky drying blood on their surface. The dog must have dragged himself to the road through the path. Following, I let the dark woodland encompass me.

Barny's voice, clearly in an argument with Ghost about where the dog should be, drifted to me through the thick trunks of old woodland. The ground cover didn't hinder me, but each step crackled with dry leaves and snapped twigs. I kept the light off, and it didn't take long for my eyes to adjust.

I wanted to scream for Heather. To fill the woodland with my entreaties for her return. My stomach felt so tight I feared it might split like a drum in a thrash metal band. Did Damien do this? Or that screaming face I'd seen down by the reservoir? I didn't know which would be worse. She needed finding; I'd rip this fucking woodland apart with a flame thrower if necessary.

Panic won't help, mucker.

My personal critic had a point. I needed help, but using those in the school could lead to more people going missing. In the dark, we'd lose people and not be aware of it until it was too late.

"Calm down and think, you bloody fool," I whispered.

Heather wouldn't wander off from Ghost by herself. She also wouldn't allow the dog to be hurt. She'd fight and make enough noise to rouse the dead in the lake if someone grabbed her. Damien might take her down without a fight, but his odds weren't great. If something had happened to her, like it had at the reservoir, then…

I took a steadying breath, trying to wrestle my heart rate under control. Right now, I had no choice. I couldn't find her in the dark in the woodlands. Not with the ground this dry and the undergrowth too sparse to see any potential damage.

"Buggeration," I murmured and dropped to the dry ground.

I sat with my back to a tree and closed my eyes. Slowly, I leashed my panic and drew the hot, wet night air into my lungs. With my hands on my folded knees, I evened out my breaths, felt my heartbeat slow, and I built my safe place. The rifle range at Stirling Lines drifted into my mind. I settled beside my favourite sniper rifle, a variant of the L96. The birds tweeted. The breeze drifted over my still body. The target ahead came into focus through the scope. As my finger found the trigger, the image drifted like torn clouds and…

Al-Ahmar's ethereal beauty came into my mind.

The ground under my arse turned from parched woodland to gasping desert sand. A tent made of dark blue canvas rose to my left and a small clutch of palm trees towered behind it, offering some shade. A tall, elegant figure walked from the tent and onto the hot desert sand. He turned towards me and, not wishing to be at a total disadvantage, I scrambled to my feet. That's when I realised I wore desert fatigues and boots. I had a rifle slung over my shoulder and a personal weapon strapped to my thigh.

"You come dressed for war, brother," Ahmar said in his soft desert accent.

"I came looking for you," I said. "Where have you been?"

His long black hair drifted over his shoulder in a breeze I didn't feel. "I am yours to summon suddenly?"

"Isn't that how this works?" I asked. I didn't have time to mess about. My girl was missing.

His full red lips twisted. "Well, it didn't take you long to make demands. What would you have of me, master?" He bowed low.

I didn't miss the sarcasm. I also didn't miss the anger building in the wind, as evidenced by the small grains of sand striking me.

Making a few mental adjustments to my attitude, I removed my rifle and lay it in the sand between us. Then I stepped back. "I am sorry, brother. I am in trouble, and I need your help. You've been quiet for the longest time since we've been bonded together."

"And you didn't think to ask if I was alright? After saving your skinny, very white backside from an angel? You didn't think I might need a little time and a little peace? You have never once sought me out during your quiet moments to ask how I am." He turned his back and strode into his tent.

I stood in the sand like a fool, confused and a little lost. Did I follow him? Or talk from here? I knew from experience that entering the home of a desert nomad uninvited would mark me as an uncouth mud dweller.

"Ahmar, I'm sorry," I said, close to the entrance of the tent. Warm spices filled the air and the smell of some kind of stew. It made my mouth water. "You're right. I ignored you and I shouldn't have done. I am sorry. I didn't understand the protocol."

The tent flap smacked me in the face as he stormed back out and turned on me. "You are rude. I saved you and your miserable family. I saved your homeland." He punctured every 'I,' with a finger to my chest. I kept backing up. It hurt. "I saved your muddy, miserable, wet, cold moorland. I did that. Not you. And you ignored me. Like I do not matter to you. I faced an angel! An angel! I did that!"

A little aggrieved, I wanted to say I'd made some contribution, but thought it wise to keep my mouth shut and not argue with the scary supernatural entity that held my sanity in his long and bony fingers.

"I'm sorry. Really. I thought you'd either left me or needed some peace. I didn't mean to ignore you. Disturbing your peace didn't seem like a good idea."

"You need to meditate more. And you need to do it without bringing your damned guns. I don't like them, and this is *my* home."

"Sorry, Ahmar."

His almond shaped black eyes narrowed, seeking a flaw in my apology. "Really?"

"Very. I am very sorry. Heather told me to check on you and I didn't listen. I am ignorant and a fool."

"Yes. You are." His body language softened. "What do you need from me?"

"Heather's missing. I have no way of tracking her. The ground is too hard."

"Use your stupid dog."

Maybe I hadn't been forgiven that much. "It hurt him when it took Heather."

Ahmar's eyes flashed. "Someone hurt your stupid dog?"

Oh, this conversation kept wrongfooting me. "Um, yes. Badly. He'll be okay, but he's hurt."

"I will go to him." Ahmar headed towards the tent.

I moved after the djinn, but the world around me faded back to an English woodland. "Ahmar, Heather…" I called out in desperation.

Yes, yes, brother. I will help you find your wife. You really need to take better care of our family. It is not my job to keep track of them.

16

THE DESERT DJINN PROVED AS good as his word. A series of images flashed through my mind. Heather walked among the trees, she climbed a sharp hillside and to the left, in the last of the twilight, I saw the vast wall of concrete keeping the mountain of water back from the valley.

"Oh, shit," I muttered. For all of two seconds, I debated which path would be quicker, the lane and then a right-angled yomp up the side of the valley, or my current direction through the trees at an angle. I had enough light to tackle the woodland. I ran.

The evening air wasn't much cooler than that of the afternoon. Soon sweat greased my skin and the sharp angle of the hill made my breathing ragged. The knot in my stomach grew tighter. I knew Heather wasn't going to the lake under her own auspices. There's just no way she'd leave Ghost or the boys in the school. Something pulled her up there and I feared where it would take her next.

Night stole over twilight and the trees thinned somewhat, making the undergrowth harder to navigate. I found numerous animal tracks, but had to keep changing it up each time I hit impassable debris. When I reached the wall of concrete, I saw a slim shadow above me.

"Got ya," I heaved. Gathering my reserves, I made for the shadow.

Scrambling almost on all fours, I reached the top of the wall. The narrow road sat maybe two metres down from the apex of the dam, sandwiched between the front and back super-structures of concrete. Heather sprinted along the road.

"Shit." I raced onto the concrete and ran. I'd never been a sprinter. I liked long distance running, where I could pick a pace and stick to it. When we sprinted in the army, we did it carrying a lot of gear and never for fun. Heather, however, being lighter and probably fitter than me these days, loved to sprint. My one advantage came from staying power. I knew she couldn't move at that speed for long.

My booted feet smacked the tarmacked road, and I realised I'd gained ground. Heather was now halfway along, about one hundred metres. I almost stumbled to a stop when I realised why I gained ground. She'd paused, and I watched in horror as she attempted to scramble up onto the wall facing away from the water. Finding purchase on a smooth surface proved difficult, and she wasn't tall enough to just lever herself up.

"Heather!" I screamed. Now only twenty metres away.

Her boots pushed into the wall, her upper body found the strength, and she climbed.

Ten metres. My legs burned, my lungs hurt, my heart wanted to explode in effort.

She climbed up onto the wall, kneeling, her feet still on my side. Five metres. She wouldn't hear me, I knew that. There'd be no 'talking her down'. I just had to stop her. She pushed one leg under her to stand. The moment she did, I knew that whatever possessed her would take her over. It wouldn't hesitate.

Two metres. She shifted her weight.

I lunged for the leg still kneeling, grabbed her ankle and yanked backwards. Her body twisted and for a horrible, sickening moment, I thought I'd made the wrong decision as she hovered over the edge. Her balance gone, I pulled harder, reached for the belt on her jean shorts, and threw us both to the ground.

She landed on top of me, making me whoof as the air exploded out of my chest. I wrapped both legs and arms around her to hold her still, then rolled so she was under me.

"Heather?" Blood smeared her face. Whether from my rough actions or some accident on the way up, I didn't know, but it broke my control. I'd dealt with missing limbs, holes the size of my fist in bodies and faces torn off by shrapnel, but seeing my girl bloodied burned my heart. "Heather, talk to me. Please… Please."

White eyes stared back, the way a corpse's eyes go white, that awful opaque stare that means the soul has left the body.

She didn't fight me. A total absence of being. I eased off her body, half expecting her to suddenly spring up and return to the attempted suicide. Or was it murder? When she didn't move any part of her body, the only sign of life in the shallow rising and falling of her chest, I sat beside her and just held her hand, trying to figure out what to do next.

It looked to be similar to what I'd seen in the field that afternoon. Maybe, in my amateur stumbling, I'd failed to rid her of the spirit. Which meant Adam could be in danger as well.

I fished out my phone and breathed out. I had a signal.

"Lorne?" Ella's voice sounded tight with fear.

"She's alive. I have her. How's the dog?"

"He's fine. The bleeding has stopped, and we've found some antibiotic cream for the wounds. Where are you?"

"On the dam. Is Adam with you? The oldest lad."

I heard Ella asking for Adam. "No, Lorne. No one has seen him since Barny and Ghost turned up."

"Shit. He needs finding. Now. I found Heather trying to throw herself off the dam."

"Oh, no…" Ella sounded faint.

"I don't want the boys going anywhere alone, but Adam needs finding. Ask Robert, he knows Adam best. Is Damien back?"

"No."

"Wellie!" I heard over the water.

I rose and turned to the sound, keeping a boot on Heather's leg so I'd know if she moved. "Crusty!" I yelled back. Then into the phone, "Scrub last orders, Ella. I'll call you in a minute. Don't move." I switched the phone off. "Where are you?" I bellowed.

A man, with a tall, rangy lad held firm by the arm, walked towards the dam on the same side of the reservoir we'd been on all day. Damien had Adam. I breathed out.

"I'll meet you," I yelled and pointed back the way we'd come.

Kneeling beside Heather, I placed an arm under her shoulders and lifted her torso. "Heather? You need to stand up."

She blinked but didn't respond.

Tucking down tight, I draped her over my shoulder and rose with a soft grunt. Shifting her about, I carried her across my back. I'd never considered her heavy, but so much of her slim frame comprised of muscle, that this exercise proved hard work. It had been a long time since I'd carried the weight of a Bergen.

At the same time, I made a call. The moment it went live, I said, "Ella, I have eyes on Damien and Adam. We'll be down at the school in the next thirty mikes. Keep everyone together."

"Are they okay?"

"They're alive. I have to go. It's going to be a tough haul."

"We can meet you and help."

"No, I don't want the kids left without you, and I don't want anyone outside in the woods."

"Understood. Be safe."

"Roger that." I stuffed the phone back into its pocket.

I reached the end of the dam and Crusty arrived just seconds later. With care, I lay Heather on the ground for a moment.

"How is he?" I asked Damien.

Damien shook his head. "I don't know. I don't understand what's happened to him." Water dripped off every part of them, staining the ground like blood. Damien continued, "I was sitting at the edge of the water over there," he pointed to the north east, "and I saw him walk into the water. I yelled, but he didn't respond. I ran in after him. He didn't even try to swim, he just walked, but he didn't stop me grabbing and pulling him back to dry land. What's going on, Wellie?"

"Did you see Heather?" I asked.

"That's how I knew you were up here. I saw her on the wall, then she vanished, so I assumed you had her. Why are their eyes like that?"

Rather than answer him, I asked, "Where have you been?"

He struggled to meet my eyes. "I just needed some space."

"You've got to give me more than that, Damien." I heard it, so did he, my sergeant-major 'I'm not taking any of your bollocks' voice.

He bristled for a moment. I'd seen him kick off at more than one senior officer. I just maintained steady eye contact. He backed down, a slight relaxation in his shoulders making it clear I'd won.

"SAS may have kicked me out, but the fight didn't end," he said. "I went on the circuit once I got my fitness back." I watched his hands flex. "The dead march in my head. It's why I drink. I can't see them when I'm drunk."

"Have you spoken to someone about it?" I asked.

Hard blue eyes burned a hole in me. "Have you?" he snapped out.

I gazed into the distance for a moment. "I talk, now. Heather, Ella, a few other people. Remember the MI6 agent they had embedded with us for a while? He lives just down the road from me. We shoot the shit sometimes."

"Then you're lucky."

"Damien, you need to talk."

He made some strangled grunt. "Yeah, because it's that easy. Fuck off, Wellie, you have no idea." He turned away and yanked Adam with him.

I made a grab for his arm. "I have a very good idea, mucker."

The fist when it connected with my head made me stumble back. My right ear rang like a fire alarm and my vision twisted sideways. I hadn't seen it coming and didn't brace.

"You have no idea," Damien hissed again. "I wasn't always a part of your unit, Wellie. I did things you can't possibly understand."

My fists ached to retaliate, but his words gave me the moment to think rather than retaliate. "What are you talking about?"

"I lied. When I left, the wheelchair only lasted a few weeks, then rehab, then I could have gone back to the medics at Credenhill and returned to The Regiment. I didn't. You know why? Because *they* offered me a job. Black ops. They liked my psych evaluation." His words came dipped in the poison of self-loathing and resentment.

I frowned. I'd heard rumours, we all had, US and UK kill squads. Black ops with private companies and government sanction. Damien had been posted away from me for two brief tours before the final one, where he'd almost lost his life. That tour he'd been different. Reckless, and bloody dangerous at times. I wondered if he'd come to the attention of a private contractor during those absences from my life.

He snarled in my face, "I don't have the luxury of talking. Why do you think I live here and work in a tiny school full of rich kids? I can keep quiet, stay fucking silent, and spend my life under the radar. It was made very clear to us what would happen if we ever spoke about what we did—a black site in the desert would be the best we could hope for." A growl of sound. "You have no right to judge me."

"Why you?" I asked.

"Because men like you would never follow the orders. You're hampered by a conscience, Wellie. I'm not."

"That's not true," I said, backing up a step, confused and hurt. I knew Damien. I really knew him…

"Isn't it? I signed on that dotted line so fast when I knew I could hunt outside the rules of engagement. You really wouldn't believe how many scalps—"

I growled, a pain low in my chest making it hard to think or breathe. "Enough, Damien. Enough. If you loved it so much, why are you fucking haunted by it?"

"It's not their dead that haunt me, you fool. It's ours. I ache for it. I ache every bloody day to go out there with a gun in my hand."

My trigger finger twitched. I'd known that ache, when I'd longed for a weapon because it makes you feel safer, but he wasn't talking about that need.

I searched his eyes in the light of the rising moon. "The man I met here is a total fake, isn't he?" I spoke quietly and with a steady grief I knew would hurt for a long time.

The feral grin from Damien said it all. "Every day I'm acting at being the school teacher. It's also a day I know I've played the game of make-believe well enough to stay out of prison. This place, it whispers to me, and I want to find out what it really wants. I can hear it, even now."

His fate resembled a warped and twisted version of mine. As if I'd walked into a Daliesque mirror funhouse. It made me shudder to think how close I'd come to losing everything. If it hadn't been for Ella…

"Lorne?" Heather's murmur from the ground snapped the terrible connection I had to Damien. Adam dropped to the ground, breathing hard, shivering for the first time.

"I'll see you around, Wellie," Damien said. He turned tail and jogged off into the trees.

I didn't bother calling him back. I didn't know if I'd ever see him again. He wouldn't be the first of us to vanish.

"Mr Turner?" Adam's voice sounded scared, but in the shadows caused by the moon I couldn't see his face.

Instead, I grasped his shoulder. "You're alright, son. You're safe. We need to get you back to the school. The pair of you."

"What happened?" Heather asked. "Why is my chin bleeding and my hands?"

"I'll explain, but we have to move." I gave the woodland one last look and wondered what Damien might do next. By taking him down into that water, I'd triggered something I didn't understand in his head. I'd broken something.

With no time to consider Damien's pit of snakes, I helped Heather and Adam up and began walking them to the school.

1 7

HEATHER SAT AT THE KITCHEN table with all of us gathered around the large room. She explained what she remembered. "I saw Barny out there and knew I had to follow him. He was going to give me the secret to the lake." She held Ghost's head in her lap. They'd had a tearful reunion. Barny saving her dog earned him a hug which then made Barny cry.

I'd seen far too many tears. Between the family chaos and hormonal teenagers, I'd had my fill of emotions. It made me uncomfortable. I ended up standing to one side with Kate, watching events with a feeling akin to indigestion in my chest.

"I wasn't there though," Barny said.

Ella spoke up, "Whatever is doing this is using images to trick us."

"I think that's what happened to Ryan," said Killian quietly.

All eyes on Killian. He shrank into himself.

"Explain," I said.

"He said he kept seeing his sister. She died from a riding accident three years ago. She'd be, like, everywhere. He'd be walking down the corridor and stop, a look of total confusion on his face. He'd call out, and she'd vanish. He said she wanted him to find the treasure." Olly looked at Heather. "The treasure the Ouija board told us to find."

Well, that story kept growing legs and walking off into places unknown. I needed to talk to Killian about poor Ryan and what happened.

Kate said, "I need clarification on what Killian has said."

I nodded. "I'll explain in a minute."

Mason, the smallest of the three youngest children, finally spoke to me directly. He usually whispered in Olly's ear. "I keep seein' my nan," he said, the big brown eyes bright with tears. "She's been dead a year."

Ella put a hand on the lad's shoulder and looked at me. "Projections of our deepest desires?"

"Maybe. Olly? You seen anything?" I asked the other boy.

"Na, but I'm about as sensitive as a brick, or so my mum says." He grinned, and I chuckled. I liked Olly. I liked all of them. They were good kids and scared half to death. In Adam's case, almost to death.

"What about you, Adam?" I asked. "What lured you into the lake?"

He shook his head. "I don't want to talk about it."

"It might help—"

His cornflower blue eyes hardened. "It won't."

On the verge of adulthood, I had to respect his wishes. "Okay. If you change your mind, vicars are good listeners, especially this one." I nodded at Ella.

I glanced at Robert, but he shook his head.

"Did you see Damien?" Polly asked. She'd been oddly quiet since our return and withdrawn.

"I did. He saved Adam. I don't know if he'll be back to the school, Polly. He's not a well man, and he's cutting himself off."

"Did he tell you? I wanted him to tell you."

"He said he lied. I know why he dropped out of our lives after his last tour—or I know a small piece of it."

Her dark skin paled and stretched over her knuckles as she knotted her fingers together. "He's not been right since before Ryan's death. It's like he can hear something I can't. Something terrible. Maybe it's those dead in the damned lake."

"I'll find him when it's safe to do so. Right now, my priority has to be the children." I had sympathy for Polly, but I was bloody angry with Damien.

Black ops usually came with a level of soldiering I couldn't countenance. I'd been approached once, by a commanding officer of all people, who took a bung for any of us he recruited, and I'd asked for permission to speak freely. When I'd received that permission, I didn't hold back. It was a dark time for The Regiment. Afghanistan destroyed more than just bodies and minds. It threatened our honour.

I pushed all this aside. Pointless noise. A quick glance out of the window told me it was full dark.

"Here's the plan. We go to the dormitories, and we get some mattresses, bring them down here and we bunk together."

Kate shifted. "I disagree. I think we should walk the kids out. Get them to the village, then I can call in backup."

I could see my inclination to behave like a commanding officer rubbed her up the wrong way. As a civilian, I had no authority. As a detective inspector, Kate's right to be in control shouldn't be questioned. Especially by a man.

It didn't stop me, though. "And tell them what? We're running from ghosts? That'll help your career. Besides, what if Killian is right and whatever is here goes with us?"

Kate's eyes narrowed. "I have two bodies and several civilian adults, never mind the children, who need my *professional* protection." The heavy emphasis on professional made several of the adults suck in a sharp breath.

"With respect, Kate—"

She turned and pointed a finger at my chest. "Don't, Turner. Don't push your luck. Until now, I've been patient, but you are a civilian and a bloody liability to these kids. Their safety is my job. It is what I am paid to do, protect and serve. You don't have command here."

I opened my mouth to snarl that none of her training in the police academy could match anything I'd done in the field when the dog rose from Heather's side. He stood looking at the open back door. A long, low growl rumbled through the silence of the room as we watched him. Barny, nearest to the back door as if he was primed to escape at any moment, stepped gingerly towards the dog and behind him. Ghost stalked forwards and for a moment I had the horrible sight of the monster that had hunted me over the moor the previous autumn.

Approaching the door on silent feet, I twisted sideways to make a smaller target, wondering if he sensed Damien out there somewhere. The tension in the room behind me made the remaining hair on my arms stand up.

Kate muttered something about everyone being overly dramatic when the backdoor swung shut, just missing my face, but catching my shoulder. Pain shot down my arm and into my head. Despite the hydraulic safety system attached to the top, it banged shut with such violence everyone but me and Kate yelped or screamed. The dog went berserk, lunging past me at the door, then racing around the room, trying to herd everyone together. I caught him on the second go. His leg was bleeding again.

"Slow down, buddy. It's okay. We're alright. Heather, he needs a lead. It'll reassure him."

She nodded, clicking the short lead onto his harness. "What's happening?" she asked, then screwed her face up. "Oh God, it's that smell again."

I coughed and gagged. The stink of dead bodies in wet and boggy conditions. "It's starting." I glanced at the younger boys. Used to fending for themselves, they pressed into a tight group near Adam and Robert. My gaze fell to Kate. "Still want to be in charge?"

She glowered at my bitter sarcasm but opted to keep her mouth shut for the moment.

"Are you feeling okay?" I asked Heather.

"You mean, am I about to turn back into a zombie? I do not know. I'm bloody scared of what's happening, though."

"You see or hear anything you don't understand—tell me."

She reached out and squeezed my arm. I should explain to her about Damien, that her instincts on the man ran truer than mine. But I needed time to eat that much humble pie.

Kate strode past me, muttering about all this being impossible, and tried the door handle. It didn't move. She yanked at the door. Nothing. I rose and crossed to a window. Unlatching it, I pushed. Nothing.

"We're locked in," Barny said. "It's locked us in." His eyes widened, and he shivered. "We need to find out what it wants."

"I think that's bleedin' obvious," Polly said, her North London accent strong. "It wants us dead."

Barny shook his head. "It could be a cry for help."

I looked at Ella. "Remember at Scob, with the witch and her lovers, we never felt like they wanted to hurt us, not really. It was Prescott who was dangerous, not the spirits. They needed our help."

She nodded. "You don't think this is the same, do you?"

"No."

"I agree. I'm going to need a quiet room where I can pray, and a bucket of water I can bless."

Polly snorted. "Yeah, that'll work."

"A pack of playing cards caused all this," Heather snapped. "So there's no reason to think someone else's magic might not calm things down. Where are those damned cards? It's time we faced this bloody thing and did something about it."

"We need to do something about this smell," Robert said, coughing.

"Do we have candles?" Kate asked.

"I have sage," Polly said. "We could burn that. It might help clear the air."

Not wishing to cause further panic, I surreptitiously checked my phone. No signal. I slipped it back in my pocket. Rather than help in the kitchen with candles and sage, I went in search of the box containing the tarot cards. A small figure slipped out of the kitchen with me.

"What are we looking for?" asked Olly.

I peered down at him, and he grinned. Shaking my head, I said, "I found Ryan's tarot pack in Medway's office. There might be something else that gives us the intel we need."

"The Ouija board is still in there," Olly told me. "Might be easier than the cards if you want to talk to the thing."

"Okay, we'll find that as well. Though I think the tarot pack might be better."

"Why?"

Ah, I'd forgotten the primary goal of all children is to ask 'why'.

"I guess tarot is like a paint brush, allowing you to paint a story with the cards and their meanings, but a spirit board is a sledge hammer." How did I know this stuff? I'd been hanging around with Willow and Heather for too long.

"And you want to paint a picture?"

"It's better than using a sledgehammer," I said.

Olly snorted. "That depends on whether you want to knock down a wall."

I laughed. "True."

"Is this thing going to kill us, like it did Ryan?" he asked. "We stopped looking for the treasure. Maybe it wants to punish us?"

The questions floored me. I was about to dismiss his fear, like you might if you spoke to an adult, but...

Stopping I turned to face the boy. Then feeling too tall, I knelt and took him by the shoulders. "I will do everything, including laying down my life, if necessary, to protect you and the others. That is my solemn promise. It is my duty."

He blinked his small hazel eyes several times. "Like a knight?"

"Maybe not that grand, but I'm going to make certain nothing happens to you. Come on, the others will worry if we're gone too long." We hurried in silence to the head teacher's office. Damien hadn't relocked the door, so we gained access easily and Olly led the way to the confiscation box, as if he knew it all too well.

"The Ouija board is up there." He pointed to the top shelf.

I fished about and found the surface of something that wasn't a shelf. The world shot to black.

MY STOMACH ROLLED, MY KNEES weakened, and I felt a gasp of air from a long distance away.

Brother?

Ahmar's voice came as a yell from inside my mind. A vast and unknowable distance back.

Brother, Lorne, where are you?

He bellowed through the darkness.

I tried to cry out, to give him a location, but the world around me turned and twisted until I found the thought gone from my mind. Just like everything else. I hung, suspended. Lost. Alone. Trapped in a void.

The void brought with it peace. An absence of existence and all its weight. No pain. No physical sensation. No grief or shame. I felt nothing.

No, brother. If you remain here, you will never return. Leave this place. Come to my voice.

If I did, I knew it would all rush back.

If you do not return, who will look after your wife? Lorne, I cannot fetch you back. Fight for her, for the children under your care. Lorne!

I considered the request. I considered for a long time and the surrounding void took on form and substance. It grew gloopy in response to my hesitation about its dominance. As it thickened, it swirled. It swirled in patterns of sweeping clouds, black on black, and I felt it sucking at the awareness of my individuality. The living mass of darkness wanted my consciousness to become a part of the whole heaving black surrounding me. I just needed to surrender. If I gave way to the black, I'd be absorbed and never know fear, or pain, or regret again.

You will never know love, either, brother!

The scream came from the furthest distance away. It barely penetrated the swirling, all-encompassing dark.

Love.

Heather. Ella. Ghost. I had such love in my life now. Three years ago I had nothing. Three years ago I was a shell of a man, broken and terrified. Too confused by the real world, I didn't know how to function, how to be human. Now… I'd changed. Now I wanted more: hearth, home, family.

I wasn't Damien.

I didn't have his terrors. I had mine, and I knew them. I knew them and I was learning to accept them because people loved me, relied on me, wanted me in their lives.

The black became viscous, and I had a sense of falling. The sense came with such terrible vertigo I thought I screamed, but all sound became a part of the swirling dark that was no longer a void. My scream couldn't be heard, but that didn't mean no sound existed as I fell.

Moans of loss and terror filled the void. Alien screams ripped around my now flailing body. Panic snatched at my mind, and I reeled in shock at the awareness. The horrors of the dark didn't hide from me any longer. I needed to flee this place. The foul stench of the dead rushed over me. Fingers tugging at my body.

The dead wanted to keep me.

Whatever held them in the dark void, it wanted to use them to keep and absorb me. Suck me in and hold me in torment forever.

Dust and sand.

I swallowed with gratitude.

"Ahmar," I croaked in summoning.

18

I LAY ON A MATTRESS in the school's kitchen. A cool cloth on my head and a fan whirring beside my naked feet.

Heather knelt beside me. "Lorne? Oh, thank God."

I groaned. "What? How?" I'd tried to mud wrestle an alligator. That was the only reason I could feel this bad, this fast. I tried to sit up. No, scrap that, several alligators.

Heather brushed a wet cloth over my face and said, "Olly panicked when you collapsed and ran to find me. Barny and Kate carried you into the kitchen. You were inert and had eyes white like a corpse. Ella prayed, along with Adam and Robert. It seemed the safest course of action."

She explained that when I'd called out Ahmar's name, she knew I'd come back. It took a while though and I didn't know how I returned.

"I think we'll leave the Ouija board where it is," I croaked, finally able to sit up.

Polly pushed a plate under my nose. A bacon sandwich covered in brown sauce sat there in all its glory. "Here, this will help ground you."

"I could kiss you," I mumbled around a mouthful. The alligators faded into the background.

"Please don't," Heather said tartly, but her eyes stayed kind.

A cup of tea came next, and the world took on its full range of colour and sound. "I'm lucky to be alive and sane."

"What happened?" Ella asked. She sat on the coffee table. Her gaze reminded me of a deep, calm ocean, fathomless and deceptive.

I shook my head. Deceptive? Ella? "Shit, it's still in my head." My rough fingertips clutched at my naked scalp. "Heather, can you feel it?"

Her lips thinned because she pressed them together. "It keeps telling me to hurt Barny. I've been thinking it encouraged the heavy drinking session you had with Damien, maybe it also caused our argument."

Her brother's eyes widened in shock. "You never said."

"Whispering poison in my head just reminds me of Dad. It's fine. I can ignore it."

Adam shifted. "I'm really struggling." His voice cracked.

Robert's mouth opened, then snapped shut, so Killian asked, "What's it saying to you?"

The blue eyes of a haunted boy looked at his friend Robert. "It wants me to really hurt you. I'm so sorry."

I watched as Robert braved the pedestal Adam sat on and reached for his hand. "It's okay. I know you won't hurt me."

"Damien touched those cards, right? And the board?" Ella asked.

We all looked at Polly. "He used them. Before handing them over to Medway, he used them. We thought it would be funny. Turned out it wasn't."

"Why?" Ella asked.

Polly's eyes grew sad. "I did a simple spread they suggested online, but when I read out the meaning of the cards, it made Damien really angry. They talked about deception and broken promises. Lost honour and pride."

I didn't want to think about the damage they'd do to a man in Damien's state. "Any thoughts about how to break its connection and control over us?" I asked. "We have no one to phone, we can't leave the building and we have no internet. I need you all to think. Every thought is on the table."

Kate sat beside Ella. "I won't let you hurt any of these people."

"Understood," I said. "I'll hold you to it as well." The pissing contest over who had jurisdiction needed to end. "Heather, did you touch the cards?"

She nodded. "I had a look at them. I wanted to know which pack they used. It can make a difference."

"And?"

She sighed and ran a hand through her dark hair. "Kicker, he said, it always mattered how the cards represented the principles behind the images. So you could get fluffy nice packs and ones that tended towards the dark. Someone gave that poor kid a pack of Aleister Crowley images. They're from his artwork. If they'd been the Waite-Smith Tarot, then I'd feel better. They're one of the most popular packs because they are calm, the images clear and simple to interpret. Smith was a wonderful artist and passionate occultist; she really understood the importance of creating the right imagery."

I looked at Killian, Olly and Mason. "Do any of you know who gave Ryan the pack?"

Two head shakes, but Mason said in his quiet voice, "It was his brother. He's called Alistair as well, but it's spelled normally. He used to go to school here, but he's been into some weird stuff since he's been in London."

"Like what?" asked Barny.

Mason looked at him. "There's this club he took Ryan to, The Horus."

"Shit," Barny whispered.

"You know it?" I asked.

Barny nodded and his eyes sharpened. For a moment, I saw the man he'd once been when he'd worked among the money grubbers in London. "Yeah. It's a fairly new club in London. Only been going for the last seventy years. It's linked to Crowley and his religion of Thelema, which is different to his time in the Golden Dawn. But that's just rumours. I knew a lot of money guys who were into some weird occult stuff. It's like they're all after the next high and if it's not sex and cocaine, it's—"

"Ritual magic," Heather said with some bitterness. "Seems it doesn't matter where you are on the totem pole of existence, there's always people after a shortcut. You're well out of that world, Barny."

"Yeah, I know. I like my rainbows and unicorns. I don't need the dark stuff. We had too much of that growing up." They shared exactly the same sad smile, and it twisted my guts. Ella caught my eye and echoed my thoughts with a silent nod.

Kate put her head in her hands. "I can't believe any of this. It's too weird. I'm a copper with a job to do."

I tried to repress the glare I wanted to toss at her. "And I'm just a soldier, but here we are. Ella, thoughts?"

She shrugged. "Well, clearly my prayers aren't enough to vanquish it. We could try a formal blessing, but that's not going to rid this place of the energy that's…"

We all winced as a loud series of bangs crashed overhead with enough pressure to cause the lights to flicker.

"There has to be something in the school it wants," I said.

"What about the djinn?" Heather asked.

"I'll ask, but I'd rather we help ourselves. He's… Um… He's not thrilled with me right now."

"Told you to say thank you," she murmured.

I didn't pursue it.

More bangs and crashes vibrated through the room, as if every door in the school was being slammed repeatedly. It scared everyone, but the boys suffered the most. They understood the consequences if the adults made mistakes.

"We need to weaken its hold on us," I said.

"I salted the doorways," Polly said. "My mum, she was into some weird stuff, Vodun mostly. It's her heritage."

"Not yours?" asked Kate.

"I'm from London. Born and bred. I've no interest in my roots. Do you?"

Kate shrugged. "I work in Bristol. We have the whole Colston slave thing happening. When they tore down the statue… It made me think about it for the first time in a long time."

Polly huffed. "I'd have thought you'd face racism every bloody day working with the police."

"We aren't all bad."

A barked laugh came back at Kate, making her flinch. Polly said, "Then you never lived in North London."

I didn't have time for this. "Okay, I know it matters, but we need to get out of this in one piece with our sanity intact. Maybe we can do the Black Lives Matter thing later." Even as the words tumbled out of my mouth, I wished them back. All eyes looked at me in horror. "Okay, white, Protestant man, and a soldier, sorry, but I have a point. Priorities are important, and right now, that priority is to stop whatever's trying to hurt these boys."

Polly and Kate relaxed first. "He's right," they said simultaneously. Then laughed.

"Guess your balls stay attached for another night," Heather whispered with a dark chuckle. "You really know how to pick your moments."

"I didn't mean it doesn't matter, of course it does, but we have to save the boys, then we can carry the banner."

"We can't do two things at once?"

"I don't know how."

"And I thought they taught you guys to multitask. You're right, though, it's a fair point. You just need to be more respectful," she said and patted my knee.

"Fire," said Kate suddenly. "Fire destroys things, right?" she asked Polly.

Polly nodded. "It's used a lot in many religions, but it's not like we can set fire to the school. Despite there being days when I'm tempted."

"No, but you and I aren't yet affected by this thing and neither of us has a strong connection to the spiritual," she avoided looking at Ella, "so maybe we can get this board and set fire to it and the tarot pack."

Barny nodded. "They have a point. This thing lives in the water from what I've seen. Fire won't be its friend."

"I don't like the thought of you going out there alone," I said, standing. "I'll go with you."

Kate's fine, dark eyebrow rose. "Really? You might think you're tough, Lorne, but she's a black woman from North London and I'm a black woman who walked the beat in Bristol for years. Trust me. We can handle this mission." The sarcasm whipped out and snapped back, the crack of it vicious enough to shock.

Heather fought to keep a straight face, but Ella frowned at her girlfriend.

"I'll go with them, but not touch anything," Barny said. "Through my visions, I'm the only one who might have seen this thing. I've also not been a victim to it."

He had a point. The dark had completely overwhelmed the rest of us.

"Okay, but in here we're going to form a protective circle so it can't get at those of us affected so far," I said.

Everyone agreed. Kate, Polly—armed with kitchen rubber gloves—and Barny went in search of the spirit board while the rest of us raided the dorms for more mattresses. They'd dragged a couple in, but we'd need sufficient for the children. With three people to a unit, I felt certain we'd be able to keep everyone safe. Heather went with Olly and Mason. Killian came with me and Robert. Adam and Ella were the only group of two, but Ella had just arrived and carried an advantage over the rest of us in the form of a dog collar.

Ghost stuck with Heather as if made of glue.

During our expedition to the nearest dormitories, the knocking stopped, but a sense of being watched kept me wound tight. I detected curiosity from the energy, or entity, hunting us.

With all the beds we needed now in the kitchen, we pushed back the moveable furniture. Then the other group returned. Polly held the board, her yellow gloves separating her skin from the varnished wood. Her eyes looked a little wide eyed and panicky.

"You alright?" I asked.

Kate shook her head. "No, she's not and I am never answering the phone to you again, Turner. Ever. You should come with a health warning."

Ella gave her a hug. "Don't worry, you get used to it, kind of."

Kate shook her off. "It's alright for you, it confirms your faith. It bloody scares me, because I'm suddenly aware there might be more out there than I want to admit."

I caught an edge to Kate's words I didn't like when talking to someone she professed affection for, but Ella clearly didn't.

"Such a tempting 'I told you so', but I'm a vicar, so I'll try to be good," Ella said, unable to hide her amusement. "Right, we need holy water, at the very least. But I think a salt circle would be helpful. I have a small Bible on me, which might come in handy. Polly, do you have a bucket I could bless?" Ella rubbed her hands together, getting down to work.

I gestured to Barny and Heather for a conference. "What about you two? Barny, you've seen this thing. Heather, you always know more than you think. We need to help these kids survive the night."

"We have to stop the thing," Barny said.

"I'm open to ideas. There's a drowned church with bodies in it. I'm aware it needs stopping," I said.

Barny and Heather looked at each other.

Polly came over. "How are we going to get outside to set fire to these things? The doors and windows don't open."

Barny put a hand on her arm. "Wait, what if it's wrong to burn everything? What if we use it to communicate?"

I laughed, not a pleasant sound, more like the one I used when someone suggested we make a run for it while under heavy enemy fire.

"He has a point, Lorne," Heather said.

Anger rose inside me. This job needed to be done and debating the issue with daft ideas wouldn't help. "I don't want to talk to it. I want it gone. Spirits don't communicate like we do. They have their own rules. We can't understand their sense of what passes for reality."

"I disagree," Polly said. "I think Barny's right. We need to know what it wants."

I didn't hide my astonishment. "But you wanted it burnt."

"I changed my mind. I think we need to ask what it needs. If we burn this lot, we'll be closing down our only form of communication."

"I'll tell you what it wants, us, dead." I would not pull my punches on this one.

They have a point, brother.

"Great, just what I need," I muttered, rubbing my forehead. Ahmar finally puts in an appearance and it's to argue with me.

"What about that sound I recorded?" Heather said, moving to her laptop. "You started cleaning it up, but we forgot about it in all the chaos."

"Will it stop you all from doing something daft?" I asked. "If we listen to it and Ahmar helps?"

Blank looks from everyone but Heather and Ella.

"He's back?" Heather asked.

I grunted. "More concerned about the damned dog than you, but yes, he seems to be back."

That is not true, brother. Your wife is always important to me, but the animal needed to be kept calm while with the strange man.

I did not know what to think or do with that statement.

"Who is Ahmar?" Polly asked.

"Lorne's spirit guide for want of a better word," Ella said. "They've taken to bickering."

I had no wish to go into the complexities of a spirit guide come hitchhiking djinn. "Let's listen to the sound. Then we'll decide what to do. Ella, if you could bless the place and, Polly, you do the salt circle, then that's another layer of protection."

"Mr Turner?" Robert asked.

I shook my head. "Lorne's fine, Robert. What is it?"

The lad coloured almost as bright as his hair. "Um, I mix music. I do the sound for the school choir and any drama stuff. It's what I want to study at college if my parents let me. Sound engineering and using it for research, not just music."

Adam said, "He's good, Lorne. He'll find whatever's on that file."

Robert coloured to tomato red.

I understood about half of what he said, so looked to Heather for a translation.

"He's going to be a lot better at it than either of us," she said.

"Have at it, Robert. Thank you for speaking up. Anyone else have some skills we don't know about?"

Olly nodded to the catapult I'd put on the kitchen unit. "That's mine. I've more stashed that old Medway didn't find, or Damien. I could teach everyone to use it."

Failing to hide my smirk, I said, "Okay, are they close by?"

He nodded. "I kept them in the ceiling of my room."

"Up for a trip to the dark side?" I asked Barny.

He sucked in a sharp breath. "I can do that."

"Heather, Ella, I want you here. If we don't make it back quickly, you're our second line of defence or our rescue team. Understood?"

"Barny can—" Heather began.

"I know he can stay, but the dog needs you and I'll not risk him out there. Also, you're another person being affected by this thing. If it attacks the two of us, Olly is alone. That's unacceptable."

Her mouth thinned, but she recognised my logic. I didn't bother looking at Kate, knowing it would end up with another argument about who should be giving the orders.

Time for a road trip into the haunted school dorms.

19

IT FELT LIKE A TRIP into the Kill House we used for training urban warfare. I took point, Olly behind me and Barny as tail-end-charlie. Keeping close to the wall of the long hallway leading to the dormitory rooms of the younger children, I moved as if being hunted. The fluid grace, brought about by hundreds of hours holding weapon sights to my eye while moving, came naturally.

It made Barny curious. "What is it you do for a living, Lorne?"

"Are you going to ask me about my intentions towards your sister?" I shot back without turning. The lights in the hall seemed dimmer than previous trips down here.

"Just making certain you're right for her."

I snorted. "Like you'd know. I'm the one that gave her options."

"I thought it might be wise to get to know you," he said.

"Now isn't the time for a catch up, Barny. If we get out of this alive, we'll go for a pint, and we can judge each other's life choices then. Right now, I need weapons and Olly has a stash."

Silence until we reached some fire doors. "You're familiar with weapons?" Barny asked.

"I'm a farmer's son. What do you think?" I segued. "Hold."

The order came without thought and I heard Barny mutter, "Farmer's son my arse."

I ignored him, wishing I'd brought Heather with me after all. Behind the double doors breaking up the long hallway, the lights flickered.

A small hand closed over the hem of my t-shirt. "That's not normal," Olly whispered.

I sucked in a hard breath and the smell of the wet dead drifted on the air, making it through the door seals. "No, it's not. I'm still finding my way around this place. Describe exactly where your room is."

Olly peered around me, looking through the safety glass. "You go along here, about half the distance we've already gone. Then there's another set of doors off to the right and that leads to our dorms. It's not long though, maybe ten metres. Another set of fire doors and the building opens up. It's like this is the trunk and when we get to the room, that's the branches of the tree. Each room is smaller as it goes to the top, where the common room is for our year. Our dorm is the first set because we share."

"A Christmas tree design," Barny said.

"Yeah, like that."

I nodded. "Well done, Olly."

"You think something is going to get us, don't you?" he asked.

"I think that's a distinct possibility." For the first time, I realised my hands hadn't ached for their usual array of weapons. Yes, I needed Olly's catapults, but I didn't need my firearms. It gave me a sense of pride in myself, like I'd grown as a person. *Stupid grunt. Now is not the time to change the habits of a lifetime.* "Yeah, well, you're wrong," I breathed out to myself.

Barny said, "What if fear is giving it strength?"

I frowned and glanced at him over my shoulder. "What do you mean?"

"It has to feed on something, everything does, except inertia, I guess, so maybe I should qualify—"

"I need a point to this, Barny," I snapped.

"Oh yeah, right? Um. Okay, everything needs food. This thing might feed on fear, at least in part."

"So going in there, bold as a set of brass knuckles, might be the best option?" I asked.

Barny nodded.

I looked down at Olly. "What do you think?"

"Me?"

"Everyone has a voice in a unit. It's how the man in charge makes the best decisions."

He looked surprised. "I think we should try it. We can always use the running away option if it fails."

I chuckled. "Good call. Alright, a few deep breaths, men. Settle those nerves. Keep eyes forward, walk quickly but calmly. Do not let the noises distract you and don't look at anything that isn't the person in front."

"What about you?" Olly asked.

"Trust me, it can't show me anything my nightmares haven't. They're far worse than whatever a denizen of hell can come up with."

"Can I hold your hand?" Olly asked, his brown eyes huge.

I nodded and his small palm slipped into mine. Not something I'd felt that often in my life. It was odd. Made me feel about ten feet tall and terrified all at once. I shook the feeling off.

"Ready?" I asked.

Two soft and uncertain affirmatives came back.

I turned and looked each of them in the eye, then repeated, "Are we ready, men?"

Olly's back snapped straight. "Yes, sir." He gave me a salute, which I returned with a snap.

"Ready," Barny said when I made eye contact a second time. His back didn't have quite the same confidence.

I pushed open the double doors.

Light blazed, winked out, flashed and settled at a level akin to the old forty-watt bulbs of my childhood. We strode in the centre of the hallway, and I damped down the rising dread circling in my blood. This was no brush of black feathers against my scalp. This was an entire flock.

We kept walking, five metres to the next set of doors, but we now splashed in stinking water.

"Lorne?" Barny's voice held a slight tremor. "The walls are leaking."

I glanced left and right. On the edge of the weak light coming from the bulbs, I saw what he meant. Water seeped through the bricks and plaster, like blood being forced through the finest silk gauze. It didn't drip down the walls like rain, it oozed, looking dark and foul. When it hit the floor, it crawled over the tiled surface, pooling together, the level rising as more gathered. It leached in thick streams from the ceiling.

"Ignore it," I ordered, even as I shrank back from the rapid dripping that formed right in front of me.

"Oh, fuck," Barny whispered.

Two metres to the door. "What?"

"Someone is behind me," his terror screamed over us despite his voice being soft.

I yanked Olly closer, turned, grabbed Barny's t-shirt and pulled him behind me, stuffing Olly between us. Then I pushed us all back to the doors.

The lights flickered and Barny groaned. The water grew restless around our feet, and I felt it soaking into the tough leather.

A figure stood in the hallway. The features remained unclear. A dull sheen of sticky black fell over his face, but he wore a coat of chainmail and in his right hand, he held a bright sword. It caught the pale light and looked capable of serious damage. The figure's legs didn't reach the floor and his height didn't equal mine, but it didn't prevent me from being struck dumb with fear. I had never, in all my life, felt such instant terror. Not even in the darkness caused by the lost souls in the hospital.

The sword rose from the Norman lord's side, because that must be who stood before us, Turstin fitz Rolf. The blade levelled at Olly.

It spurred me into defiance. "I deny you. I will not have you in this place. You are not welcome here," I shouted at the image.

It seemed to vibrate, and the cloying stink of the wet dead relaxed its grip on our throats. The fear pulled back just enough to think.

"I deny you," I repeated. "You are not welcome here. I banish you." Without turning, I spoke to my unit, "On three men. One, two, three…"

We repeated the mantra, growing louder and more confident with each phrase. Olly, most of him still tucked behind me, pointed his finger at the spirit. Barny placed a hand on each of our shoulders, joining us as a single entity.

Nine times we repeated the mantra and each time the vision before us grew weaker, faded further back, the flickering of the lights becoming less frequent. Even the water we walked through seeped away, back into the walls.

When the lights returned to normal, we stopped. The sudden silence rang loud.

"Bugger me sideways with a baguette," Barny murmured.

Olly laughed. "We did it. We're heroes."

"We won a skirmish and I suspect just a small test, not the war," I said.

"You always this optimistic?" Barny asked.

"No, sometimes, I know I'm completely screwed." I pushed him out of the way and forced open the door to the dorms.

Olly led us to his room. "Holy shit," he said.

The room had been destroyed. Even at our worst, a unit of SAS soldiers tossing the room of a suspected bomb maker couldn't have done more damage. The beds resembled firewood for tiny pixies. The fabric shredded almost to rags. Desks, chairs, the cupboards and wardrobe, all destroyed. Books ripped up and tossed, electronics smashed.

Barny said, "I guess they didn't want us finding the weapons."

"Show me where they're kept," I told Olly, pushing a path through the rubbish with my boots.

He pointed to the ceiling tile nearest the door. Clever. The least likely place for a teacher to look.

"Ready for a lift?" I asked. No way any of us could reach without help. The kids must have dragged a bed over, then a chair to reach.

Olly held his arms out, and I heaved him onto my shoulders. He tucked his legs behind my back as if he'd been riding shoulders all his life.

"Bit left," he said.

I did as ordered and heard him pop the ceiling. Some muttering and twisting ensued as I held his knees, before…

"Bingo." He pulled something out that promptly knocked me on the head. "Sorry."

I lifted him down and saw our booty. A bag full of contraband. Olly opened it and grinned. Barny and I peered over his small shoulder.

"Bloody hell, kid," Barny said. "You've got an arsenal in there."

I fished into the bag and pulled out another catapult and a crossbow with bolts. It wasn't large, the length of my forearm, but it would kill a man easily at close range. "Where did you get this and why did you bring it to school?" I asked the boy.

"Internet. I have an old credit card of Dad's. He doesn't notice much of what I do or spend. I brought it to school because we thought we'd hunt squirrels."

While I assessed the functionality of the weapon, I asked, "And did you?"

"They are very fast," he muttered. "We killed a rabbit."

"What was that like?" I used the iron sights and adjusted them. We may never need these toys, but instincts are hard to resist, and mine screamed for something to help me protect these people.

Olly remained quiet, so I looked at him not the weapon.

He said, "It wasn't very nice. Ryan thought it was funny, but I didn't like it, it was after Christmas when he got weird. I think I want to be a vegan."

I felt the urge to ruffle his hair and tell him not to worry, but I wasn't a parent, or a teacher and I didn't know the protocols with small humans. He seemed very sad though, and I knew taking a life could be hard for some.

I knelt in front of him. "Listen, Olly, it's never easy knowing you've hurt or killed something. Sometimes it's necessary, but you didn't need to eat the rabbit, so you killed for sport. And you didn't like it. You learned a lesson about yourself and I'm guessing the rabbit died quickly."

He nodded, his face solemn.

"Then maybe it taught you a lesson you'll understand more when you're older. It's good to acknowledge these things in ourselves."

"You can keep it."

"Thank you. I think that's probably best."

The lights dimmed for a moment making us all freeze. Barny whispered, "It's time to leave, people."

Olly grabbed some untorn items of clothing, and we left the room. I held the crossbow, bolt loaded, but pointed it down at the ground. I didn't know how snappy the trigger would be and I needed space to test it.

The trip back to the kitchen proved uneventful but the relief on everyone's faces when we arrived made Olly puff his chest out. We stepped over a thick line of salt just in front of the doorway.

Heather came and tucked herself under my arm. "How'd it go?"

"We met Turstin fitz Rolf in the hallway."

Her mouth dropped open. "You're joking?"

Ella came over with Kate. "Seriously?"

"Yep. We all saw him." I went on to describe the Norman lord.

"Wow," Heather said. "That's extraordinary. You saw a being from a thousand years ago." She sounded almost breathless.

"It was extraordinary, out of everything I've seen over the last few years, but I didn't like him pointing the sword at Olly."

Ella looked at the boy who sat with the others describing in lurid detail every moment of our trip to the dark side of the school. She said, "I'm worried about the boys. This is going to affect them for the rest of their lives."

Sucking in a heavy breath, I considered the implications. "I know. I thought the same thing. Sadly, there's not much we can do. It's hardly our fault they're stuck here."

Heather shifted away. "I have news as well. Killian's cleaned up that sound file. And I like this," she added, taking the crossbow away from me.

Ella rolled her eyes. "Unbelievable. You two are impossible."

"Be careful of the trigger, love. Some crossbows are considerably more dangerous than any firearms we've used."

"Understood," she said.

I smiled, watching her make a series of checks that had mirrored mine. When I approached the mattress with all the younger boys sat on it they looked up. I tapped Killian on the head. "Show me this audio file."

"Oh, yeah, it's cool. Come and listen." He sprang up, looking better than I'd seen him all day.

It occurred to me that children, just like adults, are often stressed the most when they feel out of control. Give them something to do, something they are good at and everything changes. Killian sat at Heather's laptop and began whizzing about at dizzying speed.

He looked up at me. "How much do you want me to explain what I did?"

"I don't need to know the details. I won't understand."

"Okay. Then just listen." He clicked play. "This is the original sound." An unnerving hiss came out of the tiny speakers. "It undulates, which is, I'm guessing, why you knew something else might be in there?"

I nodded. "I've seen our signallers listen to hours of static."

Barny stood nearby. "Knew it, you're army."

His tone made me frown.

Killian ignored all this, absorbed by his quest. "This is the sound after I've run it through some serious software."

An eerie wail came out of the computer.

"Bloody hell," Kate barked. "I don't like that."

She was right not to like it. The wails reminded me of the sounds I'd heard in the mountains of the Hindu Kush. The places the locals avoided because of the spirits lost and alone in those vast and empty borderlands. We were quiet because of the noise drifting around the kitchen.

The hair on my arms stood up and my throat tightened from a rising sense of fear and dread.

Killian pressed stop on the screen. "Not good," he said. "But there's more. I found other wavelengths under that lost wail. Like someone mixed a soundtrack wrong, so you lost the vocals of the singer and only heard the bass guitar."

"That wail is like the bass guitar?" I asked.

He shrugged. "Best way I can describe it to someone who doesn't understand. The wavelengths are reminiscent of—"

"Okay, I get it. It's more complicated than it looks. Let's hear the vocals."

Killian grinned at me. He pressed play.

A distinct voice leaked from the speakers. Low and gruff. I had the sense of words but couldn't make the sounds work in English.

"It's Latin," said Ella. She came over and cocked her head, closing her eyes to focus on the sound. "I went on a retreat in a monastery that allowed women to stay. That is a Latin Liturgy, or more precisely the Liturgy of Hours. It's medieval so I can't understand most of it, but I think that's what we have, a voice repeating the liturgy on a loop. Forever."

2 0

BARNY GRASPED THE NETTLE OF this idea first. "That soldier we saw, you think he's actually protecting us?"

"How likely is that?" I asked.

Heather laughed. "Seriously, that's the question? Anything is possible with this metaphysical stuff. We just have to unravel enough of it to give the spirits some peace and save the human element where necessary."

I sat, weighted down suddenly by the unfamiliar elements of my reality that no longer made sense. "I miss having hard facts I can action."

Ella clasped my shoulder. "Welcome to the world of religion and faith. Here's what I know about this rite. It began as soon as the early Church developed and was based on the Jewish sacrifice of praise. Then, as the monastic way of life became stronger in the Church, different things fell into the mixture, like The Lord's Prayer. During the Middle Ages it became a daily part of the lives of monks and if you were devout, you would also pray at the assigned hours of Terce, Sext, None… you know the kind of thing." She waved a hand.

Kate and I shared a worried look. Ella was speaking a language neither of us understood.

She continued, "So what we're hearing is some part of the *Opus Dei* from the *Rule of St Benedict*, the basis for all monastic life."

"Does that mean we're listening to monks?" I asked.

"Not necessarily. A lot of the men who took part in supporting William of Normandy came from a place of true faith and blind devotion to their God. This is before the First Crusade, but William would never have taken the throne of England without the Pope's authority. He had a legitimate claim to the English crown. Maybe, after everything you've told me, we've been looking at this all wrong. Maybe Turstin fitz Rolf isn't the bad guy. Maybe he's been reciting these psalms and prayers for centuries to keep something locked away and the only thing he can do, now that it's out, is to call for help."

That gave us all pause for thought.

"You don't think he's the one that killed Ryan?" asked Adam.

Ella's expression grew sad. "I don't know, Adam. I wish I did, but so far he's not hurt anyone. He's just pointed at Olly. Can you think of a reason?" She studied the boy.

Olly looked at Adam. "Um… I may have been there when we did the Ouija board. He might think I'm to blame."

Adam scowled at him. "You weren't supposed to be there. You little sneak."

An unrepentant Olly just shrugged.

Barny said, his expression thoughtful, "It makes sense."

"What does?" I asked, not entirely sure anything Barny thought made sense. Though, to be fair, he smoked less weed than Spud, so who was I to criticise how his mind worked? Without Spud, I'd have failed with the *Gnostic Dawn* and *The Fraternity of Nous*.

"Look at it like this: poor Turstin can't communicate with us directly, but he needs to let us know he's failing. After centuries of working hard to keep whatever it is under control, he's losing the battle. He needs to tell us why he's failing, and the only thing he can do is point at Olly to give us the clue."

Heather frowned. "But we know it's the tarot and then the Ouija board that started all this."

"Maybe he doesn't know we know, sis."

"It's the unknowns I'm worried about," I muttered. "I think that's an excellent theory though, Barny. Thank you."

"So what's next?" Heather asked.

I knew it wouldn't be popular with some in the room, but I said it anyway, "We need to talk to Turstin fitz Rolf."

Silence held sway for a bit as this information was absorbed, then the counter arguments came thick and fast. Unsurprisingly, Ella was against it. Heather and Kate supported her. Polly, who'd been silent up to now, agreed with me. The vivacious woman I'd met on our arrival might be gone, but she'd sat and listened to everyone, coming to her own understanding.

Adam supported me. Robert didn't, daring to go against his friend. The younger lads all sided with me as well. Everyone looked at Barny.

His hands came up in a gesture of peace. "Oh no. I'm not picking sides."

"You never do," Heather muttered with darkness in her voice.

He frowned, but held his tongue on whatever lay between them. Instead he said, "I think we need to talk to this ghost, but I'm concerned we'll just make things worse. It's important to strike a balance. We need to protect ourselves and this spirit of Turstin is really strong."

I gazed out of the window of the kitchen, wishing I was outside where the night air would be cool and moving around. "I should do it alone."

"Oh, yeah," Heather sneered. "That's such a good idea. The most psychic of us reaching out to a powerful ghost. That sounds like a plan." She crossed her arms and scowled at me. "You're always the one to take on the mission, aren't you?"

"It is my job."

"It *was* your job. I don't want you being the sacrificial lamb *again*. I don't want you risking everything *again*. I want you to be safe, just for a change of pace. Could you do that for me?"

I'd touched a nerve. Now would not be the time to react with anything other than care and understanding or we'd be having another knock down fight, this time in public. Crossing the kitchen, I took her face in my hands, and stared into those big blue eyes. "I'm sorry. My PTSD affects you as well, I know that, and I seem to have come out of the army with more empathy for the dead than is good for me. It can't be easy."

Despite her best efforts, her eyes filled with tears, but she held them back. With hands flat on my chest, she said, "One day the wolf will eat the lamb, you know that, right? You can't keep risking your mind and your body."

"I know, but I have Ahmar to help if I get lost."

"You don't know how much you can trust him."

I smiled. "He likes you and the damned dog. He'll get me home if I can't make it alone."

Polly spoke up at last, "I thought spirit guides helped psychics?"

"He's not a traditional spirit guide," I murmured. I didn't mind family knowing how Ahmar came into my life, but I didn't want to share that story with strangers, and I really didn't want the boys knowing about him. It meant I'd have to explain the black flags, the dead of my unit, the race to escape ISIS...

Sucking in a breath, I calmed my racing thoughts. No, far better they all remain ignorant of such things.

"You're going to do this, aren't you?" Ella asked from behind me. She sounded about a thousand years old.

I turned to face her, the least I could do considering what we'd experienced in the past. "Yes."

She nodded, but didn't hide her sadness. "I've told you how I feel about those things. I've told you what happened to me because of spirit boards and those damned cards. They are not to be messed about with and I don't think you should do it. However, I will offer what support I can. My only condition is this; I will not touch you or it. I will not use, or countenance the use of, tarot cards or spirit boards."

"Understood." I felt more nervous knowing I didn't have Ella's backing. She'd always been there, since the moment we dropped down a cliff face together, but I'd crossed a line at last. Odd that it was over something like this rather than the dead bodies I'd caused over the last few years.

"Do we do it here?" Polly asked.

I shook my head. "No, away from this room. It needs to be a safe place."

Polly donned her rubber gloves once more and picked up the board, the disc thing for the users, and the box with the tarot deck in it. "We'll go to the staffroom. It's comfortable and nearby if there's a problem. The boys know where it is."

Adam stirred. "I think I should be there."

Robert's eyes widened. "No, don't be stupid. Why would you say that?"

The older boy took the younger's hand in a gesture that touched me. "Because I started all this, or at the very least, I made it worse. Perhaps I can help because it's already found a way through me."

Their fingers laced together. Bless them.

"I'm staying. You need someone official at this end when it goes wrong," Kate said. "I'm the only authority here. It needs noting I don't think it's wise. Some mass hallucination has affected us, and I think we're disturbing the children. I can't prevent this from happening, but I don't have to participate."

Ella's mouth thinned, but she remained quiet.

Heather studied me for a moment. "I'm staying here."

"What?" I thought she'd want to come with me.

"I'd follow you anywhere in a war zone, boss. You know that. But I don't think you should risk your sanity and I've no wish to watch it happen. I'll be here and Polly will call if you need us. I'm not leaving Ella and Ghost. Also, I'm staying with the kids, in case something should kick off." She crossed her arms over her chest.

However uncomfortable it made me feel, losing the strongest members of my unit for this mission, I had to agree with their wishes. I also couldn't blame them. Too many times had they witnessed my mental collapse as reality spun away from me and I'd turned into a paralyzed jelly.

"I'll go," Barny said. "I understand enough of this stuff to help."

Four of us then. All strangers to me. We left the kitchen, careful to step over the salt line in the doorway, and Polly took us to a nearby room labelled 'Staff Room' in the same font as the school's name. Inside there were sofas, chairs, a coffee maker, and the feeling of a men's club rather than the staff room I'd known when at the local comprehensive during the late nineteen-eighties. That had a ratty sofa, hard chairs, and a kettle surrounded by stained mugs and frazzled teachers. I wondered if this was the norm, or the luxuries afforded by educating private pupils. I suspected the latter.

Together we sat around a large conference table on comfortable, well-padded chairs and Polly placed the Ouija board and planchette on the surface. "Which one are we using?" she asked, also laying down the box with the cards in it.

I sat and considered. "The cards are more subtle, but I'm not a subtle guy. I was going to use them, however, the board might get answers more quickly. So let's go all out and use the board. Also, the cards can be misleading or confusing. I've never used them."

"We need pen and paper then," said Adam. "I can take notes." He went to a sideboard and pulled out a notepad and pen.

Barny sat next to me; Adam sat beside Polly, who peeled off her rubber gloves with a crack and pop. It sounded vaguely obscene in the quiet room. My skin felt too tight, and I wondered if I'd make the same sound if someone peeled my skin off.

That's an odd thought, mucker, even for you.

My inner cynic was right. Facing the simple piece of wood with the alphabet burned into the fine grain like a rainbow of dark letters made my skin feel tight. Nothing I'd done in the army could relate to this experience. That in itself made me twitchy.

"First thing, I want you all to think about a bubble of white and blue light surrounding you. A powerful barrier covering your feet and head, also your hands. Take a few seconds now and build it really well. Fill the space between the outside of the shell and your body with more white light, a mist coating you." Since when did I sound like a guru of the mystical? "Everyone set?"

The others nodded. Adam looked pale, but composed.

"Fingers on the bit of wood then," I said, placing my trigger finger on the planchette. Then I thought about how much damage I'd done with that finger, so swapped it out for my left.

The others followed suit with their dominant hands. Four fingers now lightly touched the pointer.

In the silence, I felt the tension thicken. It seemed to creak and groan, pushing against the windows and walls of the room. A large part of me wanted to tell a filthy joke just to have them laughing or tutting to break the sense of taut expectation. I glanced up at the lights in the ceiling, half expecting them to flicker and a soft groan to fill the cavernous silence.

Nothing happened.

"Someone needs to ask a question," Polly said, looking at me.

"Sorry. Just trying to get my bearings," I muttered. "Christ, I feel like a twat."

Barny chuckled. "I can ask. I'm used to being a twat."

"Yeah, okay. I don't know what to say, to be honest. I've never interrogated a ghost."

"In that case, it should be someone else," Barny decided. "We aren't interrogating a member of the Taliban. We're asking nicely for some help from the other world."

I snapped my mouth shut. Barny either had the same uncanny ability to read people his sister possessed, or she'd been blabbing about my life. I very much doubted it was the latter. The former came from Heather's desire to navigate a dangerous world she needed to survive.

My nerves sang like over-stretched guitar strings.

Barny closed his eyes and breathed in and out, centring himself. He said, "We can feel you here, close by. We would like to speak with you in plain language we understand. We mean you no harm. Do you wish to talk to us?"

The planchette shivered. I glanced at Polly and Adam. Both pairs of eyes focused on their fingers and showed too much white. Invisible ants crawled over my skin, making it prickle. The small piece of wood moved, and I wanted to flinch back, away from the sensation. It drifted to the *Yes* the lads who made the board had burnt into the wood.

Barny nodded. "Thank you. And thank you for being so gentle. Are you the spirit of the knight we saw?"

Another shiver in the wood beneath our fingers and the pointer moved over the *Yes* again.

"That's good," said Barny. "We think you can help us understand what's happening here. Can you help us?"

This time, the planchette bucked hard into the centre of the board and shot back to *Yes*. My breathing hitched in anticipation of violence.

"Stay calm, Lorne. This man is most like you and if you're half as psychic as Heather says, then you could be a weak link in this, or a strong one." Barny kept his voice measured, but for the first time I heard a hint of steel in there that reminded me of his father's voice.

Next Barny asked, "Are you a guardian of this place?"

We watched in fascination as the little board slid from letter to letter. It jerked at times, but on other occasions moved smoothly, as if the spirit had more control depending on the word.

Adam wrote out the letters with his left hand. '*I have guarded this door for a thousand years. I am tired, and you have opened it.*' Adam looked at me. "I guess that means Ryan's cards and our stupid game?"

"Maybe, or maybe destroying the church with the reservoir water was enough. Things could have been getting worse for years," I said. A pressure in my mind began to build, and it made me feel seasick. I needed this 'interview with a ghost', over.

The planchette bucked hard, making us all startle. It moved faster over the board.

"We hadn't asked a question," Polly said, and I heard the fear.

Adam wrote, and the pressure inside me reached a critical mass. It pushed against my ribs and skull, it made my face hurt and my lungs ache at the effort of sucking in air. The small board dashed from letter to letter. When it stopped, it trembled in the centre of the rainbow as if trapped by the letters.

"What did it say?" I asked. "I couldn't keep up."

Adam read the paper. "*I must be replaced. The treasure destroyed.*"

I snatched my finger off the board. A disturbing vision of me a thousand years from now, in full battle dress and holding an SA80, pleading with someone to take my place in the spirit realm, flashed like a lightning strike through my head.

"No," I said. "No, I'm not doing that, and neither is anyone else. If you want help, you tell us exactly what this thing is you guard against." I spoke to the room, not to the spirit board, and I realised the others had removed their fingers from it as well.

A chair rattled and slid over the carpet to strike the door marked bathroom.

"Don't you start throwing a tantrum," I told the room. "We can help, we can free you, but we aren't replacing you. No one here will make that sacrifice."

The planchette moved.

Adam murmured, "Oh shit."

"Just write. You're safe enough at the moment," I said, though I failed to hide the tension in my voice.

"I'm not sure this is a good idea," Polly said.

I had to agree to an extent but... "We need answers."

"We need the questions first," she replied.

The board came alive with the rapid movement of the planchette. It dashed over the board, making a scraping sound as if pushed down hard. The pressure in my head and chest grew, and I balled my hands so tight my nails dug into my palms.

"You are a soldier, under the command of God. It is your duty," Adam read aloud. He looked at me. "Do you think William the Conqueror made him stay here and become the guardian of something?"

I shrugged. "Who knows? We just need to know what it is."

The pressure inside me snapped tight. My breath hurt and heart burned. Pain shot down my left arm and into my head. "Fuck, heart attack," I hissed, clutching at my chest. I couldn't be having a heart attack.

Barny pushed his chair back. "This isn't natural. Get Ella and Heather in here, now." He pulled me from the chair and the world turned black. Again.

21

"WELL, BROTHER, YOU HAVE REALLY done it this time," said a soft voice full of rich honey and exotic spice.

I opened my aching eyes and gazed up at the fine features of an Arabian prince from a fairy tale. Dark eyes, full red lips, skin the colour of desert sand kissed by rain. Night black hair drifted over his shoulder and tickled my scalp, where he bent over me to place a soft wet cloth on my brow.

"What happened?" I asked.

"Your ignorant and foolish self happened. You should have asked if you wished to speak with a spirit as strong and angry as this one. I remember well the passion of these ridiculous paladins. How many of them died in my deserts because of their foolish quests? Calling out to their sacrificial man-god..." He shook his head and moved away, still muttering in a language I didn't understand. Then he turned back so fast I flinched. "You know what? I think more men, women and children died during those crazy wars than they have in the latest batch of insanity over the black gold in my lands."

I opened my mouth to argue we hadn't gone to Iraq for the oil, not the second time, then realised how stupid I'd sound, so I gave up. My chest still ached, which made me want to lie still and focus on my surrounds for a moment. The rich blue of the tent walls were adorned with tapestries. They covered the wooden latticework, holding the sides of the tent in place and rose over my head to form the roof. Unlike artwork in Islam, these woven works of art had pictures of mythical beasts and beautiful women cavorting and reminded me of Hindu artwork rather than Christian or Roman.

I lay on a pile of thick, sweet-smelling cushions and blankets. Richly coloured rugs covered the desert floor. Braziers stood around the edges and a fire pit warmed the large room from the centre. Ahmar fussed over a small cauldron and coaxed low flames a little higher.

"What's happening?" I asked.

"You fell ill. I thought it wise to remove you before you really did yourself some damage."

"Does Heather know I'm okay?" I asked.

Ahmar shrugged. "I cannot speak with her directly, so at the moment, she is not a happy wife. You will have much damage to repair when we have finished here."

"Can you send me back now?" I asked, pushing myself up from the pile of cushions. My head swam and my stomach heaved. I swallowed bile.

The djinn's dark eyebrow rose. "Don't be foolish, brother. You will make yourself sick. That will annoy me further."

"You're already annoyed?"

He pointed a wooden spoon at me. "Of course, I am annoyed. Those warriors of the Northern tribes are foolish, powerful and bent on their obsession with their god. I did not like them then, nor do I like them now. I really wanted Saladin to do more... but him and his sense of bloody honour..." Ahmar muttered darkly into the pot he stirred.

"Can you help?" I asked.

His dark eyes flashed. "Of course I can help. That is not the question."

I frowned, feeling lost. "Then what's the question?"

He shook his head and made himself busy with ladling out some of the contents of the pot into a small wooden bowl. Walking towards me with the grace of a wild cat, he offered me the bowl with the order, "Drink."

I took the bowl and sniffed its contents. It smelt sweet but full of flavours I couldn't identify. "What's this?" I asked.

"Would you ask such a question if you were negotiating a peace with a tribal leader?" he asked, sitting on a rich cushion opposite me. His hands rested on his crossed knees, the robe he wore a red as rich as life's blood in colour.

"No."

He gestured with impatience. "Well then, drink."

I sighed and lifted the bowl to my lips. There are no words to describe the soft, sweet taste of the herbal concoction, and I closed my eyes as it slipped over my tongue and down my throat. It made every part of me, and I mean *every* part, tingle.

"I like that," I whispered to the bowl when I finished.

Ahmar smiled. "Good. Now you will wake strong in spirit, at least." He paused, and I dragged my eyes off the bowl and my wish to lick it clean. "Lorne, we need to talk."

"Okay. What?"

"This man, Turstin, he is a noble warrior from a time long ago and he needs to rest. However, he wishes for a warrior to replace him. That is going to be you if you don't find him someone else."

"Like Damien?" I asked.

"As you say," Ahmar agreed.

"I can't do that."

"And nor should you. It is madness. They should have brought in their magicians, not their priests, when they first discovered this monster Turstin guards. But they had killed their magicians hundreds of years before."

I frowned. "You mean the Romans killing the Druids, don't you?" I read books. Not like Heather maybe, but I knew stuff.

"Very good, brother," Ahmar said in approval. "I felt the tremors of that slaughter in my deserts so far away. The mystics, important to your land of mud and rain, vanished."

Several things fell into place. "The Iron Age fort on the hill. That wasn't just a fort, was it?" It explained what I'd seen in that field with Heather and Adam.

"No, it held men and women of power who lived with the unseen forces.

Turstin took it upon himself to conquer these forces rather than work with them. He fights with his faith and his sword. Sadly, the war is a losing one because the church is gone, the old one has risen. Others come to pollute his land and water. Steal his gifts. His rage and hate are lashing out."

I spent a few seconds unpacking all of those problems. We stood between two entities, waging a war we didn't understand. "What can I do?"

Ahmar spread his long, elegant fingers over his knees. "That is not a simple question to answer without leaving a sacrificial spirit. I gather you will not wish to sacrifice a child to find out where the spirit goes?"

I ignored him. By now, I knew perfectly well Ahmar protected children. "What is it that's living here?" I asked, trying to get a different perspective.

He gazed over my shoulder at something indefinable. "There are many mysteries in this land of myth and old woodland magic. I hear them whisper to you, begging to be heard. It is almost impossible for a mortal to listen to their songs, chants and ancient tongue without going mad. The old ones could do it, those ancient priests that walked here before the man-god died. Now, you have lost this sense, like so many others."

I'd rather he didn't keep harping on about the horrors of modern life, but that seemed to comprise of everything from the end of the Roman Empire onwards, so I guessed I'd be losing that argument.

Trying for patience, I asked, "What mystery is specific to this land, Ahmar?"

He smiled, showing teeth a little too white and just on the wrong side of pointy. I wanted to move back, but weakness or fear made him harder to deal with. We needed balance to remain productive. I forced myself into stillness.

"I do not have a name for the thing that lives in this place. Sometimes it is wise to not name a spirit, then they cannot hear your dreams if you accidentally think of them. There is a spring in this place, ancient and venerated by many of your people, but it changed its nature as it grew older." He flicked a hand over his chest, removing invisible sand. "It can even happen to beings such as myself. Over time we can... devolve. Especially when we are not cared for correctly by those using our gifts. In this case, water."

"You mean this is some kind of pissed off naiad?" I asked.

"More god, less child of a god," he said.

I felt my mouth drop open. "I can't fight a god!"

He shook his head, clearly impatient with my ignorance. "It is not a god as you think of your God. Some omnipotent deity capable of causing creation from nothing." He said this as if it were the most ridiculous thing he'd ever heard. I wished I could watch a face to face with him and Ella one day. He continued, "A local god, he is still strong and powerful, still a creator, but think of him as a hearth deity. Only now he is angry and has been for a very long time. That anger has turned a spirit of water into one of vengeance. Our natures are as changeable as man's when treated poorly. You might wish to remember that the next time you ignore me."

"I said sorry, Ahmar. It was a misunderstanding, and I won't do it again."

The djinn cocked his head and his dark almond eyes narrowed. "It is time for you to return, brother. Your wife is becoming dangerous. She has quite the temper."

"No, Ahmar, please, I need to know how to deal with an angry old god. You can't just—"

I sucked in a deep breath and my eyes opened on chaos, then my hearing kicked in. It was usually the other way around, hearing then eyes, but maybe the seriousness of the situation called for some urgent action.

Heather had Barny against a wall with a knife to his throat. Ghost stood barking like a crazy monster at her, and Ella nursed her face. Kate supported Polly, who held a rag to her arm, blood dripping. Adam had his back to the wall in the far corner, another steak knife in his hand.

That's when I realised. Their eyes held that terrible, blank white once again.

"Lorne?" Ella said as I struggled upright.

"All good," I managed to say, but my chest did not feel *all good*. Had I suffered a heart attack? I rose from the floor. "Turstin fitz Rolf, hear me," I said to the room in my sergeant-major voice. "Release these people who are nothing to you, of no use to you, and give me time to answer your demand."

A soft hiss filled the room, and the temperature plunged, making my breath fog.

"I promise, I will release you from your duty one way or another," I said to the room. "But you must release these people and the children."

Adam's head snapped back, and he snarled, "You vow?"

"I do." Though, I hoped it wouldn't mean being a guardian of the reservoir for the next thousand years.

"I release them, but you cannot leave, nor the others."

Well, I tried. "Deal," I said.

Adam and Heather hit the floor simultaneously.

2 2

IT TOOK AN HOUR TO sort through the consequences of the Ouija board, Turstin's attack, and my conversation with the djinn. Mostly my conversation with the djinn. Ella held an ice pack to her jaw where Heather had lamped her. Polly's wounded arm stopped bleeding and Kate just sat in dumbfounded silence. Her police career, thus far, had not included training on how to deal with the temporary possession of multiple people.

Ella waggled her lower jaw about but said with a great deal of dismissive antagonism, "A god?"

"Yes, but not like you think of God. More powerful than the djinn, but not like anything we'd consider able to perform the parting of the Red Sea. I guess the ancient version of a saint performing miracles for certain believers," I tried to explain.

"And it's pissed off?" she asked.

"Very."

"And because the Normans held Christianity in such high regard, they've done more harm than good."

"That's what Ahmar thinks. Kinda like locking up an innocent man and expecting him to still be a good guy when he's finally released."

"What do we do?" she asked.

"Don't know at the moment. Ahmar sent me back to help Heather." Who currently sat next to me on the floor, shivering from shock.

Her horror at finding the knife in her hand, the injury to Ella she'd caused, slicing into Polly's arm, and Ghost's fear of her, undid the last of her self-control. For the first time, I saw her collapse in a state of total hysteria. Great hiccupping, messy sobs. For a woman who prided herself on being tough, compassionate, and always willing to fight, her surrender to the huge emotional overload of the last few days didn't come as much of a surprise. But the violence of it scared me. Every box in her mental safe must have opened and vomited stored emotions and memories all over the floor. She found an even keel after I stroked her hair, whispered about love, and held her close.

"I think I've had enough," she mumbled.

"I know, sweetheart," I said. "I'll get us home."

"My dog hates me."

"He doesn't. He's just scared of the monsters and now he's confused because he doesn't know this version of you." I didn't know if I was right, but it didn't matter. The more she calmed, the closer he came. For a young dog, the poor creature had known some weird situations.

"What do we do next?" asked Barny. He stood a long way from his sister and still held a cloth to his throat, where she'd drawn a ragged slice in his throat. They could barely look at each other.

"I think we stay put and rest. We need help, and Turstin is just going to have to wait," I said.

"What if he won't wait?" asked Heather. "What if we're forced to act? There are a lot of hours between now and dawn."

Despite it being summer, she was right. Twilight had only just fallen to full dark. I rubbed my face with my hands. "I think at this point we hope for the best and just wait it out."

Heather snorted and pulled away from me. I wanted to find out how I'd angered her when Ella lay her hand on my knee and shook her head. Those hazel eyes tracked Heather, assessing and thinking.

"Quiet word," she requested.

I nodded. We rose from the mattress we sat on and stepped over the salt line at the door. "Well, that clearly doesn't work very well," I muttered, looking at it with some resentment.

"Neither did the holy water, Lorne," Ella said. "I'm not sure what's going on, but maybe we're using the wrong tools against this enemy."

I grunted. "What are we supposed to be doing, then?"

The door to the kitchen swung shut behind me and Ella sagged against the wall.

"I'm exhausted," Ella murmured. I watched her with concern as she gathered her dwindling resources. "Kate's out of her depth, not something she's used to, and it's proving difficult for her to handle all this. I'm losing her."

I put a hand on her shoulder. "Don't say that, mate. She'll come around. She cares about you a great deal. This situation is enough to melt anyone's sense of reality. I think we'd forgotten how difficult it is to understand for those who haven't experienced the supernatural before."

Ella sniffed, but didn't give herself the luxury of selfish introspection. "I'm worried about Heather."

"You and me both," I said, staring at the doors as if they could give me answers to questions I couldn't formulate.

"I've never seen her like this. It's not just what happened while you lay unconscious. She's wired, jittery, disconnected. Like she's on the edge of something and doesn't know whether to jump or not."

I studied my boots for a while. "I think it's the family stuff, but I'm hardly in a position to know for certain. She doesn't talk about it. Barny turning up like this has made it worse and I don't know why. Now is hardly the time to confront her."

"It's making her unpredictable, Lorne, and thanks to you, she's dangerous. Between you, things could go wrong here really fast."

"What do you suggest?" I frowned.

She shrugged. "I don't know exactly."

"Maybe we should get some rest and it'll come together during downtime. It's difficult to get a full picture of the situation during the chaos of contact and its aftermath. We'll reassess in a couple of hours."

Ella nodded. "We just have to survive the night, right?"

"It would be good to try," I said, giving her a smile.

She pushed off the wall. "The next time you need a priest, you can phone a different one."

"Ouch. That hurts, but I don't blame you," I said.

We returned to the others. It took a little time, everyone still jumpy, but the kids settled into sleep after Polly made hot chocolate and the rest of us just lay down to rest, rather than expect sleep.

"LORNE, WAKE UP." A FAMILIAR hand shook my chest.

I peeled my eyes open, forgetting we'd left our comfortable bed far behind. I hadn't meant to fall asleep, but my discipline was slipping. "What's wrong?"

Heather leaned over, the scent of her familiar enough to make my heart ache. She'd chosen to sleep on a mattress with the dog, rather than me. Opting not to make a big deal of the decision, I'd settled down nearby and didn't touch her.

"I can't find Barny," she whispered.

I tracked her gaze and sat up. The mattress nearest the door to the school hallway was empty.

"Shit."

"He's been gone too long to take a piss," she murmured, not wishing to disturb the others.

I looked around. Everyone seemed to be asleep, except the dog who watched us and panted. I checked the time: 01:34.

"I'll go find him," I said.

"*We'll* go find him," she hissed.

I studied her. Dark circles under her eyes made it clear she needed rest, but I could almost feel the jagged energy coming off her slight frame. "Heather, I'm worried about you."

"I'm fine. Come on." She rose and moved silently between the mattresses, just like I taught her.

Following, Ghost and I padded after her as she slipped out through the door and into the silence of the school. We approached the nearest toilets to the kitchen, and I checked them thoroughly. Nothing. When I rejoined Heather, she pointed to the floor.

"Oh shit," I muttered.

"You think it's Damien?"

The faint marks of mud dirtied the floor of the hallway. Despite it being full summer and the country being as dry as kindling, a reservoir and river dominated the area around the school. Damien could well have tracked mud into the school. The lights overhead made it easy to see the faint smudges on the floor and the two of us followed, Ghost at our heels.

The corridor turned a sharp right and we followed. Three paces in and a fire exit gave access to the outside world. I realised this door stood between two of the larger dorms. Heather gasped and pointed to the wall on the right. Large red letters stained the white surface. I approached and the smell of damp copper hung in the sullen air. Ghost jumped up and sniffed at the sticky mess until Heather pulled him down.

The letters read *'Run From This Place'* in a haphazard scrawl.

A small whimper escaped Heather. "Damien has Barny."

My worst nightmares come true. *I had to hunt one of my own.* This thought ricocheted around my empty skull like a stray bullet in a tank. It made a similar sound.

I stood as memories flickered through my head. Images of Damien, face alight with the energy of the hunt as we tore through towns and villages harbouring enemy combatants. Those towns and villages also full of innocent people. ISIS didn't exist when I served with him, but if he'd been a mercenary when they'd sprouted, fully formed, from the camps in Iraq... How much blood covered his soul? Which of us would tip the scales the furthest come Judgement Day?

"Lorne..." Heather's voice poked holes in my memories and brought me back.

"I need Olly's weapons. I can't hunt him unarmed."

She gazed at our boots for a moment before looking up at me. "Who's the better soldier?"

The question didn't surprise me, and she was right to ask. "I'm the better soldier, but he's the better killer. Always was."

"Will he kill Barny?"

We started back to the kitchen to find the weapons. "I don't know. Barny is naturally submissive, so he won't fight if he doesn't have to, that's a good thing."

"Barny knows how to handle irrational anger," Heather said. Once more, that brittle quality to her voice I didn't like to hear. We needed a long conversation with beer somewhere quiet when this was over.

Back in the kitchen, Heather and Ghost stayed by the door, but I moved among the sleeping people to Olly's stash of weapons on the kitchen table. I took two catapults, a handful of marbles, and the crossbow, along with the sling.

We retreated from the confines of the kitchen and returned to the door out of the school. I handed over a catapult. Heather tested it by pulling back on the rubber. "I'd rather have the P60," she muttered.

I chuckled. "Yeah, me too, but we don't have firearms and maybe that's a good thing. We both need to know how to solve problems without guns." I will admit, I heard Ella's voice in my head as I repeated her familiar refrain.

"Not convinced, boss."

I smiled. The causal nickname felt reassuring, like her faith in me had returned.

We both looked at the door. "Do you think it's going to open?" I asked.

"I do not know. How are we going to track him in the dark?"

"He wants to be found. He won't make it difficult," I said. "I should do this alone, kid."

Heather hummed for a moment. "Probably, but you aren't going to because it's my brother out there. We might be estranged, but he's still blood. If there're two of us hunting him, Damien's going to find it harder to win whatever game he's playing."

Walking up to the door, I pressed down on the emergency handle, and it clicked open. Dread, rather than relief, curled around my spine and climbed it, like a snake on a tree. Wanting to give the others a chance to escape the haunted rooms and corridors of the school, I held the door open for Heather and Ghost.

"Get that rock," I said, pointing to the largest lump I could see nearby.

As Heather approached it, I felt the door pressing against me. "What the…" I breathed, pushing back. The pressure continued, so I wedged myself against the door frame and used my weight and strength to keep it open.

"Hurry," I called out. With each heartbeat the weight of the door seemed to double. I gritted my teeth and Heather ran towards me, but…

I cried out and flung myself sideways to avoid being crushed to death. The door snapped shut with the violence of a rat trap. The wall shuddered. We heard voices inside the school.

Heather dropped the rock and tried pulling and banging on the door to open it, but to no avail. It remained closed.

"Lorne? Heather?" Ella called from the other side.

"We're locked out. Damien has Barny, we're going after him," Heather explained.

While they continued to talk, I scanned my surroundings. The moon, half full and sat at her meridian for the night, was clothed in a white haze. It gave me enough light without ruining my night vision, but it would take a little time for my eyes to fully adjust. When you're hunting someone in reasonably familiar rural territory, you have a distinct advantage. You can use scent, not just eyesight and hearing.

I paced and sniffed the air, seeing if anything of Barny remained in the still, sultry night. Ghost watched me with his head cocked, clearly trying to figure out what his mad human was doing this time. If I sniffed him and didn't hold his collar, he'd run off and hide somewhere convinced I wanted to drown him in the bath.

"It's alright for you, fella, you can do this blindfolded," I muttered. We'd done some scent training with him, but I had nothing of Damien's or Barny's to hold to his nose.

Opening my mouth and inhaling, I caught something at last. The very slight aroma of incense. I snapped my fingers at Ghost, and he came to my side. I sniffed again and there it was, the sweet smell of hazy days.

"Heather, I have a direction," I said.

She gave a last farewell to Ella and came to my side. "Have they gone back up to the reservoir?"

I sniffed once more. "I think so. Can you smell Barny?"

"You mean the combination of weed and sandalwood?" she asked with a smile in her voice. "Yeah. They're heading to the wall, right?"

"We don't know how long they've been missing. They could be a long way from here." I started off towards the black wall of concrete. The moon's light didn't reflect off its dull surface, rather it vanished into the artificial rock.

"Whose blood was on the wall?" Heather asked as we jogged up the sharp incline. "It was still wet."

"It doesn't matter whose blood was on the wall, we have to help both of them. Though, if it's Barny's, I'm going to be having some brutal bloody words with Damien." We dropped into silence, our breathing hampered by the ruthless climb and heat radiating off the tonnes of concrete.

Cresting the rise at last, we stood and considered our options. A track led away from the reservoir and into the woodland. In the other direction, it took us over to the dam, where I'd found Heather earlier that day. I checked the ground, but it was hard and devoid of clues.

Heather clambered down to the water's edge. "I have two sets of footprints in the softer sand," she called out.

"You sure?" I asked.

"Yep."

I didn't need to double check. I trusted her skill. I'd trained her. "Okay, then we follow the proper track through the wood. It'll be easier to run on than the sand. Get back up here."

Heather retraced her steps. "What if we miss them?" she asked.

"Then we double back," I said, already moving off.

We set a hard pace, barely hampered by the dark canopy depriving the moonlight from giving us aid. The three of us ran around the vast dark mass of water on our left. When the path dropped back towards the reservoir, we checked the sand near the water line and found the tracks once more. My beast, dormant for most of the summer, rose and sniffed. He hunted prey and there might be a fight to be had in the end. Something he definitely wanted in on.

The levels of the reservoir, being so low, meant we'd waste time by following the woodland footpath, so the pair of us splashed through the water and I couldn't help but remember the dead bodies still in the church. Had Damien put them in there? If he had, why did his reaction to their presence become so violent?

Ghost galloped ahead of us when we returned to the track once more and raced through the woodland.

Figures in the distance caught my attention, and I stopped. Grabbing Heather, I pulled her behind me, placing a finger to my lips to indicate silence. Pointing at her chest, I signalled with a brief hand signal to go right into the trees, then made a circling motion. She nodded, understanding. I'd sent her off to come back around in a flanking manoeuvre, keeping quiet.

Approaching Ghost, I lay a hand on his neck and the low rumble stopped. Not wanting there to be an accident, I clipped his lead onto his collar. A signal for best behaviour in a public place. We moved together in silence towards the trees closest to the water. Once I had eyes on the beach running around the reservoir, I stopped and waited in the treeline. The moon gave me all the light I needed. Two figures struggled at the water's edge. I frowned for a moment, not understanding what was happening.

When I twigged, I gasped. Damien was dragging a reluctant Barny into the water. The tall, thin man fought and struggled, but I knew it was hopeless. Damien's skills would force Barny to drown. I glanced around, just to reassure myself no other visible enemies lurked on the shoreline or among the trees. Then I realised the submerged road leading to Syndercombe, lay nearby. Damien wanted Barny in that church. Did that mean he'd killed Ryan while under the influence of whatever lay behind the Norman lord's distress?

In a straight fight, I honestly did not know who would come out victorious. Damien was bigger than me, and more vicious, but I had advantages he didn't, mostly my endurance. I also had the dog, but using an untrained animal to take down a human being could be dangerous for everyone. I didn't want that for Ghost. My hand tightened on the crossbow I held.

Using an unknown weapon in this situation could be a very, very stupid move. I'd never used a crossbow for a start. I could use a longbow, but I wasn't an expert.

Damnit, I'd try talking first.

23

I CAME OUT OF THE shadows and stood on the beach. "Crusty," I called out, using his old call sign. "You need to stop, mucker."

He paused, but poor Barny kept fighting in his grasp. Damien embraced his throat in an implacable choke hold, and I realised Barny was suffocating. I needed to end this fast.

"Let him go," I called out, approaching slowly. A dark figure slipped out of the trees.

Keeping Damien's attention, I said, "I need to talk to whatever's making you do this."

"You understand nothing, mortal man," growled a voice made of ancient quartz and hottest lava. How could a human throat make such a sound? I also realised, with dawning horror, the knight didn't possess Damien, the god did.

"I understand enough," I said. I noted the absence of my djinn. It annoyed me. We'd be having words if I survived the next few minutes. "Let the man go."

"He is a sacrifice," snarled Damien's face, but not his voice. "I have a right."

Heather called out, giving away her position. "No, you don't. Your time in this world is done. All things die, even gods!"

"No!" I screamed as she rushed into the water.

I threw down the crossbow. No way could I fire it now. I'd hit someone, but two out of the three, I really needed to keep alive. Heather reached Damien before I did, so I released the dog.

Ghost raced into the night dark water, the moonlight forming pearls of white as he splashed towards his mistress. He barrelled into the two men, and both fell back. Damien, body acting on instinct, released Barny, knowing the dog was the bigger threat. Ghost grabbed the tall man by the arm and tried to pull him away. Barny squealed, but Heather reached them and helped untangle man and dog, dragging them towards the beach.

Damien roared, and I charged him before the bigger man could rise from the water and follow Heather. He reached for her, but I pushed my shoulder into his chest, and we tumbled back into the water. I had my arms around his waist and rolled us into the deeper part of the reservoir.

Darkness engulfed me and the cold of the water came as a shock after the endless hot days and nights of the summer. Forcing us down, I hoped Damien would come back to his senses, but he struggled and fought me.

My only advantage came from the shock of my attack. I felt the moment that shock changed into a counterattack. Damien forced us over this time and one hand caught the back of my neck, the other found the front. Those hands tried to form a choker made of human flesh around my throat. I lost control of my breathing and bubbles filled the surrounding water. The only thing I could do was kick for the surface. Air became the most important priority.

We broke the surface, but still I couldn't breathe. Forming two fists, middle finger raised like a mountain peak among the foothills, I jabbed into Damien's ribs on either side of his unprotected body. I hit the nerves running through his flanks and his hands released long enough for me to kick back and away while sucking in a huge lungful of air.

"Lorne!" Heather screamed, and I heard splashing. I had to keep her out of Damien's grip. He'd snap her like a twig.

I rolled onto my front and made to swim to the shore. Damien snarled and grabbed my ankle, yanking me back and down. Kicking back, I made contact with something heavy and the grip on my leg vanished. Using more doggy paddle than front crawl, I fought to reach the shore.

It worked. I felt the ground under my hands and scrambled for the shore. The sound of splashing behind me forced me to turn onto my back and I watched Damien heading for Heather who, realising her mistake, tried to reach the shore before the bigger man caught her. I scrambled up and once more threw myself at Damien. We hit the sand, locked together, but he had the better position. A fist collided with my head. The world turned liquid and shiny for a moment. He turned me over and forced my face into the wet sand.

My mouth and nose filled.

I'd drown or suffocate.

Bucking and flailing, I tried to remove the knee in my spine, all of Damien's weight in the centre of my back. Colours in my head exploded and dimmed. My lungs burned. He was killing me. I clawed at his hand, the one pinning the back of my head down, fingers so strong they might crush my skull before I lost the last of my breath.

I heard a faint, "Fuck you, bastard!"

The weight over me shuddered and rolled off my spine and head. I rose, spitting sand and soil out of my mouth. At least this time, the taste of it was real. Damien rose, darkness spreading down the side of his face. Heather had smacked him with something. Just as she had the man in Scob, but it wasn't her asp this time. She stood with a branch in her hand, snarling and snapping her teeth in rage.

Damien staggered, gathered himself, shook his head, flicking warmth over me before turning away and running back into the water. I rose to go after him, but Heather gripped my arm.

"Don't, Lorne."

I watched as my old comrade swam with powerful strokes through the dark water, and I knew I'd never catch him. Putting my hands on my knees, I relaxed enough to allow my stuttering lungs to recover their full function.

In my periphery, I saw Barny trying to hold Ghost by his collar to prevent the enormous dog coming after us.

"Hold, dog," I called, still coughing up wet sand. Ghost calmed, allowing Barny to collapse back.

My eyes returned to watch the dark shape powering through the water. When he reached the far shore, the moon lent me sufficient light to see my old friend run into the woods.

"I'm sorry, Lorne," Heather said.

I pulled her into my arms, and she relaxed against me. "You have nothing to be sorry for, my love. He was going to kill me and without you, he'd have done it. You just saved my life."

Barny approached. "You saved mine too, little sis."

"Are you okay?" I asked him.

Barny looked like he could do with a hug, but Heather didn't seem able to oblige. "Not really. I thought he was going to kill me."

"He was," I stated. "Come on, we need to get back to the school. I'm worried about them."

"Why did he attack you?" Barny asked.

I sighed, once more tripping over memories and finding lost joy in our brotherhood, one which no longer existed. "I don't really understand what's happened to him," I said. "Though I have a few ideas."

Barny trudged beside me in silence for a while, rubbing life back into his throat. I wanted to do the same thing, but pride kept my hands at my sides. Damien had won. The only reason I still breathed the sweet night air was because Heather intervened. Could he be so much better than me? Was I really losing my edge? Did it matter?

"Maybe you could share your ideas?" Heather said. "Though I've a few of my own."

"He's under the influence of the old god," I said. Saying the words aloud made the rational part of me want to scream, but that rational part had shrunk considerably over the last few years.

Barny muttered something I didn't catch.

"What was that?" I asked, bending to pick up the discarded crossbow.

He appeared to be reluctant to share. "This is going to sound bonkers but…"

"I think we're beyond bonkers," Heather stated.

"Well, it's like this. The old knight wants Lorne to replace him, and the old god has chosen Damien as his champion. Clearly, no one trusts me enough to tell me the truth, but I'm guessing the pair of you were part of the same army regiment and I'm guessing it was one of the more extreme ones, like the PARAs, Marines or even the SAS. I know you have little respect for me, Heather, and I understand why. I know you don't like me very much—"

"That's not fair. I don't know you, Barny," Heather said on the other side of me.

"Regardless, I think I ought to know the truth. If nothing else, it might help me understand what's happened here. That man scared me more than I've ever been scared of anything," his voice broke, and he sucked in a hard breath.

I stopped walking and put a hand on his arm. "Barny, I wasn't going to let him kill you and he won't get to you again. I promise."

The younger man had bruises coming on his face and dark marks around his throat. He looked bedraggled, scared, and lost.

"I don't hurt people, Lorne. Why did he want to kill me?"

"I don't know why he chose you. You're right though, we worked in the same unit and yes, I was Special Air Service. Damien left a long time before I did, and I haven't seen him in years. He became a mercenary for a while and during the War on Terror, that career choice could take you to some dark places. Places even we wouldn't go. Damien is a warrior. I don't know what turned him into a teacher."

"Probably the same thing that turned you into a survivalist instructor," said Heather quietly.

I thought about that and agreed.

"If your theory is right, Barny, what do we do about it?" I asked.

Barny huffed out and hummed for a while. "I heard something in the school, not the scary noises we've all been hearing, but a weird squeaking sound. So, I thought I'd investigate. That's when I found him, in the corridor, by the door. There were rabbits in his hands, he cut their throats like it was nothing, then held them over a bowl. He didn't know I was there, watching.

Then he dipped his fingers in the liquid and started drawing on the wall. That's when I smelt the blood. When he finished with the wall, he turned to look directly at me and he said, 'You like to watch me, don't you?' He spoke in the terrible voice, and I knew I faced the same thing I'd seen in the water that day I did the drugs up here. It knows me.

"I tried to run away, but he moved so fast. He punched me and I blacked out. When I came to, he was carrying me through the wood. I tried to fight him and… Well, I failed. He smelt like that horrible smell in the school."

"But Turstin fitz Rolf caused the smell," said Heather.

I had another idea. "What if it wasn't? What if the thing keeps finding its way into the school but Turstin turns up to push it out? That's a guardian's job, after all."

"How do we fight a god?" Heather asked in a quiet voice as we again approached the dam.

Barny chuckled, then said, "We don't. We can't kill a god, but we can appease one."

I snorted. "Yeah, well, you're the next sacrifice to the thing, so unless you want to nominate someone else, we're screwed."

"We don't have to sacrifice someone. We can find a different way to appease a god."

Heather chipped in with, "Like the libations to the gods in polytheistic religions."

I'd been around her enough to know that meant Greek and Roman, probably others. "I don't think this thing is going to be happy with some ox blood and honey. We need to convince it to go to sleep—forever."

Barny, struggling with the damage Damien had inflicted as we started down the hill to the school, said, "I think we should respect his wishes and see what he wants in order to keep him quiet. We need the local deity to look after his land rather than rage against the changes."

"And we need to convince the knight to just let go," Heather said.

"Okay, but how do we accomplish this mission objective with no one else dying? And who put the bodies in the church?" I asked.

A tense silence fell. Thick and glue-like.

Barny broke the quiet. "Lorne, I think we know who left the bodies. He might not have known what he was doing."

I barked a laugh. "No, that's insane. Damien wouldn't do that. He was more shocked than me with what we found."

"Maybe he doesn't remember what he did. If he has a dissociative disorder, then his realities could be quite separate. To face one, when in the presence of another, it will cause a problem."

"No," I barked the command.

Heather crossed my path to lay a hand on Barny's arm. I saw her shake her head to stop Barny talking. She knew my moods too well.

Rage and fear for my old friend battled inside me. "You don't know Damien. I do." I strode ahead of them, back to the door we escaped through, thoughts tumbling and a sick feeling rising.

How could Damien have become a murderer? How could his mind be so shattered he couldn't tell the difference between realities?

Even as the question occurred to me, the answer came. I'd found myself curled up in a corner more than once, terrified because I had no idea which world I was in, mouth full of dust and sand, ears full of the ratt-tatt-tatt of machine-gun fire. Until I met Ella, then Heather, I felt nothing as I moved through the world without my Regiment. Was it the same for Damien?

My oldest friend, Tommy, flitted through my head. I knew I hadn't processed what happened with him, how I'd been the instrument of his death. I'd just pushed it into the box marked 'Leave this the fuck alone', along with thousands of other memories. Sometimes they spilled out in a torrent of sewage-like self-loathing, but mostly I kept them secured, hidden, buried. I desperately needed to avoid killing Damien. Living with that burden would change me forever.

I rattled the door, expecting it to remain closed, and I wasn't disappointed. Rather than be reasonable, I lost my temper. A thump on the plastic became a punch, followed by a heavy kick on the door lock and a stream of curses made of frustration and fear.

When I ran out of breath I stood back and bellowed at the building, "If you want me to free you, I need my people and they are in the damned school. Let me in."

The door clicked and swung back. Did Turstin do it? Or the prickly old god? It didn't matter. I grabbed the rock Heather had tried to get for me earlier and wedged the door. Ella and Kate stood watching me with amusement clear on their tired faces.

"Well, Sergeant-Major, that was dramatic," Kate said.

Keeping my back to the door, just in case, I grumbled as Heather, Ghost and Barny made their way past me.

"You found him?" Ella said, looking at Barny. She grimaced at the sight of the damage. "We need to get something on those bruises."

"What about my bruises?" I asked, everyone ignored me. I eyed the door, expecting it to slam shut and send a shower of pulverised rock up the hallway towards us. The door remained still; it made me twitchy.

A sensation of ice-cold air whipped over me, and the rock rolled away, the door closing fast. Kate swore and backed up the hall. Ella crossed herself and muttered a prayer, then yelped and touched her face.

"Oh, something just brushed against me," she squeaked.

"You're a priest, despite being a woman, I expect he recognises you as a woman of God." I walked back towards the kitchen.

"We tried everything to get the door open," Kate said. "I still think getting the children out is the best option."

Lights filled the kitchen, so I knew the boys weren't asleep. "Everything okay here, while I've been gone?"

"All quiet, we've just been worried about you," Ella said.

I saw Polly at the sink, washing-up. When she saw Barny her eyes tracked behind us to see if Damien came as well. "He's not here?"

It hadn't occurred to me to plan what I'd tell her or the others about Damien. "He's still out there," I said, trying to avoid details.

"Is he alright?" Polly put down the dishcloth and gave me a hard stare.

"He's... alive, and I didn't hurt him but he's not himself right now and I think I need to find out a bit more about Damien's activities over the last few years."

Polly leaned against the sink. "What makes you think he talks to me? He left The Regiment, then seven years later he's teaching in this school. It only takes a year to do the training with his experience and previous qualifications. What he did in that gap?" She shrugged. "He doesn't talk, but he has a lot of nightmares, and he never rests unless he's drunk or distracted by something more interesting." Her dark skin flushed darker, and I smiled.

Laying a hand on her shoulder I said, "I'm going to get him back in one piece, but he's not well and he might never come back to you."

She swallowed hard, fighting back the tears. "I know, he's been growing more manic and agitated over the last few months."

"Since he found Ryan?" I asked.

"Looking back, I think it started before that, but I'm not sure. It's so busy during term time I just didn't notice."

Adam came over and poured a glass of water. "What happened out there?" He looked washed out and when I glanced at the other kids, they stayed all huddled up and drained of any enthusiasm for this terrible adventure.

I put the weapons we'd taken back on the counter. "The blood in the hallway comes from a rabbit, so no one is that badly hurt. Damien isn't well so you need to stay away from him, and if he comes back to the school, you come find me. Do you guys know anything about old gods, like Celtic gods?"

The usually silent Mason raised his hand. He sat between Killian and Olly but remained mute.

Killian said, "It's true, Mr Turner, he knows a lot about old stuff. He's really into it."

I approached the boy whose pale blue eyes widened. Crouching down to their level, despite my knees groaning, I asked, "What do you think is going on?"

Mason shrugged, sniffed, then spoke at last, "We don't know much about the original gods of ancient Britain because the Romans slaughtered all the Druids. The Druids had had an oral tradition, not a written one, so they left little evidence. We only really have the stuff Christian monks wrote afterwards, and what some of the Roman writers tell us."

"Wow, okay, kid, that's useful, anything else?" I rocked back and sat on the nearest mattress. The others gathered around and sat down. It felt like story time in reverse.

He examined all the adult faces watching him and coloured, but he kept talking, "Old gods are connected to things like lakes, hills or mountains, rivers and streams. Natural places that give shelter to people or things that kill them. Then stories are built up, and that place becomes good or bad, depending. There are loads of stories about people being punished for trespassing on hallowed ground or being lured in as sacrifices."

"Can you tell me more about that? About sacrifices?" I asked.

He nodded. "The stuff about the wicker man being filled with people and burnt is probably Roman lies—"

"Propaganda," Robert added.

"Yeah," Mason said. "Anyway, we know people put offerings in places of importance, asking for the god's help in something. So, like, a woman could offer a necklace, or bracelet and ask for a baby." All three boys pulled faces at this, making Heather chuckle. Mason then said, "Or a warrior would offer a dagger, or sword for wanting victory or as thanks for a victory in battle." This met with more approval from the boys. "Then they've also found stuff like animal bones."

"Human bones?" I asked.

He shrugged. "Maybe, I don't know but I don't think so. They left sacrifices with the triple death thing but that's pretty extreme."

"What would you do if you wanted to appease a god?" I asked. Talking to Mason and watching the others, I realised something, their imaginations retained a more finely tuned antenna than most adults. They'd link ideas together I couldn't fully grasp and their instincts about this place ran deep.

His eyes widened again, and he conferred with the others, their mouths sheltered from the adults by hands, so we couldn't see their whispering. A few seconds went by before Mason nodded and turned back to his audience. "The weapons Olly has might help because we don't have a sword. Then maybe honey, milk, a lamb we could take from a farm."

I arched my eyebrow at this, and he coloured again.

"Or not," he muttered. "When we say prayers, but we don't have a name and names can be really helpful."

"Not much chance of us figuring that out," Kate said. "It would be a name in Old English. Even using location names from the Domesday Book wouldn't be wise. The entire area was Christianised by then."

Ella shifted. "True, but most of the old names remained. I think we need to try what Mason suggests."

"What about Turstin fitz Rolf?" asked Barny. "He won't be passive about us offering grave goods to a god."

Mason said, "Grave goods are for the dead person, not a sacrifice to the gods. They're different things."

Heather chuckled. "Well, that told you." Barny scowled at her.

I checked my watch, 03:04, a couple of hours until dawn. "I think we try to get some more sleep. Heads down until sun up, then we'll reassess. I'm hoping all this calms down with dawn and we get more police in here and you lot out."

Everyone agreed, and we settled back down, this time Heather and Ghost curling up with me. It felt good.

2 4

THE DREAM CAME UP SLOWLY. One moment I felt my arm draped over Heather and my fingers buried in Ghost's fur, the next I felt something digging into my back. I woke and looked around in surprise. I sat on sand, still in army fatigues, but no obvious weapons nearby. I leaned against a palm tree, heavy with dates. A small herd of white goats grazed on the grass surrounding a pool of crystal blue water.

"Ahmar?" I called out, assuming he'd summoned me for some reason.

He rose from the shadows of a tree nearer the goats. "Why are you here?" He looked cross, a small line between his dark eyebrows forming.

"Erm, I don't know." I scrambled upright. I didn't like him looming over me.

"Your life is not threatened, and I have no wish for you to be here, so why?" he asked.

"I don't know, but I need your help," I said in exasperation.

Ahmar shook his head. "I am sorry, brother, but I cannot help you. I am neither god nor a man."

I couldn't contain my growing irritation and I paced in the sand, never an easy feat because my feet kept sinking among the fine grains. "I can't do this alone."

"Mortal man has been communicating with their gods for millennia without the likes of me acting as an intermediary."

"I don't understand."

He sighed and spoke as if to a child, "I am like a fox, Lorne. I am neither a dog nor a cat. I am hated and hunted by all for my existence. I am a wild creature. I cannot face a god, however small he might be."

"But the angel—"

"Wasn't in our realm and did not wish to be. I did not win against the angel. You killed his priest with my help. That is why we won."

Forcing myself to think of the priest and not my childhood friend, I concentrated on trying to figure a way out of this mess. "Okay, but do you have any idea what I can do to prevent this from getting worse?"

"Yes, I have said already. Talk."

"Talk to a god?"

"Yes."

"Ahmar, it's not like I know what I'm doing. I didn't make this happen. Which reminds me, I could have done with your help against Damien earlier tonight. He almost killed me."

The djinn waved a hand at me and returned his attention to his goats. "I do not fight gods. We talked of this. Besides, your wife was there. She saved you." He gave me a full body look at this as though he couldn't quite believe I needed Heather to save me from a god.

I tried not to take it personally. "Well, I'm here, so you might as well help. The last time we spoke, you wanted to tell me how to appease a god."

Ahmar growled and repeated, "Talk to him."

"I'd rather not, Ahmar."

"Why not? You speak to me."

His impatience with my stubbornness irritated me. "We had no positive communication, or relationship, until last year. You and I came close to being locked up in a madhouse forever."

His eyes narrowed and one of those long, thin fingers pointed at my chest. "You were the one with weapons and death leaking from every pore. You and your kind woke me from the deserts of my land and dragged me into your latest war. *You* summoned *me*. Not the other way around." He made a sharp circle in the air, then crossed his arms and stared at the water.

"No, I did not." I didn't hide my frustration. "I wouldn't know how."

Ahmar's mouth twisted in a nasty smile, full of venom and sharp teeth. "Of course you did not know how. You know nothing, ignorant mud dweller."

"What the hell's that supposed to mean?" I wished for my assault rifle in that moment.

"Learn, foolish mortal man. Learn how to communicate with this world you are adept at stumbling into. I cannot always be your guide and protector. You are not a child, even if you behave like one. I do not serve men who chose to be ignorant."

I WOKE FROM THE DREAM with a cry on my lips loud enough to startle everyone else from their sleep.

"What happened?" Ella responded first.

Heather grunted, well used to my nightmares, rolled over and went back to sleep.

"Ahmar happened," I grumbled. "Sorry for waking you."

"You need to talk?" Ella asked.

I struggled off the mattress and checked the window. The grey light of pre-dawn filled the sky, and I felt the weight of another sleepless night press down on my head. "I could do with a cuppa tea," I murmured.

Ella came and joined me in the kitchen area. She looked drained and her hand trembled as she filled the kettle. I took it off her.

"You okay?" I asked her.

She nodded. "It's just so horrible. The more I think about that poor Christian knight feeling like he has to guard against the evil of a pagan god and that god becoming full of rage and hate over the centuries... It's all so horrible."

"Crisis of faith?" I asked, concerned for her.

She shrugged, and her eyes strayed to Kate. "I don't know. Despite the Church of England being okay with me being gay, and a vicar, and a woman—" That made us both smile because being a woman was probably the worst option for the Church. "—the Anglican communion still states gay sex is wrong. It didn't bother me so much while I was single but now…"

"It shouldn't bother you at all. It doesn't stop you doing your job, which is bringing God's words to your congregation and helping to spread that about through your community work."

We'd had this conversation many times before in some form or another over the years. It wasn't uncommon for Ella to panic about her faith and her role in Mother Church.

"But the Christian faith caused all this to happen, Lorne."

I chuckled as I made us tea. "No, it didn't. Or not your version of it, anyway." I tried to think things through from my perspective. "Look at it like this, the original goddess at the hot water springs in Bath was a powerful Celtic one, right?"

Ella nodded. "She was known as Sulis by the local tribes."

"Right, then she became…"

"Minerva, because of the Romans."

"This is a more brutal version of that. People became Christians and left their old faith, and they didn't all do it because they had to, most of them converted because it seemed like the better option. By the time Turstin came around the faith had very solid foundations in England, many abbeys and religious orders littered the countryside."

She smiled; it softened the exhaustion. "You've been listening to Heather."

"I try. A lot of what she says goes over my head, but I do try. Turstin thought he was doing the right thing. The old god didn't go to sleep like so many of them must have when things changed. New faiths layer over old ones, even in the same pantheon. Look how different the Old Testament is to the New. Or how the Greeks changed their deities over time. I don't pretend to understand the ins and outs, Ella, but this isn't on you or your faith."

"Maybe," she said, stirring sugar into her tea, a sure sign of fatigue.

"You could help with this though," I said, an idea slowly forming.

"How?"

"We need to talk to the god, and you know how to talk to God, so I think we need you. We also take offerings." A plan started to form at last and I liked it.

Ella's eyes widened. "Me? Talk to a pagan god? Lorne, half the Church already hates me, I don't think making the other half hate me is a good idea. I might as well be cavorting with the Devil."

"Think about it like this—before monotheistic faiths, people believed in everything from sun gods to ones like this, who came from a spring forming the most important river in the area. Your God formed the universe, so must have had a hand on forming all the pagan gods, who helped explain the world to His creation. Human kind. Right? Then came monotheistic religions when people's minds could absorb the concept."

She looked at me with bafflement. "You've been hanging around me and Heather for too long. I'm not sure that's how this works. I think it might take another thousand years of synods to untangle that amount of religious trickery."

"Could we say I'm right, so you can help?" I knew I was pushing my luck with the pagan stuff. Ella was pretty tolerant of other faiths, but this may well shove her over the parapet.

She chuckled and shook her head. "Sure, why not? Ultimately, I'm doing this to save some kids and to stop a furious ghost from turning you into a guardian for the next thousand years. That has to be good for my soul."

"Don't. I'm trying hard to forget that bit of the mission. Facing Turstin is the part of this I really don't know how to handle."

"It might be wise to keep it front and centre, soldier. It's what he wants from you. Okay, so I'm in. What's next?"

"We find the source of the river, then we see if we can summon the god, then we talk—or fight—depending on how things go. Meanwhile, Kate deals with the dead in the water and we get the kids out of here." I added with a grumble, "It's all she's interested in anyway."

Ella ignored my snide bitch about her girlfriend. "What if the kids take the god with them?"

"I think we have to risk it. I don't want them stuck here for another day and night."

"Most of them don't have parents and we don't have transport. We'll have to call a garage to replace the tyres on the vehicles."

"We'll get the tyres sorted, load the kids up, get them back to my place until I can arrange parents for collection. I don't want them here if Damien returns."

"Talking of which, how are we going to handle him?" Ella asked, eyes hard, mouth set in a grim line.

"*We* aren't. I am." I glanced at the others, all still in the land of nod, or faking it. "He almost killed me, Ella," I murmured softly.

Her eyes widened. "Oh, Lorne. What are you going to do?"

"He needs professional help. Barny said something about a dissociative disorder, where he's switching between realities. I don't know if it's that, or the old god playing tricks with his mind, like Ahmar did with me without meaning to because of how we met."

"I don't think the old god is as benign as Ahmar turned out to be," Ella said. "Besides, you had help in the hospital sorting your realities."

I grunted. I hadn't told any of them what Thomas Moore said about visiting me in hospital and 'healing' me. I had no proof, and I liked to think me, and the djinn sorted our shit out alone. "If we can stop the god from hurting Damien, then we can figure out the rest. I don't want to cause him pain and if he did kill those people in the reservoir..." Just the thought of it made my heart ache for my old friend. He'd be facing serious prison time. I knew I'd support him whatever the outcome. I wouldn't kill him. I just had to stop him.

25

IT DIDN'T TAKE LONG FOR everyone to wake up once the sun rose. The youngsters hovered around, restless and anxious, even Polly's fry-up not really helping them settle down, and we had a few spats. Until now, they'd been a tight unit, but stress and exhaustion broke the backs of many men under pressure, and something trapped these kids in a god's weight machine while he flexed his muscles.

Once the sunlight arced over the trees and poured into the east facing kitchen, my guess about Turstin's control proved right. The doors and windows opened. It improved everyone's mood. Even I found it easier to breathe. Kate instantly marched out of the school in search of a phone signal and Heather joined her, looking for Wi-Fi so we could find a tyre place nearby. I had the feeling the nearest would be Taunton, a good hour away for a truck. She also sent the younger lads out to make a complete list of all the names of all the tyres, so like-for-like could be replaced.

It would be a long argument with the insurance people to get any money to help pay for them, but maybe I could add it to the bill for the school.

I wondered about who might be able to help with the mission I had planned. Barny and Heather seemed to be sensible options. Heather because she'd watch my six if Damien turned up, and Barny because he understood a little of what we needed to do. He was also a calming influence on all of us, a man who'd fully rejected a life of avarice.

I watched Kate talk to her superiors and wondered how much she'd explain. When she hung up and came back to the kitchen, her countenance had changed.

"Right, I've called in the troops. My DCI is coming down and the dive team from Bristol is also on its way. We have a full forensics unit scrambling for multiple bodies." She pointed her phone at me. "I hope you're right about this and not having one of your episodes where you see things."

My jaw hardened, and Ella cringed. "The bodies are genuine enough, DI Mackenzie. You won't get a dressing down by your chief inspector for wasting resources." The sweetness in my voice made Ella place a hand over mine on the table to head off an argument. I hoped Kate and I might become friends, but we increasingly clashed to the point of rudeness.

"I need to get to the scene to make a full assessment before they arrive. Can I walk to the nearest location they'll use for the dive?" she asked.

"Of course. I'll take you to the fishing lodge we launched from yesterday. I can show you a map of where the church is under water. You'll need to warn them it's twelve metres under the surface to the church roof, fifteen, maybe more, to the floor. I didn't hang around long enough to check my gauge."

"I'll also need everyone to wait at the school, until you're cleared to leave. At that point, the children will be removed to a safe location and their guardians contacted. We will take statements from the rest of you and your full details," Kate announced, staring hard at Barny.

I said, "No." The statement arrived with all the subtlety of a war axe hitting a Norman shield.

Kate's eyes narrowed.

"Am I under arrest?" I asked.

"Not yet, but it could be arranged. I'm fairly sure I can find something your pals in the Security Services can't or won't protect you from," she snapped.

I sucked in a breath, but Ella said, "Don't provoke him, Kate. He's doing his best, as always. Just like you. Sadly, his world doesn't come with rules unlike yours and mine. We need to go to the source of the river, and it needs doing today. We'll walk to the site you'll need for your people, but after that we're no use to you."

"Are you already familiar with police procedures to know that?" Kate asked her in return. The harsh sarcasm shocked me.

Ella closed her eyes, obviously looking for patience somewhere inside. When they opened, the soft hazel had turned to green agate. "You know I'm not, but we aren't being held here for questioning unless you give us a police caution. Are you going to arrest us?"

The police officer wanted to say, 'yes', the girlfriend recognised she walked on ice so thin the cracks showed. "Fine. Go off on your little spiritual adventure, but I want you back here and I want statements by close of play today."

Ella ignored her and turned to me. "I'll have Polly help me prepare some water and food. We might be gone most of the day. I'm not sure leaving the boys here in the school is wise. It feels toxic. We could make it a field trip if Polly comes to help. You could teach them stuff on the way. Give them something else to think about for a few hours."

Kate stepped closer. "Ella, I can't sanction you removing the children from my care and the school. I really do hold the only legal authority here. Polly isn't a teacher or trained carer. Lorne is a civilian."

She enjoyed making that statement.

I thought about it. Part of me agreed with Ella. Leaving the boys alone in the school didn't feel right. I knew the place would probably be filled with police officers, but these kids were stressed and fed up with being caged. Besides, whatever Kate thought, their safety rested in my hands now Damien had vanished, and it felt right to keep them near.

Standing I prepared to face down the police officer. "I know you don't want to hear this, but events are outside of your control and experience. The bodies in the reservoir are your priority. The long-term safety and sanity of these kids is mine. You can't keep them here against their will."

Kate glowered and stepped into my space. "Do you really believe that, Turner?" She searched my eyes and I remained implacable. I'd been bollocked by far scarier people than DI Mackenzie. She hissed, "My God, you really do believe you're some kind of fucking hero." She huffed out a sharp breath. "You're nothing but a washed up, mental case, Turner. The chaos you cause, the upset, it's dangerous and you should be stopped. You are not taking those children out of my sight."

I remained calm. I kept all my instincts for violence carefully hidden. "I don't think you have much of a vote on this one, Kate. You might well hate me, and I don't blame you, but I'll not give you the satisfaction of provoking me. Why don't we see who the lads want to be with?"

As if cued by a stage direction the boys all shouted, "Lorne."

Then a chorus of cheers made me flinch and instantly regret my decision. Turning my back on the police officer I said, "Wait out, boys. We have rules. I want good boots, hats, sun screen, water, food, any weapons or gifts for a god you might have, and I need you to listen to me and obey." I gave them all my best stare.

"Yes, sir," came out of every mouth.

"Right, return to your rooms in pairs. Watch for trouble. Call out if you see or feel anything that worries you." I looked at Olly and his pals. "I know your room is trashed. So raid what you need from elsewhere if necessary."

Adam said, "I've spares of most things like hats."

"I've spare clothing," said Robert. "Some of it I've grown out of."

"Right, you have your orders, men. Go to it." I nodded at the door like my first SAS captain used to, and I watched them scramble to obey.

Kate turned on her heel and left the kitchen for the cool morning air outside.

Ella chuckled. "You're going to make an amazing dad."

"Yeah, well, Heather has quite a lot to do with that, so it's her choice, not mine."

My friend frowned. "Talk to her, Lorne. Properly. Figure out your roles and plans. She only has to carry the baby and have it. You can be primary carer."

I studied Ella. "Listen, mate, I'm sorry about Kate—"

Ella held up a hand. "You don't have to be friends, Lorne and to be honest, I agree with you. Kate can't protect them which is why I didn't back her up. It'll piss her off to the point she leaves me but it's for the best in the long run." She sighed. "We'll talk about it when the fate of five boys and your friend aren't hanging in the balance."

"Not to mention me guarding this place for the next thousand years," I muttered.

Ella smiled, a weak facsimile of her usual grin. "There is that."

Heather's return from finding a tyre company interrupted us. I could almost see the feathers she wanted to spit out. Annoyed didn't quite cover it. "Tomorrow, apparently, is the earliest anyone can come. I said it was urgent." She added in a whiny voice, *"But we're a long way from town. And we can't spare the manpower for such an enormous job. And if possible, can you bring the vehicles in?* I pointed out they had no tyres, at which point the man decided I didn't know what I was talking about. He asked me if he could talk to my husband or boyfriend."

I laughed. "Oh dear. I guess we aren't using that firm then."

"No, we bloody well aren't. Bastard."

"Leave it for now, Heather. I want you on our mission and focused. We'll sort the tyres later, or maybe Kate can ask one of her minions to call?" I smiled sweetly as the woman herself walked back in.

She glared at me.

I ignored her. Far scarier people had glared at me. Within thirty mikes we stood ready to go. Everyone had a hat, sun screen, water, sandwiches, walking boots and working comms at last. The previous night must have drained Turstin fitz Rolf of his EMP disruption, or whatever spooks did to electronics to foul them up.

Ahmar was right, I was ignorant.

THE TREK UP TO THE water proved to be easy, the boys desperate to leave the school behind. We walked over the dam to the south to take Kate to the fishing lodge where she'd meet her team. A palpable sense of relief swept over us adults when she stayed behind, and we about-faced to return to the northern edge of the reservoir. I watched Ella and Heather talking quietly, leading the boys.

"I've never seen Heather this happy," Barny said, coming alongside me. "Despite the scary ghosts."

I grunted, wanting to be alone for a while to gather my scattered thoughts. Learning what I had from Willow, I knew I needed to be focused and in control when we tried to communicate with this old deity. Talking bollocks with Barny wouldn't help at this stage.

He had other ideas. "Does she talk about home?"

I glanced at him and tried to hide my sigh. "No, not if you mean your parents' address."

"I had a lot of therapy in London, especially when I gave up the coke. It helped give me perspective."

"Is that why you live in a rainbow-coloured bus and take mescaline?" I asked, unable to keep the edge from my voice.

He chuckled. "Pretty much, yeah. It made me realise my family life sucked. That I needed to find new goals, *my* goals, and that I owed my sister a huge apology."

A warning went off on behalf of my lover. "What kind of apology?"

"I never backed her up. She fought all the time. She never caved in, always wanted her own path no matter the cost and it did cost her. I let her fight alone. I played the game our father set, and I watched her suffer. It's the biggest regret of my life." He sounded genuinely heartbroken.

"Well, I guess you can apologise, but I don't know if she'll listen. She really doesn't talk about her childhood. Sometimes I think she came out fully formed from the heart of a warrior goddess."

Barny's eyes widened. "Wow, man, that's profound. You really love her."

I watched Ghost trot along at Heather's side. "What's not to love? I wake up amazed she's still with me most mornings." I surprised myself with this confession, but oddly, other than Eddie Rice and Paul, I didn't have male friends in the area. Men like Barny, who came from such a wildly different world to mine, offered a different view on life and I'd learned to value alternative role models. Men who didn't need to battle through life with fists and guns.

Barny bumped my shoulder as we walked. "I'm not. She's loved, but more importantly, she's accepted. That's all Heather's wanted. I talked about her a lot in therapy because I admired her for fighting, but didn't understand why it made me jealous. You focus that fighting spirit."

I was touched. It never occurred to me to ask her father's permission to marry her, but it felt oddly right having Barny's blessing. "I think it would do her good to hear that, the bit about you admiring her. Leave the stuff about me out. She'll think I threatened you."

Barny chuckled. "Mate, you terrify me. The way you took out that bloke last night, that was hard core."

I wished I felt the same. "Hmm, he almost killed me."

"Yeah, but he didn't and in the process, you saved me. Awesome teamwork." He grinned, his eyes shining just like Heather's. It made me like him.

We took the walk slowly through the wood. After the night before, it felt appropriate to give the kids some time and space to enjoy their surroundings rather than continue to breathe in the fear ruling the corridors of their school, like a rabid wolf ready to devour them at every turn.

Heather and I pointed out the best places to set up small bivouacs, told them what wood to use, and we spent half an hour picking grasses to turn into twine. I promised to return in the autumn term to run survival courses for the lads, but I had the feeling their head teacher wouldn't want me within a thousand miles of the place if possible. We showed them how to pick nettles, so they didn't get stung and various animal spoor.

As we followed the path around, we saw the police divers like small, dark seals in the water.

Barny said in a quiet, almost reverential voice, "They have body bags, don't they?"

Feeling all the sadness in the world for a moment, I murmured, "Yeah, they do."

"Just this once I really wanted you to be wrong."

"Me too, mate. Me too."

Ella and Heather bowed their heads and several of the boys joined in a soft prayer for the dead. I didn't know what to think, the voice of my younger self in total denial that Damien might be responsible. The older, more cynical version of me warring with that optimistic denial, aware Damien posed a genuine threat.

In a more sombre mood, we continued on until we met up with the second branch of the 'Y' shape on the northern end of the reservoir. This point of the 'Y' held the beginnings of the River Tone. It ran between the sharp side of the wooded left of the combe and the gentle slope of the fields covering the right.

"That's not much of a stream," Polly said, pointing to the oozing water. It made a valiant effort to be a stream as it tried to navigate the sun-drenched, cracked, and very wide beach, but it didn't quite make it as a moving body of water.

I looked up the shallow combe. The official footpath continued around the large body of water, but we needed the source. Time to trespass.

"We'll walk the river, or at least the remains of it, and see where it takes us," I said.

We started, in twos, up the riverbed. At the beginning it comprised of dried silt in a crazy paving formation, but pretty soon, as the sides of the combe rose and became dense with woodland, it grew rocky. We all walked in silence, the quiet sentinels of the woodland providing us with shade, but also keeping their secrets in the shadows. It made me nervous. Damien could track us, and I'd have no way to know. I'd also be unable to protect the kids. My decision to battle with Kate loomed large in my conscience.

The path became steeper, the hillsides lower and more rounded, the trees thinner. We came to the top, and it felt calmer. I felt calmer, with the expansion of my vision. At least now I'd see Damien coming through the sun-bleached fields.

Heather, who led our strange group of refugees from the school, stopped and pointed to our left. "I'm going down there. It looks like the place a spring might... Erm..."

"Spring from?" I added with a smile. "I'll go with you. Right now, I don't want any of us to be alone. The rest of you set up camp, out of the sun, and organise lunch. We'll be back in a minute."

Matching our stride, the two of us set off for a defile in the natural roll of the valley's hills. It could be an old quarry, or it could be the location of the river's beginning, carved out of the hillside by time. The trees were old and thick here, the trunks wide and the branches low. Oak made up the majority of the copse. A strong odour crept over us as we followed an animal trail.

"What is that smell?" Heather wrinkled her nose and covered her mouth. Ghost surged forwards, but I grabbed his harness.

I recognised it. I pulled the dog and Heather back, then took the lead. "Stay here," I ordered. The animal track I followed dipped down a sharp decline that became very dark under the trees. The sound of the battlefield dead reached me, cawing and croaking through the still, stinking air. I covered my mouth and nose, knowing full well what awaited me but needing to check.

In the defile's bottom, in a small rough circle, lay bodies. Lots of bodies. Animal bodies. I almost took a deep breath in relief.

26

I WANTED DESPERATELY TO SUCK in excess air, but with it came the possibility of swallowing a million insects. The still, hot day filled the area around the bodies with a tumble of black flies. Among their swarming clouds squabbled the companions of the dead: crows, magpies and jackdaws. They picked at the bodies and the maggots. So many maggots. The birds fought like pensioners at a jumble sale, elbowing each other for the choicest bits. My stomach heaved. Puking meant breathing, so I battled the impulse.

I squinted, as if it would help the stench, and took a few more steps. Sheep and lambs made up most of the bodies, but I caught sight of red, a fox's pelt, and even a cat's skull with tufts of black. I ought to go down there and find out how they died, but…

"Lorne, get out of there," Heather called from some way back, but closer than she should be. "If they aren't human, that's all that matters."

She had a point. However, they died, it wasn't natural. I made my way back to her, and we retreated until the air cleared. We both sucked greedily at the untainted oxygen.

Heather said, "What the hell was that about?"

"Do you think the river began down there?" I watched Ghost's nose going nineteen to the dozen as he sucked in the unfamiliar scents.

She shrugged. "I doubt it. That pit went down aways. Maybe it was a quarry for the area?"

"I don't think it's deep enough for a modern quarry, but it could be an abandoned one, or one dating back thousands and not hundreds of years. Not like I'm an expert." I looked around us. "Where are we in relationship to the Iron Age hill-fort?"

"We passed below it on the walk up here," she said, pointing to the next hill over. "So this could have belonged to them."

"And be a place to lay their offerings to the god?" I asked.

We'd wandered back to the others.

Ella looked up. "What did you find?"

"Mostly? You don't want to know. Someone has been leaving animal bodies there," I said, grabbing a sandwich offered by Polly.

Heather muttered something like, "How can you do that?" Almost disgusted by my lack of empathy and desire for food. I grinned at her.

Besides, I didn't want the boys dwelling on the dead, so instead I enlisted their help. "We need to find the source of the river, so when we're done here, we hunt. I want teams of two or three and you look for soft ground and abundant greenery. Springs can look different. They babble out of the side of a hill or leak, causing boggy soil. They can rise from underground, being pressured through rocks, then seeping through the mud. We believe the original people would have left offerings for the god here, so we can look for anything of value as well."

"What do we do when we find it?" asked Adam. "We're on someone's land. We can't look for treasure without the landowner's permission."

"I'd like to know the answer to that one," said an unknown voice from behind our position.

The dog leapt up, barking like a maniac. Heather lunged for him and held his collar. I covered the distance between the boys and the stranger with the speed, if not the grace, of a roadrunner. That someone had crept up on us didn't stand me in good stead. I'd let my guard down during a picnic.

You're getting old and lazy.

I had to agree with my snarky bastard. "And you are?" I asked. The sun gave me little but the shape of a man.

He stepped closer, and the shadow resolved itself into a farmer. I made a simple hand gesture to Heather, hand flat and palm down, to show a friendly. She calmed Ghost, who responded well, considering we'd all been caught by surprise. The farmer wore a shirt and jeans despite the weather, with boots and a flat cap. Just like my father used to, regardless of the temperature. For the first time in years, I had a pang of sadness, missing him.

The flat cap came off, and he swiped at the sweat. His forearms looked deeply tanned and his face, the bit not covered by the cap, held the colour of a natural almond. The bit under the cap looked like a peeled almond, the contrast so stark I wanted to laugh. However, I valued my reputation so played it safe and honest. Or as honest as possible.

"I'm sorry, that was rude," I said, noticing the deep wrinkles in his face when I'd questioned his identity. "My name is Lorne Turner. I'm here with some children from Syndercombe Academy." Ella came to my side, the dog collar very clear in her light blue shirt. "This is the Reverend Ella Morgan. We're the appropriate adults helping at the school before these lads go home for the summer. We're looking for the source of the River Tone. I'm sorry if we've strayed onto your land."

Shrewd eyes, the colour of fresh hay, studied me for a moment. "I'm Chris Endicott, and you're right, you're on my land. You know anything about the police down at the reservoir?" The thick accent rolled, the granite of his voice gathering moss on the way.

I nodded. "It's one reason we wanted to spend the day up here, away from the school. The police will use it as a base. It's not good for the boys."

"Them police, what they doing down there?" he asked.

Olly said, "Lorne found bodies in the old church."

Heather hissed, "Shut up."

The old farmer, as square as his tractor, nodded. "Well, that's a surprise. I was thinking I was the only one havin' a problem."

"You mean the animals?" I asked.

"Why don't you join us?" Polly suggested, offering the man a slice of cake. She smiled, and I watched his antagonism slip away. A friendly smile from an attractive woman and a piece of cake can get you a long way in Somerset.

"Well, I don't mind if I do. I don't get much homemade cake these days. The missus has me on a diet. But what she don't know won't hurt." He winked at Polly.

She laughed and allowed him to settle down on the rugs we'd brought. Barny kept well back, understanding his slightly disreputable appearance wouldn't help.

Farmer Endicott bit into the cake and it acted like a magic wand, making him relax. He asked after the boys, all of whom answered politely, and Ella chatted about the weather. I wanted to press for information, but the old souls of Somerset couldn't be rushed, and if you tried, they turned as stubborn as a ram.

When he focused on me, it was all the permission I needed. "You've lost sheep down in that hole." I nodded towards the dead animals.

He hummed in agreement. "It's been a dirty business. One I don't understand. I've contacted the police, because I've lost good livestock down there, but stealing from farmers don't seem so high on their list of things to do. More interested in arresting young lads with a bit of cannabis in their pockets."

I coughed and almost choked on my cake. "So they didn't come out?"

"Do they ever? It's not like some bastard has rustled the sheep, they've just been slaughtered, poor beggars. Lot of money in that stock," he repeated. He stared mournfully at his empty paper plate until Polly offered another slice. "Don't mind if I do, my luvver. You're a wonderful cook."

"Any idea who'd do such a thing?" I asked.

Endicott sighed, sharing a small piece of cake with Ghost. "To be honest, I can't imagine, not like sheep do any harm to folk. I mean, first you gots to catch the bugger, then either haul her up here, dead or alive, which ain't easy either way, and wherever you kills her, moving her here is damn near impossible. After losing the first one, I brought my sheep closer to the farm, but me and the dogs have no idea who's taken 'em."

"Why would they dump the bodies here and not leave them in the field?" I asked.

Off came the cap, and he scratched his head, the hair suspiciously dark for the age marked by the lines on his face. "Well, that depends on who you talk to, I guess. There's them in the village who think the spirits of old Syndercombe have grown restless and come back to claim the land. Ma'be they be looking for the treasure in these hills." He spoke as if to a large audience and the boys lapped it up. "Some others say it's an old god risin' in protest at the flooded valley—"

"Is that a common story here?" Ella asked.

Endicott breathed in hard through his nose, making a faint whistle in the still air. "Well, Vicar, I knows it sounds daft, but it's a story from my grandmother. We've been farming this land for five generations—though I reckon I'll be the last Endicott hereabouts. My boys have families in the town and don't have farmin' in their blood."

If I had hair, I'd be pulling it out. I needed far more patience than a saint to prise intel from men like this. They always love to talk, but never about the subject you want or need.

Ella, though, she had a gift for digging through people's endless narratives without resorting to threats and violence. "So, Mr Endicott, what did your grandmother tell you about old gods?"

"You sure you want to know, Vicar?" He nodded at her throat.

She laughed and touched the collar. "It always pays to know the local deities, even when you only really believe in the Big One."

He seemed to like that answer and nodded. "Well, my old nan, she never left the Brendon Hills her whole life, and she knew the old stories just like her nan used to tell 'em. Us Endicotts we goes back a long way in the area. See, the old river, The Tone, that begins on our land, which is why they built the reservoir here. It was said, when you ploughed too close to the spring, you'd dig up the bones of those sacrificed to the old king of the river. I will admit to finding old coins, beads and other bits I'll give to the museum one day."

I had to bite my mouth to keep from demanding a location. It would be far better to keep him talking to Ella and Polly. We finally had proof of there being a treasure.

Polly appeared suitably intrigued. "What does this old king do?"

Endicott took a biscuit and chewed for a moment. Christ, he'd die of diabetes before I had my location out of him.

He said, "Well, that's the thing. An offering or two often pacified the old king at harvest time. The local priest would turn a blind eye to the practice. If the old king didn't get his offering, then the spring grass wouldn't grow, the crops would fail, and the lambs and calves would be stillborn. So, generation after generation of my people would come and leave a little offering of food and cider during the harvest festival."

"But you don't do it now?" Ella asked.

He snorted. "Why would I waste good cider on a myth, Vicar? It's one thing with wine in the Holy Communion but quite another to leave it out for the ants to get pissed, if you don't mind the language."

Heather looked at me and we both understood. Endicott wasn't giving anything to the old god. The church in Syndercombe had lain abandoned, and the valley flooded, so his water couldn't flow any longer. The ghost of Turstin didn't stand a chance against all that negative energy.

"Where would your grandmother have left her gifts?" asked Ella. "It's green here, but we haven't come across the spring for the river's source."

Endicott shook his head. "The source moved this last twelve months. We've been too dry for too long. This is the place the river used to start."

We all looked at the blankets we sat on as if we had x-ray vision able to see the caverns of a god beneath us. At least that's what tripped through my head.

"So where is it now?" Ella asked.

Endicott pointed back the way we'd come. "It's coming up from between the roots of an old ash and an oak. So far neither of the trees is diseased so they're healthy enough, but the little spring there, it's not what it once was from here. I remember it being good and strong in my youth."

Heather muttered, "Maybe leave some cider out this year if you want it back."

The farmer didn't hear her, being more interested in making Polly laugh.

I turned to Heather. "We need to find this place."

"Isn't it more important to find the goods left here for him? Maybe dig them up and take them down there so he has his treasure back?"

"He's not a dragon with a horde," I said.

Heather looked a little exasperated with me. "I know that, but he's been disturbed by all the changes, and they've fuelled his power by making him angry. Maybe taking his prizes back to him will make him happy?"

"Let's find the place and see what it feels like first," I said.

Endicott turned his attention away from Polly for a moment and said, "Cause, there was them men poking about some months back. I chased them off my land."

Heather and I exchanged glances. I asked, "What men? And when?"

The farmer scratched his head for a bit, considering. He nodded and finally said, "Well, I reckon it was about that time the poor young lad drowned."

The boys from the school grew silent and solemn. I noticed poor Mason wipe a stray tear from his cheek, then checked to make sure his comrades didn't notice. I wished I could spare them this, but I needed more information.

"Mr Endicott, can you tell us everything you know about the men?"

He nodded, picking up on the emotional quagmire he'd stumbled into. "I'll share with you what I knows, but I reckon I'll need to talk to the police as well. It all started in the pub. I was up at Raleghs Cross Inn, and it was the end of lambing for me, more or less, so I takes myself off for a drink. One of them school teachers was in there, giving large about his army days to some lads from Off. Then he starts on about some lads from the school looking for treasure from the Celtic people hereabouts."

I watched Polly's expression change from affable to sorrowful.

Endicott sighed. "I tried to say it was all nonsense. I don't want people buggering about on my land, leaving gates open, straying off footpaths and damaging themselves or my property. They laughed at me like I was a relic meself. That's why I remembers it. Made me feel embarrassed, if truth be told. Bloody grockles."

Ella said, "People like that make all of us feel bad, whatever we do, say or wherever we're from."

"I guess so, Vicar. Anyway. A few days later I finds them poking about. I tells 'em to bugger off and they do but that day I also finds a boy wandering about. I guess he's from the school, so I tells him to go home. I'm nicer about that one." He gave Polly a limp smile. "A week later I finds evidence of digging around here. Then another week after that, the boy is dead. That's when the sheep start turning up in that pit. I have to say, I was more worried about that than some treasure hunting."

"So that was the end of February?" I asked.

"Reckon it must have been. There's no treasure on my land. We'd have found it. What happened to that boy damn near broke my heart. I just..." His eyes grew dark with regret. "I hope those men didn't hurt that lad. I should have gone to the police sooner."

Ella placed a hand on his. "I doubt there was anything anyone could do."

I wished I agreed with her.

2 7

ACHIEVING THE GOAL, THAT OF finding the spring for the river, proved more time-consuming than I liked. Endicott wanted to postulate every thought he'd had regarding the murder of his sheep. I feared I knew who was responsible, but the kids kept their mouths shut and so did we. Removing Damien from the equation had to be the best option for the moment. I now worried about whether he'd murdered these two men. It all seemed a bit of a coincidence.

When Endicott's phone rang and he received a summons from the farmhouse, he left us with permission to nose about on his land as much as we liked. The night before, the food and the heat of the day sucked the boys dry of excess energy. To be honest, it didn't do much for me either, but I had to tough it out. We left them in the shade of trees, the plan being Polly would remain, while the rest of us went in search of a god's beginning.

Backtracking down the riverbed, we found a couple of locations with an oak and an ash near to each other, but none felt right. Not until Barny, who walked ahead, called out, "I think I have it."

Heather, Ella and I approached. Ghost hung back, tail and ears at half-mast. The trees grew stumpy, but their trunks spoke of age. Branches swept low and had a strange twistiness to them, unusual in both species. The roots, many of them exposed, wrapped around large rocks and entwined with each other, but whether locked in battle, or a lover's embrace, I couldn't tell. Little groves like this remained common on the moor but rarer out here away from the National Park. Here the land was kinder and easier to farm, so these tiny pieces of old woodland had become vanishingly small.

In the heat of midday, the air contained a softness unusual during this dry year. The smell of damp and natural decay revitalised me.

"It certainly feels special," Ella whispered as if in a church, which was odd because she was never that quiet in her own church.

"You sure you want to be here?" Heather asked, just as quietly.

"I'd rather be at home, but..." Ella smiled. "This is more than a bit intriguing."

"I keep expecting adders and badgers to appear, ready to fight. Like Cerberus guarding the gates of Hades," I muttered.

Barny said, "It should be wolves and bears, but you're right, adders and badgers are as bad as it gets these days. Unless you count the escaped mink."

"Let's try to focus on why we're here," Heather said. She approached the trees and the dark, damp ground surrounding their tough, woody toes. Kneeling in the muddy, loamy soil, she peered into a crevice. Twisting towards us, she said, "It's here. There's water coming up."

"Can you back away from there?" I asked, the tension in my voice putting Ghost on alert. Visions of some gnarled and twisting hands reaching out through the hole in the rocks to grab Heather and take her down into the subterranean world of goblins and orcs plagued me.

You've been spending way too much time thinking about the supernatural.

I had to agree with that snarky voice.

Heather did as I asked, though, without argument. Maybe it was our imaginations, maybe the sensations were real, but the air seemed to thicken, become moister, and that scent from the school clogged our throats. My scalp prickled as if those black feathers being dragged over my skin had tiny razorblades in them.

Barny and Ella backed away.

He said, "Maybe this isn't such a good idea. I thought we'd do a bit of meditation and see some things, but this feels wrong."

I agreed. It felt wrong. I'd assumed, rather arrogantly, that the old god would want help, would want to resolve the problems he faced, but that's what I wanted. In my ignorance, I'd planned this to be a simple exchange. We'd offer gifts, the old god would go to sleep. Turstin could be contacted again. We'd convince him no one needed to guard the god and done, job completed. I could go home to the farm and make sure Heather took the website down, so we'd never have to do this again.

The smell became stronger and the air unbreathable.

"Get back," I ordered, my eyes watering. It was worse than the dead sheep further up the old riverbed.

Ghost tugged on his lead, trying to pull Heather away, tail firmly between his legs.

"Shit, I can't hold him," she cried out.

"Let him go, he won't stray."

She dropped his lead, and the dog raced off back towards the children.

Ella prayed.

I touched her arm, and she opened her eyes. "Don't. Not here. This isn't a place for your God. Not yet." The light in the small grove shifted as the wind picked up, clearing the smell a little. A small shard of arrow-sharp sun hit the ground and winked on something.

A shiver passed over me. Unable to resist the spark of brightness, like a magpie to a gem, I found myself drawn to the roots of the old trees. My fingers twitched in anticipation of contact.

"Lorne?" Heather called.

"Just watch my back," I said, kneeling and reaching for the glinting... Was that metal?

My hands removed the damp soil around the shard of metal. The more I removed, the more it became clear I'd found something special. "It's a sword," I said in shock. "How the hell has it survived the river all these years?"

"Lorne, don't touch it," Heather called out, and I heard her approach. "You don't know—"

The world around me vanished.

A KALEIDOSCOPE OF IMAGES FLOODED my mind. Sharp, bright flashes of realities I didn't recognise. I tried to scream. To stop the terrible sensation of tumbling, as I crashed through the shards of flashing pictures.

It felt like falling inside endless mirrors as they shattered, each holding a distinct memory of the same location.

I tried to scream for Ahmar's help, but wherever I was, allowed no such comfort. The rolling, crashing, tumble terrified me, and I knew I held in my hand, somewhere far beyond this place, Turstin's sword. Was I about to replace him?

The thought sent deep tremors of shock through me, and controlling this madness became my mission objective. Closing my eyes against the terrible descent, I summoned the white and blue bubble I'd spent a long time developing like a suit of armour. Then I visualised my home in Stoke Pero. The place I felt safest. After that, I formed the solid image of my family. Heather, Ella and Ghost.

The sensation of falling slowed, and I worked on standing in my kitchen, back to the old range as I warmed my bones. The falling stopped. I sucked in a breath at last and opened my eyes.

I stood in the riverbed, but this time the world around me looked very different. The colours muted because the trees grew thick and strong. The woodland reached a long way into the distance. Water coursed over my feet, rising halfway up my shin. The air smelt rich and clean. Bushes rustled to my left, and I turned, ready to fight. A stag, crowned with a huge rack of antlers, walked to the riverbank, lowered his head and drank. I didn't move. When he'd taken his fill, that enormous head turned towards me, and liquid brown eyes studied me for a long time. He sniffed the air, the broad nose dark and shining. With a snort, he turned back, dismissing me, and with great delicacy, he stepped through the water and up the other side.

He'd known I was present, but didn't see me as a threat. Why?

"Lorne?" called a familiar voice.

I breathed out in a puff of air, bent my knees and put my hands on them. Relief surging through me so strongly I felt dizzy for a moment.

"I'm here, Ahmar."

More rustling, a little cursing in that ancient tongue, and my djinn came out from among the trees dressed in his robes. He didn't move as elegantly as the stag, and he lacked his usual desert grace as he yanked on his clothes to free them from a dog rose tangled around a beech's trunk.

"Muddy, foul place," he muttered, stepping into the riverbed but avoiding the water. He looked at me for the first time. "Get out of the stream before you catch a cold."

"Yes, Mother," I replied, but did as I was told. Ahmar's presence made me feel safer. I sloshed towards him.

Looking around, he muttered something, and I realised he appeared more than a little dishevelled. "Are you okay?" I asked.

He pulled his attention back to me. "No, I am not. Why can you not leave well enough alone? I am stuck here for who knows how long, because I am trying to help you."

"Erm…?"

Ahmar snorted. "Useless, you are useless. You understand nothing." He waved a hand at me in irritation and moved away. Picking a rock, he sat. "Damnable muddy country," he cursed, trying to wipe dirt off his robes. "I should make you return to the desert."

"No," I said. "I'm never going to the desert. Not until I figure out how to get you home without me being stuck in a lunatic asylum." We glared at each other for a moment before I broke the stand-off. "If you've been here a while, maybe you can tell me what the hell is going on?"

Ahmar's shoulders slumped. I'd never seen him look defeated. His dark eyes stared at the water rushing past us. "I fear for our future, brother."

"Why?" Apprehension filled me.

"Because I think we have made a mistake and I do not know how to solve it." He turned on his stone to study me and I sat on the ground so I didn't stand over him.

"What have we done?" I asked.

"We are one, for the moment. You know this. I reside in you, and you can use my gifts to your advantage in battle. My strength is yours when you learn to harness it correctly, rather than just grab at it in panic. My knowledge, a little of my magic, it is yours to do with as you wish. I am..." He closed his eyes for a moment and when they opened, I saw such sadness in their darkness, my eyes filled with tears of sympathy.

I whispered, "You are my slave."

He bowed his head in acknowledgement.

"You know I don't see you as such, right? And if I could find a way of freeing you, I would," I rushed to say as some form of compensation.

He reached out and patted my knee. "I know you think so."

"I don't think, Ahmar. I know. Whatever gifts your presence gives to me, they are yours to give, not mine to command," I said, willing him to understand.

Ahmar chuckled. "As if you could command them."

I smiled. "Yeah, well, I need to do more reading about djinn, I guess."

His eyes softened. "Let us speak of our current predicament. I would not want to leave you stuck in this place. It is very dangerous, even for you."

"Where are we?" I asked.

"From what I can tell," Ahmar said, "it is around the time your tribes invaded the Holy Land with their swords and God."

I translated. "You mean the First Crusade?"

"As you say," Ahmar replied with that familiar tilt to his head.

I tried to grapple with the knowledge we'd become stuck somewhere at the end of the eleventh century. Normans owned England, spoke French, and didn't like the locals much. I should have read more books. I didn't know enough about England after the Battle of Hastings.

Just don't panic, fella. Just don't panic. Heather's not here if you trip out and have an episode.

Yeah, okay, no panicking. I needed answers and I wouldn't get them if I had a meltdown.

First things had to go first. Like milk before cream before cheese. "Why?"

The djinn's attention remained on the water. "I think your paladin wants you here to stop his demons from escaping."

"It's a god, not a demon."

"To a good Christian, they are the same thing, are they not?"

To a Christian of the eleventh century, they most certainly would be the same thing if that person didn't understand the local dynamics. The living version of Turstin fitz Rolf couldn't speak the local language. I knew that from Heather. The locals here, who would likely be the same families that occupied the Iron Age hill-fort, would have kept the old god happy even as Christians. They certainly wouldn't have seen him as a demon.

"They would be the same to the knight," I agreed.

"I have been here, trapped in this place, since I thought it a good idea to help you fight a god." Then he muttered more to himself, "Much good it has done me." He didn't sound happy.

"I didn't know," I said.

Ahmar shrugged. "It is not all your fault. Not this time. I did not understand the significance of the spirit and the power of his call. This place, this reality, is just underneath yours. The land holds the memory of this time in its stones and gives the knight great strength. When you found his blade, it summoned you here. He will know it and he will come. He left it for you. I tried to warn you, but…" He shrugged.

"Do we kill him?" I asked in alarm. I didn't have any weapons on me. Would I need to visualise a firearm? I wasn't taking on a well-trained medieval warrior with a sword.

Ahmar gave me his best flat stare. "Always with the killing. No, Lorne, we do not need to kill this man. We need to negotiate."

"What are we negotiating for?" I asked.

"Our continued existence in your time," he said. "Turstin wants you dead so he can trap your spirit in this place. He does not know what I am, but I doubt he will be pleased to see me. If you die while he wants you, I will be stuck here for all eternity along with you. It is not a fate I am interested in enduring."

Ahmar looked like a Muslim, sounded like a Muslim and would be classed as a Saracen regardless of what truth we might try to impart. If Ahmar did anything djinn-like we'd be branded as sorcerers and killed, or demons and killed. The Normans liked to kill anything they didn't understand. Or that was my take home from films, books and, of course, my walking encyclopaedia, Heather.

"Is he here with an army at his back?" I asked.

"Not as far as I can tell. He seems to exist in this place alone. Reliving the days leading up to his self-imposed sacrifice. I have seen these days replaying. The death of the peasants in the church is an echo of his memory."

I'd forgotten about that. The vision Mrs Langford had in the church as a twelve-year-old during the flooding of the valley.

Ahmar said, "From what I have witnessed, Turstin finds the dead in the church. He is not the killer. He discovers that someone from the community is killing because the old god is angry and wants his libations. Of course, Turstin had put a stop to the community giving succour to the god. After much prayer, Turstin, who knows he is dying from some malady, comes to this place, believing it to be the location of the god's power, and kills himself while in prayer. By summoning your living spirit and, therefore me, I suspect he thinks he can pin you here and bring himself the freedom he craves."

"Can we banish the god? Send him to sleep? Cut him off from his power and leave him inert?" I asked.

"Can you think of a less destructive option?" Ahmar countered with more heat than I expected.

"What's that mean?" I asked.

"The old god protects this land, makes it fruitful and rich. All he asks in return is a little something to say thank you as a sign of respect. Perhaps we can convince Turstin to do that rather than kill himself?"

I thought about the old knight reliving this day on an endless loop for a thousand years. No wonder he wanted to be replaced. He'd earned his rest. Spent his time in purgatory.

A shape appeared downstream in the distance. Turstin, lumbering up the valley. He wore a long mail shirt, a conical helmet, greaves, and armoured gloves. At his waist hung a sword, a dagger and a purse. He was not a young man, and I saw the pain in each step.

I glanced at Ahmar. "What do I do?"

"Not die," he said. "And I should not be here."

"Can't we just go home?" I asked.

Ahmar shrugged. "If you can figure it out, make certain you take me with you." He turned and vanished into the shadowed woodland.

Turstin stopped moving the moment he saw me. I held up my hands in a gesture of peace. Even a thousand years ago that had to mean the same thing, right?

"I want to talk," I said. Medieval French wasn't on the curriculum at my local comprehensive school. "I want to help you."

A voice, as dark as when he'd spoken in the school, rolled around the small grove. "You shall serve as guardian in this place. You must be sacrificed. The demon here is killing once more."

"We can find another way. There is always a way to find peace." Ironic coming from me. I'd killed more people than this medieval warrior, I had no doubt about that. Swords against assault rifles? My body count was far worse. Maybe I deserved this fate?

"A demon cannot be bargained with," Turstin decided. "Die here with honour. If you run, I will find you. There is no escape, only delay. Choose honour over fear."

He drew his sword. The savage blade caught the light, and I stepped back into the water. No way on this earth could I fight a trained swordsman. I willed my SIG Sauer to appear in my hand, full of nice shiny NATO rounds that would turn his armour into butter and make mince out of his insides.

Whatever foul conjuring this was, Turstin controlled it because I remained unarmed as he rushed towards me. How do you punch a man in armour? All I could do was hope he stumbled, fell and I might be able to drown him. I had a vague notion of ducking under the sword and going for a takedown or disarm, but my instincts recognised another highly skilled soldier. I'd be dead in seconds.

My inner beast rose, assessed our predicament, and sat. Unable to find the battle knowledge necessary for a fight. He wanted to run. I turned to do just that, when my foot caught against a rock, and I was the one to hit the ground.

28

THE SWORDSMAN RUSHED FORWARDS, A battle cry echoing around the trees. I struggled to turn, rise, run, but failed. His sword rose over his head, the rough, sharp edge vivid and clear. I saw Ahmar run from the woodland with a branch, just as Heather had done when Damien tried to drown me.

You're going soft, mucker. You should have killed him. Laid an ambush. Peace is for the weak.

I lifted my hands in the hope I'd make him realise I meant no harm. This time, I didn't argue with my inner cynic. He had it right. My peaceful life was making me weak. My ruthless edge was being dulled by domestic bliss. I did not want to fight.

The gleam in the eye of a man used to slaughter, where there is no fear of death, only victory, is not one to witness when you're on the wrong end. Turstin fitz Rolf wanted me dead, and he had no reason to hesitate.

I knew Ahmar wouldn't reach me in time. Trapping the djinn here shamed me, but untangling us would be impossible.

The sword came down, swallowing the remaining light in the grove. I gazed into the eyes of a man who saw his freedom after a thousand years. I felt…

Agony.

The blade hadn't reached me but a pain so blinding and hard made me scream at Ahmar for help. He lunged for me, dropping the branch and wrapping himself around my torso.

MY EYES FLEW OPEN, AND I screamed again.

"He's awake," Ella yelled, smacking at someone.

I sucked in a breath to bellow when the pain relaxed and subsided to a murmur. "What's happening?" I cried out, arching in pain.

Ella held my face. "Probably best you don't look."

I frowned. "Heather?"

"I'm right here, love. Ella's got you. Just let me clean you up. Barny, I need the glue, yes, that's the one." Heather spoke, but I couldn't see her with the angle Ella held my head. Something on my left flank stung like a bitch and I tried to twist away again. That's when I noticed a heavy weight on my legs.

"What's happening?" I repeated.

Ella's hazel eyes looked soft and full of worry. "You were lost. We couldn't get you back. Barny said… I'm so sorry, Lorne. We needed to hurt you enough to call you back. I'm so sorry."

The pieces fell into place. I gripped her small wrists and managed a weak smile. "It's okay. It's okay. I get it. Heather's putting me together?"

She nodded.

"Good. I've been wanting her to practice some field surgery."

Ella chuckled, and a tear slid down her cheek. "It was terrible. We had to find a bit of you that wasn't damaged, so we knew the nerves would work properly."

"Done," Heather said. "You can let go, everyone."

The weight shifted off my legs and I saw Polly stand up. "First time I've ever had to sit on a man to keep him still." She winked at me and laughed, though she looked strained.

I sat up with Ella's help. We'd returned to the boys, who sat a little distance away, watching proceedings with fascination. The sun now sat lower in the sky. I'd been gone for over an hour. No wonder they'd freaked out.

Barny backed off, out of arm's reach. "Sorry, man. I couldn't think of anything else. It can help when someone is on a bad trip. Give them a pinch and it'll bring them back for a bit. You were so far gone, I knew it'd need more than a pinch."

"You just saved my life, Barny. Turstin had me."

Heather sat on the grass, her hands covered in what I assumed to be my blood.

"Hey, kid, you okay?" I asked her, trying to reach her but flinching at the pain in my side.

She made an odd keening sound and held out her hands. I'd never seen Macbeth, but I imagined the scene of the handwashing might look a bit like this.

"Heather," I said, finally making it to my knees in front of her. "Heather, it's okay. I'm okay." My side throbbed, but I'd known far worse. "Did you cut me?" I asked her.

A nod from a sweaty, tear-stained head.

"You did good. You did very good. Look at me." Her eyes shifted away from her hands to my face, and I smiled. "I'm here. I'm in one piece and you saved Ahmar. You and Barny and the others."

"I cut you and stuck my fingers inside so it would really hurt," she whispered, horrified by her actions.

I chuckled. "It hurt. It really hurt. You're brave and amazing." I still shook from the aftereffects.

She threw herself into my arms and I rocked back, my side a blaze of pain, but I bit back the *ouch* and took it like a man.

Heather trembled in my arms but otherwise she seemed alright.

"It's been a bit of a day," I whispered into her hair.

"Yeah, boss. It's been a bit of a day."

I released her and pushed the wet hair off her face. "You did really well."

"I never want to do that again," she said.

"I don't blame you." Then I confessed, "I failed. I fixed nothing."

"Then it's not a failure, it's a way that doesn't work," she said, using one of my favourite sayings to encourage new recruits.

Adam said, "We have his sword, and while you guys were away, we found some other stuff up here. There's a bit of a hoard. There's some kind of necklace, but we left it in the mud like they do on the TV, and some pottery, maybe what looks like a dagger. We found the treasure!" He grinned, as did the others. Then he stared at them. "We'll have to tell Mr Endicott."

Olly piped up, "Then you lot came back, and it all got weird again."

I felt for the boys having to witness adults losing their connection with reality. "Well done, boys. We'll tell Mr Endicott, but let's not steal the old god's prizes just yet. Remember what happened when Bilbo stole Gollum's ring?"

That set the boys off on chattering about films, TV and eventually the books. I tuned them out.

It gave me an idea, though. "Show me the sword," I said to Barny.

He brought it over to me. "It was wrapped in waxed leather, but how it's remained whole, I don't know. In this damp soil it should have corroded."

"Maybe it hasn't always been there," I said. "Damien might have moved it, or something preserved it. Those questions are impossible to answer. We have it, and I think I know what to do with it."

"What?" Ella asked. "And what happened to you?"

I waved the question away. "I'll explain it later. Right now, we need to think about the spiritual elements tugging at each other. Imagine this is the ring of power." I held the sword up. It was heavy and dull with age. "And the Hobbits have to throw it in the Eye of Sauron, or whatever they do." I only had the vaguest memory of watching the films during downtime in Afghanistan. I'd never read the books.

"They do it to stop Sauron from having the power of the ring," Heather said.

"What if we destroy the sword? Would that sever the connection Turstin has to this place?"

"Maybe," Ella said. "But then what? The old god runs riot through the reservoir? Makes more people turn into murderers?"

I flinched, knowing she referred to Damien.

Polly said, "Then we find a way to pacify the god."

"Prayer might banish him," Ella said.

I doubted it would go down well, but it needed to be said, "Prayer has annoyed him. I think a thousand years of prayer in Syndercombe might have driven him out, along with Turstin's sacrifice, but it hasn't. We need other options."

"It's a big thing to break a warrior's sword," Heather said. "This is a Norman sword in almost mint condition. It has to be worth a small fortune. Not to mention its historical value, which is immeasurable."

Frustration made me snippy. "Well, what do you suggest? We tried talking, and it nearly got me killed."

"Direct communication with the god," Heather said. "We have to find and trap Damien."

The air seemed to be sucked out of me at the thought. I shook my head. "I don't think that's possible. He has my training, but he's already proved he's willing to kill when I'm not. He has the advantage. It's like being a NATO soldier and having to play by the rules of engagement, rather than being the enemy that has no such control. I'm fairly sure I can't take him alive."

Heather and Ella both stared at me in surprise.

"You're giving up?" Ella asked. "With all your experience, you're just giving up? Damien's a man. He might have a god trying to control him, but he's flesh and blood like you. Also, he's alone. You have us." She poked me in the chest.

Her words made me soften and feel a measure of gratitude I'd missed over the last few days. My family stood with me.

"Alright, we'll come up with a plan. Right now, we need to get the boys back to the school. I don't want any of them here when night comes," I said.

Noise erupted from all sides. The boys protesting loudly about their right to remain. Polly explaining her responsibility to the children and that they couldn't make any parents available. I held my hands up for peace and when that didn't work, I whistled hard. The shriek silenced all opposition to my plans.

"Just listen for a minute," I said. "I know you want to stay, and I know you think this will follow you into the world outside Syndercombe. Maybe you're right. The point is, we don't want another night like last night. You're all exhausted, we're all running on fumes. It's important we don't make mistakes when we're this tired. My job is to make sure you're safe. Damien's MIA, therefore, Polly is solely responsible for your wellbeing. That's not fair to her, not under these circumstances."

All eyes fell on Polly, and I didn't miss the soft threat of tears.

"I'll call Kate and she can action your removal from the school. Then she can contact next of kin. You cannot remain in the school after nightfall." I continued, "I think it's important we do the right thing and..." I sighed, feeling like an idiot. "I shouldn't have taken you from Kate's care in the first place. You shouldn't be here. Before the sun sinks too low and the night gives the old god and this Norman knight more power, we get as many of you out as possible. Polly as well. You're all vulnerable to Damien. Barny almost died last night. Heather's been affected and so have I, which means you all need to be gone from this place."

Olly and Killian looked stricken, but little Mason visibly relaxed. Robert studied Adam's profile, trying to guess what his mentor might decide. Adam looked over at the younger students and I watched the decision settle on his youthful face.

"You're right, Lorne," he said. "We need to leave this place. I don't want to lose any of them, and we can stay together until this is over. I'll make sure we aren't separated. We can stay in a hotel nearby. I'm sure we can scrape together some money for a night or so and Polly can be our official guardian."

I sighed in relief. "Good, thank you, Adam. You've made the best decision possible. We'll sort it out."

"Mr Medway left me with a credit card for the food shopping," Polly said. "We can use that for a few days."

Ella smiled. "Right, we have the start of a plan. Let's begin the walk back to the school and set it in motion."

We packed up the picnic and I strapped the carefully wrapped sword to my daysack. It gave me an odd feeling, not because of anything supernatural in the old weapon, but rather what it represented. Warriors had carried a weapon like this one for centuries. The wars changing as the weapons changed, as they became more powerful. Even after the creation of firearms, men still killed each other with a blade, close up and personal. There's a profound difference when a soldier holds a sword over a gun. Something complex, personal, a slippery series of emotions I didn't really understand. When all this ended, I'd need to think about it some more. Maybe I'd take a few lessons in the use of a sword, and try to understand.

The walk back, in the heat of the afternoon, made the boys quiet, and I watched their exhaustion grow now their adventure was ending.

Heather and Ghost walked with them, Ella with Polly and Barny remained quiet beside me.

"Are you alright?" I asked him after we'd left the riverbed and re-entered the woodland surrounding the reservoir.

Barny's eyes strayed to his sister's back, something I'd watched happen with surprising regularity. He shrugged and said, "Not sure, to be honest."

"Want to talk about it?" I asked.

Yeah, because you really want to know what the mad hippie thinks...

There were times I wanted to strangle my inner cynic for being a pain in my backside and making me face the truth.

"If Heather hadn't brought you back, you'd have died in another realm of reality," he said. "That's big—I mean, like life changing big."

I considered what had happened from his point of view. Short of being mugged, I doubted Barny's life had ever been in real danger. He didn't strike me as the sort of person to put himself in harm's way for someone else. In fact, considering the sacrifices his sister had made to saving lives over the last eighteen months, she must be a titan in comparison.

"Stuff happens, we deal with it," I said. "I've no wish to see the world a medieval knight endlessly repeats. I've no wish to talk to some vengeful spirit or river god. Before I joined the army, I heard the dead whispering. Sometimes I saw them, then years of using some odd instinct I was born with, in war zones, honed it to the point I notice things others miss. When I was in

Syria the last time, something terrible happened to my unit and I almost died. The battle with ISIS woke a djinn." I looked at him to check he understood. Barny's expression made it clear he did. "That djinn lives inside me and enhances whatever gifts I was born with. It's a complicated relationship we're still trying to work out. He likes Heather, though, and he's given me the strength to save her more than once."

Barny's astonishment made me chuckle.

"Yeah," I said. "I know. I sound certifiable."

"Wow, that's amazing."

"It's important you know these things if you're going to be a part of Heather's life. We protect each other. She's there when I have flashbacks so bad all I can see is a hail of bullets. I protect her when people try to take advantage. We're a unit. I teach her to fight. She teaches me to understand peace."

He nodded. "I can respect that, but if you came to find me to warn me about our father, then he knows where to find her, and that's going to be difficult to handle."

I gazed at the path we followed. The well-worn track was far easier to navigate than the traitorous one provided for by a bad family. "I can handle your father."

Barny shook his head. "I know you can bury him somewhere no one will ever find him—"

I laughed and fought the urge to nod.

"But," Barny continued, "control is not always about the body and obeying is a harder habit to break than heroin. I should know. I've done both."

Considering this for a bit, I said, "Then it is coercive control?" I didn't feel right talking about this without Heather, but trying to prise this information out of her felt like pulling teeth from a tiger without a sedative.

Barny nodded. "Yeah, and it's deep. I don't think he ever sexually assaulted her, but…"

I felt him glance at me, and whatever he saw in my face made his voice fade.

"Sorry, man. I shouldn't have said anything. I don't know for sure."

"But you suspect?" I growled. The ache in my right hand for my sidearm grew so powerful I had to close my fist.

Barny shrugged. "I honestly don't know."

Heather must have picked up on something because she looked over her shoulder to check on us and frowned. I battled to clear my murderous thoughts and smile. It worked. She relaxed and turned back to the chattering kids.

"Listen, Lorne, I'd love to send you to his house, and have you drag the truth out of him, then leave his body in a field full of hungry pigs, but we need to be cleverer than that."

I looked at him in astonishment. "A field of hungry pigs? You've been thinking about this for a while, then?"

His expression turned sheepish. "Maybe. Since I was about seven, I've been trying to figure out how to rid myself of him."

That statement cooled my heels a little. If Heather's father could manipulate those around him, then the son would have picked up on a fair few tricks. He'd know which of my buttons to push to make me act. If he wanted the father gone, using me to do it would suit him very well. Just as Barny's life had never been seriously threatened, he'd never held a knife to someone else's throat. I needed to tread carefully.

"I'll talk to Heather when this is over," I said.

"She might not—"

"I'll talk to Heather." The statement made it very clear we wouldn't be talking about this again without her consent.

The journey back to the school now took us close to the fishing lodge and a burly police officer stood on the path.

2 9

THE UNIFORMED MAN TOOK SOME convincing and a phone call to Kate, but eventually he gave us permission to use the track that took us back to the school. We all wanted to know how many bodies they'd found. Who the victims might be and, sadly, who put them in the old church. However, we had five young people to protect. Besides, this time the police could deal with the dead. My job was the creature that made all this happen.

When we rounded a corner in the path, Kate's tall shadow separated from a tree and came striding towards us.

"Have you finished with all your spooky nonsense?" she snapped out. "I have statements to take and questions for you to answer." She stared hard at me. Whoever took a dump on her plate made her want to shit on mine.

My hackles rose and with them my beast. She wanted a knock down fight? I'd give them a bloody war.

A hand covered my wrist, and the beast looked down.

Ella stared at me with a calm resolution. "Lorne, leave this with me." She turned to Kate. "The children have been out all day. They are hot and tired. We need to get them safely back to the school. Then I suggest we pack them up and give them a lift to the nearest hotel or large bed-and-breakfast. After that, we'll answer your questions."

I watched Kate's nostrils flare and Ella's emotional detachment with sadness.

"The statements won't wait," Kate repeated.

Ella sighed. "Unless we're under arrest for something, they can wait. You know perfectly well what's happening here, you just want to deny it. You're angry because you fear whatever you've found in that water. Kate, you are a good person, but you are also blind."

I watched DI Mackenzie's fury rise, but she had nowhere to put it without harming her reputation as a police officer.

"One more thing," Ella said as she ushered the children along the path. "We need to get them out before dusk begins or they'll be trapped here again. I suggest you get all your police officers away from here as well."

"What will you be doing?" Kate snapped out.

"Spooky nonsense," Ella said, turning her back.

I moved with her. Heather glanced at me, worry clear.

"Don't say anything. I'll cry," Ella said. "This was always going to happen. It always does. She is too much the atheist and last night scared her in a way she just wants to forget."

"I'm sorry," I murmured, with a slight pat on her shoulder. A primed bear trap had less tension in it.

Ella managed a nod. Heather, far better at reading people than I would ever be, slipped her hand into Ella's and squeezed. They walked together hand in hand. I realised how privileged I was with Heather choosing me and believing in the weird life I now lived.

The walk back to the school turned into a sombre affair. We saw divers coming up from the water, like black headed seals, carrying sacks, but the heavy black bags used for bodies were long gone. The people in black rubber handed the sacks off to people in white protective suits, while the sun bore down, and the water sparkled. I doubted we'd find out who the bodies had been, as Kate was hardly in the mood to share. I recognised some faces of the police officers, but none of them wished to be caught talking to us by their superiors.

Making our slow way back to the school, we entered the kitchen by the back door to the kitchen.

"Bloody bastards," Polly snapped.

Two male police officers started at her explosion. I didn't blame her. The clean surfaces and floor we'd left that morning now drowned under a layer of detritus from tea, coffee, and the remains of food. I opted to wait outside while Polly took the men to task, and some hasty cleaning ensued.

Heather sat beside me. "You okay, boss?" She ruffled Ghost's ears.

"It's been a day, kid," I replied.

She bumped my shoulder. "You bonding with my brother?"

I grunted, not entirely sure how much of our conversation I should share.

"There's something you should know about Barny," Heather murmured, checking no one but us remained in earshot. "He's just as capable of manipulation as my father."

Our eyes met. "Are you?" I asked.

She smiled. "I have my moments. But I love a simple life and I don't need to bend others to my will. Besides, being part of The Devil's Mercenaries knocked it out of me." Her smile grew sad. "Just be careful."

I took her hand in mine. Its small size always surprised me because she was so strong. "He said some things that disturbed me."

Heather hugged our hands to her chest. "Tell me. I think we're about to face something very dangerous, and I want to know you and I are still one and the same."

"He told me that your father might have sexually assaulted you," I poured the words out fast, hoping they'd hurt less, like ripping off a plaster.

Heather chuckled. "I've been all kinds of victim to men, Lorne, but not that. My father is a bully. He is cruel and he is controlling. His crimes against me are many and I will never have that man in my life again, but he is only interested in sex with women who he pays to dominate him."

I looked at her with such shock she laughed. "How the hell do you know that?" I asked.

"I saw him once, coming out of a knocking-shop in Exeter. I knew a couple of the girls who worked there, and they gave me far more of the gory details than I asked for. It was funny, though. He keeps my poor mum in this locked cabinet of a house, more like a museum, where he doesn't even touch her unless he has to, but then goes off and gets turned into a puppy, or a pony, or a baby depending on the mood. He's tried them all."

I really, really, didn't want to imagine Heather's father dressed as a pony with a tail sticking out of his…

Shaking my head to clear the image, I whispered in Heather's ear, "So why did Barny lie to me? I had the impression he wants me to go after your father."

Heather murmured, "That's exactly what he wants. My brother has never had to fight for himself, not really. This living in a bus and keeping the local allotment safe from thieves and rabbits is just another game. I'm pretty sure he'll still have a tidy fortune tucked away and when it suits him, then he'll tidy himself up and go back to Daddy." She shrugged. "I might be wrong. He might have really broken free, but I remain to be convinced."

It all made sense. "What do you want me to do?" I asked her.

She kissed my cheek, then left, and I felt her soft lips. "I want you to keep being you, and me to keep being me, and pretend they don't exist. We don't need them in our lives."

"Do you want me to send Barny away?" I knew I'd always be hers to command.

"He could be useful for the moment. Just don't believe him if he's talking about our lives. I'll tell you everything you need to know when we have time and a few beers." She pushed off the low wall we leaned against and wiggled into the space between my thighs.

With her hands on my chest, we stood nose to nose, and I held her hips. I gasped at the surge of love so strong it almost choked me. "How are you mine?" I whispered, close to tears.

She kissed me with tenderness and leaned in to murmur, "Because you love me."

Captivated by the angel in my arms, I hadn't noticed her hand in the pocket of my combat shorts. She drew out the small velvet bag I'd almost forgotten about.

"Is this for me?" she asked, her smile less angel and more demon.

I laughed. "Yes, little magpie, you can have the shiny offering."

She crowed in delight when she emptied the bag into her hand and saw the cuff bracelet. "I love it!"

"If you two have quite finished," Ella said, coming out of the kitchen, "we need to talk."

Heather bounced off to show Ella her shiny prize, and I stared at Ghost. "Seems I've been forgiven." The dog just panted with a serene expression in his amber eyes.

More people had returned from the reservoir and several more police officers occupied the kitchen. I saw the boys in the corner, their space invaded by adults they didn't know or trust.

Kate, or as I should probably call her now, DI Mackenzie, had control over the scene. "Lorne, we'll be shipping you all out. The school governors are being notified, and the place is to be emptied while we deal with what's happening in the reservoir. The water company is sending a team down to help."

"How many bodies have you found?" I asked.

"We will release details to the press when it's deemed appropriate."

Ella gasped. "He's the one to find them."

"Yes, and I will need a statement about exactly what happened to all of you."

"DI Mackenzie," I fought to sound neutral, "can we have a quiet, private word?"

I watched her jaw bounce. She really wanted to deny me, because she knew exactly what we needed to talk about and her need to deny the reality facing us, wanted to fight me.

Ella turned and left the kitchen, unable to deal with the rising tension as I pushed against Kate with all the authority I'd learned to control in twenty years of service. To be fair to Kate, she gave me a good fight.

"Fine," she barked. "We'll use Medway's office." She turned on her heel and walked off.

I gave Heather a quick glance, and she nodded, going to find Ella. They needed to make sure the boys could leave fast with Polly.

Walking into Medway's office, I felt Kate's tension. I went into the cupboard where I'd found the filing cabinet and Medway kept the confiscated items, and retrieved a bottle of scotch I'd stumbled over earlier. I took the water glasses and poured two large slugs. In silence, I offered one to Kate. Her dark eyes glared at me for a moment. Then a switch flipped as she stopped fighting me and I watched her relax.

"Thanks," she said.

"You've had a terrible couple of days and it's on me... again." I knocked back the scotch and tried not to cough.

Kate gave up being the Senior Investigating Officer on site and plopped into a chair. "What the hell is going on?"

I couldn't imagine how she'd manage events from a practical point of view over the coming hours and days. Being an SIO on a case like this could make or break careers.

I sat opposite her and said, "Which version of the truth do you want, Kate?" The panic in her eyes made me nod. "Okay, we'll go for a prosaic version. Someone has been putting bodies in the reservoir."

She drank the scotch and poured another. "We found just the two you saw. Though there's evidence there might have been more in the past. It's a church so they could just be burials that weren't removed dating back centuries. We're in contact with an underwater archaeologist. The men we found had been tied by rope. Initial examination by forensics on the scene makes it look like flax of all things. No one really uses flax in cheap modern rope. It looks like non-commercial methods made it. Both bodies had been tied down, so they don't escape the nave and float away. The cold temperature and lack of a current kept them well preserved, but they've been down there since the spring.

"I had to tell them about Damien Heaney's vanishing act and his attack on Barny last night." She spoke quickly and didn't meet my gaze. "They're bringing in dogs to track him, assuming he's still in the area, and we have armed response on standby because of his past. Did you know he'd been a mercenary in Somalia? We found an international arrest warrant issued by the French, believe it or not. Though it's not under his real name, which is why he didn't flag the system during his DBS check. So, that's what I've been doing while you've been tripping about the woods looking for evil pixies." She threw back another scotch.

Somalia? I pushed it to one side. That his Disclosure and Barring Service came back clear meant something; he'd never done wrong in the UK. "Let's not condemn Damien just yet. Being a mercenary for a short time doesn't make you inherently evil. He's also been an amazing teacher. The kids here love him."

Kate nodded. "Maybe, Lorne, but I have procedure I have to adhere to and he's a dangerous man. My boss wants armed officers to escort the dog handlers as they hunt for him."

I swore. If Damien felt threatened, he'd react. "Can you hold them off?" I asked. "We need to remain in the area, just for tonight. We have a plan. This will not stop if we don't solve it. Damien's more dangerous than most, but he's not the only one this god has influenced."

Her expression sharpened, and she peered at me. "Do you really believe in this stuff? A man of your experience?"

"It's my experience that's taught me to believe, Kate. I can bring Damien in, alive, without risking your people. If you hunt him down with dogs, he'll start killing. Please, give me the night. If I don't have him by morning, then you can go for it, but take your people out of the area tonight. Whether you believe in any of this stuff or not, you know you need to leave."

She searched my eyes, and I held her gaze, willing her to listen, to deny her training and logic, to rely on her instinct.

"Alright, is there anything else we need to discuss?" she asked.

"One thing. You need to talk to a farmer, a Mr Endicott. He owns the land north of this location. He's a good man and can tell you what he knows about treasure hunters in the area. I think there might be a connection to your bodies in the church."

She nodded. "Okay, I'll talk to him. Thanks. Just so you know, I've had the tyres on your vehicles replaced," she mumbled, as if being kind to me hurt her. "I'll pull my people out and I'll make certain we keep the children together and safe. Do whatever it is you do and find me Damien Heaney. Then we're done."

I nodded in agreement. "Thank you, Kate, for the tyres and for the trust. One more thing, if you're going to break Ella's heart, do it fast."

Kate's eyes dropped to the floor, and she swirled whisky around the bottom of her glass. "I respect Ella's work, but I don't respect her faith and belief in the supernatural. She needs a woman who can work with her."

"Yeah, she does."

Kate pointed a long finger at me. "Don't get her hurt tonight."

I smiled. "That woman's pulled my arse out of more than one fire. She has some pretty serious backup when we need it."

"If you say so," Kate said, drinking the last of her glass. "Right, let's get back to it, Turner."

3 0

IT TOOK SEVERAL HOURS AND a lot of hard work on Kate's behalf to convince everyone to get out of the area, but just as I'd begun to wish I still had hair so I could pull it out, the school fell silent. Forcing the children to leave had led to a few tears being shed. I'd shaken Adam's hand, but the others had wanted hugs and promises to take care. It surprised me, how attached I'd become to them in such a short time. I really wanted to be a dad, a proper dad, and do all the dad stuff these guys missed out on because of boarding school.

We'd given them our phone numbers so they could tell us where they'd been taken and that they remained safe. I'd promised to talk to them in the morning. Their little, worried faces when they pulled away in one of the big SUVs made my heart ache. Thank God I'd never had to leave a child behind when I'd been on tour.

Polly had made me promise to find Damien and bring him in safely. It was only what I wanted, so I promised. I'd broken the news about the international arrest warrant, and she'd sighed. "I never love the good ones," she said. "All this was too perfect to last long."

I took her hands. "Don't go back to London, Polly. Don't give up on Damien just yet. We don't know it was him who killed those people."

Polly's dark eyes shone wet, but she held back her tears. She looked beautiful in her distress. "You don't believe that, Lorne. I just hope he didn't kill poor Ryan."

I squeezed her hands, but couldn't meet her gaze. With no evidence but my fear and instinct, I remained silent on the subject. I'd seen Damien kill. I'd seen him do some brutal things to people. To kill a child, though? I didn't believe that. I believed the ghosts of Syndercombe killed poor Ryan by luring him with promises of treasure and secrets. The lad was lonely and vulnerable, scared probably because his parents were divorcing. I needed to make damn sure no one else suffered under their malign influence.

In the silent kitchen I stood with Ella, Heather and Barny. Clapping my hands together and rubbing them, I announced, "Right, time for a plan."

We sat around the table with tea and some sandwiches, made from a fresh loaf Polly left for us in the bread maker.

"Barny's the only one to really see what's in the water," Heather said around her cheese sarnie.

"I was tripping, Heather."

"Doesn't make it less real under the circumstances," she replied.

Barny shuddered. "If that was a manifestation of the god, then I really don't want to meet him."

"We have Turstin fitz Rolf to deal with as well, don't forget," Ella added, picking at crisps.

I'd wolfed my cheese sarnie, like a starved dog and went back for more, this time with honey. Looking out of the window, I saw the sky, the sun now lowering towards twilight. "I think we deal with them at the same time."

"What?" Ella and Heather asked.

"See, like that," I said, referring to them speaking simultaneously. "For a thousand years, battles raged between these two and we want to stop them cold. It won't be easy. We take out one, the other instantly becomes stronger. If we allow the scales to tip, we'll lose. So we summon them both."

"Turstin's only going to manifest through one of us," Heather said.

"I know, and it's likely to be me or you, kid."

Heather cursed. "Either way, it makes us dangerous to the others."

I nodded. "First, we have to tempt them into our battleground. Ella, I think we need you to go full High Church with one of us holding that sword of

Turstin's. He'll come then. If we make a big enough noise, we'll also provoke the god into manifesting."

"Which will bring Damien into the field," Heather said.

I nodded. "That's when I act."

"Can you take him?" Barny asked.

"I have to," I said. "If it turns out I can't, then I'll kill him." I watched the faces of my companions, and they didn't react.

Ella mumbled, "Let's hope it doesn't come to that, Lorne."

So did I. During the last few days, I'd been handed a nasty reminder of how wrong a fight could go for me. I'd lost against Damien, and would have died if Heather hadn't stopped him. I'd lost against Turstin when I faced him. My battles weren't going well; my ruthless edge now lay dull in the soft meadow of my new life.

Heather interrupted my mental flagellation. "Where are we going to do this?"

"In the water," I said.

"I can't dive," Ella stated.

I shook my head. "We aren't going in deep. This god, he's attached to water, to the spring rising from the land. Everything for him has gone wrong in the last fifty-odd years. Before that, some upstart Christian from a foreign land took away a significant amount of his gifts and power. He's been relying on small donations from the Endicott family and a few others over the centuries. The local priest turning a blind eye. Now, he's completely ignored. He's angry, and rightly so, which means we have to go to him as humbly as possible. Turstin is a proud warrior. He won't listen, and he wants me, or maybe Damien, to replace him. I think that's the real challenge. I think if we can defeat Turstin and prove it to the god, we have a chance to make peace for the area."

"Meaning we send Turstin into the light?" Barny asked, referencing Poltergeist.

"Basically, yes. Ella can help, but that'll be my first job."

"And you know how to do that?" he asked.

I sat back and twisted my hand from side to side. "Kinda. It's more instinct than anything. You and Heather, or you and Ella, depending on how Turstin behaves, need to keep us in one piece."

"How am I supposed to do that if Damien turns up? I can't fight the SAS." The tinge of panic in his voice made me chuckle.

"No, you can't, but you can use the crossbow." I nodded at the weapons I'd unpacked from the daysack I'd been carrying all day. I'd kept them hidden while the police mooched around, but now, I had everything, including the old sword, on the table.

Barny's eyes widened. "You want me to shoot someone?"

"No, I want you to protect us if necessary and only if something happens to me or Heather. You're our last line of defence, that's all."

Barny didn't look convinced, but he had no choice.

"What time?" Heather asked. "That might be important to consider."

I nodded. "Fair point. Thoughts?" I looked at my unit.

"Midnight?" Ella suggested.

"Three is said to be the witching hour," Barny said.

"I think dusk, as night falls," Heather said.

"Why?" I asked her.

"The transition between night and day, or the other way around, gives power, like the rising of the moon in its different phases gives plants different strengths in herbal medicine. When the world is in flux, during dawn and dusk, realities shift. When the day or night are dominant, then that reality is fixed."

Ella looked at Heather in surprise. "Wow, okay, that makes sense. There's an argument for that."

"I agree," I said.

We all looked at Barny. He shrugged, "I'd rather get it over with, leaving it until three will send me nuts."

"What do we do with Ghost?" asked Heather.

I thought about the options. "Leave him in the truck. He knows he's safe in there."

"Too hot," she shot back.

She had a point. Even at night, it would be too hot. "Then we leave him in here," I said.

Heather didn't look happy, but she nodded. "I'll give him some of our dirty clothing, so he knows we're coming back. Hopefully, he won't chew a hole in the door."

"Again," muttered Ella, trying not to laugh.

We had lost two doors so far, one in her bungalow and the one in our kitchen leading to the hallway when I'd tried to keep the monster in the kitchen at night.

Just in case something happened in the water, I wanted the others in wetsuits to help keep the cold out. Without the correct fit, I couldn't run and fight in a suit, so I'd handle the temperature in my shorts and t-shirt. Returning to the gym without Damien's larger-than-life energy filling the hall made me feel depressed. I didn't want to think about the life he'd had after The Regiment. Being in Somalia, during the civil war, or even now, would lead a soldier down a dark road. It had left me with terrible memories just serving my country. How bad was it when you worked for private companies or governments who had no interest in protecting their 'voters'? Special Forces guys the world over had to carve out new lives; we didn't all get book deals and a TV series.

"Hey, stop it," Heather said, giving me a shove as I sorted out the wetsuits in the gym cupboard.

"Stop what?" I asked, trying to ignore her laser sight.

"Brooding. Damien's life is not your fault, love. He made choices after leaving The Regiment. He also cut you out of that life. It sounds to me like the problem with his back wasn't as bad as you were told and rather than come back to the 22nd, he ran off to play soldier in a place with no oversight. That's not on you."

"I loved him like a brother, Heather. Then I realised I was looking at a stranger."

She glanced over her shoulder. Barny was playing ball with Ghost. A loud game involving a lot of barking. "Brothers aren't always what you want them to be, Lorne."

We shared a sad smile and returned to our task.

DUSK SAW US ON THE opposite side of the reservoir to the fishing lodge and the school. We stood on the old road to Syndercombe. Heather, Ella and Barny wore wetsuits, the women fitting them well, being the same size as some of the older students. I carried the sword and had a slingshot on my belt with a few small, smooth stones in my pocket. Before we'd left the school, I'd given Barny a quick lesson in the crossbow and Heather a lesson in the slingshot. Holding these ancient weapons left a strange impression on me, especially the slingshot. I'd seen men in Arabian countries kill snakes and hare with them. I doubted I'd ever be that good, but the simple design felt right in my hand.

Ella looked at the darkening water. "This is bloody scary," she declared. "I don't know if something is going to drag me under."

"If it does, I'm coming after you," I said, trying to give her confidence.

She gave me a flat stare. "Oh, well, that's a comfort. I'm so pleased. Let's hope you get to me before I drown." Without another word, she stomped into the water.

"That's a good way of making her move," Heather said, "annoying her. I'll try it sometime." She followed Ella, complaining about the cold.

I held the sword and Barny looked at me. "I'd give anything to be off my tits right now." He gazed out at the setting sun.

"Yeah, well, I'd like to be at home with my feet up in the garden watching my wife trying to groom her dog." We'd left Ghost, howling, in the school's kitchen, or I hoped that's where he was.

Barny followed his sister. I scanned our surroundings for the hundredth time, looking for anything that felt off. So far, so normal, if you ignored all the police rigmarole left behind on the opposite bank. Walking into the water, more than just the cold crept up my legs.

Brother, Ahmar came through loud and clear, *what are you doing?*

Walking and talking to my desert companion rarely ended well, so I stopped. At least I hadn't left him in Turstin's world. *I'm going to make peace with the god. You said I needed to talk to him.*

Gods do not make peace with mortals. Get them out of the water.

You said I needed to talk. This is the only way, Ahmar.

No, it is not! I will find another way.

This is the way we are doing it. I know you don't want to face a god, so you don't have to. Just stay quiet and let me do my job.

He will kill you, stupid mud dweller.

Then I will die, and you will be free.

I thought I heard the djinn growl. *Fine, I will be here when you need me.*

I hope it won't be necessary.

He harrumphed. A proper tantrum. I pushed the sensation away. I wouldn't need Ahmar, but I would need my beast if I had to face Damien in a fight. He remained asleep for the moment, unaware of our danger.

"Lorne?" Heather asked. She had her 'Oh no, he's having an episode' look on her face.

"I'm fine. It's Ahmar, he's not happy."

Ella, who carried a daysack we'd loaded with some wafers and holy water, removed them. We wanted to replicate what we'd done at the old hospital in Horner during the Winter Sun debacle last summer.

Heather acted as curate for Ella, holding the items of the sacrament out of the water. Ella removed a large wooden cross the boys had found.

We all turned west and watched the sun as it vanished below the rolling hills. The sky turned to a bruised purple over our heads, with the wounding red of the day still trying to fight back.

Trees turned dark. The fishing lodge and its police leftovers dimmed to nothing. The water, now around Ella's thighs and over my knees, shot to black with shocking speed. The vast concrete wall of the reservoir wasn't visible from our location, so it felt like we stood in an infinite natural lake. One able to reach back in time. The caged river was the life's blood of the large valley it dominated for centuries until modern man-built railways and motorways.

"Now, Ella," I ordered. I held up the sword by the blade to match her wooden cross. The last of the light from the sun cast a shadow from the sword onto the simple cross and I almost dropped it. The blood of the blade was no match for the blood shed for the cross.

I wasn't the only one affected by the sight. Ella's eyes filled with tears and her voice came out thicker than usual as she began with the Lord's Prayer. We'd opted to take up compass points on the old road but remained close together, just in case.

Ella went from one prayer to another. She'd been learning some of the older ones to help in situations where I plunged her neck deep into something weird, so she began St Patrick's Breastplate. Then she called out Psalm 91, at which point I thought we'd blown it, and nothing was going to happen.

"Lorne," Heather whispered over Ella's prayer, "something's coming." She looked down at the water.

I looked down. It took all my willpower to remain still as a long tentacle, like an eel rather than the arm of an octopus, writhed just below the surface of the water. "Bloody hell," I whispered. Rarely did something truly shock me, but this dark manifestation chilled more than my bones.

"What do we do?" asked Barny, his eyes like dinner plates. He looked ready to bolt, and I didn't blame him.

"Hold," I said, despite the sweat prickling all over my body, which had nothing to do with the ambient temperature of the night.

A small whimper from Heather yanked my eyes in that direction. The tentacle encircled her leg and rode upwards.

Her eyes wild, Ella faltered.

"Don't stop," I barked out, dropping the blade of the sword and grabbing the hilt. I turned the weapon and cried out, "Touch one hair on her head and I'll come down there and hack you to pieces."

"Good way to negotiate peace," Barny squeaked as another long, lithe, dusky tentacle rose to encircle his waist.

Ella stumbled over the Lord's Prayer once more, the fear weakening her voice. The wooden cross in her hand trembled and blessed wine sloshed over the side of her chalice.

I needed to do something, anything, but Ahmar wouldn't help. Djinn did not fight gods.

"What do you want from us, mighty lord of the water?" I called out. "We will do all in our power to see you have what you need. Please, just tell us how to help you."

Ella let out a yelp and vanished with a splash under the water. I saw her pale face and hands being dragged away at speed. Heather screamed and Barny grabbed her, yanking her out of the reservoir. The wooden cross floated on the surface as I pushed the sword into Heather's grasp. Then I dived after my friend.

The fluid darkness closed over my head, and I pulled hard, kicking with all the power a long-distance hill runner has in their legs. I shot into the murky depths of the reservoir. Ella struggled just ahead of me, bubbles exploding from her mouth as she squirmed against the monster holding her still. I reached out, took a firm grip on her face, and made her focus on me.

Rather than fight the monster, rather than slice it with my knife, or yank at it with my hands, I stroked the thick leg wrapped around my friend. Ella's eyes, full of panic, watched, understood, and did the same thing. The monster felt smooth to the touch and cold, not slimy, just wet. The end of it swayed behind Ella's back like a piece of seaweed in a gentle tide. It relaxed the death grip it had on Ella, and she squirmed free, bobbing to the surface in seconds. I remained with the creature in the dark for a few moments longer and felt the most extraordinary sensation of gratitude wash through me. The point of the leg, or arm, rose to my face and caressed my jaw with the tenderness of a lover.

My lungs, fit to bursting, couldn't keep me alive any longer. With a last stroke on the underside of the limb, I drifted to the surface.

31

BREATHING HARD, I SWAM IN slow strokes, so I didn't look as if I'd fled the scene. I knew I'd just experienced a profound event. I'd shown the old god a little love, and he'd reacted with compassion in return. It gave me hope.

When I reached the point I could no longer swim, I rose and waded back. That's when I realised one more person stood on the sand and Heather no longer held the sword. In fact, she lay on the ground.

Damien held the hilt, blade to her belly. "Don't get any silly ideas, Wellie."

The beast rose and snarled, "Let her go, or I'll fucking rip your arm off."

My old comrade glanced at me as I stepped from the water. "That's far enough, mucker."

Heather shifted, but Damien, sharp as ever, refocused on her and tutted. She held still.

"We are not friends," I snarled. "You just forfeited any forgiveness I might have had for you."

"I have Turstin's sword. My master will be pleased with me," he said, eyes shining in the night's dark with the passion of a zealot. I'd seen that look too many times and remembered well its reflection in my mirror. Damien hovered on the edge of total mental collapse. It might not be the phrase the experts used these days, but he walked and flirted with madness.

"Yeah, well, I've just shared a moment with your god, Damien, and trust me, I don't think he'll want Heather dead."

"You do not know what he wants."

Another figure stepped from the woodland.

"He wants our souls. He is a demon," cried Adam in a voice that didn't belong to the young man. His eyes shone white, and his gait looked alien to the subtle lines of a youth.

"Oh, shit," Barny murmured.

A feral grin spread over Damien's face. "Cursed knight." He lifted the sword.

Adam, or Turstin, saw his blade in the hands of his enemy and lifted a firearm.

"Oh, God," Ella cried out.

I rushed forward between Damien and Adam. Not the wisest of my decisions. Where the hell had he found that gun? I registered it being a Glock 17, standard issue for firearms' officers in the British police. He'd stolen it from someone nearby. I hoped they still lived.

"Wait," I called out. From the corner of my eye, I watched Heather scramble backwards, blood covering her face from a head wound. Ella yanked her up and pulled her further back.

"For what?" Adam asked. "I shall kill this minion of the river demon and then I shall take your life. Once I have done so, we will force you to remain here, and I shall be free at last."

A very large part of me wanted to let them slug it out, but I knew Damien. He'd kill Adam, then he'd set about the rest of us, and I'd be forced to shoot him.

Call for parley, brother, before you find yourself haunting this place forever and trapping me with you.

The voice came like a soothing balm. Ahmar hadn't abandoned me to face the river god alone.

Ahmar snorted. *I am not speaking to that thing. I am merely making a suggestion.*

Ignoring him was easy. "I call for parley. You both have to respect the law." I had some vague recollection of the laws of parley from watching some

TV series with Heather called Black Sails. My entire rescue plan rested on a script. Wonderful.

Adam's face, occupied by Turstin's spirit, hissed at me.

Damien chuckled. "Clever. I believe you are more than you seem, mortal man."

"Let's not worry about that. Put the sword down, lower your firearm, let's talk. Battling over this land for a thousand years hasn't won either of you any peace, so we need to find a new way forwards."

"It is a demon. You cannot trust it." This from Adam under Turstin's influence.

"Christ, you sound like the bloody Tally," I muttered. I pointed at Damien and the river god. "You need to take the first step. This is your land. Make this work or you're going to be fighting me for the next thousand years and I think you know I won't be alone."

Damien, his face harder and body more graceful than the mortal version, nodded. "I can see your point." He flipped the sword so fast I flinched. He now held the blade rather than the hilt.

I breathed out and focused on Adam. "Rules of parley state, you must listen and lower your weapon."

Adam's white eyes shone with the desire of a zealot, but the weapon wavered in his hand. Was the boy fighting the possession? The firearm dropped, but the way Adam held the weapon made it clear neither he nor the spirit understood how to optimise its use.

I breathed a little easier. "Alright, let's talk." Both men began shouting. I raised my voice over the noise. "And I shall go first!" I bellowed.

Silence.

"Good. Turstin fitz Rolf, your presence here has caused great discomfort to a being who has been in this place since the dawn of man in the area." I turned to look at Damien. "Am I right?"

He nodded, once.

I continued. "River god, you have existed in this place far longer than any human culture has survived. You have known how we rise and fall. You are patient and one day this concrete wall will crumble, and your sacred place will return to normal."

"My river is drying up," he stated.

"I know. It's happening all over the world. Far beyond your valley. This is not Turstin's doing. It is not the intention of the communities relying on your water and your benefits."

I turned back to Adam, his expression belonging to a different man. "Turstin fitz Rolf. You are remembered even now as a great hero. You shall never be forgotten by history, as long as men walk this land. Both you and your king were powerful men. However, you came to a land not your own, and you forced it to your will, then you remained far beyond your natural lifespan. You have effectively tortured this poor creature for a thousand years by denying the right of the river god's existence. I do not hold to your faith. I belong to a faith that sees benefit in diversity. That sees equality in difference. I will not guard this place and you don't need to. If you leave, the river god will return to his peaceful—"

A shot rang out from the woodland.

Adam screamed and dropped to the ground.

Ella yelled and threw herself over the boy.

Damien rushed up behind me and I didn't turn in time. The sword caught my upper arm as I threw myself sideways. The powerful man crouched, grabbed the Glock, and continued running even as black shapes raced from the trees. Damien hit the water and dived.

"Fucking hell!" I screamed in frustration. My arm stung as if filled with a thousand angry bees. My fingers didn't want to co-operate, but whether from shock or damage, I didn't have time to figure out. Wet heat raced down my skin. Heather yelled, but I couldn't hesitate. I stormed after Damien, into the water. He wouldn't escape, not this time. I wouldn't watch him die from a sniper's bullet. I hadn't allowed it in The Stan, and I wouldn't let it happen now.

Pandemonium broke out on the bank of the reservoir. Armed men shouted for me to stop swimming. A few rounds cracked overhead and splashed around me until a senior officer called a halt to them taking pot-shots in the dark. It meant Kate hadn't withdrawn and she didn't trust me.

My left arm wailed, but I forced it to match the right with powerful strokes and I realised I gained on Damien. He carried the pistol, and it hampered his movements. Out into the night-kissed water I swam, the bottom of the valley far below me and blacker than the sins of the damned. I kept the white-haired man in my sights as we crossed to the far bank. Focusing on Damien made damned sure I didn't think about what lurked in the dark, under the surface of the water. How easy it would be for the old river god to reach up and suck me down into the dark, still depths of the valley floor?

It occurred to me that a god, able to manifest, might be responsible for the deaths of the men we found in the church? But why would he do that?

I felt the effort in my left arm, the blood flow steady in the water. Damien hit solid ground and waded from the reservoir's icy embrace. It urged me on. Damien stumbled and a large puff of sand blew up from the ground to his right. A moment later, the gunshot, from a large calibre rifle, boomed around the confining hills, and I realised they had a long-range weapon with a night sight somewhere nearby. If I didn't get between him and that sniper, he was going to die.

My foot struck dirt as I kicked in the water, and I scrambled up the shallow bank, the sand white in the moonlight.

"Damien!" I screamed. "Stop, or they'll take you down." After the effort of crossing the cold water of the reservoir, my breath heaved. Damien didn't stop, and I cursed, knowing I'd have to run after him. Pulling my t-shirt over my head, I ripped it in two and tied it around my arm, then raced off into the night.

The moon gave me enough light to track Damien. In his frantic struggles to gain distance, he didn't try to hide the noise of his escape. I kept at him, not trying to close the distance, just keeping him in sight and wearing him down. I needed to husband my strength, because he was bigger and stronger than I'd ever been in the army. The problem I faced now was taking him down without either of us dying. He had no such restraint.

He made it into the woodlands, and I breathed more easily. The sniper wouldn't take a shot if we ran through trees. If he had an infrared scope, I'd be surprised. I ran along the path we'd walked earlier that day, my boots squelching with every step.

Damien suddenly vanished from sight, and I put my head down and sprinted hard for forty metres. An animal track led up the hill, one that people obviously used but rarely enough to confuse me in the night. I checked the low-lying vegetation, just for confirmation, and saw it was depressed at equal distances. He'd come this way at a strong run.

"Great, uphill," I panted, pushing off the ground and heading after my friend.

Branches tore at my naked skin, the wound from Heather's attempt to save me from Turstin's blade, singing in time to the sword wound in my arm, both holding the frantic rhythm of my heart. Warm night air heaved in and out of me in gushes as I focused only on not falling in the dark. The path was steep, littered with rocks and roots. When the woodland ended, I stumbled into a barbed wire fence.

"Shit," I snarled, untangling my shorts and tearing more flesh. I found the fence post and vaulted over the evil, bloody stuff.

Checking my surroundings, I saw Damien in the distance, heading for a gate. As I ran after him, it occurred to me we headed for the Iron Age hill-fort. Why? Even as I struggled to keep my pace up, I tried to process the meaning behind his behaviour. If the god still held Damien under his control, as Ahmar had done with me in times past, then there must be a compelling reason for him to make his avatar come out into the open.

I vaulted the gate. This field resembled heathland, rather than grazing grass. Almost at the top, I realised it looked very different from below. It had terraces and many more thick gorse bushes than I thought. Navigating the difficult terrain made me lose track of Damien for a moment.

Until a heavy body slammed into me.

I hit the ground hard, the air abandoning my lungs. We rolled downhill until we hit a flat surface. Damien doing his best to punch me. Blow after blow made it through my defences, making my ears ring and my mouth fill with blood. He had the dominant position, straddling my hips to keep me down.

I put my feet flat on the ground and flipped my hips up and round, trying to dislodge his position. He reared back as if riding a horse, but didn't fall. It gave me the opportunity I needed. His weaker left arm lashed out to help keep his balance, and I brushed down the outside, then tugged hard on his wrist. That took his balance enough for his hips to rise off mine. I forced him off me and he smacked, face first, into the hard ground.

A muffled grunt came from him as I scrambled up and away. I should have rolled with him, put on a choke hold and snapped his neck.

Instead, I tried reason, "Crusty, please, listen to me. It's Wellie, mucker, just stop this. We need to talk."

You're an idiot. You should have finished him.

My inner critic snapped the thought as I watched Damien turn with elegance and rise.

"Mortal, you are no match for him," came a voice that I didn't recognise from my friend.

I spoke to a god, "Please, let him go. We mean you no harm. Turstin will leave this place and you can live here in peace. We'll reinstate the gifts of tribute, and you can care for the land."

"I have taken my tribute," the god snarled.

"Yeah, a heap of rotting sheep. But no worship, no prayers. No thanks. That's what you really want, right?" I asked. I licked blood off my lips. "Or do you mean the boy? Was Ryan your sacrifice?"

Damien snarled, baring his teeth and gnashing like a rabid wolf. "The boy heard me. The boy wanted to give me tribute. The boy found the thieves. I made them pay for their cruelty." He smashed a fist in his chest. "I avenged him."

I had to know the answer to one more question. "Did you use Damien to do it?"

Damien lifted the Glock 17, and I sucked in a breath.

"Don't, fella, don't kill me. I have a shot at a real life with Heather. How many of our kind can say that? How many can have a future after the things we've seen?"

"You don't know what I've done," Damien's voice said. His expression shifted, and I saw the man, not the god, behind his eyes.

"Whatever it is, we'll fix it."

The gun switched direction. The speed of the change shocked me. It now pointed towards the cotton white head of my friend. Damien's finger moved from the side of the weapon to the trigger.

I threw myself at him. The weapon discharged. The muzzle flash burning hot. The noise so loud and close to my face, a screaming ring started in my ears. I expected his body to go limp under me, because I still breathed, but it didn't. He didn't go limp. Neither did I. We still lived. Fingers dug into my wounded flank and tore open the wound, digging into the flesh.

I screamed and tried to lunge away, but Damien wrapped his legs around my hips and smacked my head with the butt of the pistol.

Too much. Too much.

My beast came roaring out of the dark. He'd been pacing, waiting for me to lose my temper, to lose control.

I forced a hand down between our bodies and grabbed Damien's genitals, crushing the entire package in my hand.

He bellowed in pain and released his legs from around me, so he could escape my grip. Rather than let him go, I drove my head down into his face and smashed his nose into my skull. It sent rivers of pain down my neck, but I did it again, then I punched the bastard.

And punched him.

The beast roared inside me.

A four-legged demon raced out of the dark and barrelled into me, knocking me sideways, separating me from my victim. I snarled at the dog. Ghost barked back, hackles up, but he turned and set his considerable focus on Damien. I saw the Glock among the scrubby grass and lunged for it.

My hand closed over the familiar weapon, and I pivoted to zero my focus on Damien.

"Ghost, cease," I ordered.

Much to my astonishment, he backed off but didn't relax.

"Damien, you in there?" The Glock wavered as I fought to remain upright. "Oi! You bloody great idiot. You in there?"

The form on the ground didn't move. The moon created the perfect contrast between the black of the blood and the white of the skin. A monochrome world vivid around me. There was a lot of blood.

In that moment I realised I'd beaten a man to death. Worse. I'd beaten my brother to death.

My knees wobbled at the understanding. I sagged, still trying to hold the weapon, just in case of hope.

A god filled that frail human body. He might save his avatar.

But no.

Why should he? The ancient deity of the land would move on as he'd done for countless generations and occupy someone else. He had no use for mortals beyond their worship giving him meaning in this world.

I'd murdered Thomas Moore, the man who had once been my childhood friend Tommy. Giving the news to his parents almost broke me, despite their kind understanding. I'd murdered Damien. They weren't the monsters. I was the monster. I deserved to spend the rest of eternity locked in this place, replacing the knight. Lifting the black muzzle of the Glock, I pressed it to the scarred flesh under my chin. Angled towards the back of my head. The cold surface felt comfortable, safe…

Lorne? Brother? What are you doing?

Ahmar's screaming drifted off into the distance. His panic at my actions a mist torn asunder by the bleak despair of my pointless existence.

The familiar scent of gun oil filled my senses. A comfort. This would be fast. A blessing really. A relief. No more grief, no more fighting, no more pain. I'd just end.

"Lorne?" A broken voice. A man's voice, one from my past.

The muzzle of the weapon lifted to the centre of my face. I'd look Lady Death in the eyes. I'd escaped her too many times and in the process something foul had filled me. It must have for me to murder two men who stood at my side as brothers.

"Lorne, don't. *Don't listen to him.*" A firm hand closed over mine. "Look at me. I'm alive."

The gun trembled in my hand, lowering by tiny increments.

"Crusty?" I croaked.

Blood and snot covered my mucker's face. I'd broken his nose, split his lips, maybe cracked an eye socket and cheek.

He must be in agony.

My side burned, hot, wet bodily fluids snaking down the cold flesh. Oh, I did feel cold. The tremble in my hand turned into a full body quake.

"Steady, Lorne. It's okay. We're okay, brother." Tears filled Damien's eyes and spilled over. "Please. I don't want to watch you die. Not you. I'm going to need you, Lorne. I've done some terrible things. I need help. The world makes little sense, brother." His voice, a crow's broken-winged caw for pity, mercy, help.

I lowered the Glock and reached out for my friend. He sobbed and embraced me, begging for compassion. Begging for peace.

Too shocked to feel relief, I held him close and let him cry.

3 2

I DON'T KNOW HOW LONG we sat in the old fort; the night darkening around us. Ghost vanished from my side. My mind kept circling on his sudden appearance. How much damage had he done in the school to escape? Being a dog, his wounds had closed over quickly. At this rate, I'd owe the school money rather than the other way around. At some point, I realised Damien had fallen asleep in my lap. Not the first time he'd used me as a pillow, but it was the first time his hands still clutched my legs, as if to ensure I didn't escape.

In the distance, I saw flashing blue, the police. The lights flicked on the heavy mass of water. A breeze licked at the surface, the hard white of the half-moon creating flashes of silver among the black. Light born out of the dark.

We need to talk, brother. Ahmar almost whispered his suggestion in my head.

"Not now," I murmured aloud.

A surge of energy enveloped me, and I stood in the desert oasis with Ahmar. In silence, he handed me a wooden cup. I frowned at the white liquid inside.

"Drink, Lorne. It will help. Goat's milk and honey. You need a little grounding. Your spirit is floating free, and I do not want you tempted to lift that terrible weapon again." Unaccustomed to hearing him so tender, I did as I was told.

The milk and honey warmed my mouth, brought my tongue alive and rippled down into my stomach with all the joy of life a bee has when he finds a meadow of wildflowers. I drained the cup.

"Thank you, Ahmar."

He reached out and took my rough hand in his, clasping it gently. "The god tried to kill you, Lorne. The knight has tried to kill you. I think you need to leave this place and the darkness that exists here. Your friend's mind is broken. When he wakes, the man you knew will be gone. The god has sucked him dry."

"Why is he being so cruel?" I asked the djinn.

Ahmar sighed. "I have witnessed this before among my kind. We grow weary of humanity's desires and their inability to learn. Though we are just as guilty of that as they are. So we turn on them and watch with amusement as they tear each other to pieces. Gods are no different. The men who claim to be leaders of the modern faiths are no different."

I frowned. "What about the God of the Christians?" I examined the inside of my cup and watched in amazement as it filled.

Ahmar chuckled. "You expect the likes of me to be on speaking terms with a deity so exalted by three different faiths? No. I know He is capable of fits of temper. Does your Bible not demonstrate it?"

I grunted and drank. My blood hummed as if filled with the finest whisky, but not yet the effects of being pissed.

Ahmar continued, "I liked your Jesus when he walked my deserts. I found myself drawn to him. The other prophets I did not know personally. But Jesus? He interested me because of the Romans stomping about made my people angry. I fought with a mighty warrior in those days, his name lost to dust." Ahmar picked up a handful of sand and it poured through his elegant hand.

"Why am I here, brother?" I asked. "It's not because you want to give me a lecture on faith."

Ahmar's dark, beautiful eyes glittered in the soft light filtered through the leaves of the palm trees. "Yes, it is, but I needed your mind to calm, centre and focus before we talk of river gods made of mud and hate."

"You want me to leave?"

"I do, but I also know you and, sadly, that will never happen. So we need a plan. Your friend is of no use to us."

"I didn't think you wanted to talk to the god?" I wondered if the cup would fill again, but this time it remained empty and Ahmar gently plucked it from my hand. He replaced it with a small plate of dates. To be honest, I was disappointed. I could have eaten a goat.

"I do not wish to speak with the god, and neither should you, but he must be pacified, and the knight laid to rest."

"How do I do that? When I've seen a ghost, like the one I found in that old house on my birthday, I acknowledge them, listen, then poof, they go away. I can't see Turstin fitz Rolf doing that."

Ahmar chuckled, "Poof, I like that." His face sobered. "No, he will not go peacefully. We will use his sword to summon him. The ghost will come into you, and I will drag him into the light."

"You can do that? Without being hurt yourself?"

"Your concern is comforting and yes, I can take him to the light. He won't like it, but we cannot dig up his bones. They are long rotted to nothing."

Dig up his bones? I put that to one side, and I nodded while eating a date. Oh, I was wrong about dates. These tasted rich and succulent. Better than goat meat. "Okay," I said, while chewing, making Ahmar frown at my bad manners. "What about the god?"

Ahmar gazed off into the distance. "A far harder proposition. I believe, without the knight, he will settle. However, he needs to keep quiet. If the man you spoke to, who farms that land, can be convinced, then more trees should be planted around his small home. He should be left with honey and milk at the festivals and small prayers of devotion given."

"I can't see Endicott going for any of those suggestions. That's prime arable land you want turning over to woodland. It'll cost him too much money. I don't have the money to buy the land."

Ahmar shrugged. "Then we have a problem." His head shifted, as if listening. "Your wife approaches. It is time for us to part."

My breath heaved in, and I came back to the hill-fort, slumped over Damien, who still slept. I heard heavy panting and some flowery language before Ghost, with Heather on the other end of his harness lead, appeared from among the gorse bushes.

"Thank God he wasn't dragging me to a body," she cried out as she saw me sat upright. "We need to get a camera for this harness so I can see what he's been doing."

I managed a grin, though my face ached. "Sorry to scare you."

Her face looked worse than mine felt. One side of it had turned a nasty shade of blue and red.

"Jesus, woman, how are you still standing?" I asked as she crouched beside me. Her lips looked puffy on the bruised side and her eye didn't open properly. I seriously considered killing Damien in that moment.

"I'm okay, sort of." She nodded down at the still sleeping Damien and winced as something in her neck cracked. "He attacked Barny, who went down easily, and I had to do something. I stepped up, and the bugger punched me full in the face. I didn't have time to move. Then he cracked my skull with the sword's hilt. I went down and blacked out."

"How's Ella?" I asked, stroking her poor face. "You need a hospital. Something in there is damaged." Her beautiful face was broken and her eyes didn't look fully focused.

"I'm right here. God, that girl can run," Ella huffed. "I'm going to need to go training with you two if we keep having to do this... It's no good... I need to swear... shit." She sucked in a breath and fought to even out her breaths, hands on her knees and no longer in a wet suit. "I know I shouldn't say it, but—fuck me—what a night."

The relief of having my unit restored to me in one piece returned some strength. "Where are the police?"

Ella waggled her phone. "I'm to ring if I find you. Do you want me to do it now?" She looked down at Damien. "Is he..."

"Alive, but his mind is shot. Ahmar says he won't recover properly. Touched by a god." I stroked my bruised scalp to show what I meant.

"Rather than a djinn," Heather murmured, lifting Damien's head to help me slide out from under him.

I grunted. "Yeah, well, Ahmar nearly sent me to the madhouse permanently."

Ella helped Heather drag me off the ground. "I'm not sure the djinn was the sole reason you lost your bag of marbles. You willingly threw quite a lot of them away."

Ghost maintained a wary eye on Damien keeping Heather at a distance by pushing against her. Ella had a point about my marbles. Even before Syria, the constant pressure on Special Forces UK meant they deployed far too often. The cracks were already in place.

I pushed these thoughts aside. "Call in backup. Tell them Damien's in need of medical attention, and immediate evac. The firearm is made safe. Use those words." I picked up the Glock, dropped the magazine out, and racked the slide to remove the final round safely. I then handed it over to Ella. She looked at me in surprise. "I meant it. No more guns and it's unnecessary. I have a sort of plan."

Heather sagged as Ella made the call. "I'm really glad. I just want this to be over."

"Where's the sword?" I asked.

"Barny has it. Adam's come round. Barny hid the blade in the sand before the police found it on him, then took it back to the school. The police didn't believe Adam was the attacker. They think he was shot at by accident. They missed him, hit the sand. The fright brought him down. They think it was Damien who attacked one of their firearms' officers. One is blonde, the other white, makes sense in the dark," Heather said.

"Good, it's not Adam's fault a Norman ghost used him, and we need that sword. We're going to summon Turstin fitz Rolf, before he can do anymore damage. Ahmar's agreed to step in."

Heather breathed out in a puff. "About bloody time."

"Yeah, well, we still have the god to deal with." I described Ahmar's thoughts on the subject.

We soon heard voices coming up the path to the hill-fort. By the time we'd finished with the police, an ambulance crew had arrived. Ella handed over the weapon. Damien remained asleep, and I knew it wasn't natural. Once we had him loaded on a gurney, I helped them carry him back to the fishing lodge. Kate waited for us there, but Ella opted to remain outside with Heather and the dog. I went in and wasted an hour explaining events in such a way she could use the information for a report.

"Right, now, DI Mackenzie, I need to be let loose to finish this." I added with some venom, "Without your interference."

Kate rubbed her face, looking as haggard as I felt. "When the DCI turns up in the morning, this is going to be out of my hands. The only reason I have any kind of operational control is because half the senior officers in Somerset are on their summer holidays right now. Whatever you have to do, get it done before morning."

No apology. Too exhausted to chase it down, I let her betrayal stand. She'd almost cost a boy his life with that shot. She'd have to live with that decision.

I nodded. "Roger that." I left the fishing lodge and returned to my people. "Let's get out of here. We need to do this quietly and we have until dawn."

WHEN WE ARRIVED AT THE school, exhaustion and pain rendered us all quiet and miserable. Ella's tussle with the old god's manifestation in the water left her bruised around her ribs and middle.

She vowed, "I'm never going swimming again. I'm never getting back into the water and from now on, it's showers only."

I agreed with her.

Barny's relief at seeing us alive became tempered when I explained what needed to happen with the sword. I'd told none of them I'd need to 'channel' the ghost first. I just had to hope I was strong enough to prevent him from going on a killing spree once he had his sword back.

Adam sat at the kitchen's table looking lost.

I knelt beside him. "You okay?"

When his eyes met mine, the haunted look of a man, not a boy, stared back at me. "I hurt someone."

I nodded. "He'll live. They think it was Damien, which isn't a problem."

Adam gazed at his hands. "I wanted to kill that poor police officer."

I closed my rough and bruised hands over his to break his concentration. "You didn't because you aren't a killer. Turstin is a killer, but by occupying you he found a man he couldn't force against his nature. If he'd been inside me, there would be more dead bodies out there."

"If I'm not a killer, I'm no use in the army."

"The army is made up of trained soldiers, not killers. Some of us are killers, you're right because we mirror our society, but not the likes of you."

Adam shook his head. "I don't want to hurt people and I don't want to get hurt."

I gripped the lad's shoulder. "Maybe go to college, have a life, and see how you feel in a few years. How did you get back here from where you'd been taken?"

"I don't really remember. Maybe I hurt Robert? I need to say sorry, but I don't have a phone."

"Okay, we'll get you back there soon. Right now, we could do with your help."

He nodded and gamely rose to join the rest of us.

I took operational command. "Right, listen up. We're going to do this outside. The school is infected with too much energy to be safe. We'll form a circle, me in the middle with the sword. We'll call on Turstin by name. He'll be forced to come. All of you will be inside a salt circle, so he has no choice but to come into me. Once that happens, I need you all to keep a close eye on my hands where they hold the sword. If I move, you run. I've never used a sword in an actual fight, but that doesn't mean I can't. When Turstin has control of me, the djinn will take over. From there, you just remain still. We should be safe enough."

"I hope you're right," Ella said. "It feels very wrong allowing possession."

"It's our best option. Getting rid of the knight might be enough to force the god to back down. Their battle clearly adds motivation and power to the god. Without Turstin, we might have a chance. I made a mistake thinking balance was the best option. It just isn't possible to come to a compromise with a knight and a god." I used to have operational command over men who invaded the homes of insurgents. Now, I made plans to defeat ghosts and gods. How had this happened?

"Agreed," everyone said.

Outside, the night drew to its darkest hour. We all held candles, robbed from the kitchen stores, and a big bag of rock salt the school kept for the road when it iced over. Heather, Ella, Adam and Barny took up positions on the compass points and I drew a line of salt around each of them.

Then, holding the sword, I stepped inside the circle. The others all held candles. Their small flames a weak dance of light in the heaving mass of the night.

Holding the cross guards of the sword, the dangerous end in the hard soil, I closed my eyes. "Turstin fitz Rolf, I summon thee to this place—"

Heather snorted. "Summon thee? What are you, a nineteenth century mystic?"

I scowled at her. "What do you suggest?"

Ella said, "Just call him. You're a soldier, he's a soldier."

I drew in a breath, closed my eyes again and opted for, "Turstin, I'm ready to set you free. It's time to lay down your arms. This fight is done."

The night became thicker. I heard Ella muttering a prayer and Heather joined in, closely followed by Barny.

"Come on," I called out to the night. "Come to me and all this can end. We have shed enough blood, you and I. Come and see if I speak the truth, Turstin fitz Rolf, companion of William of Normandy, rightful King of Eng—"

My chest heaved as all the air in the circle vanished and a great weight settled on my shoulders. I fought the urge to panic, and my hand tightened on the weapon.

With the last of my breath, I whispered, "Turstin, I am ready."

From a great distance, I felt my spine snap straight as if on a parade ground. *The feel of the weapon in my hand became familiar for the first time. I ached to wield it once more on the battlefield, to see the eyes of my enemies as they died. To hear the screams of the dying and watch the crows feast when the battle was done. How many wars had I won with my dearest friend William? The greatest tactician and leader. I wanted to ride into battle, the weight of my armour a comfort, the weapon in my hand an extension of my body, forged in conflicts too numerous to count. For God. For my king. For salvation in the afterlife.*

"Come, noble brother, it is time for one last journey."

I turn, and before me see a knight clothed in the glory of all I hold dear.

"Where are we going?"

"To peace. It is time. You have done your duty."

He walks and I follow. His armour is made of the finest steel. It is highly polished and shines like silver. Long black hair falls down his back from the helmet covering his face. This is no ordinary knight. He is made of the stuff of legend. I have heard the minstrels tell stories of great kings, such as Charlemagne and Arthur. He must belong to such God-fearing men. As we walk, the light becomes brighter, and I cannot see the knight.

"Sir Knight, where are you?"

I stumble into the light and peace wraps her merciful arms around me. She plucks the sword from my hands. Her maidens take my armour and I step towards my judgement a naked penitent…

33

I WOKE UP WITH A start. "Fuck, that was close," I muttered.

"What happened?" asked Ella.

"I'm not sure how much of it was real, but he's gone."

"For sure," Adam said, nodding at the sword.

We looked down and I no longer held an eleventh century weapon in perfect condition. I held a rusting piece of iron with a vague resemblance to a sword.

"Oh," Heather said in disappointment. "I hoped we'd get to keep it."

I swayed, the world tilting and Barny caught my shoulder. "Come on, soldier boy, let's get you something to eat."

"I don't like this," I mumbled. "I feel weird." Seeing Ahmar masquerade as a knight would be an image I'd hold on to for the rest of my life.

Back in the kitchen, I found a cuppa tea and slices of cheese on toast under my nose. It made life a great deal brighter.

"What's next?" Ella asked.

"Trip back to the stream's source," I said. "We need to take those libations the djinn suggested."

"What about the monster under the water?" Ella asked, her eyes betraying her fear of the thing.

I couldn't blame her. None of us understood half of what was going on. "I think it was a manifestation of the river god."

"But his possession of Damien was so violent," she said.

I considered this and nodded. "What if Damien made him more violent? What if his natural form, the way he manifested in the water, is a more natural state? He's a water god. Maybe he just grows big and plays in the reservoir? A lot of the rage we've faced is because of Damien, and he's hardly at peace with himself." I remembered the shuddering body as Damien silently relived some of the horrors he'd perpetrated after leaving The Regiment.

Ella drew circles in a puddle of water on the table's surface. "Makes sense I guess."

"It's all guess work, Ella, that's the problem. Metaphysics by its nature is unprovable."

She rose and gripped my shoulder for a moment. "I'll put together a care package for a god."

"I wish we could give the poor old bugger the peace he deserves," I said.

Adam looked at me. "What if we can?"

I frowned, the movement making my bruised forehead protest. The banging headache didn't help my concentration. "What's that mean? We don't have the money to get Endicott out of those fields."

"We don't, but I know a friend who does," Adam said, rising from the table. "I'm going to Medway's office, and I'll make a few calls."

"It's the middle of the night," I said.

"Not in Saudi, it isn't," he said.

I dismissed the boy's rambling and focused on trying to stay aware and awake. Heather sat with a bag of peas on her face.

"You okay, kid?" I asked.

She managed a nod. "Not sure I'm going to see this through, boss. You're right, I need a doctor."

"Seriously?" I heaved my sorry carcass out of the chair and joined her on the mattress she'd chosen. I peeled the bag away from her face. The swelling had become worse, not better. "You should have stayed with Kate and gone in the ambulance."

"Maybe," Heather managed. "I've been punched before, but Damien really landed this one."

I felt for her. We're trained to fight hard and dirty. A man Damien's size smacking a small woman... One strike and you're down. Ella came back from the larder.

"Can you call Kate? We need an emergency evac for Heather. Her face needs some proper medical attention."

Ella knelt and checked the growing bruises. "Oh... Heather... Yes," she said, "I'll call now."

"Sorry, boss. I just..." she struggled to put together the rest of the sentence.

"It's okay, kid. Sometimes we just have to stop fighting. I've got you. We'll go now."

She clutched my arm. "No, finish this, then come find me. Take Ella. I'll be in Taunton's hospital. Don't leave me there."

I smiled, but tears pricked my eyes. "I won't, kid. I promise."

ELLA AND I HIKED UP to the water's head together. The others remained at the school while a police officer drove Heather to the hospital. I hated being separated from her, but she was right. We needed to end this, and it needed doing now.

We made quick work of it, despite my aching and bloody body. I wanted to be at the site before the sun rose. To do this on the rising energy of the day would help. I really had spent too much time around Willow and Spud.

In silence we reached the spot, both of us breathing hard, Ghost at my heel. It wasn't like he could go to the hospital and the damage to the backdoor of the school's kitchen spoke of his desperation to find his pack. The stink from the dead animals wafted on the still air, but mostly we remained upwind of the pit Damien must have filled trying to keep the god happy.

The picnic spot we'd found the day before still had crushed grass and evidence of the boys digging for the sacrifices people had made over the centuries.

"It's quiet," Ella said.

I nodded, watching bats dance in the pre-dawn air. Simultaneously they looked really clumsy and graceful, like demented tiny black bags being blown about by unfelt wind. Not the way swifts and swallows graced daylight. The night created some wonderful creatures. We'd seen a barn owl and a badger. I really wished I could preserve this spot for future generations and bring it back to what it had once been.

Like so many others, I wanted to save the world or this small part of it, anyway.

"Will you lead the prayer?" I asked.

"Not sure I should. I feel weird about this, to be honest," she replied, taking out the offerings we'd brought.

Time to step up. I couldn't ask Ella to betray her faith. Losing Kate because of it would have ramifications. Ella needed time to process. I didn't want to add to her stress.

"Well, I've watched you pray at sites all over the moor," I said, "so I'm just going to use that as my baseline and see what happens." The first time we'd done something like this was during the *Gnostic Dawn's* spiritual pollution of our moor.

We knelt, shoulder to shoulder, and bowed our heads. The eastern horizon grew light. I summoned the blue and white barrier I used to keep me safe and spread it over Ella, despite knowing she had one of her own, and then pushed it out to encompass the glade. I heard the birds sing and knew it was time to call on the ancient power.

"With peace, and offering only friendship, we come and beg audience with the ruler of this valley, and this blessed water. It pours forth to offer bounty and life to us and in return we offer thanks by way of these gifts." I lifted the pot of Somerset honey. "I bring sweet nectar." Placing it on the damp ground I realised my knees now sank into mud. I lifted the jug of milk we'd made up from cartons. It was organic and unpasteurised; Ella had found it in the freezer. I guessed Polly planned on using it in cheese making or something. "We bring milk. Food of the lands hereabouts." I placed it down, and the earth became not just damp, but soggy.

Ella gasped as the pot of honey and the jug of milk sank into the wet ground.

I swallowed, fear crawling up my spine. How wet was the ground under our knees? Ella clasped my hand.

"Finish this," she whispered.

Nerves made me lick my lips. "Thank you, great lord, for accepting our small offerings. We will bring more, and we will maintain your peace. I vow this to you."

The ground vibrated.

"I think that means he'll hold you to it," Ella said, taut as a bow string.

I took a measured breath. "We will see you when day and night are of equal length," I promised. I guessed Heather and I would spend fire festivals here unless Barny planned on staying in the area.

Slowly, expecting the earth to rear up and gulp us down in one go, we rose and backed away from the site.

On the return journey to the school we walked more slowly, the rising sun cooler this morning, the wind shifting to the south-west and clouds gathering to resemble the promise of rain.

"Do you think it's over?" Ella asked.

Shrugging, I said, "I don't know, mate. I'd like to say yes but… We just gave supplication to a god, so I don't know."

"How do I square this with the bishop?" she asked, half amused, while the other half was obviously worried about her future.

"Pastoral care for the elderly?"

She smacked my good arm. "Idiot."

"I'd suggest not telling him. You'll never have to come and do the offering again."

"I'll have to arrange for the school to be blessed. Maybe talk to the school governors about a priest coming by regularly."

"Possibly. I think having a quiet word with the vicar of the parish might be better. Just tell him to say some prayers. I think keeping Christianity away from the old god for a good long while might be wise."

"That doesn't feel right, Lorne."

I shrugged. "I'm afraid I disagree. If you want an inclusive faith, then maybe that should hold true for these ancient places as well. With all the churches and cathedrals you have, isn't that enough land? Can't the ancient stones, wells, springs and groves have their place in the world?"

"I'll pray on it," she said as a concession.

When we arrived back at the school, we found Polly and the other students mingling with a new batch of police officers.

Polly came over and placed a hand on my arm. "Damien? The police won't tell me anything."

"First, tell me what's happening with the boys."

She glared at me for a moment before sighing and said, "We've been offered a place with Olly's grandparents who have a large holiday home in Devon. We can stay there until parents come to pick everyone up. They don't seem that interested in Olly, but I said they could invoice the school for the accommodation so they're happy."

"Are they going to be there?"

"No, they apparently need to remain in New Zealand with their other son and his children. Olly said they're the favourite ones. He doesn't seem bothered and is looking forwards to showing everyone around."

"I'll come down and visit."

She smiled. "They'll enjoy that, just make sure you bring the dog. Now, tell me the bad news."

I took her to one side and told her gently about Damien's condition. She shed a few tears, and I handed her over to a dog-tired Ella. Knowing I had to get to the hospital, I refused to relax. I had more tea and more food to help keep me upright.

When I spied Kate among the throng, I marched over to her. "What news on the bodies? Did Damien do it?" I asked, refusing to back down.

Her exhaustion showed as well, and she obviously didn't have the energy to fight me. "We'll have to rely on forensics for that and having been in the water, it seems unlikely that we'll find any. We have IDs for the bodies.

They're known in archaeological and detectorist circles as grave robbers." She shook her head in amazement. "They've been all over the world hunting treasure and selling it on the black market. Even war zones. I didn't know that was a genuine job."

Licking my lips, nervous how this information might be received, I said, "I have some intel that might be of interest if nothing else. They were here around the same time Ryan died. Endicott will tell you more."

She nodded. "I have a meeting with him in an hour or two to take a statement. It could mean we reopen Ryan's case but that'll be up to the coroner. It's not like the Crown Prosecution Service can pursue a case against the dead. Maybe you could?" She didn't hide the snarky sideswipe.

"I think that's more Ella's department." I could do bitchy if that's how she wanted to play it.

Her jaw bounced as she clenched her teeth. "I suppose so." She walked off without a goodbye when one of her minions called.

I needed to visit Mrs Langford and fill her in on all this, she'd be fascinated. I was convinced the god possessed Damien and in a fit of fury over the death of Ryan, killed the treasure hunters. The boys' games with the spirit board obviously woke the war between the ghost and the god. Damien's mental fragility made him the perfect vessel, as I did for the djinn, we just had very different outcomes.

I needed some time to figure this out or maybe I wasn't supposed to figure it out and I just needed to let it go. I looked down at Ghost who gazed up at me, worry in his dark eyes. "Yeah, I need to let this one go. We have to find your mum."

Adam came over with Robert. Polly had arrived with all the boys.

"I wanted to report in, sir," Adam said.

"About what?" I asked.

"I called my father in Saudi. He's working for a prince of the royal house who supports an NGO trying to encourage solar farms rather than oil production." Adam shook his head as if to force himself to concentrate on the relevant information. "Anyway, the prince has asked about purchasing the school, and the land around the reservoir to create a private sanctuary. He wants to buy the lake as well, but I'm not sure that's possible. He came down to Somerset last term to give us a talk on advancements in technology driven by the more progressive elements of the Saudi royal family. His son is one of the Muslim students I was talking to you about. They're going to put in an offer for Endicott's farm. One he cannot refuse. I didn't tell them about the god. They aren't that progressive, but I think we can keep the place safe. They'll want to plant trees and encourage wildlife and I'll make sure you have access to the site. My father will oversee the project, which means he can come home." This piece of news made tears spring into Adam's eyes. "I think I want to study environmental science when I finish the sixth form."

I stared at the boy stunned. "I agree. You shouldn't be in the army, lad. You need to become a diplomat. That's incredible."

He beamed. "Not all wealthy people are bad people."

34

EXTRACTING MYSELF FROM THE SCENE took a long time. First, I loaded Ghost into the back of the truck, but all the children insisted on saying goodbye, which meant Ghost escaped the truck and ran about barking, trying to herd us all up. Then the police caught wind of my attempted escape and decided I needed to remain on site. As tempted as I was to pull a fast one by taking on the remaining firearms' officers with my bare hands, I battled to keep control. Kate finally gave the order I could leave, but once again, I had to remain local so I could answer any follow-up questions.

I saw Medway's sleek car arrive and knew I'd be sending an invoice in the post. He might pay me. Though, considering the odd accounts Heather had found on his computer... The penny, dropped, clanged once and rolled into a bright corner full of light.

Marching over to Kate, I pulled her to one side. "Listen to me but don't react, we're being watched. Medway is going to head straight to his office. You need to get onto his computer. Heather found some stuff on there that might not be appropriate."

"Oh, finally, someone I can arrest. You're off the hook, Turner. Get away from here before I change my mind." She turned away, a look of gleeful anticipation on her tired face. Turning back for a moment she said, "Thank you, Lorne. For everything."

"You still going to ignore my calls?" I asked.

"God, yes. I never, ever want to think about the meaning of existence again and I never want to be that scared. I'd rather go back on the beat in St Paul's in Bristol." With that she strode off snapping orders to her detective constables to detain Medway.

Ella came up beside me. "Your good deed for the day?" She nodded towards DI Mackenzie who zeroed in on the head teacher.

I put an arm around her shoulder and gave her a hug. "No. My good deed is giving you the keys to the truck while I take Heather's bike to Taunton. I need to find my girl. Can you take Ghost for a few hours?"

"Only if you promise to come to Luccombe and report in," Ella said. "I'll have food and beer."

I laughed. "Done."

Dixie, Heather's bike, sat with her new tyres, facing the mighty wall of the reservoir. I saw Ella drive out of the school without saying goodbye to Kate and felt sad for my friend. She deserved more from life than to be alone. I turned back and surveyed the wall. Behind it lay secrets. Behind it lay myths. A Norman lord gave his life to protect this place. A god dwelt in the soft, damp soil and just wanted to do his duty to his land. I marvelled at the weird and wonderful world I now inhabited.

No more blood and bone. No bombs and bullets.

I had mysteries to solve and for the first time, I could feel myself embracing the opportunity. It made me chuckle at the oddness of life.

ON THE WAY TO TAUNTON, I'd swung by Mrs Langford's place. The old woman sat outside watching the police and ambulance vehicles buzzing around.

She smiled as I pulled up and walked towards me, so I didn't have to clamber off the bike.

"Well, you made it then?" she said.

I chuckled. "Only just, for some of us."

"I can already feel the difference to the area. Thank you."

"I have to get to the hospital, but I'll come by when the dust settles and tell you what happened. For your records."

She smiled so brightly, ten years or more dropped off her. "I would love that, Mr Turner. I'll have cake and tea ready for you and your lovely young woman."

Shortly after that, I left and wove through the narrow lanes. They gradually opened up into the major arteries of Somerset heading towards Taunton.

I DID BATTLE WITH THE nearest supermarket and bought some essentials like chocolate, clean underwear, toothbrush, more chocolate. I'd already taken Heather's phone and Kindle from where it'd been left in the school. Arriving at the hospital, I found Dixie a safe place to remain and went in search of Heather. It took all my navigation skills but eventually I discovered the love of my life scowling at a wall.

When she caught sight of me and turned, I almost stumbled to a halt. The side of her face nearest the window looked like the gathering clouds outside. A deep purple-black, the colour of dread and great pain. Manfully, I pushed on, with a plastic smile.

She chuckled. "I look that bad, huh?"

"I'm not sure how to answer that," I admitted. With great care I kissed the healthy side of her mouth. "What did they say?"

"I want my rewards first. I've been sat here for weeks with nothing to keep me occupied." Her one good eye narrowed.

"You've been here for six hours."

"Exactly! It's been weeks! Now convince me that you're going to make the best husband ever."

I handed over the bag of goodies. When she found the Kindle and the charger she managed a crow of delight so loud she woke the old woman in the bed next door. I pulled the curtain across.

"You are worthy of my hand in marriage," Heather declared.

I kissed said hand and smiled, my heart aching. "Come on, spill, how bad is your face?"

"Concussion, they won't let me out until tomorrow. I've a few, tiny, hairline fractures to my cheek and eye socket but nothing that won't heal.

I've a headache worthy of a demon's hammer trying to turn my brain into corned beef and I hurt all over. Basically, I'm going to be fine. They'll do another scan on my head tomorrow, make sure I don't have bleeding anywhere bad."

"Like the brain?" I said, my concern obvious.

"Don't overreact. I'm fine. I'll ring you tomorrow when you can come and get me. What happened to Barny?" she asked, a blatant effort to distract me.

"Oh…"

"You forgot all about him, didn't you?" she laughed, then winced as her lip threatened to split.

"Yeah. Do you want me to swing by Wivvy to check on him?"

She shook her head. "No. I think I'd like to leave him behind for a bit. Let the dust settle. See what my family's next move is before I decide whether or not to let him back into my life properly."

I nodded. "Okay, you'll guide me on this one."

She squeezed my hand, and I described what Ella and I had done at the river's source, what the god said, and how Adam had saved the day. I also told her about the dead treasure hunters and that Damien might be responsible, but they'd have a hard time proving it.

"That's good," she said. "Damien's here, somewhere. They're going to section him but they're waiting for a place to be available."

I said nothing and concentrated on waggling her engagement ring around her finger.

"Lorne," she rapped my skull with her other knuckles.

"Ouch."

"Go see him."

I felt the depth of my frown.

"I'm serious, Lorne. He needs you."

"He broke your face."

"Lorne." Her insistence made me sigh.

"Fine."

"Good. Now, I need to rest. So go find your friend, then our dog and give Ella a hug from me. When you get home, phone me."

I nodded.

It took more tracking skills and some fast talking to the police officer on duty, but I gained access to Damien's private room. They'd cuffed his hand to the bed, the lights burned very low.

He didn't react as I entered the room. I stood still and looked at my old friend. What had happened to him in Somalia? What turned him into the dangerous weapon I'd faced? Had he killed the men or merely found Ryan's small body? Would we ever know the truth?

"Damien?" I squeezed out between the rocks of anger and sadness blocking my throat.

No response.

The door opened behind me, and a nurse gasped when she saw me standing in the room.

"Oh, sorry, I thought I saw a ghost," she said with a small laugh. She looked like a blonde elf with her sharp features and short hair.

"I'm an old friend," I said. "His only contact, I think."

"I see. Well, um, you might want to talk to the doctor." Her face became schooled in the art of managing expectations.

"Why?" I asked.

She glanced at the door. "He's unresponsive. We're still in the early days, but at the moment they think he might be catatonic. It's a complex syndrome so it'll be a while before they're sure. He can breathe, but that's about it for now. It's a complicated problem and I'm not the expert…"

Something in my face stopped her talking. "We served in the SAS together," I blurted. "We survived the War on Terror."

Her eyes shone with sympathy, but she didn't understand. How could she?

"I'm sorry. From what I understand he could recover; he just needs time and a reason. The brain is a funny thing. Sometimes, it just needs to reboot."

I gazed at the bed and the figure in it. "We went through so much together. He's my brother."

She patted my hand. "He can hear you. Talk to him. Let him know you'll be here when he's ready to come back."

So I did. I took my old mucker's hand, and I talked to him. I told him about missions I'd been on after they had discharged him, the ones I couldn't share with Ella and Heather. Sitting with him for hours, holding his hand, gave me an odd sense of peace. Almost as if he'd found his quiet place and wanted to share it with me. When I left, I promised he wouldn't be alone. I meant it. He was family.

AUTHOR'S NOTES

HOW DID CLATWORTHY RESERVOIR BECOME a focus for this story? That's down to my dad. He used to tell us stories when we walked to places, probably to stop me and my sister from squabbling like seagulls over a bag of chips (French fries to my American friends).

This visit would be back in the seventies and the safe paths running around the reservoir didn't exist in those days. I remember walking over the dam and being told: "There's a drowned village down there in the bottom."

"Really?" I asked as Dad hung me over the edge of the wall to peer into the endless black of water. It was winter and parents weren't quite so safety conscious in those days.

"On a cold and misty night, it's said the church bell rings out over the water, even though there is no bell in the drowned tower."

The story went on, as they always did, becoming grander with each sentence. It's a story that never left me. The thought of that lonely bell…

So, that's where this story began, over forty years ago. I even found a version of this story on the web, which means Dad might well have picked it up in the pub. He even knew the man who designed the mighty wall. During my research for this book, I went back over the oldest maps I could find, from the early nineteenth century and discovered there was no church in Syndercombe. The nearest is Clatworthy, and it still stands today.

Just goes to show.

A quick history lesson on the word, *knight*. During the Norman invasion and shortly afterwards the knightly class didn't exist as most people think of them, that came much later and is mostly because of Edward I. The mounted fighters of the Norman invasion were generally landless warriors known as *cnivet* (there're lots of ways of spelling this word). This is one theory, though I've read several over the years: "The word originally meant 'boy or youth', and was later extended to mean knight, a feudal tenant bound to serve his lord as a mounted soldier. Hence, it came to denote a man of some substance, since maintaining horses and armour was an expensive business." Read more: Surname Database. I've used knight because it's the common form of address in a modern context and this is a novel, not an academic text on Medieval Norman history. Turstin fitz Rolf was gifted Syndercombe and Clatworthy Hundreds by William I.

Also, there is no private school nearby. There is a house down there, which inspired the school, but it's a private house and nothing at all to do with the story. As far as I know, it's not haunted. The source of the River Tone is up there, but I might have moved it slightly, so it was easy to reach. There is also another spring the other side of the hill that supplies the river as well.

Phew, I think that covers my stealing and literary amblings over the facts. I hope none of these spoil the story for you. I love Clatworthy Reservoir and it's a fantastic place to walk around. A joy to the local wildlife and any old gods who might have been worshiped by the people in the Iron Age hill-fort up there—they sleep peacefully.

AUTHOR THANKS

MANY THANKS FOR READING THE fourth of Lorne Turner's books. If you have a little time, I would appreciate a review. I really value my readers' thoughts about a book. It often helps me craft future stories. They are vital for indie authors like me. You are always welcome to get in touch directly at:

joe@joetalon.com

www.joetalon.com

Insta @JoeTalonBooks

Follow on BookBub!

I have FREE STORIES for you as well. All I'd like in exchange is your email address and you can unsubscribe from the newsletter at any time.

The first is called *Forgotten Homeland*. Just follow the link. It takes place just as Lorne leaves his regiment and returns home.

The second is *A Meeting of Terrors*. It's the fateful meeting between Lorne and Ella for the first time.

I'd like to keep in touch. Either via the newsletter I'll send out every few weeks, or you can join my Facebook group: Joe Talon Books. If you join either, there will be notifications of new stories, releases of covers and the occasional giveaway and special deals just for you. There will also be an opportunity to join my *Advanced Reader Team*.

ACKNOWLEDGEMENTS

ONCE MORE MY THANKS GO to David Luddington for his dedicated editing work, he always finds a layer I've left crumbs for but not quiet turned into a proper part of the cake. He also writes the most amazing gentle British comedy. They are some of my favourite books. Here's the latest: <u>The King of Scanlon's Rock.</u>

Also, Jeff Jones for his, very swift and skilled wrangling of my dodgy grammar.

I might write the books but I owe a great deal to the support of my ARC team, Facebook group and newsletter readers. You guys have no idea how much strength you give an author who does the whole thing alone! Thank you for your continued support, guys.

Stick around for the next, *The Alchemist's Corpse*.

COUNTING CROWS

THE MOOR IS DARKENING.

Lorne Turner's army days are over, but his haunting memories never rest. One fog-bound morning he stumbles across a murder. The crows feasting on a sacrifice.

Detective Inspector Tony Shaw tries to tell him the occult symbols on the dead man are nothing but faked staging. Lorne's honed instincts scream in warning. There is darkness and it's spreading.

The first person he turns to for help is the only friend he has, Ella Morgan, vicar of his parish. Together they reach out to the pagan Willow Hunter, and they begin to unravel the crime.

Corruption, greed and the abuse of occult mysteries lead Lorne into a world he never thought existed in Somerset. Trained to stand strong against terrorists, now he must fight the ghosts of his mind and the darkness of a madman.

An old soldier once more goes into battle. What will break first, his mind, or his enemies?

Counting Crows on Amazon

MONEY FOR OLD BONES

LORNE TURNER NEEDS A BREAK, so when he's offered the job of security guard and handyman at an old rectory in the Lyn Valley he takes it.

He thought he'd gain a little space and perspective. A little quiet from the noise in his head, from his demons, from his beast. Sadly, The Rectory doesn't provide the haven he needs.

As the rain falls, waters rise, and old graves move.

The grave of a witch, who cursed the village. The grave of a soldier, who tried to escape the Hanging Judge after the Monmouth Rebellion. The grave of a priest, broken by love and grief.

When the whispering of Exmoor's dead turns into a scream, Lorne has to act.

The original families of Scob must face their debt.

Lorne, Ella, Willow, and Heather need to find a way to balance the scales before more lives are lost.

Can they survive the haunting misery of the old bones? Can they save each other from the beckoning darkness?

And the rain. Always the rain.

<u>Money for Old Bones on Amazon</u>

DEAD OF THE WINTER SUN

LORNE IS BEGINNING TO UNDERSTAND that the dead might not stay in the graveyards where they belong. He also knows it's time to start facing this disconcerting reality in the same way he faced his enemies in battle.

So, when Eddie Rice buys a rundown cottage on Exmoor, and an old graveyard, which should be empty, things become increasingly weird. It isn't empty for a start. Not of bodies, or the whispering dead.

After an elderly woman is murdered nearby, Lorne, Ella and the others begin to uncover a plot that links this quiet corner of the world with Cold War espionage. Soviet secrets unravel and the more Lorne discovers the closer to breaking point he gets.

The Winter Sun burns in his blood, eating his mind. Can his desert hitchhiker save him? Or will his sanity fold under the weight of Cold War madness?

Dead of the Winter Sun on Amazon

SALT FOR THE DEVIL'S EYE

LORNE'S HOME IS TURNING INTO A dream. He's happy and at peace for the first time in his life. The nightmares are releasing their grip on his mind and he's learning to cope with the whispering dead.

Sadly, that's not the case for everyone.

An old friend calls about a missing boy from a traveller's camp on the Quantocks. They've been living on the site of an ancient hillfort, near the burial grounds of long forgotten souls.

These people don't trust the police, but they do put their faith in an old soldier to bring their boy home.

When Lorne discovers this disappearance has a link to his childhood friend vanishing, more than thirty years before, his oldest fears start to rise and take form.

The ancient sites of the Quantocks, the modern world of Hinkley Point's new nuclear reactor, and ex-police officer Tony Shaw, start to weave a tapestry of darkness that threatens all the peace Lorne's worked so hard to find.

Salt for the Devil's Eye on Amazon

BAD WATERS RUN DEEP

LORNE ISN'T CONVINCED HIS NEW psychic detective agency is a good idea but when he receives a call from a boarding school, sat in the shadow of Clatworthy Reservoir he reluctantly agrees to help.

The wisdom of teenagers has caused a problem at the school. The students decided the Ouija board they made in class might be fun to use, but when their call is answered, everything changes.

The results have opened a door Lorne has to close or lives will be lost.

The team discover a dark secret. The rising waters of the reservoir that flooded an ancient village called Syndercombe concealed a twisted, evil mind who took the opportunity to hide his dead.

But his evil didn't surrender when age robbed him of life and he's returned to the school, seeking new victims for his twisted desires.

If Lorne, Heather and Ella can't stop the rising evil in the reservoir then more than just the water will be polluted, the souls of the innocent will be lost to the bad waters of Clatworthy.

Bad Waters Run Deep on Amazon

THE ALCHEMIST'S CORPSE

THE COLD OF WINTER WRAPS sticky fingers around Exmoor as Lorne, Ella and Heather learn of Saint Decuman and his healing well in Watchet.

It seems the old saint is trying to send a warning to those able to listen, the elderly of his ancient parish.

When Lorne and Heather offer to help the spooked pensioners, little do they realise they're walking into a warzone.

The local motorcycle gang, The Devil's Mercenaries, are now peddling designer drugs. While a new cult, The Watchers, is offering a different kind of high.

Lorne, Ella and Heather must untangle the links between an old alchemist, the designer drug and the cult before the hauntings claim more lives.

War is on the horizon for this small seaside town and Lorne is a man who knows how to kill. The question is, can he?

The Alchemist's Corpse on Amazon

A freebie!

A MEETING OF TERRORS

AFTER TEN MONTHS OF BEING alone on his moor, Lorne Turner receives a panicked call.

He needs to rescue some teenagers from an act of stupidity. Nice and simple. Fast rope down to a cave entrance, see if they are still alive, and get them out. Piece of carrot cake for an ex-operator.

When Ella Morgan is also 'roped' into helping, Lorne begins to understand the importance of friendship outside the military. The pair descend into the cave complex and that's when Lorne realises the dead don't always whisper.

Sometimes the dead scream!

This short novella takes place before Counting Crows and gives us an insight into how Lorne and Ella first begin their friendship. It's also how I first started to get to know the pair. I hope you enjoy it as well.

A Meeting of Terrors Free on Story Origin

And finally, the original story!

FORGOTTEN HOMELAND

COMING HOME AFTER EIGHTEEN YEARS of service in the elite 22nd Regiment of the British Army should give Lorne Turner a sense of pride. Instead it fills him with dread. The shock of his last mission haunts him, rising from the dust and sand he never quite left behind.

The farm, in which he grew up, is isolated on the edge of a Somerset moorland. One covered in the barrows of the ancient dead, but he's more concerned with the recent dead.

Night after night a storm sweeps in from the north and Lorne can hear the crack, the bang, the scream of the wind… It is just the wind, right?

When his tolerance runs out, he ventures into the darkness, to the church, as lonely as he is on the edge of the moor, and he discovers that not all ghosts live in dust and sand.

Not all ghosts live in the nightmares of a tormented and haunted man.

Make sure you are part of the newsletter team and thank you for reading my books, it means the world to me.

Forgotten Homeland Free on Story Origin

Printed in Great Britain
by Amazon

22254057R00172